Keeping French Time

By

Sophia Worden

Little Red Hen Books, Cornwall, UK.

French Proof Reading by David Madell.

Copyright © Sophia Worden, 2024.

Copyright notice © 2024 by Sophia Worden.

The right of Sophia Worden to be identified as the Author of the Work has been asserted by her in accordance with the Copyright, Designs and Patents Act, 1988.

All rights reserved. No part of this book may be reproduced, stored in or introduced into a retrieval system, or transmitted, in any form, by any means (electronic, mechanical, photocopying, recording or otherwise) without the prior written permission of the publisher, except in the case of brief quotations embodied in critical articles or reviews.

A catalogue record for this book is available on request from the British Library.

Published by Sophia Worden, Little Red Hen Books, Cornwall, UK.

LittleRedHenBooks75@hotmail.com

Cover by Sophia Worden

Interior Design by Sophia Worden

French Proof-Reading by David Madell

ISBN: 978-1-4461-0959-5

Published by Little Red Hen Books, Cornwall, UK.

Prologue
Ver-Sur-Mer, Normandy, 1923

THE OPEN BOOK

I've never seen a coffin that size before.

Maman said I could choose one bunch of flowers - just one - and she would tell the undertaker. So I chose bluebells, because that's what he was like. Only, as the man carries the coffin to the bier on the altar, I can't see them. Too wintery for bluebells, maybe.

Maman nudges me forwards. 'Go and say goodbye,' she whispers. She stays where she is, herself.

I don't want to look. I don't want to look. But the sight of that broken, bleeding body on the cross above the altar is even worse. So I glance down at Pierre. The bunch of bluebells rests against his cheek. Hiding the bruises.

But not his face, as pale and wrinkled as a blanched almond, from being in water too long.

My eyes slide away, towards Maman in the front pew. She pulls her veil down. Its slight blue haze conceals her flame of hair, the cut on the side of her face - as if she's beneath the waves of the sea. No-one except me is watching her. Monsieur le Curé can't spare a smile for us, like he does on normal Sundays.

He reads aloud from the Bible, 'In my Father's house are many mansions. If it were not so, I would have told you. I go now to prepare a place for you.'

Maman's hand shakes when she turns over the page in her prayer-book.

But I'm dizzy with watching her; my eyes blur and strain, start to water. Suddenly, she's too near, and too far away. Then she scatters into patches of black, a drift of petal shadows across the stone floor.

Someone grabs my arm. Someone whispers, 'Don't worry, Odette. I won't let you fall.' One of the altar-boys. Augustine's older brother, Jacques.

He loves me. He loves me not. A little girl pulls petals from a bunch of flowers. He loves me.

Jacques guides me back to Maman. I rest my burning cheek against the cool skin of her arm. She still smells the same. Vervain tea and attar of roses. A whole garden has given up its flowers to make a few drops. But I don't like it anymore.

Maman shivers. The Church of Sainte-Marie swells with hymns. The sound reaches the vault of the roof with its interlocking beams. Sorrow perches in an eave above my head, sings to me, then flies away. *'Ky-witt, Ky-witt, what a beautiful bird am I.'*

Jacques steps forwards to light a tall candle. The short ones splutter: flames extinguish in a pool of wax.

We are sending you away from us, Pierre. And how will you like that? In a boat that only a child can fit.

Though you never said, I always knew you were afraid - of the sea...

Part I
Ver-Sur-Mer, Normandy, 1915-23

THE CHILD'S BIBLE, 1915

Every move he makes, I watch, to know he's safe. He fumbles for the white gate's clasp, finds it, passes through, stumbles away from the house. Our house, shaped like a lighthouse, at the end of a promenade which stretches out like one of its beams. And sometimes in the evening, I take a candle and shine messages from the window to sailors far across the sea. Or mermaids. Whoever might be watching. After all, our home used to be a coastguards' lookout, positioned at the apex of a crooked row of cottages where the seawall begins. A wall of stones, rolled up by the tide onto the beach. Shingle.

He drags himself along the path by the seashore, resting his weight, first on one leg, then on the other, sometimes leaning on his cane. The sunlight glints against his spectacles that he polished at breakfast this morning. The sea, frothing the colour of old coffee, splashes away from his shoes. But once he's past the Egg-Rocks, '*oolithique*,' he calls them, I know he's safe.

Papa.

I let go of my breath, shut the back door, and clatter through our kitchen that curves like a crescent moon. Then past the staircase, that coils round and round like the spiral shell we keep on the window-sill - next to the seaweed, that lets us know what the weather will do. Then straight on, into the parlour.

In the parlour alcove, I open the illustrated Bible, and there's my name on the family tree. *Odette Angèle Elise Rivière*, written in Papa's grown-up, swirling flourishes. Though he hasn't written in any of Maman's relatives.

The cover's heavy, the pages are musty. Perhaps God, this strange person or being, is a book. Solid and musty, like this book, like Papa? Full of pictures or close-set print? Is God in the pictures? In the clouds? In the sky? Or is he the little book, with his lightning-bolts, the sharp, flashing things inside?

No, the little book is Maman's needle-case. The sharp gleams are her needles, with the sun on them.

I turn over a few pages of the Bible and there's a watercolour garden, intensely green. At the heart of the garden is the Tree of Knowledge, of Good and Evil, with its full, ripe fruit hanging heavy from the branches.

Eyes full of apples, I flick back the pages. Genesis, the dawn of creation, a ball of orange paint flaming against a black background. If I half-shut my eyes and twist the page, there's a face in the halo of flame.

Maman.

THE SILVER-BACKED BRUSH

Later, from behind the window-seat's wine-coloured draperies, I read aloud from the Bible. My mother, Marie-France, lets down her hair. She's caught the sun in it, down by the sea today. Red and gold needle-lights. Red hair that crackles with life of its own. She brushes it away from her face. It falls in waves, far below her waist.

'Very good, *chérie*,' she says. 'Now put the book down and come here.' She gathers the thick tail of my hair in one hand and draws the silver-backed brush through it with the other, over and over again. Soothing.

There are freckles on the backs of her hands. Each year, there's more.

She re-plaits my hair and then I'm ready for bed. She covers me over with the blanket, turns the light down low, and begins to sing.

'*Monique a perdu son grand pierrot, toujours en satin blanc.*' 'Monique has lost her clown-doll, always dressed in white satin.' Then the chorus. '*Ne pleurez pas petite chose.*' 'Don't cry, little one.'

'I wasn't,' I protest.

'Not you, *chérie*. The little girl in the song. And her doll. A pierrot's eyes are always full of tears.'

THE SNOWSTORM

Maman promises we'll see clowns at the circus. She's taking me, for my sixth birthday. But only if I'm good, and don't chew the ends of my hair.

Or perhaps only if Maman's good. 'I'm not always am I?' she says, sighing ruefully. *Non. Pas du tout.* When we're by ourselves, she sings loudly and discordantly all over the house. She whirls me in wild dances across the parquet floor when she's supposed to be dusting. She tears scraps of silk from her old dresses for dusters, then stops in front of the cabinet and unhooks the clasp. The glass-panelled door swings open, like a doll's house door. Inside are my father's china ornaments, their paleness gleaming against the cabinet's dark mahogany. They're all called *pas-pour-toi*.

'Papa's nesting,' she says.

She dusts them gently, gingerly, as if she's scared of what she might break. Porcelain and Promises.

Papa was nearly sixty when he married Maman. She wasn't even twenty. Eighteen, in fact. *Petite Maman.*

'My good girls,' he calls us on Sundays when our hair is brushed, and our shoes are shined. He takes my mother's arm, holds out his hand to me, and we walk to church, proud despite the whispers.

'*Son père, c'est une antiquité,*' someone whispers in the pew behind us, loud enough for me to hear. Jealous because her father was conscripted to fight in the war, but mine was too old, so stays behind and runs his antiques shop.

Papa often says, 'Your Maman's the most precious object in my collection sought, wooed and won.' Now he wipes the dust from her porcelain face, now he smooths the cobwebs from her hair. But sometimes she sighs with the good care he takes of her.

Maman reaches inside the cabinet, then holds out the snowstorm to me. 'Our little village, Ver-Sur-Mer. By the sea. In a glass dome. Shake it and watch the snowflakes settle. Only, don't shake it too hard, Odette,' she adds. 'Think how bad you'd feel, if it slipped and broke. It's very old and very precious. Here,' she says, reaching for it, 'Let's put it back inside the cabinet, on the high-up shelf, out of harm's way.'

'*Mais non,*' I say, 'It's mine, it's mine.' I stamp my feet and put my arms behind my back. It nestles there, inside my fingers, smooth and warm as a hen's egg.

The snowstorm, *c'est moi*. It's part of me and I won't give it back. *Non non non.* You can't make me.

But Maman coaxes the snowstorm out of my reluctant hands. She places it back inside the cabinet, on the highest shelf. The door slams shut.

Now the snowstorm shines down on me. Blue, sparkle, blue. It makes me want to be a collector, too.

THE MIRROR

On Saturdays, Maman promenades along the seashore, her parasol looped over her slender, gloved wrist. I leave her to it. Because, 'Come and help me in the antiques shop, *ma grande petite fille,*' says Papa.

He hands another book to me. The books without spines go into one cardboard box, those with pages missing into another. Here we only sell what we like ourselves: ladies' fans, clockwork mice, glazed dishes, and, inside glass bottles, sailing ships, with string rigging. But not the stereoscope with the double-imaged cards. Papa wants to keep that for himself.

And not the stopped clocks that can't be started, though they look so fine.

'Sometimes when it's broken, it can't be fixed,' says Papa, smiling sadly and shaking his head. Then he snaps open his snuffbox, takes a pinch, gasps, flicks his fingers and wipes his eyes.

The pride of his collection is a curly haired statue of Pan, cast in bronze. But me, I like the length of white silk he says I can have for a wedding dress, if I don't grow any taller. Though my real favourite is the oval mirror. A plaster frame covered in gold-leaf curlicues surrounds it, really special. Froth framed, but the glass is rust patched. Three, four, five, six, no seven stains the colour of tea.

I blow on its speckled surface, then polish it with my cloth. Then I squint at my reflection: the frowning girl that's me. Skinny body, hazel eyes, mass of dark hair. Appearing, disappearing, playing *Cache Cache* in the glass. Which of us is which?

The mirror doubles and freckles everything: the shop, the antiques, me.

On Sundays, when we walk to Church, I tell Maman she should wear a sunbonnet. Because her freckles mark her age, and Papa is old enough for both of them. She laughs. 'Who's the mother and who's the daughter?' she says, '*ma drôle de petite fille.*'

Petite Maman. I wish she were really tiny, like a doll. Then I could keep her safe, inside my pocket.

THE MASK

One time, a mask comes into the shop. It's white, impassive, with sharp features. Its' eyes are closed.

'Plaster of Paris,' Papa says. He takes off his glasses, and then slips the mask over his face. He disappears, all except for the tips of his grey moustache.

Papa's little joke, like when he takes his false teeth out and displays his pink gums. Except it isn't funny.

I scream.

'*Eh bien*, no wonder, *la pauvre*,' says Maman, clutching me to her, glaring at my father. I'm comforted by her sweet, familiar smell. The vervain tea she drinks, and something like flowers - attar of roses, she says. 'You'll scare her into nightmares with that death mask.'

Death mask? I raise my head from my mother's lacy bodice. 'Who is it?'

'I've no idea,' Papa says, carelessly, removing the mask from his face. 'Maybe the Unknown Soldier.' And then he frowns. 'I can't sell this thing here,' he continues. 'There's been enough death already. My customers will find it morbid.' He reaches for another pinch of snuff. It stains his fingers brown, this dust that might be powdered flesh and shining bones.

'When I was a girl, there used to be a museum full of death masks in Rouen,' says Maman. 'I wonder if it still exists? You might be able to sell it there.'

'How do you know about it?' asks Papa.

'Well, it was also the Musée Flaubert. Since the nuns at my school forbade *Madame Bovary*, I read it under the desk and one day I went to his museum.'

'Always the reader,' mutters Papa. But this time it's him, not Maman, who travels to Rouen. There he sells our mask, and there he finds a toyshop, and then he comes home again, with a green and gold striped bag.

'I'm very sorry I scared you before, Odette,' he says. 'Here, shut your eyes and hold out your hands. *Un petit cadeau pour ma grande petite fille.*'

My fingertips touch lace, stroke satin, slide over porcelain. I open my eyes. A Pierrot doll. I'm so happy happy happy I make the doll dance across my wrist.

But he's a bit battered from the journey. 'I'll glue the frill of crepe back round his collar. I'll re-paint his *chapeau*,' says Papa, watching me anxiously.

I smile at Papa, but I put the doll behind my back.

I don't want him to spoil my Pierrot, like he did with the headless Madonna. He glued her head back on, but then he painted her sash, seaweed green. More a mermaid than a Madonna, after that. And then nobody wanted to buy her, not even after I tied a ribbon round her neck to hide the crack and the patches of glue.

THE APPLE

Yvette Calombe's a very ugly little girl with frizzy hair, squinting eyes and pock-marked skin. Her father is the Mayor's cousin. She doesn't like Augustine, and Augustine doesn't like her. At all.

But Augustine Solange, ah! My best friend, with her sweet, mocking smile and her straight, dark hair, just like mine. But she's a little bit taller, a little bit older, and her eyes are green.

May is the month of Sainte Marie, and so it's also the month of my mother. She's Marie too, so that must be why I'm chosen to be Queen of the May. I'll dance round the maypole with Yvette and Augustine. Afterwards we'll present flowers to the Mayor.

'*Mary, we crown thee with blossoms today, / Queen of the Angels and Queen of the May*,' I warble into the speckled mirror. My voice frosts the glass. The fleshy bit at the back of my throat bobs up and down.

'Such beautiful singing,' Papa beams at me from across the counter. That's because I'm pretending to be Augustine. Her voice is better than mine.

She leads me through her farm's apple orchard to a hole in the fence. At first it isn't big enough. It gets bigger after we've wriggled through it a few times, anxious to avoid the nettles' acid bite.

On the other side of the fence is fairyland. Drifts of apple blossom blow over, looking like snowflakes. Dainty petals of white satin. Shy bunches of blushing buds.

'The trees are getting married,' Augustine says.

'The trees are making their First Communion,' I say.

We make ourselves garlands and practise being the May Queen. First me, then Augustine. In case I'm sick and not able to do it, she says.

She fixes me with her green-eyed gaze. 'You mustn't ever come here by yourself,' she says. 'We're both in charge here. The soldier obeys us both.'

'What soldier?' I say.

'It's all right,' she says, kindly. 'He's not here at the moment. He knows that fairyland is safe because we're both here.'

But one evening when I run up to the farm to play, her mother, Madame Solange, says she's busy feeding the hens. So I creep through the hole in the fence by myself. Ssssh! Don't tell Augustine.

A seed has blown over, taken root and become a sapling. It casts a circular shadow on the sunlit ground. The setting sun throws threads of golden silk downward through the crimson edged leaves. I slash at them with my hands, but they never waver.

I stay for ages, striding round the patch of wasteland, wishing that it belonged to me, and me alone. Among the bright leaves, there's a flurry of feathers, the first trills of evening birdsong.

Then, on the other side of the fence, tramp-tramp, rustle. The stinging nettles, all *piétinés,* trampled underfoot.

A screwed up face, acid and bitter, peers at me through the hole. All the little hairs stand to attention on the backs of my arms. Goose-bumps. And I can't tell who it is in the fading light. I can't tell if her eyes are green.

'Augustine?' I whisper.

No answer. *Mon Dieu,* what if it's the death mask, come back to haunt me? I scream.

The face disappears.

I never do find out if it's Augustine, or Yvette, watching me. Hating me. I'm afraid to ask. Because the next time I go to the farm, the hole in the fence has been boarded up.

THE PIP

'Maman, Maman, Papa, look at me! I'm Queen of the May. Watch me. Watch the ribbons criss-cross. No, come on, watch properly!'

My parents clap and cheer, and I burst with pride and importance.

After the ceremony, Maman reaches for me, to spin me round, as she often does.

'*Mais non,* Marie,' says Papa, reaching between us. 'Have some sense, for once.'

He fetches wicker chairs and places them in the shade. We all sit together: Papa, Maman, me, sipping orangeade. My legs, my white socks, my shiny patent shoes, dangle backwards and forwards. A long way from the ground.

But after May Day, Maman doesn't ever try to swing me round again. She spends long afternoons reclining on the *chaise-longue,* not even reading her novels. I'm scared she's sick.

Augustine and I bring her apples from the farm, ripe and rosy as Maman used to be. She bites into one. Her white teeth leave a perfect circlet in the apple's firm flesh. Then she swallows the pips. Papa sighs. Will she never learn? There's arsenic in them.

Maman's belly swells up over the top of her skirt. She grows round as the glass dome on the high-up shelf. She must be poisoned.

Then my baby brother is born. '*Comme il est beau,*' Papa declares, smacking kisses on both my cheeks. 'As bronze, as beautiful, as my statue of Pan.'

But he doesn't look like the statue of Pan to *me*. He's red and wrinkled, with a shock of hair, black as Pierrot's *chapeau*. So black, it's as if Papa gave it a lick of paint in the middle of the night.

Yvette says that babies come from men and women in the middle of the night. 'Don't you know *anything*, Odette?'

But when I tell Augustine, she says that her mother says they grow like fruit from tiny seeds. So I know that Yvette's lying.

And I know that's why Maman ate the apple-pips. To grow a baby. It's true then, what they say, there's always fruit inside the seed.

I'll have to be careful not to swallow any pips myself. We don't want any more babies here. My brother's such a handful.

I want to call him Pierrot. But my mother says that Pierrots are always crying, and she doesn't want a crying baby. And the little girl in the song loses her doll.

'But we can call him Pierre, which sounds almost the same and means rock. Nothing can harm him with a name like that...'

THE PEBBLES

We take the baby to church to be christened. I dip my hand in the stoup and then cross myself. I like to splash the holy water all over my face, or, when there isn't any, the holy dust.

'*Bah*, does she want to bathe in it?' mutters a churchgoer behind me. Maman turns and glares at her, then ushers me inside.

Monsieur le Curé sinks the jug into the rose-veined marble font. Then he tips the holy water over my brother's head. Now he has a name.

Pierre screws up his eyes and howls, his face, a disgusted wrinkled almond.

Sugared almonds for weddings, or christenings. But once you suck the colour off, they're just ordinary, like pebbles.

When he's older, we follow a yellow path of sunshine all the way down to the sea. We skim pebbles. Mine soar across the waves; his sink into the water. He cries, big, glistening tears, like the Pierrot.

'It's all right, Pierre,' I whisper. 'It's only a game.' And I won't ever throw you into the water, not even now you're wailing, and I'm tempted. No, I hold you tight, I keep you safe.

The toddler, the waves, the screeching gulls. Such a *boucan* they make. My head aches.

'*Eh bien*, stop that,' I say, finally. 'Don't you know your tears are made of seawater? If you cry too much, we might drown.'

He stops, instantly, catches a tear on the end of his finger, and licks it off. Then he smiles.

THE SABOTS

I help him take off his sabots and we slither barefoot over the wet sand. We scramble across rocks, peer into rock pools, watch the velvet swimmer crabs with their dead men's fingers, the devilfish with their bright red eyes. We wrinkle our noses at the sea's stewed tang.

Seaweed unravels at the water's edge, like Maman letting down her hair. And the corrugations in the sand are like Maman's frowns, when Papa tells a bad joke. Then she laughs and tries to stroke the lines away.

So we decide to draw a face in the sand, with seaweed for its hair. Then Pierre takes a stick, wobbling beneath its weight, and scratches a smile.

Later, we mould eggs, squelching the sand through our fingers, feeling the sting of salt water on little, invisible cuts. We place what we've made in the shadow of Bathonien, the Egg-rock.

'Papa calls it '*oolithique.*' That means it's shaped like tiny eggs,' I tell Pierre.

'Let me see,' he begs.

I lift him up. But he's heavy now that my arms are tired, and he sags against me.

'You eat too much,' I say.

He raises his hand and runs his fingers against the miniscule rock-buds, as rapt as I am with rosary beads. I hold him there, against the rock, for a long time. I don't want him to be frightened. I don't want him to turn and see the waves, stealing away the face in the sand.

THE EASTER EGGS

An awful day. I'm in disgrace, searching for dock-leaves near the boarded-up fence. Maman sent me to find them, whilst she tends to Pierre. His legs are raw with nettle stings.

And that's not all. Madame Solange says we can't hunt for Easter eggs in her orchard. Ever again.

The morning began so well. Augustine and I, scrambling around, searching for hens' eggs to paint. But then we go to feed the fowls. One hen, with her yellow chicks, is in a coop. Augustine fills her hand with maize.

'The Governor of Normandy says we're not allowed to use wheat or corn for them,' she says.

'Why?' I ask, but Augustine doesn't know. She holds her hand out to the hen.

The bird eyes it with her bright, hard eye, and makes a sudden peck at the hand. Rap rap rap. Augustine laughs.

'She pecks at you, but it doesn't hurt,' says Augustine. 'Do you want to try?'

'No,' I say, shrinking back.

'It doesn't hurt,' she says. 'It just nips nicely.'

I shake my head. Co-*ward*, co-*ward*, the hen shrieks. I flush crimson with shame and misery. Deep inside, I know something bad is going to happen.

We take the eggs and hide them in the orchard garden. We decide we'll let Pierre find them, because he's only little.

Besides, the real prize is a duck's egg, glazed to retain its blush of blue. Augustine will hide it. Then the girls from school, and me, we'll try to find it.

She smirks as we hunt for the hidden duck's egg. Her eyes gleam.

Yvette shrieks and runs round and round the orchard, like a headless chicken. Her school pinafore billows round her like a flour sack, from neck to knee. Her frizzy hair tries to jerk free from the two plaits looped behind her ears.

There are days when the grown-ups predict Yvette will be pretty. Today is not one of those days.

The rest of us jostle, elbow, bump into each other. Our faces flush, our cheeks shine, our eyes blaze. We look like our papas, coming back from the tavern on High Days and holidays.

But after half an hour or so, our excitement fades. We can't find it. We're bored.

'Tell me where it is,' I whisper in Augustine's ear.

She jerks her neck away. 'Your breath tickles,' she protests. Then she places her finger on her lips and looks mysterious. 'Ummmmmm,' she says, enjoying her little moment of power.

But Augustine never can keep secrets for long. Not from me. She giggles and points to the topmost branch of an ancient apple tree. There's the duck's egg, hanging suspended by a thread.

But I'm not the only one to see it.

Yvette approaches us, clasping Pierre's grubby paw in her hand.

Tears streak clean tracks down his face. His ankles are covered in a weal of blisters.

'He fell into the nettles,' she says. 'You ought to take better care of him.'

I snatch his hand from Yvette's grasp. He's my little brother, after all.

Yvette surveys us coolly for a moment, then nods towards the duck's egg, swaying slightly above us. 'Good hiding place,' she says, and then she adjusts her pinafore and shimmies up the tree.

Once she has it, she yells, 'It's mine. It's mine. I found it!'

Augustine glares up at her, eyes flashing dark as pistols, as Yvette clutches the duck's egg in her hot little hands.

Pierre starts crying. Is he upset because we didn't find the prize egg? But then he kicks off his sabots. His nettle stings are worse. The blisters stand to attention on his thin ankles and the skin around them is swollen, livid red.

The image stays with me as I carry him home. It's my fault that he's hurt. Maman doesn't say it, but that must be what she's thinking as she tries to peel off his socks without touching his blisters.

And then - as I pick dock-leaves, things gets worse. Madame Solange tells me to leave. I try to explain that I need them for Pierre's nettle stings, but she flaps her hands and won't listen. Her bonnet strings stream behind her, all undone.

She's like the witch that wouldn't let Rapunzel's husband take the lettuces.

Or else she's the hen with the horrible face, who pecks with malice.

I run all the way home and only find out later that Monsieur Solange has been killed by German soldiers, at the Plateau of the Chemin des Dames.

Pierre's nettle stings get better: the kind of hurt that heals.

Another woman from the village, Madame Sabatine, also loses her husband in the battle. She sets up a foundation in memory of him, the Saint Martin Association, which donates money to our school so we can have new notebooks and fountain pens instead of pencils.

'But was Martin Sabatine really a saint?' I ask Maman.

'Everyone deals with grief in their own way,' Maman sighs. 'To Madame Sabatine, her husband has become a saint.'

But Madame Solange's grief is different. She attends her husband's funeral but after that, she refuses to go to church. She tells Maman, 'The sight of that wounded body on the cross doesn't console me at all.' She takes her own crucifix down from her bedroom wall and locks it away in a linen cupboard. She doesn't want to see it, ever again.

And months later, when I glance up at the crucifix on the altar, above the child's open coffin, I understand what she means.

THE WRITING DESK

Nom de Dieu! It's raining again. Inside our village school, the blinds are pulled up so that the wide windows throw leaden grey light all around our rectangular shaped classroom. It spills evenly onto the white-washed walls and across the wooden floorboards. Heavy, solid, mahogany desks are ranged in rows away from the white marble fireplace with its bulbs of hyacinths perched on top. At the front of the classroom is a raised dais with the teacher's desk placed upon it, more impressive, shinier, than those of us children. Here sits Mademoiselle Madeleine, our teacher. From time to time, she looks up from her novel, a copy of Zola's *Germinal*, and glances through the large window to her right at the pouring rain.

Mademoiselle is a very pretty woman with dark hair, in a bun. She looks like Sarah Bernhardt in Mucha's poster of Medea. Clutching a dagger over the prostrate body of her murdered child. I wonder if she likes being a schoolteacher? Madame Solange tells us that Mademoiselle belongs to the Groupes Feministes de l'Enseignement Laïque. So she's almost a Communist. No wonder she has such strange ideas.

Now she puts down her novel and tells us to stop what we are doing and get out our joined-up handwriting books. Before, when we used to write in pencil, the inkwells were empty. I used to keep daisy-chains in mine. But they were always brown and bedraggled by the end of the day.

And that is a poem which Mademoiselle recites to us, eyes flashing, gripping her bun of dark hair. '*Rose, elle a vécu.*' Has lived, girls, note the use of the *passé composé*. To convey sorrow at the passage of time.'

My school desk's made of pine, with its ink-well in the top, right hand corner. It has three long grooves, much longer than they need to be, where I lay my pens. The pine is covered with scratch-marks from some long-ago penknife. Engrained with dirt and splattered with ink. Someone started to scribble down the verb *Aimer* on it. *J'aime. Tu aimes.* Who loves who? Perhaps she was making notes before a test. But then she realised she knew it already and didn't need to cheat.

I wouldn't cheat. I'd be too scared. Mademoiselle's mouth and her dark hair are sometimes so severe. As if she's put her school-teacher's mask on. And then her abrupt, strict, musical voice. How it makes us all deliciously tremble. Especially when she recites. Today it's from a play by that great baldy, the Ennngleeesh Shakespeare: 'The evil that men do lives after them.'

Peculiar emphasis on evil, and on men. As if women never do anything wrong. 'And certainly not you young girls,' says Mademoiselle, beaming round at us. 'You're all so young, you're still in a state of grace.'

State of Grace. How nice that sounds. Gentle, gracious, lighter than air. Airier than light. *Si belle.*

The class lets out a sigh of rapture.

Mademoiselle raps her knuckles on her desk's sloping lid. She opens our textbook, le *Petit Manuel Lavisse*, then wrinkles her lip. 'Bah! The primary school teacher of the nation, indeed!' Now she reaches for our reading-book. *Le Tour De La France par Deux Enfants.* Written in 1877. But no. She thumps the palm of her hand against her forehead. She can't bear its sweet, trite phrases. It's not as if we're still in the *école maternelle*.

'What's your favourite book, *mes enfants*?' she asks.

Augustine raises her hand. '*The Three Musketeers*, Mademoiselle.'

'That's quite advanced reading for someone of your age. I don't want to hamper your intellectual development, but I'm not sure if it's entirely suitable…'

Maybe she's thinking about D'Artagnan, who loved Constance Bonacieux, even though she already had a husband. Or Milady de Winter, the English woman with the *fleur-de-lys* branded on her shoulder for all her unspeakable crimes. But what were they? And why can't we speak of them?

Mademoiselle frowns. The fine wrinkles about her mouth become prominent, then smooth themselves away. 'Oh hang it all! Do you know, girls, I have to be so careful what I say to you. There's so much I want to teach you about the world, but you're all… quite young still.'

Someone towards the back of the class titters.

Mademoiselle smiles a bright, impatient smile. She turns her head towards the noise. She doesn't see my hand, waving forlornly at the front of the class.

'I notice none of you said the Bible,' she adds. 'I thought you were all such good little Catholic girls.'

Mademoiselle, isn't, oh how can I say it, she isn't Catholic. Sometimes it's as if she envies us our religious certainty. She has to find her own way, she says. So we pray very hard that she won't burn in hell.

But now my hand falls to my side. She pre-empted me. The Bible was what I was going to say.

THE CHILDREN'S READER

Instead, Mademoiselle reads us a translation of a fairy-tale by the Brothers Grimm. 'A German fairy-tale,' she mutters. It reminds me of the story of the Garden of Eden, a bit. It begins with a woman standing beneath a juniper tree, peeling herself an apple. She cuts her finger and blood falls into the snow. She wishes for a child as red as blood, as white as snow, and then nine months later, her son is born, and she dies. One day the little boy wants an apple, and he leans into a chest. His stepmother beheads him by slamming down the chest's lid. His little sister thinks it's her fault that his head falls off, and weeping bitterly, she gathers up his bones and buries them beneath the Juniper Tree. He is transformed into a beautiful bird with red and green feathers, and this is his song:

*'My mother, she killed me,
My father, he ate me,
My sister, Marlene, loved me best of all.
Gathered all my bones,
Tied them in a silken scarf,
Laid them beneath the juniper tree,
Ky-witt, Ky-witt, what a beautiful bird am I.'*

But Augustine is bored. She's eighteen months older than me, too old for fairy tales, she says. Instead, she passes me a note. A sketch of a girl's smiling face, with 'You are as pretty' scribbled underneath. The handwriting is Augustine's, but I think the drawing must be one of her brother's. It's too good and Augustine can't draw.

The picture reminds me of the face in the sand. It's sister, perhaps. Since I'm listening to the story, I don't pass the note back. The face smiles up at me from the sheen of my desk and I'm lulled by the sound of Mademoiselle's voice. *My sister loved me best of all...*

Outside, in the schoolyard, I try to shake off the spell of the German fairy-tale. I remember that the Boche, *les Pruscots*, are savages, our sworn enemies. Our hearts weep for the loss of Alsace and Lorraine, and we always colour them in violet on our geography lesson maps. Violet, the colour of mourning.

So now we decide to play at soldiers. Augustine will be the General, and I'll be her second-in-command. When we go home tonight, we'll ask our mothers to sew special buttons for medals onto our collars. We sing a patriotic song that the school superintendent taught us, swinging our arms from side to side, marching in time to its beat. One two one two: *'Mourir pour la patrie/ C'est le sort le plus beau.'*

There is no finer end than to die for one's country.

But half-way through, Augustine changes her mind. She decides to sing a different song, one her brother taught her. It's about a Captain, returning from war, who has to marry one of three sisters. The first sister is too quiet. The second sister is ugly, with little, squinting eyes. But the third sister is as beautiful as a summer rose.

'*Belle comme une rose,*' she sings in her sweet, clear voice: '*Belle comme une rose d'été, tu es la fille pour moi;*' '*Beautiful like a rose, a rose of summer, you are the girl for me.*' After a moment, we all march to the new tune. Then she repeats the second verse. One two one two: '*Trop laide toi, trop laide, tes petits yeux, trop laide, trop triste pour moi.*'

'*Too ugly you, too ugly, your little eyes, too ugly, too sad for me.*'

She aims the words like bullets, directly at Yvette.

THE LITTLE BLACK NOTE-BOOK

The Minister of Education says that Mademoiselle and all the other schoolteachers must write an account of how people feel about the war. Mademoiselle doesn't want to do it. 'Not my vocation or my inclination,' she says. But in the end, she decides we will all keep journals, to improve our writing style.

She hands out notebooks with stiff, dark covers. But in mine, I write down all my sins, and then I confess them each week to Monsieur le Curé.

I like kneeling down on the *prie-dieu* beside the mesh of grille, and making my voice sweet and pure, like Augustine's. A good girl's voice. 'Bless me Father, for I have sinned. It's been one week since my last confession. My sins are…' The words roll off my tongue, like flecks of communion wafer.

I *know*. I made my First Holy Communion last year, and now there's another photograph of me in the parlour. Ethereal beneath a net veil and a band of lilies. Clutching my white muslin skirt with gloved hands. A bible tucked under one arm, a rosary looped over the other. The hint of a beatific smile

But it's wasted on Monsieur le Curé. He can't see my smile, my holy, prayer-clasped hands, through the grille. Instead, I rifle through the notebook, and tell him:

'I pushed Yvette in the corridor. I made fun of her voice when she spoke in class. I tied the belt of her apron to the back of her chair, so that the chair came with her when she stood up.'

Actually, I made that last sin up. But thank goodness for Yvette. Otherwise I wouldn't have hardly anything to confess. Sometimes, for good measure, I add that I gave Pierre a shove. But generally that isn't true either. I just think that the more I confess, the better I'll feel afterwards.

'Girls, you're all still so very young. You're not old enough to have done anything terribly wrong yet,' Mademoiselle says, frowning as she waits for us, wondering how we manage to stay so long in the confessional box with Monsieur le Curé.

I could show her my ink-stained notebook, if she's curious.

THE PHOTOGRAPHS

Maman smiles as I lift Pierre up in my arms so that he can get close to the display, blur it with his breath. The parlour photographs. Pressed onto vellum paper, edged with a metal frame. Protected by glass, like *Blanche Neige* in her coffin.

Maman's auburn hair haloes her white oval face. It looks black in the photograph. She's raised her wedding veil, so we can see her large eyes, her pointed chin. She's pinned a polite smile to her lips, like a butterfly or a pressed flower. She's fastened her lace bodice with a topaz brooch, pulled her skirt over her white, high-heeled shoes. One heel peeps out beneath the swathe of cloth. And her glove buttons, which by squinting, we can just about make out, are tiny seed pearls.

Papa stands next to Maman. He poses stiffly in a dark serge suit, hands tucked into his pockets, creasing the cloth. His mild face is decorated with a pair of round-rimmed spectacles, and a drooping moustache, which counteracts his smile.

Pillars and plants sprout behind him. Maman's *beau prince*, with a snuff box in his pocket. You can't tell from his face that once, a long time ago, Papa had another wife. But they had no children. And then the lady died, and he was sad, so sad. And then he married Maman, and that was that.

'*Eh bien*,' she says. 'I was so proud that day. Before then, I thought no-one would have me.'

I stare at my beautiful mother. 'Oh, but why?'

'Because…' she shrugs. Her mouth twitches. 'Well, because I was born two years after my father died.'

Pierre wriggles. Baby smell of tarte-tatin, his eyes, dark gleaming raisins in his wide face. He wants to know why there's no picture of him. 'Or Minouche,' he adds. Our poodle. Now she has fleas, she has to live outside in the yard. We don't see her so much.

'When you can manage to sit still,' Maman promises, 'We'll take one of both of you.'

It's a promise she's never able to keep. Minouche is very old, the same age as Papa in dog years, and she dies a few months later. We hold a funeral for her. And Pierre -

No.

I think that what Maman says about her Papa makes no sense at all. But Augustine says, 'Your mother means that – her father was not her mother's late husband.'

'Eh?'

'Your Maman,' she pauses.

'Your Maman,' she says, trying again, then smiling. But it's not her usual grin of mirth and malice. There's something older, kinder in it. Finally, she takes a deep breath and forces out the words. 'Your Maman was illegitimate.'

Illégitime? Maman? Comme Guillaume le Batard? Impossible.

All the little hairs stand up on my arms and I shiver. I read a story once about an unmarried girl who had a baby. Her family drove them naked out into the snow and they died. At least they didn't do that to Grandmaman, and my mother.

But 'That explains why they packed her off to convent school for so long,' says Augustine. 'Ugh! All that Latin and learning. Wouldn't suit me. I bet she even has her *baccalauréat*, like Mademoiselle.'

I nod. For a moment, I'm suddenly, fiercely proud of my clever Maman.

But thereafter one of our favourite games is *'Qui est grandpapa?'* Augustine and I dart in and out of the village shops, sizing up the customers, or else we scrutinize the elderly men sitting outside the tavern. With their crow's feet, watery eyes

26

and broken veins, it's hard to tell which one sired my mother. Where is the *vrai* grandpapa, where is the one with blazing blue eyes and astonishing red hair?

Though I can't help but notice that none of these greying men look much older than Papa.

THE SLIPPERS

During our weekly outing to the confessional box - crocodile line, grey felt hats, polished shoes - I often think of becoming a nun. To atone for the sin of my mother's conception.

To be forever spotless and holy and pure.

Perhaps I'm inspired by Maman's tales of her convent school. 'When I was very little,' she says, 'The nuns used to take me to chapel to entertain me. The dear Sisters of Charity. But I'm afraid I was never very attentive to the Mass. I liked the pictures in the prayer-books better. And the hymns, so beautiful...' She gazes into the parlour fire, then pauses, shakes her head.

'I'm miles away,' she says. 'I was remembering how I used to beg to be allowed to light candles for the Holy Souls. And they, the nuns, used to let me.'

'The Holy Souls?'

'The ones in Purgatory. The ones who aren't good enough for Heaven, or bad enough for Hell. Like most of us, really.'

'And what do they do in Purgatory?'

'Well, do you know, Odette, I'm not really sure. Maybe they sit around and tell stories about their lives, like old people do. Like Viscountess Agathe.'

'Like Papa,' I nod.

Maman frowns, then continues, 'And we pray to set them free. "Let perpetual light shine upon them," that's what we must say.'

'Perpetual light,' I repeat. The words taste sweet as communion wine. 'Is that like State of Grace?'

'State of Grace?' says Maman, arching her eyebrows. Then, 'Perpetual State of Grace. That's what I thought it would be like for my school-friend Thérèse when she became a nun. Do you know, after she'd been a postulant for six months, she had a nun's wedding day.'

'Didn't you want to be a nun too, Maman?'

She gives me a half smile, then picks up Papa's slippers, to toast them in front of the fire. 'Ah, when your Grandmaman went to the angels, to the Holy Virgin…'

'To Purgatory,' I interrupt.

'I was forced to leave the convent,' says Maman. 'No more money. Anyway…' She shrugs. 'A while later I received a letter from Thérèse, saying she'd left, that she thought she could do more good in the outside world than shut away in the convent.'

'And did she?'

Maman sighs. 'After that, I never heard from her again. So anything at all might have happened to her…' She rests her cheek against the slippers' burning soles, then holds them up to the orange haze. 'He mustn't be allowed to have cold feet, must he?' she murmurs. She fixes on me the burning points of her pupils, like two flaming arrows, ready to fly.

THE TEA-CLOTH

Yvette won't ever become a nun. All she talks about is her future married life: 'My husband will have brown eyes and a hunting rifle. We'll have two boys and a girl, Celeste, to help me wash the dishes.'

'You want a large family, do you?' asks Mademoiselle, eavesdropping on our conversation.

'It's my patriotic duty since so many people were killed in the war,' says Yvette, smugly. 'And I'll get more money,' she adds.

'Yes,' says Mademoiselle. 'The Parisian fund always sends the postal orders to the mothers. Women aren't allowed to vote, but they are allowed the government's money.'

'Why's that?' I ask.

Mademoiselle shrugs but comes up with an answer. 'The government worries that the fathers would drink it all away. Such stereotyping!' Then she frowns. The number eleven creases her brow. 'Beware of stereotypes, girls. And never feel trapped by biological destiny. My little sister-in-law makes herself so ill trying to have another baby. And there are ways to prevent it. Other alternatives. I have some pamphlets somewhere…'

She smiles at us. 'Maybe we'll look at them when you're older. Just remember there's more to our lives than sewing, cooking, and caring for children.' She counts off the main subjects of our curriculum on her fingers, then shrugs again. 'And perhaps one day the government will realise it and give us the vote.' Her mouth twists into a mocking grin.

But Yvette takes no notice of Mademoiselle. She just carries on practicing her wedding, with a teacloth on her head for a veil.

THE HEAD-DRESS

But this year, I don't know how or why, Yvette's to be Queen of the May.

'Never mind. It'll probably rain and then no-one will come to see her anyway,' says Augustine, with sudden, spiteful relish. It animates her face, which otherwise would be as doleful as mine. We don't really care that Yvette's mother had to go into a clinic for lung disease. Tuberculosis, they think. Before the war, people said that TB was the disease you caught when you didn't have enough rest, because elves made you dance too long at night. But now we know it spreads rapidly among our soldiers, that Yvette's mother might have caught it during her husband's leave from the front line. She might even die.

'Swollen eyes, pale skin, hates the sight of bright light,' mutters Augustine. 'But is she coughing blood? That's the key symptom. And if she is, then she's a vampire.'

'But I thought vampires sucked blood, not coughed it.'

'Silly,' says Augustine. 'The only way she can make up for her loss of blood is to suck it from other people. Like this.' She bares her teeth and approaches my neck.

I slap at her, but her sharp little canines nip the skin beneath my ear. Later, when I check in the mirror, there are two indentations, and a soft mauve bruise.

Augustine drops an apologetic kiss on my sore neck. She pushes her face very close to mine, so close I can feel her breath against my cheek. Her eyes are sparkling.

'Now Yvette's mother's a vampire, she'll drain the life away of everyone else in her family. And you know what that means,' she adds.

'No more Yvette,' I say.

'Thank goodness,' says Augustine. 'Because of her, we weren't even picked to be the May Queen's attendants this year.'

Then her eyes flash green with a wicked plan. Every year, Mademoiselle stitches together a head-dress of clustered cloth flowers and paper leaves for the May Queen. And we know where it's kept. Inside the drawer of her desk on the platform at the front of the class.

The next day, we arrive early at school. The blinds inside the classroom are still pulled down. Yesterday's sums still on the blackboard. And nobody sees us go inside.

Augustine pulls open the drawer and throws the blameless white head-dress towards me. I drop it as if it had burned my fingers.

'Don't be so stupid,' she hisses and picks it up. I run to the classroom door to keep look-out. Each little noise makes me nervous.

'I don't think we should do this,' I whisper. I step forward and try to pull the head-dress from her grasp.

She snatches it back. The ribbons rip, and before I can stop myself, I enjoy the sound, the sudden moment of destruction, the relief, then the release. The antique dealer's daughter likes to break things, does she?

Loud footsteps outside. We stare at each other, but the sound fades away down the corridor.

Augustine pulls a few more flowers from the head-dress. Her nimble fingers complete their task. She shoves the ruined thing back inside our teacher's drawer, beneath the pile of new exercise books, the pens, the withered apple. Then we dart outside to join the others arriving in the yard.

Augustine's cheeks are guilty red, and she sparkles with malice. But I think I've gone white with fear. My lungs have stopped breathing. There's no blood in my veins. There's a stake through my heart.

It doesn't take Mademoiselle long to discover the destruction. At first, she tries to cajole us into confessing the crime. When that doesn't work, her voice rises an octave.

'You pretend to be such good little girls, who go to confession each week, but you're not brave enough to own up to what you've done,' she sneers. Finally, she tells us all to shut our eyes. The guilty person or persons should then open them.

I can't help it. I squint at everyone through half-shut eyes. But Yvette's eyes are wide open. She's staring at Augustine and me in the front row. Her expression is stricken, ghastly. Her mouth trembles. She knows. She *knows*.

'Oh not you, Yvette, *chérie*,' says Mademoiselle. 'Of course, I didn't mean you.'

I shut my eyes tight. The sight of Yvette's horrified face is more than I can bear.

We don't confess, and so Mademoiselle keeps us all behind an extra hour after school. She dictates a long poem to us and then shouts at us for our mistakes. 'I don't need to tell you girls, I'm very disappointed in you. Very disappointed indeed,' she says before she opens the door and lets us out.

I run into the yard. I don't wait for Augustine. I hear her calling after me as my feet pound the promenade. As the sea crashes over the rocks.

But she soon catches up with me, throws herself against me, knocks me from the sea-path. Then there we both are, crouched down, heads bent, panting and dizzy, when Yvette rounds the corner.

If I keep my head down, stare at the long grass, she won't see me. She won't speak to me. She'll go straight past, and I won't have to witness her accusing expression.

'That's right, bury your heads in the sand,' calls Yvette, striding up beside us.

Yvette, she can read my mind, she's the all-seeing, all-knowing, all-powerful God. I gulp, start to giggle, put my hands over my mouth. I know what this feeling is. When Maman sings too loud, weeps, then laughs, her emotions all mixed up, it's *hystérie*. Papa said so, and I wrote the word down in my notebook.

Yvette glares at me, and the giggles subside. 'I'm sorry,' I mumble. 'I can't help it.' She turns away, looks straight past me, at Augustine.

But Augustine's recovered her breath, and her composure. Her eyes are narrow, and she gives nothing away.

'Just you wait, Augustine Solange,' says Yvette, 'Just you wait.'

'Until when?' says Augustine, using the same voice her mother uses when she speaks to tradesmen and hired farmhands. 'Until you know your twelve times table? Until you can spell *'j'accuse'*? I'll be waiting a long time. Besides, you've no proof it was us.'

Thanks for the *us*, Augustine. You've as good as admitted it, and now Yvette knows I was definitely involved, as well.

But Yvette smiles. 'Oh, Odette isn't like you, Augustine,' she says, 'She feels more, so she hurts others less. But you, you're something else. You just wait…I won't tell Mademoiselle, because after all, a few detentions won't solve anything. But one day, when you're least expecting it…'

I wish she'd stop smiling. That's how the farm cat looks, when we pour him some cream. Or when he pulls apart a mouse.

But now there's a feline look to Augustine as well, her eyes, all green and round and glittery, and suddenly I'm scared of both girls. I remember the death mask. Someone peering at me through the hole in the fence. Yvette, Augustine, they're each as bad as the other.

So now I run, run away from them, back to Maman and Papa and Pierre, and our curving crescent moon house, and our tea-times in the parlour, and the drop of cream that falls from the lip of our porcelain jug, which I catch and lick, but no-one minds. Because, at home, that's about the worst thing I could do.

But now, I go straight to my room and write down the crime in the notebook. The ink dries quickly. It looks even worse like that, even more unforgivable.

Then I hear my mother's tread upon the stair. The third one creaks. I quickly scribble out the sin. Then I throw the notebook underneath the bed.

Maman's face peers round the door. 'There you are,' she says. 'I was just looking for you to tell you about Yvette's mother.'

I catch my breath.

Maman places a cool, cologne scented hand against my forehead. Even though she's a wife and mother, not a nun, it still feels like forgiveness. The state of grace after confession.

I don't deserve it.

'Poor little girl. You're really worried about her, aren't you?'

I stare at her with imploring eyes.

'I talked to a nurse I know from the clinic. It was bronchitis, not tuberculosis. They're letting her go home tomorrow.'

Oh. No vampires. No dancing elves. I sigh, a long, drawn-out breath.

'I'm glad you have such a kind heart,' says Maman. 'Come downstairs and I'll make you a *tartine*. A special treat before you start your homework.'

I follow my mother out of the room without a backward glance. I don't need to. The telltale notebook is throbbing beneath the bed.

THE PAIR OF WHITE GLOVES

That Sunday, Maman comes running into my room, all out of breath. Her cheeks are flushed, and her eyes sparkle bright as diamonds.

'Oh Odette,' she gasps. 'There you are. I've misplaced…that is to say, I've lost my white gloves. Could I borrow yours for church, please?'

'But Maman,' I say. 'When did you ever wear gloves to church? You'd go barefoot if it weren't for Monsieur le Curé.'

'Not Monsieur le Curé,' she says, and darts me a warning look, before continuing, self-consciously, 'But your Papa, you know, he can be so particular about these things.'

I shrug. 'Well, if it's that important to you…'

Maman nods. 'It is,' she says. She smooths her white skirt flat against her legs, and I note her glossy hair, her immaculate appearance. So different to how she looks during the week, when she wears an old blouse covered in Minouche's fur, and never wets her unruly hair. In fact, her weekday self makes me wonder why Papa married her at all.

But, 'I only want a wife for Sunday best,' I imagine him saying.

I pull open the drawer of the rosewood *armoire* and root around for a pair of cotton gloves. There they are, scarcely worn, resting against each other like weary sisters. I take them out, and then they are so sleek with their tapering fingers and delicate folds, that I don't want to lend them.

'I'll be careful,' Maman murmurs but when she snatches at them, I don't believe her.

She gives me a quick, apologetic look, and then she dashes out of the room again. I stare at the empty space in the drawer where the gloves had lain, whilst the church bells give out their hurried peals for morning Mass.

THE STEP-LADDER

'Papa,' I begin.

He raises his head from the catalogue. His eyes peer out from behind his spectacles. He blinks. 'Yes, Odette?'

'Papa, why did you marry Maman?'

His eyebrows edge higher into the grey thatch of his hair. 'Why, Odette,' he coughs. 'Don't you know? She was left to me in a will.'

'A will, Papa?'

'Yes. My dear friend, Constance Duchene, your grandmaman, bequeathed me her youngest daughter. 'You will take good care of her, Emile, I know,' she said. 'You see beauty in such unlikely places."'

'But did none of her brothers and sisters want her after she left the convent school?'

Not wicked stepsisters, like in *Cendrillon,* but half-brothers, half-sisters. They should have done *something* for her.

'Well, Odette,' says Papa, lowering his eyebrows. 'It's like this, you see. Your Maman's relatives were kind enough to her, but... remember your Pierrot doll. There he was, with the company of all the other toys in the toyshop, and still he wasn't happy.'

I nod, uncertainly.

'It wasn't until we brought him home and cared for him that he stopped feeling so lonely. That's just how it was with Maman.'

Mais non. It can't be. But then perhaps that's how the grown-ups think.

Although Maman, when she married, was she a grown-up? 'Quite old enough to know her own mind,' like Papa says? Or was she still a doll, to be taken out of her convent-school toy-box and dressed by her guardian in pretty clothes, a pearl choker, a wedding gown?

Old enough! He can talk. As he reaches for another book to catalogue, I can't help but notice the white hairs clustered beneath the knuckles, the prominent wrinkles and veins, the slight tremor. That last trip to Rouen aged him.

He went again to the Musée Flaubert, to find out whether they had managed to identify the death mask. But instead he saw a head, an actual mummified head, of a man guillotined in 1793. The man had fine pointed features, and good teeth. Only his eyes were glass.

'*Mais mon Dieu - son visage!* A look of unbearable terror. You can tell he looked like that when he was taken dripping from the scaffold. More than a century ago, Odette, just think of that.'

But I shake my head. I don't want to think of it.

'Of course, you're young,' rasps Papa. He takes another pinch of snuff, then enters the name of the early edition in quivering copperplate in his ledger. Malory's *Morte D'Arthur*. Then he forces the book in between some tightly packed volumes, next to a French translation of *The Interpretation of Dreams* by Sigmund Freud, *sans couverture*. And *sans illustrations* too, just lots of close-set type – so I haven't tried to read it yet, though I think the title's pretty.

Next Papa decides to climb a ladder, just to set a picture straight. As if anybody cared.

'Odette,' he says after a moment, in a very small voice, 'The ladder's wobbling. Can you hold it steady for me, please?'

I glance at him. It's only the little stepladder with three wooden steps that we always use. Perhaps he's too old to climb it.

But there isn't time for me to reach it, before Papa gasps and topples. Then he's lying on the floor, with the elongated numbers of the shop door painted over him.

He's pretending. Another one of his little jokes, surely. Look, he's smiling.

No. He's grimacing. His lips are turning blue. His chest labours but he can't force the air inside.

I step forwards, fast as I can, but it takes forever to reach him. I pick his hand up. It's so cold. He groans. I want to go and stay, both at the same time.

'I need to fetch help,' I tell him.

Heart attack, they say later, and a lung infection. Pneumonia.

My shoes clack along quiet, disinfected corridors. I enter the ward, with its white, identical beds on either side, its sweaty old men staring at me as I pass.

Papa is propped up against some pillows. The sheets trap him against the mattress. His woollen nightcap lolls against his face. He tries to smile but his lips tremble. His tongue strains to form words.

I pour him some water from the jug. But it leaks in tears from his glassy eyes. Too old.

THE POTATO MASHER

Without Papa, Maman isn't coping well. She hasn't got out of bed for three days. I've made Pierre all his meals, but 'Not omelette again, please, 'he begs.

'Well, what would you like?'

'Roast duck and jam,' he says.

'You can't have duck with jam.'

'But we did, we did,' he says. 'At Augustine's, for her Name Day.'

'Oh, you mean plum *confit*,' I say.

He nods, his eyes round as his belly. 'Duck, jam, *pommes frites* and *petits pois*.'

'But there's no duck here. What do you want me to do? Go and pull the neck of one up at the farm?'

Pierre flaps his arms, jabs at me with his nose. Bony little nose, his nostrils flaring. 'Quark, quark,' he honks. 'Duck jam, duck jam. *Pommes frites* and *petits pois*.'

'No *pommes frites*' I say, quickly. 'I'm scared of the frying fat. It hisses, sparks, leaps out at you,' I say, making a grab for the duck, holding him close. 'But I can do mashed potatoes and boiled peas. They're easy.'

'As long as there's no lumps in it,' he warns, struggling to set himself free. 'Don't make it like Maman does.'

That's a bit much, I think, considering it was Maman who taught me how to cook. 'Since you're so fussy,' I say, 'You can mash them yourself when they're ready.'

I add salt, pepper, milk and butter to the boiled potatoes in their saucepan. Now a white and golden lake nestles amid pale yellow hills. The land of milk and honey. Then Pierre swoops down with the masher and destroys it.

'Just like God's plagues,' I say.

Pierre gives me a look, and grips the metal *presse-purée* harder, his knuckles, white and strained. 'No Pierre,' he mutters as he mashes. 'You're too little.' 'No Pierre, leave me alone.' He pulverises another potato. 'No Pierre, I'm busy.'

'Do you mean me, Pierre?' I ask, stung. 'I have to do my homework, you know.'

'Not you. Maman. Too busy sleeping to play with me.'

After all, he's only five. It isn't fair. And as I watch him pound the potatoes, shell the peas, I realise, something has got to be done.

THE DECANTER

So the next day, I tell Mademoiselle at school what's happened.

'I'm so sorry,' she says. 'That's a lot to cope with at your age. But don't make it worse for yourself.'

'How do you mean?'

'You feel too much, Odette,' she replies, her eyes bright, her hair glossy as crow-feathers. She tips her head to one side. 'You're too aware of other people's pain. And then you absorb it and hold onto it.' She takes my hand, gives it a squeeze. 'It becomes yours and hurts you.'

Her voice drops an octave. 'Little *oiseau*. It's right that you should care about your mother, but you also need to care about yourself.' But she agrees to come home with me after school.

I knock on Maman's bedroom door and enter the room. She's shuffled all the pillows into the centre of the bed. She lies still, straight down the middle, her head facing the wall.

'Maman? Mademoiselle from school is here.'

She should get out of bed. She's not the one who's sick.

Maman turns her head away from the wall. She brings me into focus. 'What have you been telling her?' she says. Then she reaches for her handkerchief and blows her nose.

Finally, I persuade her to put on her *robe de chambre*, come downstairs and greet our guest.

Mademoiselle Madeleine. I never knew her name before.

'Like Magdalene, the fallen woman?' asks Maman, tightening the belt of her robe.

'Like the little cake,' says Mademoiselle, trying not to smile. It's true, she's become a squat, plump, delicious little woman. She always says she eats too much because she remembers when the Catholic shopkeepers refused to sell her bread and milk.

'Ah, Proust,' says Maman, showing off. Showing that she's a cultivated lady, too. 'Dipping madeleines into spoonfuls of tea and feeling shivers of exquisite pleasure.'

Mademoiselle raises her eyebrows. The arched brow, the curve of her cheekbone, all she needs is a spotlight trained upon her.

And it seems Maman and Mademoiselle share an interest in French theatre. Moliere, Racine, Corneille, they swap the hallowed names, then their favourite dramatic quotations. "Books and marriage go ill together," says Maman.

"I prefer an interesting vice to a virtue that bores," parries Mademoiselle, her eyes snapping messages I don't understand. Then she nods towards my father's finest dust-covered decanter of Calvados on top of the cabinet. 'And what you need, *chérie,* is a little drink to cheer you up.'

Who is she? A dedicated teacher or one of those flappers, the *garçonnes* Papa reads about in the newspaper, who like to dance and party?

Maman finds some glasses, retrieves the decanter, pours them both a drink.

I stare at her. That's Papa's best Calvados. His brandy made from the farm's cider apples, a special present from Monsieur Solange before he went away to war. It's to be sipped only at Christmas and christenings, I *know*. Papa isn't going to be happy.

After her second glass, Mademoiselle intones a male lead, the bourgeois Nobleman, Monsieur Jourdain. Fencing, dancing, singing, she sports the most killing manner. Then she seizes the decanter and pours herself another drink. 'And for you, *chérie?*' she says to Maman, waving the glass in lordly fashion.

Come on Maman, enough's enough. Tell her no. After all, you know you can't drink. Just one glass of watered-down wine on your birthday and your head starts spinning.

'D'you know,' says Maman to Mademoiselle, 'Normally if I drink one glass, just one glass, mind you, of diluted wine, my head starts spinning. But with this Calvados, I feel per-fect-ly fine.'

'Must be it's superior quality,' says Mademoiselle, smacking her lips, tilting her glass towards the light.

'Oh we're all very la-di-dah superior today,' agrees Maman and the fiery trickle of Calvados disappears straight down her throat. Then there's a hectic flare to her cheeks and her eyes glitter.

'Perhaps you should go back to bed,' I say, very quietly.

'Oh you,' says Maman, breathing fast. 'You're far too serious for a child your age. You should learn how to enjoy yourself.' She takes another gulp of her drink, then snatches the heavy velvet curtain, drapes it round her waist, joins it with her topaz brooch.

In her new, flowing skirt, she curtseys to Monsieur Jourdain, then giggles, the image of the maidservant, Nicole. "Oh beat me, Monsieur! Please, just beat me and let me laugh! I can't bear it. I'd rather laugh my fill and take a beating for it."

I compress my lips. I don't know what to say.

But Maman understands. 'Well, after all, your father wouldn't want me to sit and mope.'

No, but I want you to. As long as you don't mope too much. As long as you're still my mother, and not some unreachable stranger.

'Little *oiseau*, little thundercloud, little *citron*-sour *tartine*,' sings out Maman, then leans across me to chink glasses with Mademoiselle.

THE TOPAZ BROOCH

Later that night, loud laughter wakes me, followed by the sound of a lullaby. *'Monique a perdu son...'* My lullaby. My mother's voice, completely out of tune.

I creep down the spiral staircase and press my eyes to the crack in the parlour door. Maman is slumped forwards in the rocking-chair, still laughing, still trying to sing. '*Son grand pierrot, toujours en satin blanc.*' Mademoiselle stands behind her, her arms resting on my mother's shoulders. She dips her head and drops a kiss on the back of Maman's neck. The bare white patch of skin at the base of her upturned hair.

Mademoiselle points to the wedding photograph on the wall, says something, laughs. She reaches for it and places it face down on the occasional table. Then she steps forwards and pulling the curtain across the window, shuts out the night.

Maman's topaz brooch darts a sudden, warning gleam at me. Glittery green blue. I shut my eyes, overwhelmed. But the image of the two women, together, remains superimposed on my eyelids.

Am I dreaming?

THE COPPER PAN

When I next visit Papa in hospital, I look for his beloved pot of black paint beneath the bed. Of course, it isn't there. Just a copper bedpan.

For some reason, this makes me angry. Furious. I straighten up and glare at him. You're too old. That's all that's wrong. You're just too old and tired.

Broken, and can't be fixed.

And it seems he agrees with me, his head dips low on his chest. He sighs and then he seems so small, so lost. His eyes shine with tears, and just for a moment, he reminds me of Pierre.

Papa's last breath mingles with the breeze that stirs the orchard leaves. And then, that's it, he's gone. Not even *au revoir*.

I call for the nurse, the doctor, anyone who can help. But it's too late. Thirty, forty years too late. Papa, I wish I'd known you when you were young. Your arms always ached when you lifted me. The tremors grew so bad, you were frightened to handle your antiques. It was all wrong.

'Wrong,' I say to the nurse as she approaches the bed. She gives me a quick, startled look, and then lifts Papa's wrist. No pulse. I could have told her that.

'Go and wait for me in the room at the end of the corridor,' she says. '*Ma pauvre*,' she adds. She's wearing black woollen tights. They make her legs look scrawny, like a crow's. Will we all have to dye our clothes black, live in perpetual mourning now? But Augustine didn't, when her father died. She just wore a black armband with his initials on it. Very proud of it, she was. Though she doesn't wear it anymore.

But Augustine, I think, as I drag myself down the corridor, measuring out its silence. I want Augustine. You're the only one who can understand me, now. Not the nurse. I'm not going to wait for her. She must have seen hundreds of people die. Papa isn't special to *her*.

I disappear between the hospital-doors, then trail through the village, my shoes heavy on the pavement. My shadow follows behind me.

A horse and cart trundle past. The horse has a black mane and shining hooves. He's breathing fast, plumes of white mist. I want to climb on his back and ride away from here. To Augustine.

Someone grabs my elbow. 'You ought to be more careful, *ma fille*,' he says. 'You don't want to get knocked down.' He escorts me towards my father's shop, tips his brown felt hat and smiles. Then I recognise him. Mademoiselle's brother, Monsieur Carpentier. The undertaker's assistant, before he lost his job. I scowl at him from beneath my fringe, but he's already gone.

Since I'm here, I may as well check the shop. I push open the door - I must've forgotten to lock it. But it's all right, I don't think anything's been stolen. Everything's safe. The mirror, throwing my reflection back at me. The bronze statue of Pan. The ship in a bottle. All present and correct. But perhaps I'd better make a list, an inventory, to be sure. That's what Papa would want me to do.

Papa. I gulp, then reach for the little, stiff-covered notebook where I used to write my sins. I stop at a white page and rule off some new columns.

THE METAL COMB

Coming home, I breathe in deeply, then push open the parlour door. I exhale, a great, shuddering sigh. Thank God everything's still the same. Same shutters, curtains, cushions, daylight. Same snowstorm gleaming on the high-up shelf.

Same curving crescent moon house.

But not Maman. She'll never be the same again. I must stay with her, comfort her, and then it's too dark. Too dark and too late to leave the house and find Augustine.

And then that night, I see Papa. He still looks the same, kind smile, tired eyes, but he's thinner, more shadowy. He walks through the house, daubing black paint everywhere. While Minouche howls ceaselessly in the yard. Like when she had fleas, and we wouldn't let her inside.

Though one night, I tiptoed downstairs. The third stair creaked. My bare feet were cold against the parquet floor. I opened the back door and threw my arms around Minouche's neck. Then I fetched a metal comb and a bucket of water. I started to brush the fleas out of Minouche's bobbly fur. I watched them float on the surface of the water. But there were so many of them, they made me feel sick.

And when I went back up to bed, it was worse.

She wouldn't stop howling.

THE BAND OF GOLD

Maman twists the gold band nervously round her ring finger. Her hands are so thin now beneath their freckles, but that isn't why she's selling it.

It's because, without Papa's earnings, we're poor.

Even the furniture is being sold. And if things don't pick up soon, we'll have to sell the house. And then where will we live?

Maman starts to rock herself backwards and forwards, her head bent low, biting the ends of her plaits. She won't look up.

She won't look up for me, but she will for Mademoiselle. She'll smile for her, let herself be soothed and comforted.

Maman needs a mother. I'm not old enough, not wise enough.

But then Mademoiselle's sister-in-law dies in childbirth, and the poor little baby too. She must not have read the pamphlets. Or else, she didn't understand them. And Mademoiselle is taking her brother and nephew away for a holiday, a rest.

'Don't go,' Maman implores. 'Your brother is strong, a man. He can manage without you. I can't.' She slumps forwards in her rocking-chair, more tired than she can say. 'Death comes in threes,' she whispers. 'I'm so afraid. All the time.' She twists her wedding ring round and round.

If she sells it, will she still be married to Papa?

THE MOTHBALL

Like Augustine's mother, Maman has stopped attending Church, at least for the time being. But *I'm* in need of spiritual sustenance, so I'm going to go to Mass by myself. Maybe I'll have a crisis of faith. Then Jesus will come and put his arms around me. He'll show me the roses on the backs of his hands and feet, and say, 'My love, why sufferest thou?'

But no. Just as Monsieur le Curé is saying, 'Peace be with you,' the back of my thigh begins to itch. The sensation travels higher, makes me squirm.

One of Minouche's fleas.

Cautiously, I wriggle my leg to make the flea drop off. But it crawls up towards my drawers. I squash my thigh against the hard wood of the pew, hoping to crush it to death. For a moment, the itching stops.

In the pew in front of me, Viscountess Agathe starts to twitch. Her fingers stray to the small of her back. They disappear beneath her waistband. The flea must have jumped from me to her. I wonder if she finds it. Or perhaps it drops dead, asphyxiated by her odour of lavender, mothballs, and old lady's sweat.

After Mass, on the church porch, the Viscountess stops me. 'When I came back from communion, I noticed, child, that you couldn't keep still. You must be suffering a great deal at this time.'

I bow my head and try to look saintly. It must work, because she clasps my hand and says, '*Ma pauvre*. I feel for you. You must come up to the *château* in the afternoons and read to me.' Her palms are warm, moist, but she has liver spots on the back of her hands. That's worse than Maman's freckles.

'My mother needs me at home,' I stammer. 'She's not well at the moment.' Though now that I'm thirteen, I'm always at home. I've reached the end of my compulsory education and that's it. Never mind that I wanted to stay on and try for the *baccalauréat*, like Maman once did: now, we're just too poor.

'Your mother needs some money in her pocket,' says the Viscountess, her eyes narrowing as she pats her reticule, releasing another waft of mothball. Though perhaps they smell so strong because we don't have any at home. Maman doesn't care about mothballs. Or moths.

'I'll pay you,' continues the Viscountess. 'And besides, it'll be entertainment for you, and company for me.' I nod, unable to think of any more excuses. I'm sure if I had more education, I'd be able to think of them. But without it, I know I'll always be thirteen inside my head, and never any wiser.

'Good, then that's settled.'

So one afternoon, I find myself trudging up the hill. I pause to take in the Château de Courseulle's cream granite columns, blush-pink walls, lordly turrets and ninety-nine windows. Just one more, and the Viscountess would have had to pay a higher rate of tax.

One of the walls facing the fields is round. 'Is it a tower?' I later ask the Viscountess.

'No child,' she says. 'It was built like that to avoid damaging a beautiful tree.'

'Oh,' I say, and for the first time, I think perhaps this job won't be too bad. But it is. The Viscountess pretends to doze, but beneath her fleshy lowered lids, her eyes are sharp. Sharp enough to notice my wandering attention and call it back to her. The stories in *Lettres De Mon Moulin* are certainly monotonous. The windmills are all disappearing anyway… And the sound of my own voice lulls me into a dream, whilst the mellow light of the afternoon splashes round us, golden as cider.

Until it's time for me to go and I curtsey to Viscountess Agathe. Like Nicole, with Monsieur Jourdain. Then I run home and when I get in, I pick Pierre up and squeeze him half to death. I'm so happy to see him, after my afternoon with the old lady.

With all our make-do and mend, Maman and I have managed to save enough to buy him a model fort for his sixth birthday, from the big toyshop in Rouen. We'll all help to make it; we'll cut out all the little cardboard pieces, and glue them, together. But for now, he's content enough to be left to himself, sorting out his toy animals onto the different squares of the patchwork rug.

THE SNOWSTORM

But a few months later, when I arrive home one afternoon, Maman isn't sitting squinting over the sewing she takes in, giving herself a migraine. And Pierre isn't sprawled beside her on the patchwork rug, playing with his Noah's Ark. Two *by* two *by* two.

Instead, when I enter the parlour, Augustine and Augustine's mother are there, standing by the fireplace. Augustine reaches out her arms to me. But as I approach her, she looks frightened, and puts them behind her back. And Augustine's mother says that I am coming to stay at the farm with them, because my mother is in hospital.

And Pierre is dead.

Someone is screaming somewhere in the room. I lose myself in the sound, and then I'm far away. Why is that bird screeching? But the mist and flames and fire pass, and the bird disappears, and there, beneath the juniper tree, stands the little brother, and he takes the father and the sister by the hand, and then they all three go inside the house and rejoice.

That's how the fairy-tale ends, but it isn't true, it isn't true, and the waves are covering over his face, and this time, I can't hide it from him. He isn't coming back, and I can't make the sea stop, can't stop screaming, please help me, please, somebody do something…

Augustine's mother puts her hand on my shoulder, presses down, hard. I shudder and then the screams stop. She takes her hand away.

She wants to make me a camomile *tisane*. To calm my *hystérie*. '*Camomile pour les vieilles filles*,' she always says. It's for old ladies. I don't want it. I want Pierre, with his dark, shining eyes and his baby scent of *tarte-Tatin*.

'Bring me back an apple,' he'd begged this morning. But on my way home, it was cold, and I hurried, and forgot. And now it's too late. Now my hands swing empty, useless at my sides. Unless…something glints, catches my attention. The snowstorm. I'm tall enough to reach it now.

I throw it to the ground before Augustine or her mother can stop me.

Ver-Sur-Mer lies shattered all around us. A broken church steeple. A patch of painted blue sea. And all the snowflakes, falling, falling.

The tears will never stop falling.

And I think it must be my fault because of what I did to Yvette when her mother was sick.

Or because I minded so much about having to read at the *château*.

Or else it's my fault, because I wasn't with them when they went down to the sea. I always warned Maman not to swim when the waves were high. She and Pierre, tossed about like seaweed, to be washed up on the shore with the tar-streaked feathers and the bits of broken glass.

But then Augustine runs to me and hugs me so tightly that I can't breathe. For a moment it seems as if all the broken pieces might fit back together again. Like the bones in the story of 'The Juniper Tree.'

Then I look at the shattered glass around us and realise - they will not.

THE NIGHT LIGHT

When Augustine's family have gone to bed, and the farmhouse is quiet, I sit by their kitchen fire. The apple branches catch alight; arching, quivering; they send a shower of sparks up the chimney.

Or perhaps the crackling sound is a woman, shaking down her hair, gleaming red from the flames. She holds out her arms to me, embraces me, then covers me with a shawl. Laughing as it catches in her loosened braids.

A woman with my face, softened in the circle of light. A woman with the scent of green apples in her hair.

The last few embers from the gnarled bark glow. Soft lips brush against my face. A farewell.

And now, darkness. Where's the night-light Maman promised to keep burning? The stump of candle floating in a saucer of water?

Maman, who doesn't keep her promises.

In my dream, I reach to open the shutter, to let in the moonlight. But from the window, I see a figure picking her way through shadow and silhouette of leaf and hedge, then running down the shingle path towards the sea.

The waves tug at her cloak, the hood falls away from her face. Her loosened braids spill out. I call, and she half turns, but her eyes are already glazed over with strange determination. Already deaf and blind to me, to everything except the underwater existence she's chosen, already white and dark as the sea.

She holds out her arms to the water and it covers her over.

Salt of tears stings my eyes. The moon floods the floorboards of my dream.

I wake to find the kitchen fire's gone out. Someone kind has thrown a shawl over my shoulders. Augustine, Jacques or their mother.

Beneath the prickle of new wool, my dream makes me shiver.

Maman wasn't just bathing in the sea: she wanted to drown. But why did she take Pierre?

THE GREEN MADONNA

Maman is away a long time. They let her out of hospital once, for Pierre's funeral, but then she has to go back inside. There's a cut on the side of her face that won't heal. She needs a rest. She isn't mended. Whilst she's gone, I can't stop thinking about 'The Juniper Tree.' What if it wasn't his evil stepmother who killed the little boy? What if it was his real mother?

Winter gives way to spring, snowflakes to apple-blossom. But when Maman finally comes home, for good, she's no longer the same person, anyway. A green Madonna rather than a blue one.

One afternoon, I leave the *château* early. I run home through the farm's orchards, panting, gasping for breath. And when I finally arrive, Maman is sitting on the patchwork rug, with my Pierrot doll on her lap. All around her are red snakes of her hair. She snips off the last strand just as I'm shutting the front door.

Silently, I hold out the apple and she smiles at me. An upside-down smile.

And I'm the mother and she's the daughter. I help her into her cotton night-dress, the one with the *broderie anglaise*. I tell her she can keep Pierrot to cuddle, for now. Only, when I wake at night, I'm lonely without him. I creep into their bed, and put my arms around her, and listen to the quiet sound of her breathing.

Sometimes it's so quiet, I think she's stopped breathing completely.

THE BASKET OF WILDFLOWERS

Maman's hair is longer now. She attends Church again. The women from the choir take her for Sunday walks, picnics, gathering wildflowers in woven baskets slung over the crooks of their arms.

Mademoiselle returns to the village school. Her compassionate leave is over, and she wants to keep her job. Besides, when she isn't teaching, she'll be her brother's housekeeper, in his cottage with its white-washed stone walls. I suppose if you don't have a husband, you might as well take care of your brother.

'You ought to take better care of your brother.'

I ought to have, yes.

And then, one day, Maman decides that she will open up the antiques' shop again. And who does she ask to help her run it? Why, Mademoiselle's brother, of course. But I know I can't let her out of my sight. So on the first day of the shop reopening, I announce that I will go too, to make an inventory.

'You're so clever, Odette,' says Maman. 'I would never have thought of that.'

Inside the shop, everything is present and correct: the freckled mirror, the bronze statue of Pan, the ship in the bottle. I tick them off on the list on my clipboard, frowning at the grown-ups who have left me to do all the work. Maman has tucked her hair behind her ears, but she keeps pulling at a strand that has come loose. Monsieur Carpentier smiles at her, then polishes the same three inches of counter, over-and-over again.

'Aren't we lucky that Monsieur Carpentier is here to help us, Odette?' Maman says.

'He gets paid, doesn't he?' I mutter.

Maman gives me such an uncharacteristically sharp look that I wonder if she heard me. 'There are hardly any men of any use left since the war took them all from us,' she says. 'But Monsieur Carpentier was here for us in our hour of need.'

'Oh, do call me Bertrand, please,' says Monsieur Carpentier.

'Call me Bertrand, please,' I mimic, *sotto voce*.

50

'Oh Bertrand,' says Maman, 'your sister has told me so much about you. She is my dearest friend, you know.'

'She speaks highly of you too,' says Monsieur Carpentier. 'Since my wife died, I haven't been much in the way of company, but Madeleine was saying you should come to our house for Sunday lunch.'

Maman stops twisting her hair in order to clasp her hands together. 'Oh, that sounds delightful!' she says. 'The very thing, isn't it, Odette? A lovely family Sunday lunch.'

'The mirror's cracked,' I say, 'and the ship in the bottle is missing its cork.' But, and, I don't know why, they both start laughing, and all I can do in response is scowl.

Maman often visits them at the cottage. Her face blooms and she is young again. And in the end, I wonder who she's visiting, the sister or the brother. Because it's the brother she's going to marry, and the women in the shop laugh and say, 'She's lucky to find one. There aren't many men left, since the War.' A sixth of the men from the village are dead, but, 'Your turn next,' they grin when I go to buy bread.

At the wedding, my eyes slide away from their smiling faces. They're sore with weeping, as red-rimmed as Mademoiselle Madeleine's eyes, before she pulls down her hat's veil and hides them.

She doesn't want to stay here, after all; she doesn't want to keep house for the newly wed couple. She'll look after her nephew Paul until they get back from their honeymoon, but then, after that, she's leaving for her new position, in Bayeux. Besides, the school superintendent wasn't too impressed with the letter she wrote to the local newspaper, about the importance of teaching birth control methods to young women.

Mademoiselle Magdalene. No State of Grace for her.

Still, I can't blame her for wanting to go. She loved Maman. Like a sister. But it wasn't enough. All we did for Maman, all of us, it was never enough. She had to have a husband.

Monsieur Bertrand Carpentier.

THE POSTCARD

He's scrawled his name at the bottom of the postcard Augustine waves in front of my eyes. 'For you,' she says, smiling. I bet she's read it. Not that I care.

And, in my mother's handwriting, 'Love you lots *chérie*, and wish you were here. *Bisoux*.' No, Maman, of course you don't, not on your honeymoon. And it's a long time since I wanted you here.

Because I hate her, hate her so much now. 'She's *definitely* like the stepmother in 'The Juniper Tree." I say.

'What do you mean?' asks Augustine.

So I fetch my notebook, with the quotation I've copied out from the fairy-tale.

Augustine peers over my shoulder and reads. *'The mother sprang up, with her hair standing out from her head like flames. 'I will leave as well,' she said, 'and see if the bird will lighten my misery, for I feel as if the world is coming to an end."*

'See?' I say, turning my face towards her. 'Doesn't that sound exactly like Maman? And here's the best bit,' I add, reading aloud. *"As the mother crossed the threshold, crash! The bird threw the millstone down on her head, and she was crushed to death."*

Augustine doesn't reply. Her eyes narrow and her face looks strange, as if she's frightened of someone. But there's no-one else here today, just us.

Though it's true, I want to push Maman over, so she falls and cracks her head on the hard stone hearth. So that she breaks into little pieces, so many, that she can't be mended. I wouldn't care, no, not even if she tumbled into the flames. I want her to *burn*.

But no, I can't do that.

Though I am taking back my Pierrot doll. She shan't have him in her bed. She'd only roll over and crush him.

I crumple the postcard. Its' black and white towers fold over, as if they've been set alight. Goodbye Maman's *vie de château*. Goodbye Bertrand's castles-in-the-air. I snap shut my notebook, turn towards Augustine.

'It's all right,' I say, smiling. 'Nothing to worry about. I've just made a very important decision, that's all. When they get back from their honeymoon, I'm going to tell them. I'm not going to live with them.'

And when I run into Maman in the village, I won't smile at her and say hello. If she tries to kiss me, I'll turn my head away, blind to her entreaties and her basket of flowers. Because who'd want a betrayer's kiss, with her mouth all bristling, sharp as needles? And Judas in the illustrated Bible had red hair.

Augustine raises inquiring eyes towards me. So beautiful, her eyes. Green as early apples, before the sun ripens them. 'What will you do, then?' she asks, although surely she already knows the answer.

My smile widens. 'I'm going to stay here on the farm, with you,' I say.

Forever.

Part II
Ver-Sur-Mer, Normandy, 1923-7

THE CAMEO BROOCH

Beneath the veil of the moon, the bible-black sky, I often dream I'm walking along the road leading to Ver-Sur-Mer. If I turn left, it becomes a shingle path down to the sea. But if I turn right, past the sacred spring, eventually there are two white stone pillars. The entrance to Augustine's farm.

I pass through them, then into the courtyard. On the far side are the barns, the outbuildings, the hayloft. Nearer to me are the steps, beside them, a white gate. Behind it, there's a pond and a henhouse. Just beyond that are the orchards, then wide, green fields. But I don't want to go that far, today.

Instead, I creep back round the fence, past the wasteland's boarded up hole, easy to spot because the wood's a different colour. Then I climb the steps. They lead into an enclosed garden, surrounded by a stone wall. Here the grass is coarse-grained, and the air is sweet.

Breathe in the aroma of roses, the scented stocks, the snapdragons.

When I pinch the velvet, the dragon always snaps.

A pear tree entices me with its branches. But I'm not going to climb it today. Instead, I crunch over dead leaves. Their musty odour mingles with the fresh, living smell. I tilt my head and then the house rises up before me.

Les Hirondelles, for the birds nesting in the grey-thatched roof. One morning, a swallow flew through the open window, and into my room.

Beneath the roof, the attics, then three solid storeys of leaf-covered stone. The leaves look like ivy, except they're paler, brighter. In autumn, they're a riot of red, and even now, they're crimson-edged.

I walk towards the side-door and push it open. Pass quickly through the parlour and into the dining room, neglected, unpainted. Nobody uses it. Run alongside the shabby horse-hair *chaise-longue,* the mahogany table, the straight-backed chairs

- only the black and white tiles on the floor are beautiful. Then I clatter past the staircase, down the passageway and stop at the kitchen-door.

I can't help knocking, though I've lived here for a few months now.

'Come in, you daft thing,' calls Madame Solange.

I push open the door. Madame Solange is frowning over the kitchen table. Our wax crayons and drawing books are all piled up there, where they shouldn't be. She smiles at me, then sweeps everything onto the dresser, the books, the chestnuts, the dried, strung berries. She pauses to adjust the canisters. Coffee for Monsieur le Curé, when he calls to debate women's suffrage, or tries to persuade her to return to church. Thin, bitter chicory for everyone else.

She wipes her hands on her apron, sprinkles flour over the surface of the table, slaps down a lump of dough.

Madame Solange is nothing like my mother. Baking, for a start. And severe and gracious as the cameo brooch she wears. A classical profile, a lady of the Manor rather than a farmer's wife. She rolls the pastry out evenly using a transparent glass bottle. A bottle emptied of cider, and minus the label, that showed an apple tree in full flower. From a watercolour painting by Jacques Solange himself.

The side door bangs shut. Then there's the heavy thump-thump of Jacques's boots across the tiled floor. He comes in, dumps his schoolbooks on the floury table, sits down next to me. A hopeful, starving little boy look on his face. Wondering if she'll let him have a *tartine* before Augustine gets home.

Our knees brush beneath the kitchen table.

We smile at each other.

But I look away first. I stand up, warm my hands at the hearth fire. Red flames lick and curl round the heaped wood. One of the ancient apple trees struck by lightening in the recent storm. Not my wasteland sapling, thank goodness.

The smoke's as bluely fragrant as the incense Monsieur le Curé swings round the altar. But I don't search for faces in the leaping flames. I don't need to. I'm home, after all. Everyone dear to me already lives here.

THE WIDE-BRIMMED HAT

In front of me, Augustine trails her wicker-basket, so that it keeps bashing the backs of her legs. Slim, bare, legs, stained the colour of walnut juice, by sun and sea. But Augustine, so deft at swimming and climbing, can barely lift one foot in front of the other.

'I'm tired,' she says. 'Why do we have to do this?'

At the head of our procession, Madame Solange halts, turns, and faces her daughter. 'You know why,' she says. 'And if it's bad for you, it's bad for all of us. Odette and I aren't complaining.'

Augustine mutters something beneath her breath.

'What's that?' says her mother.

'Nothing,' says Augustine.

We continue to pick our way, single file, through the undergrowth. A brown lattice of twigs breaks up the view ahead. I'm just straining for a glimpse of it, when Augustine lets go of a hawthorn branch. But when it hits me, she's so sweet, so contrite, I'm sure it must be an accident.

Besides, her apologies are soon lost in the renewed sound of the river, very near to us. And all around us, gently sloping hills.

'Here we are,' Madame Solange exclaims.

I stumble past them, wanting to be the first to see the valley of yellow flowers.

But Augustine pushes ahead of me, the weight of her basket forgotten, her face radiant with joy. As the flowers close round her, she stretches out her arms and starts to spin. When she stops, she's lost her wide-brimmed hat, and her mass of jetty hair is escaping from its comb. Her cheeks are red. Her eyes dart over our faces, as if she can't see us.

Madame Solange, coming up behind me, nudges me in the ribs.

'See what a beautiful daughter I have,' she whispers. Then, more sharply, 'Augustine, are you going to help us or are you just going to stand there?'

The pupils of Augustine's eyes settle, and she gives a long, slow, sigh. Then we all three start to gather the golden flowers.

'Camomile pour les vielles filles,' Madame Solange always says, but now she wants them for herself - and for me. Because night after night, we meet, heavy-eyed, at the kitchen table. Then she declares we'd sleep better for a poultice of valerian, an infusion of camomile flowers.

Though now, as I gaze at the yellow petals beating in waves against Augustine's dress, I've never been more awake.

THE NOTE-BOOK

Jacques likes honey drizzled on his croissant in the morning. He likes large squares of dark chocolate with a stale baguette in the afternoon. In the evening, he likes *café au lait* in a porcelain bowl large enough for soup. Just a hint of brown sugar.

Jacques likes to spend Sunday afternoon watching the old men play *boules* in the village square. Sometimes he joins in, striding up beneath the lengthening shadows of the chestnut trees. Then he spends the evening fishing, his cap pulled down to shade his eyes, whilst church bells peal in the distance. He likes the quiver on the line when the fish bites the bait. Then the way they slide into a pan slick with butter. A squeeze of lemon.

He likes the dazzle of kingfisher, orange and azure, amid the trees. He likes the way fronds of willow dip into the water, lightly rippling its surface. Sometimes he takes out a notebook and a chewed, stubby end of pencil and tries to sketch them. Though all of his sketches are unfinished: he says it's because an artist once painted a pheasant so perfect, so realistic, that it came to life and flew away.

I *know*, because he often shows me his notebook, though I never show him mine. He blushed to the roots of his hair when I turned the page and saw doodled there, my initials intertwined with his own, over and over again. In the same Gothic style as the initials of Margaret of Anjou and Philibert the Fair in the Church of Brou.

But then, Jacques likes church history books, with illustrations of stained glass windows, and prayer books, and the lives of saints. Dead, buried, but not forgotten.

Jacques has fair, transparent skin, which flushes easily. He has light brown hair and a light-hearted disposition. A deep voice, a lazy smile, and eyes a dazzle of kingfisher blue.

I like Jacques.

THE BUCKET OF MAIZE

Jacques and I slip through the swing-gate that's used to keep out the chicks - so they don't come pecking round the kitchen for their special treat of cider-soaked breadcrumbs.

I crouch down in the low-roofed henhouse, biting my lip. I reach inside the bucket, then hold my hand out to the hen. It's filled with maize. The hen eyes my fingers and bobs towards me. Her comb waggles, and the flaps of skin beneath her beak. Wattles, Jacques calls them. But to me, they're flapping bonnetstrings, like Madame Solange's, the day she found out her husband had been killed. The day the nettles stung Pierre.

The hen advances another step. I draw back, with a cry.

'She won't hurt you,' says Jacques. 'You'll have to get over this fear, you know, if you want to be a farmer's wife.'

I flush crimson.

'Anyway, it doesn't hurt,' he adds, and he puts two corns in his palm. Then he lets the hen peck at his bare hand. 'There, look,' he says.

My own hand jerks forwards and then, just as quickly, pulls away. I try again, start back, again.

Jacques watches and frowns. Finally he grabs my hand and pushes it forwards. The bird pecks, pecks, pecks from my fingers.

'There, you see,' says Jacques. 'It doesn't hurt, does it?'

'No,' I say. It doesn't, though I'm still scared. But I smile at Jacques, then straighten up, and smooth down my skirt.

THE BOOK OF HYMNS

'What shall we do today?' sighs Augustine, fanning herself with her hands.

'Let's go and search for the lost chapel of Saint Gerbold,' says Jacques. 'I've been reading Canon Michel Beziers, and he reckons…'

'No, thank you,' says Augustine. 'Not that again. Not in this heat.'

'How about prawn fishing?' I suggest.

But Augustine shakes her head. 'Let's play Egg,' she says.

'How do you play that?' I ask.

'Each one of us has to scream 'Egg' and the one who can shout it the loudest is the winner,' she says.

'What's the point of that?' asks Jacques.

'We might snap our vocal cords,' she says, hopefully.

'No,' I say. 'Let's go swimming instead.'

Though to reach the stream, we must walk past the sacred spring that runs parallel to the farm. *Les Sources de Saint Gerbold.* The rush of white makes me wonder. Are the old legends true? Is this where Saint Gerbold arrived in Ver, floating on his millstone, miraculously turned to flowers?

And is it the same millstone that crushed the mother to death in 'The Juniper Tree'?

Probably not.

Though the chapel is supposedly founded where he landed, on a Gallo-Roman cemetery, Jacques says. Ugh. The back of my neck prickles. I don't like the idea of Saint Gerbold disembarking on buried bones.

I shake my head, alter my thoughts. When the saint climbed up the stony path, the very pebbles blossomed, giving you the name 'Mount Fleury.' And Jacques says that because of Saint Gerbold's flowers, Ver is named for 'springtime' in Latin. *Vers.* Or else, he says, assuming a knowledgeable air, it's named for a Gallic word, meaning 'alder tree.'

No. Ver is always *Verre*, because of the glass snowstorm with our village inside. That I broke.

Soon we reach the stream. Jacques pulls off his shirt and wades into the water. Augustine and I tuck our skirts into our drawers and follow after him. He throws water over us both, indiscriminately.

The wet, flimsy cotton of Augustine's frock clings to her. She isn't as flat-chested as me. I'm skinnier than Minouche, who pined away after Papa died.

Pierre and I had a funeral for our dog. We buried her in the back garden, said our own prayers, sang our favourite hymns.

*'J'irai la voir un jour.
J'irai loin de la terre,
Sur le coeur de ma Mere,*

Reposer sans retour.'

*'I will go and see her one day,
I will go far from the earth,
On the heart of my mother,*

Resting without returning.'

I don't want to think about Minouche. Or Papa. Or Pierre. Not about any of them. But as the water rushes past my ankles, slips backwards through my open fingers, I can think of nothing else.

THE FOUR EAR-DISHES

Madame Solange bakes bread early in the morning. The warm scent permeates the house, giving rise to yeasty dreams. But by day, this mother of sweet-toothed children is preoccupied with deserts. The bread pudding of Normandy. *Clafoutis aux Abricots. Pomme au foit. Tarte aux poires. The Gratin de Fruits Rouges.* The Berry Gratin. The recipe says you can use cherries, raspberries, or strawberries. She sends Augustine and I to pick blackberries.

We stain our fingers and brambles catch our stockings. We fill our mouths with the plump, luscious fruit. Her open mouth, my open mouth, blackberries jewelled against our tongues.

In the distance, Jacques slashes the hedgerows with his stick.

Madame Solange places the berries into four ear-dishes. In a clear glass bowl, she mixes egg yolks with sugar, so that the mixture froths. She stirs in sour cream. She pours the mixture evenly onto the fruit, then sprinkles granulated sugar on top. Then she places it at the heart of the stove and grills it for ten minutes until it's brown. She calls out to us to come quickly and serves the desert straight away. The hot fruit mix slithers down our throats.

But I wake in the night with cutting pains in my belly. Too much ripe fruit perhaps - knotted in an indigestible lump in my intestines. Then the cramps start, so severe that they force me from the bed.

I run to the bathroom and turn on the new electric light. Bright red stains on the cotton gusset. And streaked all down my legs. Ugh.

I grab a wodge of cloth and try to clean myself up. Poor Augustine. She's had to put up with this for six months already. Then I go back to bed. I pull the covers right over my head. The cramps get worse. I don't cry out, though. I bear it for the Holy Souls in Purgatory.

I won't be able to go swimming with Jacques today.

THE STEREOSCOPE

But anyway, at breakfast, Madame Solange asks me to stay at home. That suits me, my stomach still hurts. She wants me to receive a parcel for her. Or is it for me - my birthday's next week.

So I drag the grey tabby cat onto my lap, and we sun ourselves in the parlour window-seat. Dozing, purring at each other.

A loud rap wakes us. I open the front door to a woman bending over a large cardboard box, shifting it in her arms. She raises her head. A familiar face. In vain, I search for sunlight in the haze of red, but she wears her hair shorter now. Maman.

'I was clearing up,' she says. Then, more firmly, 'I thought you might like some of your Papa's things.' She thrusts the box towards me.

I try to take it and almost stagger. Beneath the woollen scarf and clean handkerchiefs, I catch a glimpse of Freud's *The Interpretation of Dreams*. Perhaps I'm old enough to read it now. But the book, minus its cover, isn't what's making the box so heavy. It's the stereoscope. After the statue of Pan, my father's favourite possession.

I incline my head inside, towards the kettle on the stove. I'll at least make her a cup of chicory. Yet without the protection of the cardboard box, she's vulnerable. She hesitates, twists her hands in her skirt, mumbles, 'I have to get back. Another time.'

But what if now is the only time? Our only chance to reconcile?

Maman walks away without looking back. Her bravery only brought her so far. I watch her go without calling after her. I can do that, because I'm not quite fourteen, and don't yet understand the effort it has cost her.

I shut the door.

I take the box over to the kitchen table, lift out the book, leaf through it. Still incomprehensible. Then I remove the stereoscope from beneath its black velvet cover and root around for the double-imaged cards. When you place them inside the stereoscope, they merge into one three-dimensional image. Places, people, fully rounded, like actors on a stage.

The quaint titles, written in Papa's neat, copperplate handwriting, make me smile. *'How Biddy served the tomatoes in her dressing-gown.'* That one's from England. *'That Pesky Mouse again!'* 'That's one for you, Moïse,' I call to the cat, stretched out on the window-seat.

Then, *'Seaside Belles.'* A group of young women pose in a sand dune near some bathing huts. The little one in white with a big hair ribbon looks a bit like me. I rummage through the pile of images. *'La Bande Joyeuse.' 'La Ronde Champetre,' 'L'Oiseau d'Alain.'* All like pieces in a puzzle, fragments in a story I haven't invented yet.

One card catches my attention. Its title, *'Positively No Admittance,'* seems vaguely prurient. But the image doesn't seem so, to me. I slot it into the machine. And there are two young girls, peeping out from behind a heavy brocade curtain with tassels on the bottom. They wear their hair up, perhaps for the first time. A glimpse of white stocking, a hint of shoulder, bare arms, light summer dresses. Two young girls, sisters perhaps, about their *toilette*. They could be Augustine and me.

How strange it is, that rummaging through the box, looking for my old life, all I can find is the new one.

THE ROSARY

My rosary is amethyst and silver. I know every glint of colour, every chiselled facet, even with my eyes shut. Especially with my eyes shut, as I say my prayers. '*Je vous salue, Marie, pleine de grace…*'

The Holy Mother racks up another prayer-bead for her celestial necklace. Is it amethyst and silver, like mine? Like my prayers, deep, sorrowful purple, filtered through with silver light?

Half an hour every morning, half an hour every night. That's what Monsieur le Curé recommends in the weeks leading up to our confirmation. At first Augustine and I toyed with taking each other's names. But of course, we can't do that. We're not little children anymore, we're proper *jeunes filles*. So we each settle on Marie, after our church.

Not for my mother, Marie-France. Of course, not for Maman.

One time, Augustine and I try to make rosary beads by boiling rose petals in an aluminium saucepan. It has to be aluminium, I'm not sure why. But anyway, we do something wrong, or else we forget about them, and they rot.

Monsieur le Curé takes our confirmation classes, hears our catechisms in the parlour of his house, with its gnarled wooden crucifix next to a portrait of the Pope. It's strange to see him outside of his proper sphere, the church, the confessional box. The new curé I mean, Émile Hamelin. Émile, same name as Papa, but a much younger man: dark, dapper, with a faraway look in his eyes. Ordained in Rome. An odour of sanctity, or at least of heavy incense, clings to his black soutane. Impossible to fantasise about him as I do about Jacques, hugging his image to myself in bed at night.

Mon Dieu. I've lost my place on the beads. I'll have to start my prayers over again.

One bead for each person that I love.

THE WHITE PETAL

The almond blossoms cascade in pink and white waves above our heads. One white petal falls against his cheek. I brush it away. Jacques leans up on his elbow.

'You should have kept it,' he says.

'What would I have done with a bit of almond blossom?'

'Kept it. Pressed it as a souvenir of your fifteenth birthday.' He twists his head round to look at me.

'You, Odette, you're like the almond, too.'

'What do you mean?'

'Well, you know, you're a tough nut on the outside,' he says, 'but there's always the promise of a flower within.'

'Like Saint Gerbold's millstone?'

Jacques's brow creases and then he smiles. 'Exactly like it. Saint Gerbold, who washed up on these shores with his millstone turned to flowers.'

'Some day we'll find his chapel's foundations,' I say, and squeeze his hand.

'The promises of some day,' he replies and starts to recite an old riddle:

'Tell me, my pretty one, tell if you know,
What needs no rain and yet it can grow,
What can blossom, bloom through the years?
And what can yearn, cry without tears?'

I try, not very hard, to guess the answer: 'A spring. A stone. A meadow.'

'You're thinking too literally,' he replies. 'You need to think *met-a-phor-i-cal-ly*.' He teases out the syllables, refuses to tell me the answer.

THE SILVER CROSS

We lie together. The sun is heavy and warm on our eyelids. The long grass closes over our heads like green water. The bushes stretch their flowering branches over us. Tendrils of bright, green vines curl round us. Our hair is still wet from swimming in the stream.

'Supposing we'd drowned today and woken up together here… wouldn't that be perfect?'

I didn't mean to say it out loud.

I hear a long, drawn-out sigh. Then a voice. 'Your little brother,' Jacques says. 'That's who you're thinking about.'

'I wasn't,' I say. It's true. These days, Pierre is always on my mind, which somehow absolves me from consciously having to think of him. 'I was thinking about us. And of what it feels like being here. Our private green world.' I gesture with my hands, annoyed that I can't find the right words, that I can't make him understand. I shut my eyes, frustrated.

He sweeps the green leaves out of my wet hair. He runs his fingers lightly along my forehead, then down to the hollow of my throat. He touches the silver cross his mother gave me for my confirmation. Then, a soft, full pressure on my mouth. He's kissed me.

Everything is green and vivid behind my eyelids. Above us rustle the tops of trees. Then a flurry of feathers, the sound of birdsong.

'Of course I'm here. Of course I'm here,' pipes a red and green bird.

Little Pan god Pierre.

THE LINEN CAP

'Moise, Moise,' I call into the long, grey shadows. But no grey, brindled tabby cat appears. Instead, a young man steps forward and stops in front of me.

It's Paul, one of the men from the village come to help with the harvest. He has dark brown eyes and the same russet, leathery skin as every other worker in the region. His mouth is very red. But his hair is what makes him memorable: it glints white-blond in the early afternoon sunlight.

I nod, and am about to walk away, when he speaks to me.

'S'cuse me, Mademoiselle,' he says, in quite a gentlemanly tone of voice. 'You don't know me, but…'

'Yes I do,' I interrupt, but he continues,

'I'm Paul Carpentier. That is to say, your mother's husband's son.'

Her *beau-fils*. Her stepson. Now there was news I wasn't expecting.

'What I want to say, Mademoiselle, is that your mother and my father are thinking of leaving the village…'

'Why?'

'There isn't enough work here. They're thinking of leaving to go and be servants in a *château* in Noailhac. To a relation of the Viscountess Agathe.'

'Oh,' I say, 'So far away.'

'And I know your mother would appreciate the chance to say goodbye to you before they leave. She's a good person, always been kind to me…' He finishes on an awkward note.

Out of the corner of my eye, I see Augustine open the side-door, carrying a bucket of grain for the hens. She wears a big linen cap to cover her hair, with flaps hanging down to protect her forehead and neck, but the sun has crept beneath them, and reddened her skin.

The sight softens me. 'I'll come,' I say.

Paul follows the direction of my gaze. Augustine's hair is escaping from her linen cap. She reaches up to re-arrange it, her smooth brown arm contrasting with the jetty mass of hair. Her forearms are brown too, and the little V at the base of her neck. And her eyes sparkle, bright and clear as tourmaline turned to the light. She's so beautiful and yet, at the moment, she's not even aware of it.

'Mademoiselle Solange,' says Paul, an answering gleam in his dark brown eyes. He also reaches up, and quite unselfconsciously, smooths down his own hair. 'Please introduce me to your friend,' he says.

I call Augustine over and mutter words of introduction.

They go for a long walk together round the farm. Then, that night, Augustine creeps into my bed to tell me what he's like. She whispers her confessions in the still darkness, against the smooth cheek of my pillow.

'And then he kissed me. And then he touched me - here. And it felt like....'

Almond blossom petals. She wants to share it with me, this new experience of being in love. As if I didn't know.

But unlike Augustine, I keep my secrets.

THE BRONZE HUNTER

Through the chinks in the shutters, bars of sunlight slither across the table. Dust-motes hang suspended in the sharp, gold light. A polite sip of orangeade, the rearrangement of a badly folded napkin, and here we are, staring round at each other.

I can see us all reflected in the froth-framed mirror above the sideboard, doubling the size of the parlour. Maman sits at the head of the table. I'm wedged in between Paul and Augustine. His elbows take up too much room, he gesticulates violently with his large hands. Augustine, in contrast, is demure in a pastel frock. As for me, I peer at myself in the glass.

My face is oval and elongated, my skin, creamy porcelain save for the light splattering of freckles across the bridge of my nose. I smooth my scowl away, and concentrate on my eyes, two hazelnuts, Jacques says. I bring him into my thoughts as a defence against Paul and Augustine's sidelong, amorous glances.

Besides, Augustine's not being much help today. Normally content to chatter away, now she's silenced by Paul's presence.

She steals another glance at him, and then at the bronze statue of the hunter on the mantelpiece. His rifle is slung over his shoulder, resting against his tricorn hat. A greyhound's head and the tip of his nose rest on the hunter's lap.

So Maman kept a few of Papa's antiques, didn't have to sell everything, then. I wonder if she still hates dusting them?

Maman's second husband Bertrand isn't here, out for the day, perhaps not wanting to witness this awkward reunion. Or interrupt it.

I glance across at another bronze on the sideboard, between the pale green glass vases covered in grapes and vines. The statue of Pan, curly head bowed over his pipes. Little Pan god Pierre. Papa used to say that Pierre looked like this statue. But that was when I was quite little. Later, my weekly trips to the confessional box taught me that Pan was a pagan god, blasphemous.

Besides, I knew Pierre was the Pierrot doll, with dark, sorrowful eyes.

'Let's have a little light in here,' Maman says suddenly, throwing open the shutters.

Paul casts a worried glance at the green leaves on the immaculate wallpaper.

'Just this once, Paul, won't hurt,' Maman says. But beneath his stern gaze, the olive branches start to wilt. I'm not sure I like you much, after all, Paul.

'That's better,' she says, brightly. 'Now I can see you all clearly. Odette, Augustine, you both look so pretty. Surely you didn't put on your best dresses, just for me?'

The clock on the mantelpiece ticks loudly in the ensuing silence. Impossible to answer. Augustine has dressed herself in honour of Paul, and not wanting to be outdone, I've followed her example. But my mother's steady, expectant look unnerves me, and I nod.

She pinks with pleasure and clasps her hands in front of her. 'Well, eat up girls,' she says. 'You always did like my *tartines*.'

I swallow another mouthful, wondering how old she thinks we are.

Din dan don. Din dan don. The parlour clock chimes the hour. Twelve.

Or perhaps she imagines time has stood as still for us, as, judging by her looks, it has for her?

Maman takes another sip of orangeade, and it loosens her tongue. She tells us how working in a *château* will be a wonderful opportunity for her. Her eyes gleam as she begins to give herself airs, to see herself as its mistress rather than its housekeeper.

I want to shout, 'You're just going to be a servant, that's all.'

I want to shout, 'Don't go. Stay and be my mother.'

But I'm too old for all that now. I'm fifteen, Maman. Too old for *tartines*, orangeade and finishing my homework in time for supper. I glance back at the bronze Pan. He's just a statue and there's an empty place at the table where Pierre ought to be.

After we've eaten, Paul offers to walk us back to the farm. At first he strides down the centre of the lane, looping arms with both of us. Engaging us both in conversation. Polite enough, I'll grant him that. But presently his head bends low over Augustine's as he tries to catch her whispers, her giggles, her entreaties. The moonlight glances off his silver-blonde hair.

Augustine darts me a look of her own. I know how to interpret it. I unhook my arm from Paul's and dawdle far behind them, in the lane darkened by their shadows. As if I'm the foolish bridesmaid, following after them, with no lantern to guide my way.

THE WICKER BASKET

I clamber among the bushes, clutch the dark jewels, slip them into my basket.

But the brambles catch my dress: the skirt tears at the hem. I run home, hoping to change before I give the blackberries to Jacques. But then I remember, he won't be there. He and Paul are spending the afternoon mending a barn roof.

And I've not even had time to wash my face when Augustine knocks at the door. 'May I come in, Odette?' she asks.

She must want something.

'Of course,' I reply, turning away from her voice, towards the mirror.

She slips behind me and puts her hands around my waist. She peers at herself over my shoulder, adjusts her headscarf, then presents her face to be kissed.

But I don't want to. It's all very well for her, bright and blooming as ever, but me… My lips are stained with blackberry juice, my hair's tangled, my dress is torn.

It doesn't matter. She loves me anyway.

I turn and rest my head on her shoulder. For a moment, I'm tempted to tell her how I feel about Jacques.

'Oh, you've picked them for me,' she says, reaching into the basket.

I sigh. The moment's passed.

Augustine drops a ripe berry into her mouth. 'Let's go and visit your mother again today,' she says.

'I don't want to,' I reply, so startled I say what I really think.

'But Paul…' she entreats, tugging at her scarf.

'Paul won't …' I begin. Be there, silly.

'Paul won't what?' she interrupts.

'Paul won't make any effort if you make it all for him,' I end up saying, parroting her mother. Besides, Paul's only a farmhand, and Madame Solange must want better for her daughter. Even if she sometimes says another pair of strong arms around the farm would be no bad thing.

'You sound just like Maman,' says Augustine, tossing her head. Then she throws me another pleading look. So I wipe my stained mouth, change my dress, find my scarf. I know it'll be a wasted journey but perhaps it'll teach her not to go running after him. Where's her pride? After all, the more Emma Bovary chased Rodolphe, turning up dripping with rain in his bedroom, the less he wanted her.

THE LAMPSHADE

The air is crisp and cool, and I breathe in, deeply.

'Do you remember that day when we wanted to go sailing?' asks Augustine.

'We never managed it though,' I reply. We weren't able to find a fisherman who would take us out on the sea, give up his day's catch for our few coins.

'There's been too much of that,' says Augustine, almost wistfully.

I glance at her in surprise. 'What do you mean?'

'We never end up doing what we want to do. There's always too much work. Yes Maman, I'll do the dishes. No, Maman, I didn't let the bread burn on purpose. All that sort of thing, and hardly a moment to ourselves.'

'It's a lot of work for her, running the farm without your father,' I say.

'I know,' says Augustine. 'And I suppose most of the time I'm happy. But, you, Odette, you're not bound to the farm like I am. Don't you want more out of life?'

I'm not sure how to answer. I've never been able to think of a future that didn't somehow involve the farm, and Jacques, and Augustine.

'It turned out all right in the end,' I say, evading the question. The day we didn't go sailing, we watched the sunshine through the chinks in the pier's wooden slats, dappling the waves beneath us. And every time a man over fifteen and under fifty passed by, Augustine would say, 'That's my husband.'

'Don't let him get away then,' I'd reply, but really, I couldn't see anything special about any of them. All village boys. None of them anything like Jacques.

But now, as the clouds scud ceaselessly above us, I'm suddenly light-headed, dizzy. The broad expanse of sky seems to suggest other possibilities than the farm, the courtyard, the fields that I know.

Then I notice a dark shadow wheeling over us.

'An eagle,' I say.

'You and your birds,' Augustine replies, turning her face upwards, squinting against the sunlight. 'I can't see anything.'

'Must've disappeared behind a cloud,' I say, but she's not that interested and soon we're knocking on my mother's front door.

There's a cry, and then a thud. The door swings open.

'*Mes filles*, what a lovely surprise,' Maman says, almost as if she means it. Her mouth brushes against our cheeks.

Oh. She's still in her night-dress, the one with the *broderie anglais*, and only a shawl slung round her. Her bare feet scuff against the stone flags.

'Forgive me for being *déshabillée*,' she says. 'I was just catching up with Monsieur Flaubert.'

Augustine's eyes widen, and she peers past my mother, as if she's expecting to see a strange gentleman, similarly undressed. But Maman gestures towards the *chaise-longue* with a creased copy of *Madame Bovary* lying on it.

The movement raises the shawl, reveals her little, round belly. She's gone the way of Mademoiselle Madeleine, been eating far too many cakes.

Unless she's...

'*Enceinte*,' hisses Augustine, while Maman fetches us some tea.

'We shouldn't have come,' I hiss back.

But we settle ourselves on the *chaise-longue*, and Maman takes the rocking-chair. And Augustine soon recovers her social poise. In between sips of vervain, her fingers curled round the porcelain bowl, she murmurs,

'And so Madame Carpentier, how are you? What of your plans to leave us for the *château* in the South of France?'

'*Eh bien*,' says Maman as wisps of steam settle in her hair, 'That will have to wait.' She glances at us, then drops her eyes, suddenly shy. 'I'm going to have a baby.'

My heart contracts. What to say? For the moment, nothing, though Augustine finds plenty of compliments.

Then Maman raises herself from the rocking chair, rubs the small of her back, and reaches for the lamp on the windowsill.

Lit up, its red and gold glass shade casts a halo round her. Now her face is like the copies of Leonardo paintings Jacques shows me - like *La Jocande*, all smiling and gleaming because she knows, she *knows* what it means when she craves three russet apples all in a morning.

I should say that to her. I should say, 'Maman, you look like a painting by Leonardo Da Vinci,' and then see how happy she'd be. But somehow, I can't. With her, my heart is always heavy, my mouth trembles, won't utter a word. Not even now, when she turns towards me, her blue eyes scanning my face, waiting...

She turns back towards the window and nods at the dark-edged sky.

'Clouds gathering,' she sighs.

Then there's a peal of thunder.

'Paul's at the door,' Augustine says, darting up with sparkling eyes.

But then she pauses. Would it be better to welcome Paul into his own home, as if she were his wife? Or should she sit back down and tweak the hem of her skirt to reveal her pretty ankles?

'It's thunder,' I say, but then there's another rap. Augustine sits down, elbows me to one side, arranges her skirt just-so.

Maman opens the door. The man's voice is unfamiliar. Augustine's face falls. It isn't Paul.

Well, of course not. Paul must have a key. Only strangers need to knock.

And the man at the door is speaking such a peculiar *mélange* of French and English. At least, I *think* it's English. It's nothing like Papa's crisp vowels when a rare old book from over the sea appeared in his shop: "A grete multitude of angels bare hit up to heyvyn' – just listen to that, Odette.'

Non. Pas de tous.

'American,' the man says finally, nasally.

What's an American doing lost in Ver-Sur-Mer?

'My husband or stepson may be able to help you,' Maman replies, in her most immaculate convent-school English. 'You can stay here until they arrive.'

But he takes her at her word, this American on the doorstep, for *un deux trois quatre étrangers!* crowd into the parlour, lugging great sacks behind them. The bottom corners of their sacks are stained dark, wet.

Did they all fall from the sky?

Because beneath their flying jackets, they're wearing dark, military uniforms - with badges shaped like eagles sewn above their blazer pockets. They bring with them the smell of outdoors, of petrol, fresh air and salt water. Their trousers are drenched as far as the knee.

The first man, the one who spoke to Maman, holds out his hand to me. 'Admiral Richard E. Byrd,' he says as I take it.

THE PACKET OF CIGARETTES

His handshake is firm. His smile displays white, even teeth, and a pleasing cleft in his chin.

'Sorry to disturb you all,' the Admiral says. 'We went to the lighthouse first, but we couldn't make the keeper understand us. Poor fella, he looked scared outta his wits. So we ended up here.' He gestures to his companions and introduces them.

Bert Acosta is also tall, with broad shoulders and springy hair that stands up in wet tufts.

Bernt Balchen is thin, with iron-grey hair plastered to his scalp, and a wise, quizzical expression. He, unlike the others, greets us in perfect French. *'Bonjour Madame, mesdemoiselles.'* And his accent isn't American. Jewish perhaps - does it matter? In fact, we later learn he's Norwegian.

And finally, there's Lieutenant George O. Noville, the shortest of the four. His wire-framed glasses magnify his eyes and his lop-sided face twists into a manic grin. Local gossip later reveals a blood-clot was once removed from his brain when he crashed a plane in New Jersey.

'Please make yourselves comfortable,' Maman murmurs, especially polite now she's speaking English. Her education must have been so much better than mine.

Augustine rises up and shakes hands with all the pilots. Then she gestures to the *chaise-longue*, so that they can take her place. The men squelch against the cushions, shivering while Admiral Byrd settles gingerly against the spindles of the rocking-chair. Noville sneezes.

Maman disappears into the kitchen, and I follow her.

'I don't have enough food for so many visitors,' she whispers.

'Just give them something to drink so they can warm up,' I reply. 'Cognac? Calvados?'

'*Ma grande petite fille*,' Maman sighs. 'You're all grown up. But there's no alcohol here. Tea will have to do.'

Augustine pokes her head through the kitchen doorway. 'I'll help you carry everything through,' she says. She glances at the tray. 'Nothing to eat?' Then she plants herself in front of the copper kettle, scrutinises herself in its convex mirror. She tucks a stray curl behind her ear, and pinches her cheeks red.

A light blush suffuses Maman's pale skin. 'I'm not even dressed,' she says, glancing down. 'You girls will have to entertain the gentlemen while I sort myself out.'

'We don't know much English,' I call after her, but she's already vanished up the backstairs.

Augustine shrugs. 'I don't care,' she says, and carries the tray into the parlour.

The pilots clutch the warm porcelain bowls, slurp their drinks. Steam begins to rise from their damp clothes.

Augustine takes my hand, swings it backwards and forwards. Deliberately girlish. She tilts her head, smiles and says to the Admiral,

'We saw your aeroplane up in the sky. We thought it was an eagle.'

I glare at her. She didn't see anything at all.

Admiral Byrd smiles back. In a mixture of French and English that we somehow understand, he says, 'Well, pilots are like eagles, Mademoiselle. We volunteered to take airmail from New York to Paris.' He nods towards the bulky sacks resting against the white-washed wall. 'But the fog made it impossible for us to land. Hell, we nearly hit the Eiffel Tower. So we flew back over this way, towards the lighthouse, and when we ran out of fuel, we had to make a water-landing.'

He stands up and paces towards the window. 'I hope the plane's okay. It's so dark out there, and that wide stretch of water…'

'A whole ocean between us and the U S of A,' sighs Noville.

'Hey, don't you start,' says Balchen. 'When we flew out of the fog, it was beautiful, Mademoiselle, the sea bathed in beams from the lighthouse, guiding our way. Before the storm started, I could clearly make out each farm and field, each house and hedgerow.'

'Yeah,' says Noville, wringing out his wet sleeve. 'Beautiful. Specially when you shoved me into a rubber dinghy and Acosta here thought he'd snapped his collarbone.' Drops of rain and seawater disappear between the cracks in the stone flags. The Admiral frowns at him.

'And where in the hell are we, anyway?' Noville adds.

Augustine drops my hand and turns towards him. She opens her eyes very wide. '*Mes pauvres*, can it be that you don't know? You're in Ver-Sur-Mer.'

'Ver-Suuuur-Mer? Where's that?' says the Admiral.

'Normandy,' replies Augustine. '*Nor-man-die*,' she repeats slowly, then sings a few words of the song. *'I love to see my Normandy/ The country where I saw the light of day.'* Now all the men are staring at her, and she lowers her eyelashes. She murmurs, '*Mes pauvres*. You're all wet.' She turns to me. 'Odette, you should find them some of your stepfather's clothes. Or perhaps Paul's would fit better.'

But that's the last thing I want to do, root round in the Carpentier wardrobe.

'Who the hell comes to Normandy?' says Noville 'Specially in a baked bean tin of a plane?'

Acosta reaches into his breast-pocket and draws out a packet with *Gold Flake* emblazoned on the cardboard. 'Smokes?' he says.

Augustine turns back towards me and frowns. '*Fumeur*,' I say.

'Oh yes, please,' she says.

Acosta grins at her and reaches for his lighter.

Augustine takes a cigarette and leans towards him. A little flame spurts from the lighter, then the ash glows orange. She inhales.

Oooh - *le petit poseur.* How is she managing not to cough? Yet she and Acosta lose themselves in the smoke's curling tongues.

But Balchen coughs and frowns. 'I should've thought,' he says, 'you'd want to keep your lungs fit for flying.'

'We're not all like you,' says Acosta. 'Clean-living, rice-and-vegetable-eating, if you can believe it, Mesdemoiselles.'

'He looks well on it,' I say.

'If you like older men,' mutters Acosta.

'But there's a reason for it,' says Balchen, frowning.

'What's that?' asks Augustine, politely enough.

Balchen is silent for a moment, then murmurs. 'Before I retrained as a pilot, I was a foot soldier during the war. And when I killed someone for the first time... well, it changed everything for me.'

Admiral Byrd interrupts. 'I'm sure the young ladies don't need to hear about this.'

'No, tell us please,' I say. 'That is, if it's not too painful for you.' Because I need to know. I need to know how it feels to kill somebody. And then, how you can live with yourself, afterwards.

Balchen considers me for a moment. 'The man I killed,' he says slowly, 'was my age, or thereabouts. And I still can't forget his look of surprise. Or the colour of his guts, spilling out of him.'

I glance quickly at Augustine. Is she upset? Because soldiers aren't supposed to say things like that. Not to a young lady whose father was killed in the war.

But she gives me a small, reassuring smile and then I think, perhaps soldiers should say things like that. Otherwise wars will keep happening and men will keep on being killed.

'Anyway, after that I couldn't bear to eat meat,' continues Balchen. 'Couldn't bear to think of wounded flesh or blood of any kind. So there you go.'

We're all silent for a moment. I glance at the bronze hunter on my mother's sideboard, with the brace of pigeons at his feet, and I nod. And the next time we eat game, I feel queasy, and leave half of it untouched on my plate.

Not that I could ever be properly vegetarian. Augustine and I both have a tendency towards anaemia, and sometimes we crave *rosbif*, for the iron. Little vampires, Jacques calls us.

'There, what did I tell you,' says Acosta. 'Balchen's an animal-lover. A regular Saint Francis of Assisi.'

'You know your saints? You're Catholic?' I say.

'Some of us are,' grins Acosta through the halos of smoke. 'Some of us have Saint Christopher medals glued to the control-panel.'

'We're all Catholic when we hit some turbulence,' pipes up Lieutenant Noville, grinning and displaying a gold filling. 'Because, my God, you should hear our prayers then.'

I nod again, but wonder if that's the true definition of faith, that you feel the need for God most strongly when you're in trouble. Or perhaps that's just using Him like an insurance policy, like if your barn burns down or your pearls get stolen. Perhaps that's not real faith at all. I'll have to ask Monsieur le Curé - though I haven't been to confession for months now, not since Jacques first kissed me.

It was all so much simpler when I was a little girl, with my notebook full of sins.

Balchen waves away the blue smoke, so like incense. Then he points to the nearest sack and says, 'We held them up, as high as we could, so they wouldn't get wet. And we managed not to lose a single envelope. No mean feat, mesdemoiselles, I can assure you.' But he reaches inside his jacket-pocket and takes out two envelopes. Despite his words, the handwriting is slightly smudged. And they're both missing their stamps.

'Perhaps the stamps are trapped among the other envelopes,' I say. 'We'll help you look.' Augustine nods and stubs out her cigarette.

Noville upturns the sacks. All the letters spill out. Like bird-markings, different handwritings speckle the envelopes. As we start to sort through them, the feather-thin paper rustles, quivers.

Now I feel a sudden urge to stretch my wings too, to soar away to other lands. Airmen, airmen, teach me how to fly... But Augustine grabs the empty sack, gropes around inside. Then she smiles and draws out the two lost stamps. Lindbergh's 10 cent plane nestles, twice, against her white palm.

Noville takes her wrist and drops a kiss on her fingers. 'Thank you, Mademoiselle,' he drawls. 'You've done us a great service.'

Suddenly there's the sound of voices, and a key turns in the lock. Paul stomps into the parlour. The sight in front of him - Lieutenant Noville still clasping Augustine's wrist - pulls him up short. He stands very still.

Jacques enters the parlour behind Paul. And he's the first to recover his composure, moving forwards to shake hands with the pilots, smiling at me.

Paul drags Augustine into the kitchen. I hear a furious whisper, 'Just what were you thinking of?' and then he shuts the door.

Jacques offers to escort the pilots to the Mayor. They finish their tea, they murmur, '*Au revoir*,' and then they leave.

As soon as the door has shut behind them, Augustine rushes out of the kitchen and throws her arms around me. When she looks up, her eyes flash fire and tears. Paul emerges from behind her and then she grabs my arm, won't let go. He nods to me and offers to walk us back to the farm.

Augustine's so upset, I forget to call out goodbye to Maman, still hiding upstairs.

Us girls huddle together in the damp night air, anxious to avoid the puddles, with their captured full moons. The sudden hoot of an owl makes Augustine shriek, and she clutches me again.

And now it's Paul's turn to walk on the outside of the lane. Then, at the entrance to the farm, he bows stiffly and leaves us to proceed alone through the white pillars, into the courtyard.

Still, I'm glad they've fallen out. 'He isn't right for you, anyway,' I tell her, putting my arms round her. She rests her head against my shoulder, but now she's crying so hard she can't hear me.

THE UMBRELLA

The next day, it's still raining. Dreadful weather for July. And just as Augustine and I are racing raindrops down a windowpane, we glimpse Paul crossing the courtyard.

Which is faster? Who will win? The raindrops merge together in one large, glowing bead.

Paul runs his hands through his rain-slick hair. He tells us that the French Navy have hauled the pilots' precious plane to shore. Of course, the souvenir hunters have already reduced it down to its metal frame, paying no respect to the name 'America' painted on its cabin side. But the planes' three engines have been recovered and the rest of the plane will be sent to Cherbourg. 'And the men themselves,' he adds, giving Augustine a searching look, 'they've already left Ver-Sur-Mer.'

When she doesn't reply, he takes my place beside her on the window-seat. He whispers that he's sorry. And then they both stare at me, willing me to go.

I fetch my umbrella and walk out into the courtyard. It's *still* raining.

And I know, I just *know*, Paul's going to propose.

So I hover and shiver, wondering whether to go back inside, or just trudge around out here. Puddles merge with mud. The gravel glistens. The water barrel, green with moss and lichen, reflects the dark sky, broken up by the orchard trees.

Suddenly I sneeze. The next day, I have a really bad cold.

THE FOUNTAIN-PEN

Maman always said my colds were emotional. With her, migraines, with me, *les rhumes*. *Mon Dieu*, I ache all over. My throat hurts. But Augustine makes me some tea, marshmallow root, with honey and lemon. Then she perches on the end of the bed, and whilst I'm drinking, she shows me some pictures she's cut out of the illustrated magazines. *Man Cottage Cat Sky Kingfisher Crocus Mirror.*

They make me smile.

'There,' she says, 'the sun's come out, after all that rain.'

'I'm sorry,' I say. 'If I've been a bit funny with you. It's not that I don't want you to be happy.'

'I know that,' she says. 'But I'm fine. You're the one we need to sort out. That's why I cut the pictures out for you. I thought you could paste all the ones you like into your notebook, and then, if you sort of think about them, wish on them, you might be able to make them come true.'

'Whose idea was that?' I say.

'Mine - well, mine and Jacques,' she says. 'Only Maman's keeping him busy today and there's only me to entertain you.'

But perhaps it's just as well that Jacques isn't here. He's so artistically refined, he'd only laugh at our *bon-bon*-box dreams. Whereas Augustine and I, well, you can't really call either of us artistic. She's cut crooked some of the pictures' edges and when I paste them into my notebook, they bubble up. Splodges of glue ooze from their sides.

First of all, I paste in a picture of a cottage..

'Not that one,' says Augustine. 'There's no flowers.'

'There will be,' I say, glancing at the pen-and-ink drawing. 'They've been planted, they just haven't come up yet.'

Next, I paste in a picture of a black-and-white dog, and then a tabby cat and finally a man with a white beard.

'Who's that?' asks Augustine.

'That's my husband,' I say.

'So old?' she says, a little frown puckering her brow.

'We've grown old together,' I reply. I ink in the colour of his eyes with my fountain pen.

Augustine squints at the picture. '*Bien-sûrrrrrr*,' she drawls, 'Blue eyes. Like Jacques.'

But now I put down the notebook and pen. I'm still not ready to talk about Jacques yet. And it's difficult to think about him when his sister is near.

'I wish I could be more like you,' I say, in a rush.

'How do you mean?' she asks.

'Well, sort of lighter, brighter, not so worried all the time.'

'We're just different, that's all,' says Augustine. 'You're a thinker, and I'm a do-er. If I get a spare moment, I try on a new dress. If you get a spare moment, you go and discuss ornithology with Jacques.'

'I don't have so many new dresses to try on,' I say.

'No, but even if you did, you'd still be sitting in a corner, nose in a book. All that Molière stuff at school, you really used to like it. And Keats and his quatrains - *bah!* It meant nothing to me, but you... I used to envy you sometimes. No wonder Mademoiselle wanted to start you on Goethe.'

I stare at her and shake my head. I can't believe she envies me.

'It seems a long time ago now,' I say.

'That's because you gave up. Why did you, Odette? Even if your Maman couldn't afford for you to stay on and do the *Baccalauréat,* I'm sure you could still have had some language lessons.'

'And what use would they have been?' I say, 'We never go anywhere or see anyone.'

'No, not unless pilots tumble out of the sky,' says Augustine. 'But Odette, you shouldn't think like that. For me, it's fine, I'll marry Paul and be happy. But you, you want more out of life, yet you don't do anything about it. Why?'

'I think,' I say slowly, 'that after Pierre died, it felt wrong to try and be happy, to make something of myself. Or else... else I didn't want to tempt fate.'

'And now?' says Augustine, taking hold of my hand, trying to warm it between her own.

'Now,' I say, shrugging, 'I don't know. When I try and imagine the future, it's like there's a big stone wall blocking my thoughts.'

'Well, you're still young,' says Augustine, smiling. 'There's still time to sort out your future.'

She lifts a strand of my hair, dull and listless, like it always is when I'm sick. 'First thing we'll do,' she says, 'We'll mix some beef bone marrow with rosemary and rum. Then we'll shampoo it into your hair, and add some lemon juice - or no, cider vinegar is better. That'll bring back the shine. After all, you've got to look your best for my wedding.'

Augustine can sometimes be so, well, so sweet. 'Don't worry about me,' I say. 'All eyes will be on you, anyway.'

Then I remember that in the box in the wardrobe, beneath the stereoscope, there's that length of white silk from Papa's shop. It's so fine he said it must have belonged to the Viscountess Agathe. And then, one day, he said that if I always stayed small, like Maman, there was enough material there for my wedding dress. From then on, I willed myself to stop growing, and when I was thirteen, it happened.

Augustine's always been taller, older than me. But now she has more chance to use the material than I do. Should I offer it to her or keep it for myself?

After she's gone, I take out the cloth and give it a shake. Then I can't resist draping it over my head, as if it were a veil. But no. Just look at the state of that hem. Moths have bitten part of it away. It's my own fault. I have little muslin bags full of camphor and thyme in my chest-of-drawers, but nothing in the cardboard box. And I know rosemary spirit, which you're supposed to use once they've laid their eggs, would only spoil the silk. Even if I sponge it with cold water afterwards.

No. I'll have to trim the hem and then wrap the rest of the material up with pimento berries.

It's just as well I pay attention to Madame Solange, or else I wouldn't know half these things. Maman didn't have much idea, after all. Never even knew that to protect her own silk dresses, or that she should iron them on the wrong side. Once they were burnt, she just tore them up into strips for dusters.

Now I hold the silk against my cheek, let it breathe against my skin. It's mine. It's mine. More mine than the snowstorm used to be.

I exhale slowly, imagining myself beneath a miraculously repaired glass dome. All the pieces glued back together again, but with no cracks showing. And I'm trailing slowly towards the church with its painted steeple - a miniature bride, behind a veil of drifting snowflakes.

My blue-eyed groom awaits me.

THE PILLOWS

They had to take the tram to Caen to order the double bed. Where Paul and Augustine will sleep after they are married. Where Augustine and I sleep, together, in these nervous days before the wedding.

I creep into the room we share at the top of the house. It's small and square, with oak beams and white plastered walls. The shutters are open and folded back, to let in the summer air.

Two big square pillows lie quietly side by side. I pace round the bed. I press my face briefly onto each of the pillows in turn, cheek to cheek with the smooth linen, then smooth out the traces with my hand.

The white coverlet is folded back over the wooden foot of the bed, revealing the blue patchwork quilt. Slung across the corner of the bed is Augustine's cotton nightdress. I reach towards it.

Then I imagine the heads of the bride and groom resting against each other, dark and blond, their hair mingling on one pillow. My hands fall to my side.

THE WEDDING SLIPPERS

The kitten-heeled wedding slippers keep slipping off her narrow feet.

'Never mind,' Jacques says, 'Your feet will swell up on the day and they'll be fine.'

'But they're uncomfortable, too,' says Augustine, frowning over them. Then she smiles, puts them on her hands, and makes them dance. Gleams of light lend a rainbow sheen to the pearl beading, pick out the detail in the embroidered flowers. She turns to me.

'Odette,' she wheedles, 'Will you wear them in for me? I'd do it myself, but I promised Paul I'd see him this evening.'

'But my feet are even smaller than yours,' I protest.

'It doesn't matter. At least the shoes will mould to the shape of a human foot. Please...'

I nod.

Before she leaves, Augustine sweeps the stone floor with a twig broom and throws an old sheet over it. When she's gone, I step into her shoes and shuffle across the floor. Slip-slop-wobble. Jacques starts to laugh.

I lift the hem of my skirt an inch or two off the ground. Walking is easier when I no longer have to worry about it catching.

Jacques watches my ankles, transfixed, as I prance across the sheet in his sister's slippers. Suddenly he grabs my arm and tucks it into the crook of his own. Together we practise the Wedding March. When we reach the kitchen table, he kisses me. And again in the dark hallway, before I turn on the light. And again at the top of the stairs. Before I dart into the attic bedroom, kick off the slippers, and throw myself onto the empty double bed.

THE EMBROIDERED CUSHION

When I wake the following morning, a feeling of intense happiness floods me. It's as if I've taken a strong medicine: it begins to take effect, and all the pain has vanished. Happy happy happy, there it is, a secret song bubbling away inside me. The rain has gone and it's getting light.

I run to the window and breathe in the cool, clean air. The glittery sunlight, the deep, blue honey of the sky. The pointed pear tree leaves, the red and pink snapdragons. On the branches of the apple-trees, birds perch, ruffling up their feathers against the light breeze.

Then Augustine appears, walking across the courtyard in her linen cap, its corners sharply starched. She turns and waves at me, but before I can wave back, the sun shines directly into my eyes. Blinding me. But the white light haloes her face, rendering it so pale it seems to shine, frozen and still, as if captured in stained glass.

She steps through the light, and I smile at her.

I take up the cushion I'm embroidering in fire-red stitches. My wedding gift to Augustine. *'In the church of Sainte-Marie, Ver-Sur-Mer, on 31st July 1927, Augustine Adèle Solange married Paul Gaston Carpentier.'*

I've just finished when I hear Augustine's light tread upon the stair. I quickly wrap the cushion in tissue paper and thrust it into the drawer. Then she enters the room, loops her arm through mine, and starts to pull me towards the door. She needs my help, she says, to make sure everything's perfect at the church, and in any case, she's so nervous, how could she possibly sit still?

It's true, there's a hectic flare upon her cheeks, a warning sparkle in her eyes, and a return of the peremptory manner to hide her conflicting emotions. Augustine, I know you so well.

On the way to church, we meet, of all people, Yvette. She's running a stick along the fence, lost in her own thoughts. Her hair is neatly tied back with a blue hair-ribbon. Her heavy colt's mane no longer falls into her eyes, which are brown, heavy-lidded, and gentle. In her light blue dress, she is certainly presentable, almost pretty. She stops abruptly when she sees us.

'Yvette, Yvette, do you know that I'm getting married tomorrow?' sings out Augustine, dropping my hand, and impulsively reaching for that of our former classmate.

'Yes,' says Yvette. Her hand lies slack in Augustine's grasp.

'And what would you say if I were to invite you to the wedding?' says Augustine, her voice the caress of honey. She gives Yvette's hand a little squeeze, as if it were soft, white bread.

'I'd say that was very kind of you,' says Yvette, flatly. 'Only my young man is visiting me tomorrow, and I wouldn't want to disappoint him. You know how it is with young men.' She releases her smooth paw from Augustine's capricious grasp, and I notice the dazzle of an engagement ring. Good for you, Yvette.

'But he could come with you,' says Augustine.

'You don't need the entire village at your wedding,' says Yvette, trying to smile. 'We're not children anymore. It's not like those old May Queen days when everyone we'd ever met had to tell us how pretty we looked. Though you will be pretty, I'm sure.' Her smile falters, and she continues, almost as if she can't help herself, 'Do you have everything ready, your gown, your veil, your *head-dress*?'

Augustine drops her eyes at the final word, but I continue to gaze at Yvette. There's a sudden flash of indignation in her mild eyes, then she steps back from us. She gives me a dignified little nod.

'I wish you well, Odette,' she says. 'Your turn next, maybe.'

'Or yours,' I say, as politely as I can.

She nods at us both, and then Augustine drags me away, to the dark porch of the church. I'm glad of its shady coolness. I place my hands against my burning cheeks, a child again, eight years old, and guilty.

'Stupid little girl,' mutters Augustine. For a moment, I wonder if she means Yvette, or me.

THE PAIR OF SCISSORS

Inside the church, a nun is changing the flowers in preparation for the wedding. A gentle smile on her face, she slowly removes the shrivelled stems and replaces them with big bouquets of fresh roses. Her silver scissors click and catch in the candlelight.

Snip snip and all my mother's hair falling onto the patchwork rug.

An elderly priest walks towards the confessional box. A stranger to this village. Monsieur le Curé is away, on sabbatical in Rome. I imagine entering the confessional and behind the anonymity of the grille, telling the unknown priest... what? That I never wanted my mother to get married again? That I don't want Augustine to get married either? That she's my friend, my sister, the first person I see in the morning, the last I talk to at night?

The wedding service that this old man will read tomorrow flashes into my mind. If any person knows of any reason why these persons should not be joined in holy matrimony, she should speak now or forever hold her peace.

An old woman is sleeping in a pew, clutching her rosary beads.

I imagine snipping them right out of her hands, so that a cascade of beads tumbles across the floor. Some roll under the pews. Some fall down the cracks in the stone paving. We will never be able to find them all again, never.

A shaft of sunlight dazzles against the whiteness of the walls. Between the two windows, a tablet with a crest on it, and a motto in Latin. Then the gleaming letters of the names of people who died in the war in 1914.

A cascade of tears.

'Why are you crying?' asks Augustine, striding rapidly down the aisle towards me.

'Everyone cries at weddings, don't they?' I sob.

Don'tleavemeDon'tleavemeDon'tleaveme.

'At weddings, yes,' she says. 'Not before them.'

Part III
Ver-Sur-Mer, Normandy, 1927-45

THE SNAP DRAGON

On the morning of her wedding, we both wake early. Through half-shut eyes, I watch as Augustine finds her petticoat, throws a shawl round her shoulders.

'Come and keep me company in the garden,' she pleads.

I pretend to be asleep, but she pulls the blankets from me and laughs at my shivering.

Our bare feet pad down the stairs, then cross the cool black and white tiles. We throw open the double doors, let in the sunlight, let our feet imprint the sun-baked earth. But now she's so radiant I can't bear to look at her. Instead, I follow the swing of her silk petticoat, the poise of her walk across the grass.

She pauses by the bed of snapdragons. Smiling, she reaches her hand out to the flower, closes it round its crimson throat.

'There, that'll teach you to poke your tongue out at me,' she says. She turns her flushed face towards me. 'See if you can do the same,' she says.

I put my hand to the flower's throat. Augustine stands very still. She watches my hand, and I let her watch.

I pinch the flower until its head lies back, its teeth aimed at her. She laughs again, a sudden, convulsive trill.

'I can't tell if it's a vampire flower, or a hapless maiden,' she says. 'Do you remember how we used to pretend Yvette's mother was a vampire?'

'Poor Yvette,' I say. 'We were so horrible to her.'

But Augustine isn't listening. She plucks her own bruised flower, presses it to her lips. 'Poor little thing,' she whispers. 'I shall be like that to-night.'

I raise my eyes towards her, finally forcing myself to meet her gaze.

'My wedding night,' she explains. 'My deflowering.'

'Oh,' I say.

And now she can't stop laughing, the sound mingling with that of the silver- throated bells across the fields. 'Come on,' she says. 'It's time to get dressed.' Her white reflection is briefly painted on the dark glass of the double doors.

THE PEARL DROP EARRINGS

Late on the evening of their wedding, I can't sleep. I wish I'd stayed and danced for a bit longer with Jacques, like he'd wanted. If only he'd asked me first. But it was Augustine, and that spoilt me for anyone else.

I put my arm around Augustine's waist, fitting my hand into the silken folds of her wedding dress.

'We can't both lead,' she says, laughing.

Her face is very close to mine. Her breath is hot and sweet, her teeth, white and pointed in her pink mouth. I'm awkward, fumbling and bumbling against her.

'No,' says Augustine. 'Not like that.' She gives me a little shake and suddenly it's easy. We glide away together.

My heart beats fast from the dance, until I'm not sure where we are anymore. The cobblestones wheel round us as we twist and turn. The fence, the steps, the apple trees are all mingled horizontals and verticals. And then, sudden, dizzying glimpses of green fields, and rippling, feathery grass. The house's shawl of red leaves whirls by and the snapdragons appear and disappear, like exploding fireworks. Everything is spinning and alive.

'Augustine,' I say to the white shape in front of me. 'Augustine.' I start to laugh.

And then we realise that the music has stopped. Slowly, the courtyard settles back into its customary stillness. Only Augustine's pearl-drop earrings dangle backwards and forwards, in the empty space beside her jaw line.

'My turn,' says Paul.

And suddenly I remember, pearls are for tears, the tears everyone cries at weddings.

After Paul cuts in, Jacques steps up. But I can't help it: I want to leave. I try and ignore the hurt look that springs to his eyes when I say I have a headache. Still, it's only a half-lie. Once I'm in bed, the insistent music, the dancing feet clattering against the cobblestones outside, soon make my head pound.

It's unbearable - and I wake up the next morning with swollen eyes.

'You look like you've been crying,' says Madame Solange. So I make my excuses and run back upstairs to splash more cold water on my face.

THE LENGTH OF RIBBON

But the first night after their honeymoon, I *still* can't sleep.

I can't sleep because I'm back in my old room beneath the attic. In my old, single bed. Less room to stretch out in. Less warm, without Augustine beside me. That's all that's wrong, all that's different, I tell myself.

But really I can't sleep because of the creaking sound coming from the double bed in the attic above me. The noise, it's as loud, regular and rhythmic as the dancing in the courtyard on the evening of their wedding.

I bury my head in the pillows, but it's no good. I can still hear them. I try to pretend it's just the *charivari*, that serenade of rough music when villagers bang kettles and drums under the newly-weds' windows. But of course it isn't. The villagers have far too much respect for the wealthy Solange family to behave like that.

Charivari. Charles Bovary. Marriage to a mindless bore. How could she?

I get up and root around for a broad length of ribbon. I cut it in half and shove each piece into my ears. Now the world is pleasantly muffled and at bay.

I shut my eyes tight and think of our bed in the attic room above. How Augustine and I curled up close to get warm. Clasped together like spoons, we were soon fast asleep.

THE VASE

Maman gives the wedding couple an embroidered tablecloth and hand-crocheted napkins. Augustine and Paul will use them for the thank you dinner they will hold. To help them out, I make a list of who gave what. Really, it's a secretly covetous inventory of all their gifts. Because apart from my father's stereoscope and a few dresses hanging in the *armoire*, I don't have much. Whatever cast-offs Augustine deigns to give me. I won't have anything more until I'm married myself.

You'd think that being poor would make me less materialistic, but somehow it has the opposite effect. Still, the villagers have been generous with their gifts. Not for Augustine, because, after all, she's flighty, and too wealthy to be well-liked - especially since her mother took advantage of low land prices at the end of the war and increased her holdings.

But for Paul's sake, there's crockery, china, decorative baskets and practical baskets, and such a quantity of linen. Viscountess Agathe sent a pair of vases garlanded with roses from one of her trips to Paris.

A pity they're so ugly. Blotched and speckled, like the liver-spots on her rheumaticky hands as she picked them out. Bless her. Or perhaps not bless her. There's a record Jacques likes to take from its cardboard sleeve, twirl on his finger like a magician's plate, then play on the wind-up gramophone. The needle wobbles, settles into the groove, then starts to spin out, '*Tout va très bien, Madame La Marquise.*'

One servant after another sings on the telephone of all the catastrophes that have occurred in Madame La Marquise's absence, but as if they were nothing, *un petit rien*. Your favourite horse is dead in a fire that destroyed the stables which caused the death of your husband which caused another fire which destroyed your *château*. But apart from that, everything's fine.

Bah - how we like to see the aristocracy suffer. Hmmm... My old dog died. My father and brother are gone. My mother re-married. My sister abandoned me. *À part de ça, tout va très bien*. Everything's fine, *absolutment*.

THE DECANTER

I add a handful of sea-salt and two teaspoons of cider vinegar to the decanter. I suppose I could've used crushed eggshells instead of salt, but Jacques wants them saved to paint.

I shake the decanter. I rinse it carefully in cold water, and then dry it with a linen cloth. There. I place it on the windowsill, marvelling at its sparkle. Vinegar in cold water always makes it shine.

The one chore I never mind is washing-up. Beautifying bleary glass, wiping away smeary fingerprints, all the while imagining the dinner party over again, with those same glasses gleaming in the candlelight.

Only this time it's *my* dinner-party and *my* marriage that's being celebrated. I imagine the guests toasting me, a blushing three weeks' bride. My face is rosy in the heat of candle haze.

'To Odette,' they say. 'To Odette and Jacques. Long life and happiness.'

'Haven't you finished drying up yet?' calls Madame Solange.

I pull out the plug and watch the water drain from the sink.

THE TABLECLOTH

But that night, I have a strange dream. I dream that Paul and Augustine are hosting another party. The double doors of the rarely used dining room are thrown wide open; every surface of every sideboard is covered in vases of flowers. The wine flows, the glasses sparkle, the crockery shines. The candles on the two-branched candelabras are burning. There is water in the crystal water jugs and napkins in the silver breadbaskets. The guests are animated, even laughing. But as is the way of dreams, I'm not sure who they are or what we're eating.

The only thing I am sure of is that the beautiful, embroidered tablecloth is covered in cat's fur. Not just a few stray hairs, but a veritable mane. Yet nobody notices or says anything. They just carry on eating and drinking, laughing and talking, as if nothing at all is wrong.

THE STONE JAR

I've never seen her like this before, her face, glowing, her eyes, so happy. Like Mademoiselle, lit up with Calvados and longing, that first night she came to stay. But no, Augustine is drunk on admiration and cider, from helping Paul and the farmhands with the late August wheat harvest.

'Come with me,' she says, breathing sweet fumes against my cheek. 'I've something to show you.' She takes my hand and propels me towards the hayloft. She pushes me towards the ladder, slumped against a bale of hay, and I climb.

There, in a folded teacloth, is a stone jar of cider. An unexploded bomb: huge and squat, with a brown painted rim. She lifts it up, unscrews the stopper, holds it to my face.

Sharp, unmistakeable whiff of winey apples.

She puts the jar to my mouth.

'Go on,' she says.

I hesitate.

'I dare you,' she says.

And I take a deep gulp.

It's not the first time I've drunk cider, but it tastes like it is. A rough fermented drink of russet summer, of fire and orchards, of red apples and green leaves, of Augustine's cheeks and sparkling eyes.

I put down the jar and gaze at her. Her hair is burnished like cider-flame, her eyes are two mysterious ovals in the hayloft's gloom.

I want to drink her up.

'Augustine,' I say, on my knees and shaking.

Quick and assured, she crawls towards me. She takes my hand. Her touch burns me. Then she pulls me down, into the hay, into her wide, drunk smile. I kick against something. The stone jar of cider. The last few drops soak into my skin. And then Augustine is there, dabbing me with her fingertips, putting them in her mouth, sucking them.

Her mouth. I can't stop staring at it. Too near and too far away. Augustine lowers her head. She kisses me once, full on the lips. Her mouth is cidrous and sweet. Then she rests her pointed chin against my shoulder. I breathe in her hair, but her eyes never leave my face, her pupils narrowed to their points, sharp as beestings.

She's waiting for me to decide what will happen next. Then, 'Augustine,' Paul calls.

Augustine sighs, then sits upright.

'We're here,' she calls back.

She turns and watches me, pressed against the hay, relishing its prickle against my spine. And the memory of the cider, soaking into my skin, and the feel of her lips against mine. Her mouth curves into a tender, amused smile. She leans towards me. But, 'Nothing happened,' she whispers. She drops a kiss on my forehead.

Paul enters the hayloft. His shadow is thrown between us as he stands at the foot of the ladder, staring up.

THE EARTHENWARE DISH

From the kitchen window, I see the farmyard, drenched in sunlight. Their feathers gleaming, the chickens hop beside the henhouse and peck at grain. Bits of straw, feathers and pollen float in the air. It's nesting season.

Jacques walks towards me across the courtyard, shielding his eyes from the sun. His neck is sun-tanned against his white shirt. Sunlit hair upon his arms. He smiles at me, then glances away, suddenly shy. I remember the sensation of his skin against mine.

It should be softer.

Then, at midday, there's a dead chicken on the kitchen table, its head hanging over the side. Paul knocked it down with his wheelbarrow. Not on purpose, Augustine says, her eyes round, sparkling, mysterious. But I wonder.

She lets out an exaggerated sigh and starts to pluck. Soon the table is lost in whirling feathers. Like snowflakes, perpetually gliding, drifting.

Augustine reaches inside the chicken but starts to retch. The stench of its guts is unbearable.

I take over. Amid the entrails, my fingertips brush against something smooth and round. My palms sweat. I'm not sure what to do. My voice is wavering and high.

'That's enough,' I say and grab an earthenware baking-dish. I shove the chicken inside the stove, as far away from me as I can.

In an hour or so, I take down a cloth, and bind it round my hands. Gingerly, I reach towards the stove's glowing heart. Then I prise the chicken free from its dish and put it on a plate.

'Chicken chasseur,' says Paul, coming into the kitchen. He smacks his lips and reaches for the carving knife. His large hands bear down. But the knife's progress is suddenly impeded. Paul turns the chicken round and makes a slit from its neck down to its belly.

As I feared, all the eggs are inside. All boiled whole, all without their shells. Eggs of various sizes: the tiniest one, the size of a pea. And inside them all, the treasure of a bright yellow yolk.

THE WISH-BONE

At lunch, Paul crunches down on a bone, then takes it out of his mouth and puts it on the side of his plate. A shattered wishbone. Ugh.

'Oh,' he says, carelessly, turning to me. 'I forgot to say. My father came into the fields just now. Your mother's asking for you. He didn't stop to say why.'

That's odd. And it's Bertrand, not my mother, who opens the cottage-door. Normally he'd be out looking for work. But perhaps he needed a rest today. There are shadows beneath his eyes, and he hasn't shaved.

He nods. But then his eyes glaze over. He can't see me. And his voice is pitched so low, I have to dip my head to catch the words:

'She lost the baby early this morning.'

I run up the stairs, then tiptoe along the corridor, trying not to disturb her. But, 'Odette, is that you?' she calls.

I peer through the open door, remembering how Maman used to take to her bed with migraines, how she used to turn her head away from me, towards the wall. There she is now, smothered in blankets, her hair loose behind her, her face white against the cloud of pillows.

She sees me and leans forward, tries to sit up.

'Maman.' I say. I reach out and help her upright.

She rests her head on my shoulder. Her hair smells faintly of lavender, from the pillows. But, for the first time, I notice a streak of grey.

'Can't have that,' I whisper. 'Can't have my mother getting old. You should comb red wine through your hair, that would hide it.'

'Isn't my hair red enough already?' says Maman, with a tired smile that doesn't quite reach her eyes. Then she tells me that she's changed her mind, that she's never going to leave Ver-Sur-Mer. Bertrand can ask the haberdasher for work if he can't find anything else. 'Because one thing I'm certain about,' she says, 'I'm not going to lose any more people that I love.'

I squeeze her hand. My eyes drop to the dog-eared copy of *Madame Bovary* lying beside the bed.

Maman follows the direction of my eyes, nods at the once-forbidden book. 'I want something better for myself,' she says. 'I want a happy ending, not a tragic one.'

For a moment, I'm tempted to give her that happy ending. I want to say, 'I'm so sorry, Maman, for everything. I love you, have always loved you - '

But it's no good. My heart aches but the words won't come out. They're buried too deep, like bones beneath the roots of the Juniper Tree.

THE PIERCED TIN BOWL

I reach for the little oval dish that we need for the *hors d'oeuvres*. Magenta radishes peep out from beneath their white bonnets. How Augustine hates you. Never mind, she shan't have to eat you.

But thinking of her reminds me to swing the salad dry.

Augustine has a terrible craving for spinach at the moment. Perhaps for the iron, because she's been so tired, languishing on the *chaise-longue*. Her eyes are ringed with mauve, transparent circles. She's like that girl in the fairy-tale that wanted to eat lettuce from the witch's garden. Rapunzel's expectant mother. And whatever happened to her after her flaxen-haired darling was taken away from her and shut up in the tower? Nobody ever said.

There are some things which nobody ever confesses.

But what's this? There's grit beneath my fingernails. That won't do. Not for Augustine. *Madame la Marquise*, I call her at the moment, like in the song. Bobbing a curtsey to her like I used to do to the Viscountess Agathe up at the *château*. *Petite-Mere-Madame*, for you, I'll clean my nails. I reach for the pierced tin bowl next to the sink that holds the nailbrush and soap.

I'm just scrubbing the crescent moons of green soap out from underneath my fingernails, when someone grabs my shoulders. I gasp and drop the brush into the sink.

Jacques's arms reach round me. He leans against me and gropes for the brush in the soapy water. He restores it to the bowl, then drapes his wet hands on my forearms. His touch makes me shiver.

'Goose bumps,' he says, and starts to rub me warm.

I turn in his arms and rest my head against his shoulder. I can't help it, I start crying. Soon there's a round, damp crumpled patch just beneath his collar.

'What's wrong?' he says.

'Thank God,' I gasp. 'Thank God you still want me. You haven't forgotten me.'

'Forgotten you?' he says, laughing, but there's a concerned look in his kind eyes. 'Odette, we live in the same house. Which is certainly convenient.' He stares at me intently for a moment, then gently presses his cheek against mine, to soak up my tears. His clean linen, sweet tobacco smell reassures me. And just for a moment, I stop looking for Augustine in his face.

THE LINEN CAP

'Can you do anything with this?' asks Augustine, poking her face round the door with an almost comical expression of dismay.

'What's that?' I say.

She steps forward and drops her linen cap into my lap. One of its flaps is half torn away, and there's a row of uneven stitches where she's tried to mend it. Dark navy thread against a white, linen cap. Really, Augustine, you should stick to embroidering flowers. You're no good at anything else.

She places her warm hands on my bare arms, and pushes her bright, appealing face close to mine.

'Please,' she wheedles.

I glance down. Her hands are larger, squarer than mine. Elegant, but almost masculine. The hands of a gentleman dandy, if they hadn't been roughened by farm-work. I give the calloused fingertips a light squeeze.

'Very well,' I say, and sigh. 'I'll see what I can do.'

'Thank you. Thank you,' says Augustine, joyous, sparkling, grazing her knuckles against my cheek.

'But why's it so important to you, anyway? It's only an old linen cap.'

Augustine blushes, looks straight ahead. Her eyes take on an abstract, dreaming gaze. 'Paul says that the one perfect moment in his life was five years ago, when he first saw me wearing this cap, walking across the yard.'

My eyes narrow and my facial muscles contract. 'And how did it get torn?' I say.

Augustine laughs, and all the dreams fall out of her eyes. She gives an exaggerated shrug. 'Well, you know what men are. Sometimes I wear it for him…and one time, he was a little bit rough…'

She steps close to me again, interrogating me with her laughing eyes. To see whether I'm shocked or share the joke. But I'm not sure how to react. How much does she mean what she says and does?

Still, my cheeks burn. Because I want to know how her hair feels in my hands. Her rich, abundant hair, even thicker, even glossier, in the early days of her pregnancy.

I can smell the warmth of her skin, the sweet almond oil she wears in her hair.

I inhale her fragrance so that she travels deep down inside me, entering my bloodstream, inflaming my nerves.

I want to rest my cheek against the gently swelling curves of her belly.

But all I can do is grasp the linen cap tightly against my lap.

THE BIRDCAGE

A curious gift for a husband to give his pregnant wife. A white wire birdcage, with the wire twisted into shapes of palm trees. The love-birds twitter inside the cage, whilst the palm trees mock them with the freedom they no longer possess.

'What shall we call them?' asks Augustine, clapping her hands in girlish glee.

'Paul and Augustine,' suggests Paul, in a deep, unnatural voice, as proud and clumsy with his gift as a big dog with a small slipper. Just for a moment, I glimpse something of what it is Augustine likes about him.

But Augustine darts him a scornful look, then lowers her eyelashes. 'I know,' she says. 'How about Napoleon and Josephine?'

Paul nods. Of course, the names appeal to him. After all, the Napoleonic Code is the family law that makes the husband its absolute despot, an Emperor strutting on his little perch. Under this law, a father can put his own child in prison for a month, and not even explain why. And a mother has no power at all.

Though, round here, a little boy can drown, and his mother remains forever silent...

Augustine, delighted to have her own way, makes a great show of cooing at the birds, and trying to kiss them through the bars of the cage.

It doesn't last, though. Pregnancy accentuates her anaemia, so that even mounting the stairs causes her to breathe very fast. The crimson tips of her ears turn white, and the veins in her temple throb. Then she's too tired in the mornings to feed the birds, and it becomes my job.

She's so big that we joke she must be expecting twins.

One morning, when I approach the cage, I can only see one of the birds, beating its wings furiously. But as I get closer, the other bird is lying on the floor of the cage, its legs in the air, its body quite stiff. Poor Napoleon.

Augustine insists on seeing the poor little corpse. I wish I hadn't told her. The least thing sets her all in a quiver these days. But now she emerges briefly from the isolated pool of her pregnancy, like a swimmer coming up for air. She darts a reproachful look at me.

'It's not my fault,' I mutter.

We bury the bird near the grave of my old dog, Minouche. But we don't know what to do with the one lovebird left in the white wire cage. Without her mate, she is sullen, disconsolate. She refuses to sing.

Finally Augustine opens the cage door and lets the bird soar out into the sky. She follows the trajectory of its flight with her eyes, and for a moment, she is the bird, sunlight on her wings.

'Don't tell Paul,' she whispers. Then something stirs inside her. She gasps and bites her lip. Madame Solange and I help her to bed and then I run for the midwife, Madame Rolland.

THE TIN KETTLE

Augustine's and Paul's bedroom has wooden floorboards and a light oak bedstead. There is a large mirror on the whitewashed wall which doubles the size of the room, a rocking-chair with a crocheted baby's cardigan resting on the plump cushion and two dragonfly Tiffany lamps on either side of the bed. Augustine lies on top of the bed, pillows behind her back. She is clenching her fists, grimacing.

Flames lick round the wood beneath the charred base of the tin kettle. Hot haze against my face. Bubbles burst against the kettle's metal sides.

A fitful red light gleams on the midwife's sabots. She shifts her feet. Waiting is the worst part.

'You should tie your hair back,' she mutters to her daughter. 'So unhygienic for a delivery, slopping all over the place like that.'

The girl, Louise, lowers her head over her needlework, hides behind her curtain of hair. But I see the tips of her ears flush pink.

'Her hair's so beautiful,' I say, feeling sorry for Louise.

'Yes, the colour of money,' sniffs Madame Rolland.

Madame Solange fingers her rosary beads. She's halfway through her tenth Hail Mary when Augustine starts to swear.

'Hail Holy Queen. This is much worse than I thought.' The contraction subsides and she darts a reproachful look at her mother. Then a new contractions starts to build. She suddenly writhes and arches her back upwards. Then a scream loud enough to tear the house in two.

The baby's membranes rupture spontaneously.

Madame Rolland frowns. 'The cord might be tangled,' she says, but does not tell us about her secret fear until later, 'tangled around the baby's neck.' She makes a tent over Augustine with a blanket, then rinses her hands in a bowl of water beside the bed. She reaches inside the tent and slips the cord over the baby's head. 'Skin the rabbit,' she mutters to herself. And then the baby slithers out from between Augustine's legs, bloody, raw and blue.

Quick slap. Sharp intake of breath. The air of indignation swells baby's perfect lungs. She shrieks. Madame Rolland takes a cloth and wipes the baby clean.

'Juliette!' says Augustine. Her face glistens. The pupils of her eyes are dilated, eerie, triumphant. The girl I knew is lost in them. She reaches out her arms for her daughter, but then her face contorts as she is wracked with another contraction.

Madame Rolland hands the baby to Louise, then begins to poke around inside the tent. 'You knew you were having twins?' she asks. 'Head still down and just above the spine.'

Augustine lets out another unholy groan. But she has faith in the midwife, we all do. Madame Rolland is the mother of three sons and a daughter of her own.

Augustine's muscles contract and her eyelids flutter as another baby slides out into the world. He is much smaller and browner than his sister. His legs thrash about, streaked with mucous and dried, clotted blood. Madame Rolland takes the baby boy, slaps him, frowns over his whimper, then wipes him clean. This baby, the one they will always worry about, she hands to his mother.

She looks into his eyes, a blaze of blue, as if he's angry at being born. 'Jojo,' she says.

Juliette is the duck's egg twin, large, blush blue and wholesome. And Jojo is the hen's egg. Looks as good to eat as his sister, but never really hatches. And so even though his first moments are not as traumatic as Juliette's, Jojo is always the one we'll worry about.

THE CHANDELIER

In the lobby of the town hall, the chandelier's lit candles halo the bust of Marianne. They turn to blond the panels of rococo flowers, whiten the vases of lilies. They make the posters' writing shine.

'MARCELLE CAPY FOR ONE NIGHT ONLY' the black letters promise. And beneath the chandelier, the staircase uncoils. I wish I were a child again and could race Jacques up its steps. Then we could slide down the smooth black balustrades that eventually curve into question marks.

Perhaps I should say that to him, see if I can make him smile. But no, he's gazing up at Marianne. Then he hunches his shoulders, and sighs. 'We'd better go inside,' he says. 'We've already missed the start.'

'Peace above all,' booms Marcelle Capy, I presume. The key speaker tonight for the *Ligue Internationale des Combattants de la*

Paix, the LICP. Yes, that's him, looking down on us from his platform.

A war veteran reaches for his crutches, pulls himself up and cheers. Some of the war widows nod and clap. Madame Solange, sitting beside them, shuffles over to make room for us. We clamber over black skirts and sit down, hemmed in between the bulk of bodies.

In the front row, a small, plump woman in a cream blouse stands up.

'Whilst I'm all for peace, I don't believe the LICP goes far enough in denouncing Nazi Germany,' she says. 'We need to boycott Fascist regimes and provide economic support for anti-Fascist refugees.' She gestures to the woman sitting beside her. 'Stand up Anna and tell them what it's like for Jews in Nazi Germany at the moment. Tell them what it's becoming like for Jews in *France*.'

The woman, Anna, turns in her seat and clutches her friend's lacy sleeve. Her brown hair reaches just past her shoulders, and flops forwards into her large brown eyes. She has olive skin, olive eyelids and straight, dark brows. But if she were less dark, she'd look like the bust of Marianne.

'No Madeleine, I can't,' she says, in a low voice. 'Not in front of all these people.'

Madeleine? Oh, of course it is, it's Mademoiselle Madeleine, still supporting her precious causes.

I stand up.

'You're wasting your breath,' I say. 'Nobody here wants another war. Nobody here wants to lose another brother, son or sweetheart.' I pause for a moment. Then I glance at Jacques and I'm suddenly able to continue. 'Aren't there already enough people whose names we only see on war memorials and gravestones?'

Madame Solange tugs at my skirt

'Votes,' she mouths.

'What?'

'Say something about the vote,' she hisses. 'It's one story when they want us to sacrifice our husbands and sons, and another story when they don't let women have the vote.'

'That's hardly the issue,' I hiss back.

Mademoiselle Madeleine jerks her head. Her dark eyes flash. 'I'm truly sorry for your losses,' she says, 'But I don't believe that following a policy of appeasement with Germany is the answer. The Fuhrer is more dangerous than you can imagine.'

And she's not the only one to think like that. We read in the *Gringoire* that Renouvin, a Parisian barrister, struck the Foreign Minister Flandin across the face in front of the dignitaries assembled under the Arc de Triomphe. Flandin's crime? To send a telegram to Hitler congratulating him on signing the anti-war petition at Munich.

'Not worth the paper it's printed on,' Augustine said, at the time. Though I'm not so sure it's the atrocities in Nazi Germany that stir her. Sometimes I think she likes the idea of, not violence exactly, but power. The bronze statue of the hunter, her father with his bayonet. If she can't be a General herself, then her menfolk must fight for her.

'In the countryside, do you hear.
The roaring of these fierce soldiers?'

blares out the gramophone later that evening. Augustine joins in the chorus as we cross the black and white tiles of the dining room floor. *'Grab your weapons, citizens! Form your battalions! Let us march! Let us march! May impure blood water our fields...'*

'Donnez-moi la patience,' says Jacques, looping his coat over the hook just inside the door. 'Augustine, we're not all like Paul, you know.'

'No,' she sniffs as the needle lifts from the record. 'As it is, I've had to give Papa's bayonet to Paul, because you don't want it.'

Jacques sighs. 'I'll fight if I have to, even if I do attend peace rallies from time to time.'

Augustine rolls her eyes as he unwinds his scarf and hangs it up.

Jacques frowns. 'If you were the one who had to go to war, *ma petite soeur,* you might be singing a different song,' he says.

'Children, please,' Madame Solange begs. She takes my hand, holds it to her forehead. 'I've got a terrible headache. And I can't bear it when you two fight. Aren't things bad enough already?'

Beneath the electric light's unforgiving glare, Jacques bows his head. Augustine mumbles something and chooses another record.

THE VOTIVE CANDLE

'Come with me to church,' says Jacques, a few weeks later. 'I want to pray, but I don't want to go there by myself.'

We walk along the narrow lane into the village and past the tavern. There are two old men seated at a little table outside. They're just setting up their pieces on a wooden board. Black is lined up against ivory, knights and rooks guard their lieges, pawns face each other in battle formation - the same arrangement of war the world over.

Jacques takes my hand as we near the church. In a rush, he tells me that when his father was away during the Great War, his mother used to guide the plough, and he used to lead the horse. He was only ten, but he didn't mind. He liked it. But now, if France declares war on Germany, he'll have to stop writing, painting and working on the farm.

He'll have to become a soldier.

'Can you imagine,' he says. 'I'll be forced to kill men I've never met before, who've never harmed me.' His blue eyes are anxious beneath his widow's peak of brown hair. In the church porch's subdued light, his gentle face is much too thin.

We pass into the church. The Roman. The Gothic. The nineteenth century pastiche. It's as mixed up as you are Jacques. *Un mélange.* But then I always thought you belonged in another time. Papa used to say that even thirty years ago, there were art salons in Ver. I like to imagine Jacques wearing a paint-splattered smock, discussing Impressionism with our leading Parisian actor, Monsieur Marc Rouge, in the Hotel des Arts down by the sea.

Today, as a salt tang follows us through the open door, the church reminds me of the sea. The bell tower, after all, has a fish bone formation. Then there's the curving spiral staircase that reminds me of the shell we used to keep on the windowsill. And above us, the arched roof with its interlocking beams is like some great boat with all the apostles safe inside…

I walk away from Jacques, genuflect at the altar, screw my eyes up at the sudden blaze of stained glass. Saint Gerbold again, with his wheel, the chapel, a boat on the sea. *Mon Dieu.* The little four-foot boat we sent Pierre away in. And now, when conscription is introduced, fishers of men, all the others will be sent away too…

I start to pray to the statue of the Virgin. Haloed by golden stars, she holds out her arms to me in gracious welcome. But then images of all the Pietàs I've ever seen, in prayer books, on Monsieur le Curé's postcards, force their way into my mind.

So I look down. Roses bloom in the holes in her feet. Like Saint Gerbold and his eternal blossoming pathway.

Footsteps echo behind me, then Jacque stands besides the altar.

'Let's light a candle,' he says. A one franc candle: it doesn't cost much to deflect such a lot of fear. He guides my fingers with the taper of light. The wick casts its glow across his face and my heart contracts. Everyone else has been taken from me. What's so different about Jacques that he should be spared?

Everything.

But his face is no longer troubled. He's smiling.

'Just look at that,' Jacques says, nodding at the statue of the Virgin. 'How can anyone take it seriously?'

'What do you mean?'

'Only that the sculptor must have modelled it on the prettiest girl in the village. His own passion for her must surely surface in the minds of the worshippers.'

He nudges me with his elbow. 'Odette, he must have modelled it on you.'

'This is a church,' I say. 'This isn't the right place to say things like that.'

'Where is the right place, then?' he asks, as he takes my hand, and leads me back down the aisle. 'This is the church where we might get married, one day.'

'One day soon,' I say. 'I'm not a girl anymore. I'm twenty-seven.'

I let him put his arms around me and kiss me on the porch.

We walk back home together, arm-in-arm. The two old men are still playing chess outside the tavern, their sun-tanned skin the colour of cider. One of them lifts his head from the board long enough to nod and smile. And I remember the old game Augustine and I used to play, *'Qui est grandpapa?'*

But, 'War veterans,' says Jacques, and shivers.

THE BAND OF GOLD

Spring is here and suddenly everyone is getting married. With the approach of war, no-one is taking any chances.

Besides it's May, the perfect month for a wedding. From my window, the high narrow lattice beneath the attics, I watch as the sun shines through the gaps in the orchard leaves. It makes shadow-patterns, a veil falling over me. And the trees' branches interlock, like an architrave.

A visionary bride and groom pass beneath it, beneath a shifting haze of blossom.

Yvette Calombe and Frank Delmare.

They've invited us, Jacques and me, that is, to their wedding. Not Augustine, though. They must think it would be too much for her, what with the twins getting over the chickenpox they caught in their first week at *l'école maternelle*.

Anyway, Augustine is perfectly sweet about it. She reminds me that Monsieur le Curé hates sweeping up confetti. She gives us handfuls of runched-up rose petals to pelt the bride and groom with instead.

I want to think well of her. I want to think it's her penance for the destruction of the long-ago head-dress.

After the ceremony, the reception. The White Lion tavern is decked with green and white garlands for a wedding reception. Happy couples dance the length of the tavern, where tables and chairs have been pushed back to the walls to make floor-space. The counter is decked with green and white garlands, and glasses of cider are lined up all along it. Opposite, a rostrum, where the perspiring father of the tavern-keeper wraps himself round a violin. Yvette has looped her long train over her arm, and is dancing with her groom, Frank.

This time, I make sure I dance every dance with Jacques.

There's a moment when the music stops, and he takes my hand.

'Odette,' he says. 'There's something I want to ask you. Will you…'

'Of course you must keep playing,' trills the bride. 'That's what we're paying you for.' The fiddler puts down his glass, sighs, and picks up his violin.

Yvette catches sight of us and waves. Then she drags her new husband away from his brother Michel, and steps forward. She lifts her veil and, well… But I kiss her on both cheeks and offer her our sincere congratulations.

She squeezes my fingers. I feel the cool pressure of her wedding-ring.

I glance at Jacques, expecting him to say something. But he's gazing, transfixed, at Yvette. Not because she's beautiful. She isn't. But because the bride in her cloud of tulle… The groom in his dark serge suit… It's as if we're facing our doubles, our future selves. It's all a bit much.

My heart sinks. And I end up saying the first stupid thing that comes into my head. 'What's it like, re-living your old May Queen days?'

Yvette is suddenly wide-eyed, alarmed. Her smile falters.

Fortunately, the violinist starts to play 'Soldier's Joy.' The groom whirls the bride away. Her veil, her mane of frizzy curls, streams out behind her. The skin on her cheeks shines like a polished walnut. And a white starry flower falls from her headdress, to be crushed by dancing feet.

But none of that matters to her, because she's happy.

I wish I hadn't said anything. I wish I'd kept quiet, like Jacques.

Though now, he's altogether *too* quiet. But perhaps he'll propose when we're alone.

THE BOWL OF PLUMS

But as it happens, more than young couple in the village has to postpone their wedding-day. On 3 September 1939, France and Great Britain declare war on Germany. Our government orders a general mobilisation. All men between the ages of twenty and forty with fewer than four children are drafted into uniform.

On the day before Jacques and Paul must leave us, we all eat lunch together out on the veranda, beneath a large, white parasol. Beyond its circle of shadow, the orchard glistens with pointed leaves and ripe fruit.

We're all quiet at the table, not wanting them to go.

I steal a glance at Augustine, sitting opposite me. Surely you know? But of course she doesn't. She's too preoccupied with Paul. And so I don't tell her that I love her brother.

But then, I never tell Jacques that I love his sister.

We eat onion tart and tomato salad. The dressing, three parts oil to one part vinegar. Seasoned with garlic and black pepper. Afterwards, Madame Solange sets down a bowl of dark blue plums. Those are for you, Jacques, I think, for your blue eyes closing beneath their heavy lids as our mouths meet.

But is it onions or vinegar I taste when Jacques kisses me goodbye? Away from the others, in the shadow of the hayloft. Because there's something disquieting about that kiss.

A farewell kiss.

'Wait for me,' he says. Nothing else. But I make him a solemn promise that I will. And at the time, I mean it.

THE BOOK OF GERMAN FAIRY-TALES

Months pass. Without the men, the village is empty, quiet. I try and pretend that it's just haymaking season, that they've just gone to the fields, that's all.

But really it's Easter and whilst we're waiting for news from Jacques and Paul, Yvette's husband has his first leave. And he's lucky because their baby arrives early, and he's able to meet his daughter. Little Celeste Delmare, born on Good Friday. Frank spends three days with them and then returns to battle.

We decide, for the first time in years, to celebrate Easter, to try and cheer up the children. Juliette and Jojo go off to collect the hen's eggs, like Augustine and I used to do. When they return, I take one, wipe away the feathers and fluff, and pierce a hole in the top. I make a bigger hole in the bottom. Then I blow out all the egg white and yolk into a saucer, plop. I rinse the eggshell, dry it, then paint it. I paint the entire egg, apart from its base. When it's dry, I paint the base.

There. My little round canvas. My strange eye on all the world. What shall it be? Green and red, an apple? Or no, ruffles of yellow petals, like Van Gogh's sunflowers? Or…

'Why have you painted a snake?' asks Juliette.

'No, it's an elephant,' I say. 'That's its trunk.'

'What's that?' asks Jojo.

I try to explain. An elephant is big, like a barn, and it has two tails. One tail is behind, and the trunk is the name of the one in front.

The twins exchange puzzled glances. They don't quite believe me.

'*Mes enfants.* Your education,' I sigh. I offer to read to them instead.

Juliette chooses the book. The Brothers Grimm again, a gift from Tante Madeleine. Very striking, with its red leather covers embossed with gilt flourishes, its crisp white pages, its stark, black ink.

A couple of months later, I'll see those colours again. The *swastika* flag.

Jojo falls asleep with his head in my lap. Juliette leans against my shoulder, peering at the pictures. A piper in a multi-coloured costume is followed by dancing girls and boys. *"They all disappear into a cavern in the mountainside and are never seen again,"* I read.

'Never seen again?' says Juliette, biting her lip.

THE EBONY CROSS

Though we tell her not to, Juliette gives her grandmother one of the painted eggs. But Madame Solange doesn't seem to mind that this year, we're celebrating Easter. Though her husband's death made her temporarily lose her faith, the absence of Paul and Jacques brings her back to Jesus.

One morning, I think I catch her praying. She's leaning against an open cupboard door with a dazed expression, mouthing silent words. I try to pass without disturbing her, but then she speaks.

'Look at that,' she says.

I poke my head inside the cupboard. And there's Jesus, unwrapped from a linen cloth, as if he's just been resurrected.

Well, not really. He's still attached to the ebony crucifix. The painted blood still oozes underneath the nails.

'His poor feet,' Madame Solange whispers. She reaches out her hand, strokes them.

Suddenly she shakes her head, turns to me. Her pupils settle. Her eyes focus.

'You must think I'm going mad,' she says. 'I came up here to find my savings book. I had a letter this morning, from the Viscountess Agathe in Paris. She asked if I would make a donation so that some rosebushes can be planted along the Maginot Line. Those poor soldiers, with nothing to look at except concrete walls.'

She smiles. 'Of course, it's all nonsense. Soldiers need good food and stout boots. But I think if Jacques saw a rose blooming, it would make him think of home, and think of you, and he'd be a little bit happier.'

She leans forward and touches my cheek. She knows, I think, she *knows*. Perhaps Jacques said something to her before he went away.

Later that day, Madame Solange sends me to post her donation to the Viscountess Agathe. And the ebony crucifix returns to her bedroom wall, covering the patch that has been bare for so long.

But by the time the roses open on the Maginot Line, the Battle of France is over. Less than six weeks after it begins, Marshal Pétain, our new Prime Minister, announces that he's asked Germany for armistice conditions, and that 'the fighting must stop.'

'They'll be coming home, then,' says Augustine.

But I shake my head.

THE FAMILY ALBUM

The Germans are coming to Ver-Sur-Mer. Marching down the Place d'Or into our village with their horses, their tanks, their *swastika* flags, their flags with skulls-and-bones. Paris is already occupied. At the cinema in Caen, there's a film of Hitler looking from the Palais de Chaillot at the Eiffel Tower, slapping his knee with delight.

I should be frightened, but I don't know what to think, really. Most of our young men haven't returned yet, and now they're to be replaced by this plague of foreign soldiers.

'Plague of rats, more like,' hisses Madame Solange. 'And that pushover, Pétain, and all that Vichy lot, they're just as bad. Give us the gift of himself, he says. *Pah*. What makes him so sure we want it? *Putain* more like.'

'*Putain. Putain,*' says Jojo. The words ring out like bullet shots. 'What does it mean?'

'It's very vulgar,' says Augustine, frowning at her mother. 'Never use that word again.'

Marshal Phillipe Pétain, the great victor from the First War, even greater in defeat. Some of the villagers are reassured that he's taken over the destiny of France. But the rest of us are tired of seeing his white moustache, his bushy eyebrows, wherever we go. His gaze, blue-grey as new-cut steel, stares at us from every shop window. Even the bust of Marianne has been removed from the lobby of the town hall, to be replaced by one of him.

Madame Solange sniffs and insists we lock everything away, not only all the important papers, but the family silver, and all the books.

'Jacques's books,' she groans. 'To see them in the hands of Germans. I'd rather burn them.'

'They'll think we're very uncouth without books,' I say to Augustine, and she nods. We stare round at the empty rooms, without a single cushion or painting. Not even a flower in a vase. In the large linen cupboard, beneath a pile of sheets, Madame Solange buries the family photograph album. The Germans shan't see Augustine in her First Communion dress, or Jacques, aged three, naked on a rug.

The twins enter into the game of packing everything away with relish. Juliette bustles about with a white plaster shepherd and his swain that she's not normally allowed to touch. And Jojo... he reaches up to the mantelpiece for the wedding gift vases with their garlands of ugly roses. But his sleeve catches against them and sends them toppling to the floor.

'Mmmm-aman, Mmm-aman, Mmm-aman,' he stutters, looking like he wants to cry.

But Augustine kneels down beside him and pats his shoulder. 'I always hated them anyway,' she declares. 'Well done, Jojo.'

I don't think he understands but just for a moment, his face is wreathed in smiles.

'They won't want Blondin, will they?' he says, with a lob-sided grin. His pet rabbit, white, with pink-tipped ears and nose.

Augustine looks at him for a moment. 'No Jojo, they won't want Blondin.'

'I think that's everything,' says Madame Solange at last, turning and facing us all. The piano is locked, the curtains have been taken down, bottles of blackberry wine are crammed into the gardening shed. Paul's hunting rifle is stowed away. The gramophone is shut up inside the *armoire*. ...So no more listening to Louis Poterat warbling, '*J'attendrai,*' to Augustine matching her voice to his. 'I will wait,' she used to sing. 'Day and night, I will wait forever for your return...'

Like me, I'm sure she meant it.

THE BOOK OF ITALIAN FAIRY-TALES

There's nothing to do now except wait.

Monsieur le Curé lends us a book of Italian fairy tales for the children. Stiff, blue cardboard covers, battered and cracked, pages of coarse paper, yellow at the edges. White letters stamped upon it. *Il Pentamerone* or *The Story of Stories*. By Giambattisa Basile.

One afternoon, I take it down from the shelf and sit om the chaise-longue in the parlour. Jojo sits on my lap and Juliette curls up beside me, peering over my arm at the book's pictures.

'Jojo,' I say, 'stop wriggling. Now, are you both listening?'

'Yessssss,' says Juliette.

'And you, Jojo?'

He pauses, then copies his sister. 'Yessssss.'

'Very well then, I'll begin.' And I clear my throat and look down at the page. 'Once upon a time there was a pair of sisters who longed for a man. So they shut themselves up inside their chamber and began to make a great quantity of paste of almonds and sugar, mixed with rosewater and perfumes. In this way, they formed a most beautiful youth: his hair was golden thread, his eyes were sapphires, and his lips were rubies.'

'What are rubies?' asks Jojo.

'They are very, very red stones...,' I say. 'Anyway, then these sisters sighed over him. They prayed over him. They wept over him. And as their tears hit the doughy mass, at last it began to breathe. After breath, words came out. Then, finally, disengaging all its limbs, it began to walk. And he was more beautiful than any man they had ever seen, this sugared almond man.'

'Oh,' says Juliette, but all the same, I hear her tell her mother the story later, when Augustine is helping her get ready for bed. Augustine nods across the counterpane at me, and from the mischievous glint in her eyes, I know she has a plan.

At midnight, Augustine and I creep downstairs into the kitchen. Following the fairy-tale as if it were a recipe, we fashion for ourselves a sugared almond man. We bake him in the stove. Then we break him in half, devouring him equally, piece- by-piece, our own blasphemous communion ceremony. And then we laugh and laugh at what we have done, until we must hold our aching sides, hold each other, until we are crying.

'Hush, *chérie*,' Augustine says at last, wiping the tears from her face, 'we'll wake everyone up.'

'I know,' I reply, 'but it's so funny. Will we tell the children in the morning?'

'Maybe,' says Augustine, reaching for the mixing bowl to wash it in the sink. Then she sees the corner of some thin paper poking out from beneath a placemat. 'But what's this?' She slides out the sheet of paper. It's a telegram, addressed to her mother. She glances at it, then her hand trembles and she turns white.

'What does it say?' I ask.

'It says…' Augustine takes a deep breath. 'It says a German soldier is going to be billeted with us.'

THE MIRROR

From my bedroom, beneath the attics I hear their boots cross the courtyard. Augustine, the Captain and his Lieutenant. Tramp tramp tramp. The sound mingles with the Germans' harsh, guttural voices. But I remember enough from Mademoiselle Madeleine's lessons at school to understand what they're saying.

'Fraulein,' says the Captain to Augustine, 'Please ensure you do everything to make my Lieutenant comfortable during his time here.' He's used '*du*,' the German familiar form. Augustine won't like that.

'Why are you being so familiar?' she replies. 'You don't speak like that to married women.'

'I beg your pardon,' says the Captain, laughing, and clicking his heels.

I strain to catch the rest of their conversation, but the sound of their footsteps retreats.

From my window, I see the vines are stripped bare of their grapes. The apple trees reach out their arms to me. The wind disperses their blossom. It drifts over into the boarded-up wasteland, to settle beneath my crucified tree. Because jagged spikes have been nailed into its bark. The soldiers made it into a lookout point, since it's the tallest tree on the highest point of the horizon. But it will grow and gnarl around the metal, clutching the alien rungs and dragging them into its body.

How dare they? I glare at the ceiling above me, at the attic where the Lieutenant will sleep. Next door to Augustine.

Or rather, as I realise that night, can't sleep. The ceiling quakes and shudders. My lamp is set swinging by the thud and scuff of his boots. They cross the sparsely furnished room. They pause, perhaps before the mirror above the fireplace. He contemplates his reflection, fingers the scar above his mouth, turns back towards the bed.

In my own mirror, my face is white and startled above the frill of my nightgown.

When I was a child, playing *Cache Cache* in the glass, I used to believe that all mirrors were really connecting doors. If I passed through one, I would end up in some great, mysterious corridor. I could walk down it, peering through each mirror in turn, until I found the one which led to the room of my true love.

THE LADLE

I won't forget his blue eyes darting round the parlour this evening, narrowing in disbelief.

'No books for such handsome shelves? But perhaps you ladies keep your favourites at your side?' He smiles, a lazy, compelling grin which reminds me irresistibly of Jacques. And his hair, just one shade darker than Paul's.

'Perhaps we should make a bargain, mesdemoiselles,' he continues. 'My Goethe for your Rimbaud.'

'We wouldn't be able to read it,' Augustine says, making her eyes very wide, then letting their lids drop.

'Ah, then I should teach you German,' he says, as if he himself speaks French like a native. Though his odd pronunciation has a certain charm.

'*Danke schön*,' says Augustine, with a demure smile.

'*Bitte sehr*,' replies the Lieutenant.

Later that evening, Augustine keeps turning away from the soup she's heating on the stove, to steal glances at him. But then, I suppose he's worth looking at. His metallic blue eyes, his sharp, pleasant face, his flaxen hair, are all so striking. The leather and steel of his boots and belt-buckle sparkle in the steam-filled kitchen.

Augustine tries to recite a German verb. '*Pfeiffen, Pfeiffe, Pfiff, Gepfiffen.*'

The Lieutenant throws back his head and laughs.

'Isn't that right?' she says, smiling despite herself.

I kick off one of my slippers and rest my instep against the cool tiles of the kitchen floor. The swelling starts to subside, the tingle of nerve pains cease. I exhale slowly. No Augustine, it isn't right. As the Lieutenant smiles back, I remember you and Paul walking down a darkened lane together. And me forced to dawdle a long way behind.

Juliette is watching me. Eight years old and eyes as bright as a blackbird's. She copies my sigh and thumps her hands down on the kitchen table.

'Don't do that,' I say. She's much too sharp, this one, as if she's inherited a double dose of wits. Her mind is never still. Her eyes gleam with sweet malice. She laughs, and the sound kindles a spark of animation in her brother's vacant eyes.

He too bangs his hands, arms, elbows against the kitchen table.

The Lieutenant laughs again, a resonant sound, like metal being crushed. 'Little monkey,' he says to Jojo. 'Was it you who stole my razor?' He grins and rubs his hand against his stubble.

The boy frowns, emphasising the chicken pox scars on his forehead. His mouth turns down. 'Mmmm-aman, Mmm-aman,' he stutters.

Augustine sighs, then kicks back the peeling linoleum, faded pink by the stove. But she turns and faces the Lieutenant. 'I'm sorry,' she says. 'We've tried to teach Jojo not to take things, but he doesn't always understand.'

Juliette's plain, elfin face creases into a scowl. Like me, she dislikes the way Augustine refers to Jojo in the third person. As if he's not even properly there.

The girl turns and pats her brother's arm, and he grins into her face.

'Don't worry on my account,' says the Lieutenant. 'Only worry if he tries to shave.'

Augustine nods and the tension eases round the kitchen table. Then she fetches the crooked porcelain ladle, turned the colour of ivory after years of use. There's a bluebird painted and glazed onto the bowl of the spoon. A Prussian blue bird, like the one in the children's fairytale, which dips through the steam and ladles soup into our shallow bowls. Clutching the ladle, Augustine turns towards the Lieutenant to serve him. She smiles full in his face. A bold, sensual smile that transforms her delicate features, as if she's lit up from within.

Jojo gazes at the strange woman in consternation, then at the Lieutenant.

'Is that our Papa?' he whispers to his sister.

Juliette shakes her head and for the rest of the evening, won't look at her mother.

But the German soldier can hardly tear his eyes away from Augustine.

THE SUMMER DRESS

Augustine is humming a tune to herself as she bends over her sewing, embroidering flowers onto the skirt of her summer dress. Red and gold, the colours of flames. The light from the window catches the nape of her neck, makes a few stray curls glisten.

She stands and holds the dress up against herself.

'How do I look?' she asks.

'Why not try it on and see?'

So she slips the cotton over her head, then turns to the mirror above the dresser, and pinches some colour into her cheeks. In the mirror, I see her steal a sly glance at me. She reaches into the drawer and fumbles inside, then takes out a lipstick and adds a slash of red to her mouth. She blots it on the back of her hand.

'Do you think Franz will like it?' she asks, then drops her eyes and bites her lip.

At the sound of his name, I run up to my room. I drag my best blouse from the clothes chest, take my one silk skirt from the *armoire*. I brush my hair until it shines. Then I glide downstairs, luxuriating in the breath of silk against my bare legs. And for the rest of the evening, Augustine and I sit and stare at each other from opposite ends of the room. Like reflections in a mirror. And neither of us says a word.

THE SOUP TUREEN

Today, Madame Solange's eyes are red, ringed with black circles. She shuts them, rubs her temple. 'Is that three kilos of maize or eight?' she mutters. 'I can't read Augustine's handwriting.' She opens her eyes and pushes the black leather ledger across the kitchen table towards me.

'No more can I,' I say. 'But let me do something to help you.' I get up and rummage around in the drawer of the oak dresser for the paper packets of herbs. I weigh out equal quantities of rose petals, cornflowers and camomile flowers.

Then I mix them in a saucepan and boil them in water for five minutes.

I tip out the water, let the petals cool. I crush them between pieces of gauze, then give us a compress each for our eyelids.

'I usually use rounds of raw potato myself,' Madame Solange says, companionably enough.

But her voice sounds a long way away to me. I like it behind the gauze, a white mist where I can hide. It's nice not to have to think about anything, to let my mind wander down a fragrant, flower-strewn path. I don't normally like the scent of roses, but mixed with cornflower and camomile, it's something else…

But Madame Solange can't relax.

'My eyes are fine now,' she says after a moment or two, and removes the gauze. She gets up, goes to the stove, starts to heat the evening *potage*. Her hands fly from cupboard to spice rack like zigzagging swallows.

Later, she ladles the leek soup from the china tureen into white soup plates. We push our spoons across the pale, green ponds, back and forth, like swimmers. I think of the three children racing each other to the far side of the stream, of Jacques, the winner, pelting us both with water.

The big, silver-plated spoon suddenly feels heavy in my hand. I put it down.

Lieutenant Franz Liebhart drinks his soup heartily, stuffs down mouthfuls of bread, calls for a second helping. You won't stay slim for long if you eat like that, I think. Madame Solange hesitates for a moment, then serves him some more soup.

Augustine picks up the bluebird ladle and waves it at the moths butting against the glass dome of the lamp. She isn't really trying to drive them away. She just wants to draw attention to herself. She steals a glance at the Lieutenant, a slight smile playing about her lips. How fair his hair is in the light from the glass dome.

Franz gazes back at her. How pretty she is in her light summer dress. Like a little Dresden doll.

You're caught now, I think, and fly inexorably to your fate.

Memories re-formulate in my mind. Surely it was Augustine who always used to win our swimming races, who emerged from the water, the panting, dripping victor.

Beyond the circle of light, the rest of the garden is swallowed up by night.

THE RED CROSS CARDS

Weeks pass and still our men don't come home. We don't know if they're alive or dead. No news. No news. No news, and other women have already heard, have already received cards from temporary camps. Half-pitying, half-despising us, they say, 'Don't you know, for you, it's hopeless.'

I imagine a rose blooming beside a concrete wall, and I tell myself, nothing is ever hopeless.

But we don't hear anything until January of the following year, 1941, when we finally receive Red Cross Cards. The French Army had collapsed so quickly. So many soldiers were captured that it took the Germans that long to count the number of casualties, to identify those killed in action, or taken prisoner, and to notify the families back in France.

One card from Paul, one from Jacques. Cards with the lines crossed out that don't apply, leaving just the seventh to read, 'I am a prisoner and in good health.'

No further communication is permitted on them. And yet now we know. They're alive. They're alive. Joy and sadness mingle, like wine and water in a communion chalice. And Madame Solange prays, kneeling each morning by her crucifix, never mind the arthritis in her knees.

'Dear Lord, the war is finished for France. Surely they must come home soon? When will we see them again?'

Though they're not the only prisoners from Ver. Several other wives also receive Red Cross cards - including Yvette Delmare.

THE HALF MAILGRAMS

A few prisoners manage to escape. But when they return to Ver, the Germans make them dig trenches, carry sandbags and bags of gravel and water for fortifications, and guard the railways for six hours a day.

'Might as well have stayed where we were,' they grumble, though they get used to the work, in time.

But not to all the restrictions on our lives. Now we need permission papers to move around. Only doctors are allowed out after seven at night. Our lights are painted blue, and our shutters are permanently drawn, so as to give the Allies no clues to bomb us - those friends who sometimes behave like our enemies. Even our station signs are painted out, to confuse the Allies. And access to the beach is forbidden. *Verboten* say the signs. The Germans mine the sand and plant large iron crosses and posts vertically.

Rommel's asparagus, we call it.

Not in German hearing, though. We have to be very careful what we say. Everything might be interpreted to our disadvantage. Even Monsieur le Curé must carefully choose the words for his sermons.

Carefully chosen words. Like the mailgrams which Paul and Jacques write to us from their prison-camp in Germany. We read and re-read them. And now we're allowed to write back on the return halves.

A social worker from the *Famille du Prisonier* turns up at the farm one morning, to advise us.

'It's Vichy policy, 'says the woman, with a curious smile. 'The government wishes us to help you write your letters, so that they'll be more interesting. So that in their hour of need, your men will be entertained rather than disheartened.'

Mon Dieu, such cheek. Surely this policy just strengthens the bond between the prisoner-of-war and the social worker, rather than the man and his wife? Besides, no-one has ever told me what to write, not since I was a little girl at school. I scowl at the social worker.

But beneath the brim of her hat, she carries on smiling.

'I know I've lost weight, and you can't see my hair, but don't you know who I am?' she says. 'I asked specially to be assigned to you, *chérie*.'

And then I do. It's Mademoiselle Madeleine.

THE HOLLOWED-OUT CIGARETTE

How did she get this job, I wonder? Especially since her friend Anna is Jewish and has to wear the yellow star. They try to find her tutoring work, but no-one wants a Jew teaching their child. It's just too dangerous.

Still, Mademoiselle always was clever.

'*Bah*,' she says, as I make her a cup of chicory. 'I just had to swear an oath of loyalty to Pétain, that's all. Easy enough to do, with my fingers crossed behind my back.' She scans my half mailgram reply, 'Perfectly acceptable,' she says. 'You always were one of my best students, Odette. Such a shame you couldn't stay on and take your *baccalauréat*.'

I flush pink with pleasure. Perhaps Mademoiselle's not so bad. Better than Yvette's social worker anyway, who tries to take over the duties of the head of the family, tells her how money she should spend, where she should live, how much work she should do, even how her daughter should be educated and disciplined. Mademoiselle Madeleine doesn't meddle quite so much, and really she has righter, since she's Paul's aunt, and my step-aunt, after all.

Not that Augustine is happy. 'Half a mailgram,' she retorts. 'Pathetic. How can I tell him everything I want in twenty-seven lines, and a postcard once a month if I'm lucky?'

'Perhaps you could pretend you were writing poetry,' says Mademoiselle. 'You know, condensing much into little.'

Augustine darts her a scornful look. But after Mademoiselle has gone, she writes her undying love onto a tiny piece of rolled-up paper. Using her tweezers, she removes the tobacco from a cigarette. Then she places the paper inside it and replaces the tobacco.

A month or so later, Paul replies.

'Please *chérie*, don't send me any more messages in hollowed-out cigarettes. The guard confiscated the last one.'

And sometimes I wonder how Augustine can make paper love to Paul and still flirt with Franz in the kitchen.

THE FIVE KILOGRAM PACKAGES

Madame Solange keeps a wooden box beside photographs of Jacques and Paul, where we can all place items for the monthly packages we send.

Our packages are much better than the standard Red Cross parcels. We post dried flowers, books, drawings, snapshots of the children. And, even better, knitted gloves, bread, if we can spare it from our own bread ration tickets, cigarettes and *bonbons*. The children are encouraged to give up their chocolate rations to their father and uncle. Madame Solange takes it and melts it down into a tin for the package.

'I don't want to,' says Jojo. 'We always send them all the chocolate and then I don't get anything. I'm only allowed to lick the pan.'

Juliette glares at him. There are dark stains round his mouth. She punches his arm.

His hand flies open to reveal a silver wrapper and four sticky chocolate squares.

'They won't want your horrible old chocolate anyway,' says Juliette. 'Because I'm going to send them *all* of mine.'

'That's right,' says Madame Solange. 'A little self-sacrifice is good for you. And with every gift, you also send a piece of your heart.'

'*Bah*,' mutters Augustine, who has been known to protest at the weight of the five kilogram parcel when it's her turn to take it to the Package Centre. She complains she already works too hard, that she's run-down, *fatiguée*.

Madame Solange and Juliette both frown. Then Juliette smiles her sweetest smile, and quotes something, a problem page reply I remember reading in the latest edition of *Pour Elle*. 'Papa will soon come home, Maman. If I say it and think it every day, it will happen, perhaps sooner than you think.'

Only, *Mon Dieu,* the way she says it, it sounds more like a threat.

Because your sharp-eyed daughter knows you're not too tired to unlock the piano and sing with Franz, Augustine. Not too weary to sigh and flutter your eyelids when he reads you Heine, *'sadder and sweeter, like pain dipped in honey.'*

'Don't be so harsh,' she tells me when I try and say something. 'You're just like those gossips in the village who mutter if I wear lipstick, if I sing, or even smile.'

'But what about your father?' I reply. 'He died, fighting the Germans. And your brother and husband are both prisoners-of-war.'

'Jealous are you, Odette?' she flashes back. 'Because Franz likes me more than you?'

I don't know how to reply. She gazes at me fiercely for a moment, then drops her eyes.

'I'm sorry,' she says. 'I shouldn't have said that. But you don't understand.'

'Tell me then,' I say.

'None of it, not my father, or Paul, or Jacques, is Franz's fault. I've been *so* lonely. Besides, every moment I enjoy with him, I pay for ten times in remorse.' She shakes her head, shakes away her bad thoughts, doesn't want to talk to me anymore.

THE LETTERS

Without Augustine's messy love-life to judge and disdain, I'd have to look a bit closer at my own. Because Jacques has written to me from his prison-camp. I imagine the blue light flaring up in his eyes as pen crosses pages. Then, at the bottom of the mailgram, an obscure scribble it takes me ages to decipher.

'Je t'aime.'

There - he's finally managed to write it. But somehow I can't find the right loving phrases to reply. So I write round this tender feeling which is between us. Lots of crossings-out.

Like skating patterns on a frosted lake, sweet and perilous such writing seems.

The first part of Jacques's reply is more articulate, and more frustrated. As if I've hurt his feelings. *'Did you read.' Swann's Way' in the end?* he asks. *'The character of Odette is as full of contradictions as you are.'*

Even though I haven't read it, I know it's not a compliment.

But in the postscript, there's my surname *'Rivière.'* He's put a line through it and written *'Solange?'* beside it.

That question mark haunts me still. Shaped like the neck of a swan. His marriage proposal. It makes my heart pound, pound, pound throughout the night. Keeps me wide awake. Then, finally, at first light, I take his letter out from underneath my pillow. I walk over to the window, unfold it and read it again.

'Do you remember, Odette, the day we walked out and saw a warbler's nest in the fork of a black hawthorn bush? You knelt down, and holding out only one finger, barely touched the soft moss. Then, anxious not to frighten the bird, you withdrew your finger, leaving just your hand outstretched.

That was the day I knew I loved you.

Whenever Van Gogh paints a thatched roof, it reminds him of a bird's nest. I promise you, Odette, one day we'll have a home of our own. It'll be a house formed from our bodies and our hearts, our separation and our reunion.'

But somebody else can't sleep either. Footsteps cross the courtyard. Then Franz appears beneath my window. He pulls down the handle of the wash-pump, splashes cold water over himself.

He sparkles beneath it, throws back his head, smiles.

His teeth are white as pearls.

His hair is burnished, like spun gold.

His muscles are taut, disciplined, beneath the pull of his white shirt.

Yes, bathing, glistening, in water and sunlight, he's a bronzed god, a chessman of ivory and gold.

And just for a moment, I think I've never seen anyone so beautiful. And more than anything in the world, I want to be loved, by someone like him, the way that he loves Augustine. I turn away from the window and start to write my consent to Jacques. If my words aren't as elegant as his, they're enough. I sign my letter 'with all my love, *Odette Angèle Elise Rivière,*' then crosses out my surname, to be replaced by an underlined <u>*Solange*</u>.

THE WEDDING DRESS

It isn't quite the right colour. Ivory silk, it's true, but tinged with misty grey. A faded dream of cloth, from the previous century, kept too long at the bottom of the wardrobe. Another relic in the cardboard box beneath the stereoscope. I shake it out and sigh over it, and in the end, I decide it'll have to do.

Because, somehow, I think if I have a wedding-dress hanging up in the wardrobe, waiting for him, he'll return to me. So I smooth my hands over the ivory silk and take it to the village dressmaker. Daughter of the midwife and the pharmacist, Mademoiselle Louise Rolland, whom, they say, keeps company with a German soldier.

The dressmaker finds her *lunettes* on an inlaid table, amongst her scissors and needles, threads, buttons, and braids. She nods her head over my material.

'You're lucky to have silk like this now. We don't have anything left.'

She jerks her head past the naked mannequin, towards her *chaise*, which looks remarkably new and clean. Pink flowers bloom on the cream upholstery. But the seats are covered in worn tea-towels and then I realise what she means. Even the furniture covers have been taken away, to be made into clothes.

I'm about to mumble something apologetic, when I notice a man's wallet on the *chaise*. The German soldier's wallet? I stare at Louise. For a moment she drops her eyes, but when she looks up again, her glasses magnify their wary expression.

Sly green eyes, that turn brown in shadow, and edged with long, dark lashes. Just for a moment, she looks very like Augustine.

'How can you?' I murmur.

And her expression is that of a cat's, who's afraid someone will deprive her of her prey. She shrugs eloquently, and we stare at each other in silence.

'I love him,' she says at last, her mouth full of pins.

'But his regiment will go away one day,' I say.

She scrutinises me carefully for a moment, weighing her words. As if she's trying out different versions of her story, like the material to be fitted to me, lengths of ivory silk twisted this way and that.

Then she spits out the pins, and her words tumble over each other, like bolts of satin.

'I know that. But Hans said he'd send for me after the war.'

'And you believe him?'

'Yes, I believe him.'

'You're mad,' I say, wanting to hurt her. As if she's Augustine, and I can finally tell her exactly what I think. 'He'll forget about you the moment he's gone. And what you're doing is very dangerous. When your brothers come home...'

Though if it's dangerous for her, it's even more so for Augustine. Adultery is a civil and criminal offence, grounds for divorce, punishable by fines and even prison sentences. And adultery with a German soldier, whilst your husband is their prisoner...

Louise jerks her fingers through her hair. Her one real beauty, thick as Augustine's, less excessively red than Maman's, varying according to the seasons between deep gold and bright copper.

'Dangerous...' she murmurs.

The bell above the shop door jangles. Her hand drops. Another customer.

Madame Yvette Delmare, the buttons on her skirt straining beneath her little round belly. She never re-gained her figure after she had her daughter. She'll be wanting her old dresses to let out, no doubt.

Yvette nods at me, giving the dressmaker time to hide the soldier's wallet beneath a cushion.

'What did you want me to do with the material in the end, Mademoiselle?' Louise says to me, smoothly and carefully. A silken voice.

'Oh, don't worry about it,' I say. 'I've changed my mind.'

It isn't the right time for wedding dresses.

THE SILVER ROSES

Augustine is no-where to be found.

Or at least Augustine might be found, in a certain harvest hayloft. In the company of a certain German soldier, telling her he has never before seen eyes so intensely green. But I'm not going to betray her. So when Madame Solange calls and calls her to come along, it's time to go to the cemetery, I offer to accompany her instead.

We're quiet as we walk along. I admire the silver roses in her pierced ears.

Her wedding earrings, she tells me, shortly.

We push open a pair of tall, wrought-iron gates with a sign on them, *'Accès interdit aux chiens.'* Then we're inside the cemetery. The path runs all the way round, tombs on both sides. Some of the graves are very old, with fragile, blackened crosses crumbling at their heads. Others are thick, polished stone bearing gilt vases with tiny, ornamental roses.

Some graves have stone angels. One, a carved stone chalice. And one gives me a start because it's a stone in the shape of a book, with incised letters, filled in with gold, which spell out my own name: *'Odette.'*

I scan the gravestone rapidly. To my relief, in smaller, engraved letters, *'Beloved Wife of-'* and some dates, half a century back.

Madame Solange kneels beside a gleaming slab of black granite. She inserts chrysanthemums from her garden into a vase on top of it. I look over her shoulder to read her husband's name. *Charles.*

'It doesn't go away,' Madame Solange says, almost to herself. 'Missing him, loving him. The feeling doesn't go away.'

She stands up and steadies herself. I give her my arm. She looks at me for a moment. Water shines in her eyes, tips over, flows down her cheeks.

'You see,' she says, 'Time isn't such a great healer, after all.'

I know that, I think. You don't have to tell me. I pat her arm awkwardly, and she takes my hand and squeezes it.

'And if you knew,' she says, 'how it makes me feel to have that German boy in the house. And all those arguments with Augustine. She insists he's just a young man like Jacques or Paul, forced to live in a foreign land.'

I nod. I've heard their arguments. Slammed doors. Muffled sobs. Notes pushed under doorways. Then the cups of camomile tea that herald a tentative reconciliation.

'Well, Odette, you're not as volatile as us Solanges,' she continues. 'You keep your feelings more to yourself. And perhaps you're right. Because all this fighting with Augustine doesn't do me any good, at all.'

No. And Augustine always gets her own way, anyway.

Madame Solange lets go of my hand and fishes for her handkerchief from the pocket of her blue woollen skirt. She mops her eyes. Then she blows her nose.

We shut the tall gates behind us, and the church bells begin to peal out the Angelus. Tongues beat against bells, a beautiful silver unstoppable onslaught.

And I suddenly think that the hayloft is like a church, with sunlight pouring through its high windows. Here, Augustine whispers the litany of her new love. She gives herself to her fair-haired lover in that profane and sacred place. Then they rise up, these two who are one, this golden image, molten and fused, in their own secret church.

THE TELEGRAM

Beneath the uncertain sliver of moon, it's hard to work out what's happened. But the planks that cover the hole in the fence have disappeared. The bush that sprouts over them has been trampled down. And the nettles beside it are bent, broken.

I straighten up, and there is Yvette, lurching across the courtyard towards me, her skin blotched, her eyelids swollen. She reaches inside her pocket, and her shaking hands take out… a handkerchief?

No. Suddenly, flimsy paper with smudged, grey print is thrust in my face. I squint and read: *'Our deepest sympathies. Lieutenant Frank Delmare succumbed to typhoid fever and died in our hospital in the early hours of the morning.'*

Yvette snatches back her telegram whilst I'm still trying to understand it.

'I didn't know what to do,' she gabbles. 'Celeste's with her grandmother. But I just had to get out of the house. I walked and walked and walked and ended up here.'

'Let me take you inside and bathe your face,' I say, patting her shoulder. 'Maybe give you some camomile and honey. You've had a terrible shock.'

'*Ma pauvre*. You know about terrible shocks too, don't you?' says Yvette, with so much compassion that I'm ashamed. 'Perhaps that's why I came here. Because you know how it feels.' Her eyes shine with tremulous sympathy, then she reads the telegram over again.

'I don't understand,' she says. 'Typhus? I thought the government sent out quantities of vaccines. And do you know what's worse? I'm sure they were going to let him come home soon.'

'Don't try to understand,' I say. 'Let's go inside. It's cold and it's late. I'm sure you can stay the night if you don't want to be alone.'

'But what about Augustine?' asks Yvette.

'Oh, don't worry about her,' I say. 'She won't trouble you.' She's barely a thought for anyone these days, except Franz.

'Why not?' says Yvette. 'Where is she anyway?' She glances round, unnerved by the sharp shadows from the orchard trees. Then her eyes alight on the old fence, the trampled down shrubs

'Let's go inside,' I say, trying to propel her towards the house. But she shakes off my hand and stands still, listening.

A girlish, high-pitched peal rings out in the cool, night air. Augustine's laugh, but to us, it's the jangled cacophony of nightmare, coming from the other side of the fence.

'Laughter?' says Yvette, more bewildered than angry. 'What is there to laugh about?'

'She doesn't know… what you've suffered,' I say.

'She never did,' replies Yvette, suddenly grim. She marches over towards the fence, and I trail after her.

Now we realise the planks have been prised off. They're lying in a flowerbed further up. The hole in the fence gapes wide.

Yvette bends as low as she can and peers through it.

Then her head jerks back, pale as the long-ago death-mask. She vomits into the patch of nettles.

Then I look.

On the other side of the fence, Franz leans against the trunk of the apple-tree, just beneath the iron spikes. Augustine lies in his arms, bathed in moonlight.

Yvette wipes her mouth, lurches towards me, grasps my sleeve.

'Her mother,' she says. 'We have to tell her mother. She's got to be stopped.'

'You can't,' I say. 'I know it looks bad. Terribly bad. But I'll talk to her. And you don't know what she's been through. With Paul away…and her little boy not right…'

'But they're alive, aren't they - not like my baby's father.'

'Augustine lost her father, too,' I say. 'And hasn't her mother suffered enough? Why give her something else to worry about?'

Yvette's face looks lost, inward. She clasps her arms round herself. Finally, she nods.

'I won't tell her, then. Not today. As long as you do.'

My heartbeat speeds up. I don't know what to say. I shut my eyes and there they are again, the grey letters, stark against the spectre-thin telegram. But if Yvette were less grief-stricken, less wholesomely good, I'd suspect her of seeking revenge. And I know I have to get her away from here.

So I nod. I let her think I'll do what she wants.

Another promise I can't keep.

THE UMBRELLA

I take Jacques's latest letter from my apron pocket. But then, on a whim, I climb the stairs to read it in his room. Here, the picture railings are painted gold. The wallpaper is a tangled profusion of sunflowers. Normally, I don't like yellow, but now it makes me feel as if Jacques is with me.

Because he loves sunflowers. They're dotted all around the village, in front gardens where children play. On our way to school, we used to stop and stare at their lions' faces, their starry clusters of mane. And if later, birds come to steal the seeds, it's because they're trying to feast on sunshine.

Like I am, when I read his letter. He writes: *'I dreamt it was raining. You were beneath the umbrella. The drops fell on its taut fabric. But the sun shone through the silk, through the clouds. Colours spread across your cheeks. Rainbows everywhere.'*

He's lucky to see the world so clearly, in such vivid colours. Though surely there must be other days, when he feels depressed, when the colours are less bright. Only he never writes about them.

That afternoon, I dip a soft cloth into a shallow dish. I grit my teeth, then stroke the cloth over the yellowing piano keys. I imagine Franz's caressing hands. How he loves to play.

Of course, *I'm* not musical myself. The notes come out, tuneful enough, but my lungs run out of air, and can't sustain them.

And what use is it thinking of Franz anyway? He isn't mine. And perhaps I only want him because he's Augustine's.

Now I wipe away the remnants of previous players. I snap shut the case over the piano keys, lock it all up. Because I can still feel Jacques's letter inside my pocket. And isn't it better to give love where it can be received, rather than wear myself out with an aching, fearing pain I don't even understand?

'*Merde*,' I mutter. The dish is full of lemon juice. The acid stings my fingertips.

THE NEEDLES

Later that evening, I decide to knit Jacques a scarf. Red to keep him warm, and blue for the colour of his eyes. I'm just losing myself in the gentle monotony of click-clacking needles when Augustine bursts into the parlour.

'You remember Père Lelédier? Whose sons used to come here and help with the harvest, before the war?'

'What about him?'

'Well, he decided that their cottage wasn't providing enough shelter from the bombing…'

'Oh, hush a minute, I think I've dropped a stitch. No, it's all right. Carry on.'

'Well, so they could have better shelter, the family decided to finish digging a trench that the Germans started. Near to Mont Fleury and the sacred spring. And whilst they were digging, guess what they found?'

'Buried treasure?'

'No. Lots of old bones, desiccated, but not powdery.'

'Ugh,' I say. 'What's so special about that?' *My sister loved me best of all/ Gathered all my bones/ Tied them in a silken scarf/ Laid them beneath the juniper tree…*

'Well, the bones weren't just thrown there. They were carefully separated, and placed at such angles, and at such a depth, that the Lelédiers think…'

'What?'

'The Lelédiers think they've found…that is to say…'

The Juniper Bird's Tree.

'…they think they've found the ruins of a little square building, an ancient religious site.'

'The foundations of the chapel of Saint Gerbold,' I say, slowly.

Augustine nods, and her eyes sparkle, not so much with the news itself, as with the pleasure of telling it. How pleased Jacques would be, too. All those summers, when we read old books, drew up maps, went exploring, but we never found the lost chapel. In the end, Jacques thought the Calvinists had destroyed it, burnt it to the ground. So we had to content ourselves with the saint's spring, the hill, the ancient rock.

Now I feel as if an ancient mystery has been solved, but not the one I wanted to know.

'Oh, look, you've dropped a stitch,' says Augustine. 'Silly girl, to miss it like that. If we were still at school, Mademoiselle would make you unravel the whole thing.'

I shrug, make a mou of disdain. It's only a dropped stitch, after all. But I glance down again at my knitting. *Plain. Purl Plain. Purl.*

THE WASHING LINE

The next day, a message is delivered to the farm. German labour demands are forcing Vichy to conscript female labour. Like the rest of the unemployed women in this village, I'm to be sent to a work-camp, fifty miles away.

Because getting up at five in the morning in summer and seven in winter, lighting the fire, going to the dairy, isn't work, after all. No matter how little sleep I might have had. Cleaning the house, the stables, is just a type of holiday.

Then I milk the cows, put the milk in the creamer. Prepare the breakfasts for the farmhands. Feed the children, then the chickens. Sometimes, the chickens, then the children.

Then time is getting on, and I need to fetch vegetables from the garden, draw water from the well, not to mention giving the calves their feed. Then I see to the pigs, whose rations have to be weighed and carefully distributed. Next, the scrubbing of floors and boots, of arms and necks, of red and white vegetables. I chop carrots, radishes and chives. Strip the potatoes of their mud coats. Flour and mould the pastry into the shapes of the day.

After the midday meal, everything starts again with the dishes. Some days of the week, there's the washing, the mending, the ironing - if there's time. After that, Augustine or I help Madame Solange prepare the dinner. And the garden must be watered. The clothes, pegged out on the washing-line. Then the lights in the henhouse must be lit. And there's yoghurt to make.

Even when the children have gone to bed, there are still urgent repair jobs. Jojo's overall, Juliette's apron. Then Madame Solange and I wear out our heads with the accounts. At the end of all this, after clearing all the papers away, I'm often the last to bed.

And I'm still classed as one of the unemployed, *sans profession*.

A farm girl, good-for-nothing. *Une bouche inutile*.

THE GRAMOPHONE

I open the side-door, and Franz is there, in the parlour, resting his arm on the mantelpiece, his head tilted to one side. Music blares out behind him.

He's discovered the gramophone in its hiding-place: Augustine's wardrobe, with its finely wrought hinges and bird heads all around the lock. I don't ask him what he was doing in her bedroom. It's right next to his. Perhaps he heard a noise and...

Perhaps the gramophone sang a secret hymn. Save me. Save me. From this wooden wardrobe coffin. Let me play my music again.

I imagine myself as a Jewish girl, with dark, shoulder-length hair and mournful eyes. Like Anna, at the peace meeting. Every time there's an alert, they hide me in the wardrobe.

'Save me, save me,' I whisper to the deaf knots of wood, the little islands in their sea of blood-coloured varnish.

Save me. Save me, Franz. Save me and I'll do anything. My heart contracts, then speeds up its count in my chest.

Franz turns away from the gramophone. His blond head swivels in the looking glass above the fireplace. He smiles at me, and his blue eyes are gentle.

'So I spoke to my Captain today. I told him how useful you are to Madame Solange and her family. To Augustine,' he adds, as if he can't resist saying her name.

Once I thought if I passed through the looking glass, everything would be backwards. And Franz wouldn't belong to Augustine anymore. He'd belong to me.

'He agrees that you will do better on the farm than in one of our work camps. So you don't have to go.'

I reach for his hand. I hold it to my lips. Thank you. 'Thank you,' I say, and Jacques's image swims before my eyes, this man's smile just like Jacques's, as good and wholesome and pure.

But his hand drops. The kind light fades from his eyes. The sugared almond man isn't mine.

'You should thank Augustine,' Franz says, pointedly. 'I'm doing it for her. She was the one who begged me to let you stay here.'

There's a stained glass window in our church, depicting Joseph and Potiphar's wife. But Jacques once told me it really represents Saint Gerbold, resisting the advances of his temptress.

'I'll g-gg-go and find her,' I stammer.

Merci, Ray Ventura sings. *Tout va bien, Madame La Marquise.* Then the needle gets stuck. The stylus skips a groove.

THE GLASS JARS

The cupboard is a house within the house. It's a secret space, with red walls that remind me of the long-ago window-seat's crimson curtains.

It's a space that makes the children want to break in and steal the riches of their grandmother.

Because the cupboard is where Madame Solange keeps her treasures: apples and grapes, bread and cheese, willow-pattern cups and saucers, fine diamond-paned decanters. But later, we'll discover something there that shouldn't be.

A lady handed Jojo the envelope at the orchard gate, to give to his grandmother. But he wanted a handful of raisins from the cupboard. He forgot about the letter, left it tucked between two glass jars, next to Franz's stolen razor.

For the moment, the jars sparkle. The apples sit in scarlet rows. The knives are polished and sharp. And nothing is cracked or chipped. But now a very particular bomb waits for Madame Solange.

THE SATCHEL

Augustine and I can't afford Elizabeth Arden's special, waterproof, paint-on stockings. So we dab our legs with diluted gravy. I paint hers and she paints mine. She's not as good as Jacques with a brush, but she does manage a convincing seam up the back. We're just twirling our skirts, admiring the effect, when someone hammers on the door.

Augustine sighs and adjusts her petticoat, so it won't stick. Then she undoes the latch.

Monsieur Rolland, the pharmacist, and *Pétainiste*, enters the parlour. After him trails twelve-year-old Juliette, dragging her satchel.

'Tell your mother what you did,' he hisses from behind his half-moon spectacles. 'Go on, tell her.' He gives Juliette a little push towards us.

The girl's eyes are wide in her small, squashed face. She stares at him, stares at her mother, then runs to me.

'Where's Grandmaman?' she whispers.

'She's upstairs, resting. Oh Juliette, what have you done?'

But Juliette bites her lip, won't tell me.

Monsieur Rolland jerks his head forwards. 'They picked *her*,' he says, stabbing a crooked finger at Juliette, '- a special honour, see - to raise a flag to Joan of Arc and Marshal Pétain. And she, what does she do…' He pauses, wipes away the thread of spittle dangling from his lower lip.

'Well, what does she do?' asks Augustine.

'Your daughter goes to the flagpole in the centre of the schoolyard, before all the pupils and teachers, and shouts, 'When Marshal Pétain drives the enemy from France, like Joan of Arc did, I'll raise the flag. But not before.'

'Did you do that?' asks Augustine.

The girl nods.

'And who put you up to it?' quavers Monsieur Rolland. 'Eh, who put you up to it? That's what I'd like to know.'

'No-one,' says Juliette.

'I hope you're not trying to be some precious heroine of the Resistance,' he mutters. 'Resistance, eh? Do you know what that means, *Re-sis-tance*?'

Juliette shakes her head, then hurls herself against me. I wince as my skirt sticks to my gravied legs. I don't have a petticoat to protect it.

'Ask,' he snarls. 'Ask one of your classmates when their parents are arrested. Or look out for your friends' empty desks. *Mon Dieu*. Lucky they sent for me, a volunteer *gendarme*. Otherwise it might have been a night in the cells for you.'

'Oh Juliette,' sighs Augustine, giving her skirts a sudden, concerned twitch. 'I can assure you Monsieur Rolland, this is not what we're teaching her at home. But we're very grateful to you for bringing her back safely. Say thank you, Juliette.'

But the girl refuses to turn and face Monsieur Rolland.

THE ENVELOPE

A few weeks later, Madame Solange and I are paring apples in the kitchen. The peelings lie in red and green coils upon the table, exuding their fresh, tart odours. Jojo and Juliette pounce upon them. They chew the juicy ribbons, working their jaws. 'Fetch me another cooking apple, Juliette,' says Madame Solange, rinsing her fingers beneath the tap.

The girl reaches inside the cupboard's cavernous depths. But instead of an apple, her hand draws out the envelope tucked in between the glass jars. The name 'Madame Solange' is scrawled, snake-like, across it.

'For you, Grandmaman,' says Juliette.

'Oh,' says Madame Solange, wiping her hands on the back of her apron. 'Another one of your Valentines, Juliette?'

The girl shakes her head.

'The lady gave it to me,' says Jojo.

'Which lady?' asks Madame Solange, reaching for the letter. 'Do you know, Odette?'

140

I shrug, but my heartbeat speeds up.

'The f-f-ff-at l-ll-l-ady,' stammers Jojo, in between mouthfuls of apple. Madame Solange balances her *lunettes* across the bridge of her nose and starts to read. Suddenly she turns white as the sheet of paper in front of her.

'Leave that peel alone and go and feed the chickens,' she tells the children. 'Go on, hurry up, it's already past the time.' As soon as they've gone, she thrusts the letter at me.

Chère Madame,

I thought you should know. One of your girls has been seen keeping company with the German soldier billeted with you. She is a disgrace to he village, to France, and to the memory of your late husband.

Such a short letter to cause such a lot of pain. And it is, of course, unsigned.

Is it always like this, that the choices we make demarcate the shapes of our lives? Even when we are no more than children, the evil that we do lives after us. The May Queen head-dress re-appears in my mind's eye, ghostly white and flimsy as the paper of the anonymous letter.

For by writing *'One of your girls'* Yvette is giving us a choice. Either I betray Augustine, or I lie for her, and betray myself. Because Augustine is wrong to love Franz and maybe I'm wrong to love Augustine as much as I do.

At any rate, Yvette is having her revenge, on both of us.

THE CAMEO BROOCH

'Which one of you is it?' she spits. The cameo brooch with her husband's portrait in it trembles at the V of her lace blouse. 'Which one of you is behaving *comme une putain*? Which one of you is sleeping with the German boy?'

Augustine and I stare at each other, aghast, as Madame Solange rains down insults upon us. Neither of us says anything. After all, when it came to the really big sins, we were never much good at confession.

Madame Solange leaves the parlour to wipe her face, to compose herself.

'We could deny it,' says Augustine, her face flushed with guilt.

'*You* could deny it,' I say. 'I haven't done anything wrong.'

'But I have a husband, children. It's far worse for me if I'm found out. We should lie - or - or, no, you should say it was you. After all, it can't really matter to you, since there's no-one except Maman to mind.'

But what about Jacques? Though perhaps now isn't the right time to tell Augustine about him.

I feel a sudden sense of helplessness, as if I'm being swept away by waves. I look past Augustine, through the window, into the orchard. I'm not sure how long I look.

Then I gaze at the sky. It's pale blue and all my life is in it, spilling out among the clouds. I see the silver hairbrush, the Pierrot doll, the statue of Pan. I see the confirmation cross, and all the books, and the crystal and amethyst rosary. I see the bronze hunter and the night light and the curving spiral staircase.

My whole life swirls out into the sky, everything I have ever been or wanted to be.

I see a little girl dressed as a May Queen, crunching an unripe apple. I see a nine-year old, duster in hand, polishing the froth-framed mirror. And my face is in the mirror, a little older, wiser, sadder, as I pin a black ribbon to my hat. I hear my brother calling, '*Ky-witt, Ky-witt,*' and my father saying, 'Odette, come and look at this.' His oval spectacles gleam as he glances up from the stereoscope. And Minouche is by his side, wagging her tail, and I think, 'Is this where people go when they die?'

And then Jacques appears and shows me a box of paints, all colours, and I say, 'How did you get here?' But I turn away from him and my distant past, towards my unknown future. Because beside me, all the while, there's a girl with imploring green eyes, only inches from mine.

I find myself saying, 'Yes,' to her.

And then, somehow, my husband is here, a stranger with a soldier's hat, and then my unborn daughter is staring at us, and my grandchildren jump up and down and wave. And a woman unwinds a white silk scarf from her flaming red hair and holds a finger to her lips.

When Madame Solange returns to the parlour, I bow my head and say, 'Madame, I am so sorry. It was me.'

She does something I'm not expecting She slaps me.

I put my hand up to my sore cheek, cradle it against my fingers.

Madame Solange looks at me coolly for a moment. 'Odette,' she says, 'you can't stay here anymore.'

'Maman!' says Augustine.

Madame Solange looks at her daughter, then back at me. 'Oh, I think Odette knows me well enough to know I can't tolerate any kind of lie,' she says. 'She must pack up her things and go back to her own mother. I've tried my best for both you girls and this is the thanks I get.'

'I'm a better person than you think I am,' I say at last.

'You don't know what I think,' says Madame Solange.

I wonder then if she knows. That I've just confessed to a sin I haven't committed. Though Monsieur le Curé would say there's no difference between thinking a sin and doing it.

Later that day, I stand in the front courtyard, surrounded by bags and valises. I glance round at the barns, the outbuildings, the hayloft, the steps, the white gate, the pond and the henhouse. Then I stare back at *Les Hirondelles*. My gaze travels upwards, to the birds nesting in the grey-thatched roof, then down past the attics, the three solid storeys of leaf-covered stone.

Once again, there's the pear tree in the garden, reaching out to me forlornly. I walk over to rest my head against the trunk of the wasteland apple tree to say goodbye. The scars weep rust and sap down the bole.

All of a sudden, Madame Solange comes to the parlour window and peers out. When she catches me gawping, she draws the heavy brocade curtains across.

THE BEEHIVE

My mother's house. The white-washed cottage in the village, where faded ivy leaves vie for space on the trellis with clusters of honeysuckle. Where, blinking, dazzled by sunlight, I step into the gloomy parlour and then my heart sinks. I long to throw open the shutters, to let in fresh air and daylight, to vanquish Paul's mother's wallpaper, and other ghosts.

Of course, Maman and Bertrand are kind enough, try their best with me.

'I'll talk to Hélène Solange for you,' Maman promises. 'I'll make her realise it wasn't you.'

'Don't,' I say, 'I'm sure she'd rather believe it was me than Augustine.'

'Well, in her heart, she must know the truth already,' says Maman. 'Of course, a mother knows her own daughter.'

Not always, I think.

At night, when I have nightmares and call out, Maman sits beside me and strokes my head, static fireflies shooting out from her nightdress.

How can I tell her, 'It's you I was dreaming about?'

Though one night, I dream of something else. I dream I'm back at the farm, walking towards the beehives. My mouth waters in anticipation of the honey. But as I get closer, I realise that the buzzing comes not from bees, but from flies. Thousands of them, swarming over the pulpy, bloody carcass of a dead calf.

I turn away, round a sharp corner, and there, just past the hayloft, is Jacques, standing in front of an easel. Then I remember that he once told me about a painter called Soutine, who fetches dead animals from a slaughterhouse, to paint in his studio in Montparnasse.

Jacques smiles at me and turns his canvas round so that I can see it. It's filled with swirling shapes and vibrant colours: the calf and other animals resurrected and floating over the rooftops of Ver-Sur-Mer. And we are floating with them, hand-in-hand, borne aloft by my umbrella into a cloud of golden bees.

I can still feel the sensation of his fingers, curled around mine, as I wake.

THE TELEGRAM

But of course, bees only fly away from the hive when someone dies.

I remember this a few weeks later, as I'm reading the telegram that Augustine, white and trembling, hands me in the doorway to the cottage. The carbon paper is too flimsy to bear the import of its message. STALAG IX. WE REGRET TO INFORM YOU OF THE DEATH OF JACQUES SOLANGE. DEEPEST SYMPATHIES.

So, Jacques has died in the German prison camp. His life, an unfinished sketch.

'Oh Jacques, Jacques. How? Why?'

Augustine replies, 'W-w-w-ee don't know.'

I reach for Augustine, crush her against me, then step back. It's no good. She always did look so much like her brother. I turn away from her and stumble towards my room. I lock the door and throw myself onto the bed.

Finally, towards evening, I unlock the door.

The fire has sunk very low in the hearth, and Augustine is shivering on the *chaise-longue*, waiting for me. I fetch the blanket from my bed and together we burrow beneath it.

'Did you love my brother, Odette? We never knew for certain,' she says.

'Yes. Very much,' I reply.

She takes my listless hand and begins to chafe my fingers.

My tears start falling again.

'You never told me before,' she says, wistfully. 'Always you had to have your own enclosed garden, your walled-in, secret garden where none of us are allowed.'

She squeezes my hand. I try to smile at her through my tears.

But after all, it's months before I see her again. Her mother forbids it.

THE HUTCH

Throughout that long Autumn and Winter we wait for the Allies to arrive, wait so long that the *débarquement* becomes a tired joke.

Then, suddenly, there's news of a British plane flying over Mont Fleury. Of course, one swallow doesn't make a Spring, but in April, there's the sound of bombs falling. And then in May, bombardments and machine gunnings. In early June, the aviation activity increases.

Before we know where we are, it's the 6^{th of} June 1944, *Jour-J*. Early in the morning, the Allies land on our beaches, to liberate us. Bursts of fire everywhere. I pull the blankets over my head every time I hear them.

But the noise is interspersed with staccato raps on the front door. A familiar voice calls, 'Odette! Odette!'

Augustine. 'Let us stay here,' she begs when I open the door. And sheltering beneath her shawl, Juliette and Jojo, dressed in their Sunday best, and silent as apparitions.

Jojo carries a large wooden box with bars and bits of straw poking through them. His rabbit hutch. Behind the wire mesh door, Blondin's pink nose and pink-tipped ears twitch.

'The Canadian officer says we're not safe up at the farm. It's too close to the *château*,' Augustine continues.

I throw my arms round her. I've missed her so much. She's thinner now and her ribcage knocks against my heart.

Slowly she eases herself from my embrace.

'The Canadian officer?' I say. 'But what about your mother? And Franz?'

'Franz is gone. Yesterday, he was hiding in a hedge, begging us not to betray him. Well, begging Maman anyway. Just imagine, that field where we used to keep the sheep, there's the English in one hedge, and then the Germans opposite, and they're all shooting at each other.'

'Shooting?'

She nods. 'Yes. Then, at lunchtime, the noise gets worse. I open the window to check that Franz is still safe, and a bullet flies past. Then I see all the German soldiers bent double, going over the village bridge. And Franz is with them.'

Her mouth trembles. 'I didn't even get to say goodbye,' she murmurs. Her eyes fill with tears.

I take her hand. Because after all, in times of war, any gesture of affection is extraordinarily beautiful, a sign of the love which the whole world so desperately needs. At least, that's what Augustine always used to say when she tried to justify her relationship with Franz.

'But the Canadian?' I say. 'Where does he come into it?'

Augustine wipes her eyes with the back of her hand. 'Well, I could see soldiers swarming over the fields, but I couldn't tell whose side they were on. They were on their stomachs in the leaves…'

I nod. 'Hard to tell if their uniforms are khaki or green…'

'And so I grabbed a coffee pot and went outside and very deliberately walked along the edge of the field. And then the soldiers hidden in the laurels, among the almond bushes, come out. And they're Canadians! All laughing, shouting, speaking at once, chewing gum, of course. And they give me some chocolate for the children. Then their officer arrives and tours the house, looking for delayed action bombs. I pull open all the doors and cupboards, and of course, all the things we hid before Franz arrived spill out. Even some bottles of champagne.'

'Champagne?'

Augustine smiles. 'Well of course Maman sees the bottles, and insists we toast the Canadian heroes. So we sit on the outdoor steps and have a drink. What's that, Jojo?'

'Even me,' he repeats.

'Even you,' says Augustine.

'And I smoked a Gold Flake cigarette,' says Juliette.

'You did not,' says Jojo. 'You liar.'

Juliette reaches inside her pocket and pulls out a stub of cigarette. She sniffs it.

'Smells lovely,' she says. Then, 'Why are you smiling, Odette?'

'You just reminded me that your mother liked to smoke too, when she was young,' I say. 'Remember those American pilots, Augustine? But where's Madame Solange?'

'Maman?' Augustine pauses and the tears start back to her eyes. 'We couldn't get her to come with us. Not even the Canadian officer could persuade her. She says it's her home and she's never going to leave it.' She pauses, then gulps. 'But at least the Viscountess Agathe is with her.'

'The Viscountess Agathe?'

'She turned up today, early this morning. We were so surprised to see her. She thinks the *château* is too much of a target but that the farm is safer.' She gulps, 'Let's just hope she's right... *Mes enfants*, stop that, please. Jojo, give Juliette back her cigarette. Hasn't there been enough fighting already?'

Jojo whimpers. Augustine strokes his head, absent-mindedly, then turns her eyes back to my face. 'Do you think the old ladies will be all right?' she whispers.

'I don't know,' I reply. 'But I think you did the right thing to come here, all of you.' And I lead them to the *chaise-longue* in the parlour and wrap the blanket round them. Maman makes everyone *tartines* and Bertrand fetches a pack of cards and teaches the children to play *bézique*.

'Careful not to knock the spots off,' he says as Juliette shuffles, and she laughs.

THE HEADSCARF

Though the feeling of being safe doesn't last long.

Augustine sits up suddenly and says, 'I forgot to tell you - guess who we saw on our way here?'

I shrug. 'The Lelédiers?'

'No, you'll never guess. It was Mademoiselle. But I hardly recognised her. Her hair was wild, and her eyes were everywhere. She clutched my arm and begged me, yes begged me...'

'To do what?'

'Well she kept saying the name 'Anna' over and over again. Then she said that Anna's papers were all in order, that they were supposed to be going to Switzerland together. But that someone must have informed on her, because she'd been taken away.'

I swallow hard. '*Mon Dieu.* How awful. What did you say?'

'I didn't know what to say. She looked so scared. I gave her my headscarf, wrapped it round her. Then she started to mutter something about Franz. *Your* Franz, she said.'

'What did she mean by that?'

'That's what I wanted to know. *My* Franz? I said. Then she asked me to ask Franz to rescue Anna. That she'd heard he saved you from a work-camp and that she knew not all Germans had bad hearts.'

'The poor thing,' I say. 'She must be out of her mind with worry to say that.'

'Yes,' says Augustine. 'She must be. Because she told me to tell Franz that she used to read us the Brothers Grimm when we were at school.'

'What did you say?'

'Well, I told her I couldn't tell him anything. Not because I didn't want to, but because he'd gone, over the bridge, with the other Germans.'

'Would you have said anything to him if you could?'

'I might have done. Because she looked so, well, so - *desperate.* And then she told me there were forty-five camps in both zones and that she'd never be able to find her friend.'

We're both silent for a moment. I imagine Mademoiselle Madeleine pulling the headscarf tighter round her head, saying goodbye, stumbling once, righting herself, then walking away.

Of course, Anna is never seen again, either in Ver or Bayeux.

But when the war is over, they restore the bust of Marianne to the alcove in the lobby of the town hall. And they pin a poster outside, which shows our heroine standing in front of an execution post. Her body is bloodied and martyred, and one stigmatised hand shields her eyes as she looks into the glare of the future. Her other hand pushes back the recent past.

I still think she looks like Anna.

THE GAS CAPES

Later that day, Augustine decides she wants to go and check on her mother.

'It isn't safe,' I tell her.

'But the noise is coming mainly from the beach,' she insists.

I pause to listen, but all I can hear is sudden birdsong outside the window. I shake my head. 'You should just stay here,' I say.

'But Maman will be missing us by now. Maybe I can persuade her and the Viscountess to come back with me.'

'Not if I'm with you, they won't,' I mutter. 'Your mother hates me.'

But Augustine flings her arms round me. 'You're coming with me?' she says.

'Well, I can't let you go by yourself,' I reply.

She gazes at me for a moment. 'Now might be the right time for you and my mother to settle your differences. I mean, with all this going on, I'm sure I can convince her that it hardly matters whether you did or didn't sleep with a German soldier.'

Merci beaucoup, Augustine.

The twins stay behind with Maman and Bertrand, and together Augustine and I set off along the shingle path that turns into the road to *Les Hirondelles*. She's right, the noise is coming mainly from the beach. Heavy machine-gun bullets cut up the sand. It sounds like a giant swarm of bees.

Then, as we near the farm, there's a huge, deafening bang.

Augustine's fingers dig into my wrist. Through the white pillars we watch as the farmhouse starts to tremble. The windows dance.

Then the whole sky lights up. Flashes, fires, tracer bullets, shells fall all around us. A fire breaks out some way away - the Château de Courseuilles. Then the church steeple folds into itself, like a penknife closing. The farmhouse windows shatter, sounding like music. And suddenly I remember the snowstorm. All the pieces, falling, falling. They'll never fit back together again, never.

Something hurtles towards our heads - a piece of burning paper? We dodge it, and then I realise. It's a bird, with blazing wings.

'Maman,' Augustine screams, and I have a sudden vision of my own mother, outlined in flame. Because as the north wing, the kitchen and the attic bedrooms catch alight, we realise that Madame Solange and Viscountess Agathe must be dead.

I raise my hands to my face. My skin is tender where I press it. And my hair feels strange, coarse, singed by sparks.

Now we can't even see the outbuildings because there's so much dust and soil flying around. But we hear branches breaking, twigs snapping. And much later, we find a fragment of cloth hanging from the wasteland tree. The pocket of Juliette's apron.

British bombs destroy the curving house by the sea, where I used to live with Maman, Papa and Pierre. They also wipe out the Hotel des Arts, the cafés, restaurants, and concert hall along the pier - and damage the lenses in the lighthouse.

And the beach itself… Tank trucks rip up the turf. Barbed wire rolls of steel matting and stacks of rusting rifles litter the sand. The shingle wall is completely destroyed. Dead soldiers lie down. A few are covered with gas capes, concealing the look of surprise on their faces. And corpses white as snow float past on empty rafts…

THE BOWL OF SOUP

Until the British caterpillar machines arrive, German prisoners are made to de-mine the fields with their bare hands. And British soldiers guard the path outside our cottage. Maman invites them inside to share a meal with us, then realises we have nothing to give. Nevertheless, we all sit down to some soup with a little meat in it.

Whilst she's waiting to be served, Juliette takes out her Gold Flake stub and puts it between her lips. Then she inhales, for all the world as if it's lit.

'You shouldn't smoke cigarettes,' says one of the officers, Stanley Morgan, in passable French. His hair is thinning on top, but he has a kind, intelligent expression. 'I knew a Corporal who doused himself in petrol to get rid of the mosquitoes. Then when it came to a stand-to, he thought he'd have a cigarette, lit a match - and whoosh! Blew himself right out of the ruddy trench. Proper Charlie Chaplin, he was.' He taps his jacket pocket. 'That's why I only smoke a pipe meself.'

Juliette stares at him impassively, then places her cigarette stub back in her pocket, and holds her bowl out for a spoonful of soup.

Meanwhile, her brother sits in the corner with huge tears falling from his eyes.

'Why's the boy crying?' asks another of the officers.

'We're eating his rabbit,' says Augustine shortly, and sends Jojo upstairs.

She and the children remain with us for another few weeks, until another cottage can be allocated to them. In time, they receive compensation, and then the slow, painful task of rebuilding *Les Hirondelles* begins.

THE PIPE

After they've gone and we have a little more room, one of the English officers decides he'd like to be billeted with us. The pipe-smoking Stanley Morgan. Still, better a pipe than Papa's snuff, I suppose.

So Stanley sits in my mother's kitchen, waiting for his boiled egg. And I'm smiling, smiling all the while. And as the hot water takes its time to boil, I think, Hurry up, hurry up, fall in love with me. You're my only chance to escape this village where everyone hates me.

When I think he's not looking, I dunk a loaf of day-old bread in cold water and put it in the oven - just on the shelf, not in a tin. Soon the sweet smell of dough permeates the kitchen. I wrap a cloth round my hand, take out the bread and cut off two, thick crumbling slices. Then I cut them into strips to accompany Stanley's egg, an English custom to which he's very partial.

'I heard of a soldier once,' says Stanley, smashing the top of the eggshell, 'used to keep chickens inside his tank. In a little wire-mesh box. So he always had an egg for breakfast - and then, sometimes, chicken for lunch.'

He dips the bread into the egg yoke, gives his 'soldier' a yellow hat, then bites into it.

'Day-old bread?' he says, with a sweet smile. 'That's one of my mother's tricks, too.'

'What sort of soldier are you, Stanley?' I say as I start to wipe the bread-knife free of crumbs. 'You weren't here for the Jour-J landings.'

He pauses in mid-bite and winks. 'It's all strictly hush-hush, Mademoiselle,' he says. 'Though I did have to arrest Monsieur Rolland the other night, for being outside after curfew.'

'Oh Stanley!' I put the breadknife down suddenly, with a clatter. 'His daughter Louise is a sort of friend of mine.'

For the first time since I've known him, Stanley frowns, a number 11 frown that makes him look serious. 'From what I hear, she's not the best sort of friend to have. Her and her German fancy-man.'

'The heart wants what it wants,' I say, with a sigh.. 'And the war made all of our lives so... complicated.'

There's a look in Stanley's eyes I might like, if only… if only I could get Jacques out of my mind. Perhaps it's Stanley who's the sugared almond saint? After all, Saint Gerbold was originally English. Though Augustine always reminds me that he has a German name.

Suddenly from outside comes the sound of cheering, 'VIVE TOMMY,' 'VIVE L'AMERIQUE.' Stanley and I rush to the window of the cottage and stand together there, gazing out as the crowd lets loose a cascade of flowers and flags.

'They're throwing rose petals,' I say.

'Look Odette,' says Stanley, 'there's the Tricolore, the Stars and Stripes - and the Union Jack.'

THE TRICOLORE FROCK

I rush upstairs and pull on a different frock. Then I step outside, run towards the crowd, their flags unfurling, red, white and blue against a cloudless summer sky.

My bare feet form hills and valleys in the wet sand. As soon as they're made, they fill up with water and are erased. The sea beside me is clear. But far away, it seems deep blue. Or glittery green. Squinting against the bright sun, I can't decide. Topaz perhaps. It doesn't matter.

My skirt is blue. My bodice is red. My sleeves are white. The breeze ripples in the folds of material. I run faster, my blood surges, my head grow light.

I imagine myself dancing with Jacques in the courtyard, on the evening of Augustine's wedding. Arm-in-arm, leaping in time with him and the music. His hot glance upon my face. Then suddenly, he's gone... The circle breaks up. The dancers re-group in new patterns, to be swallowed up by the cheering crowd.

THE BRACELET

A month after he arrives in Ver-Sur-Mer, Stanley takes me for a walk along the seashore. He points out the devilfish, the velvet swimmer crabs, and I pretend I've never seen them before. Then he points at some oyster shells. 'Where I'm from,' he says, 'a little village called Fitz in Shrewsbury, they put empty oyster shells inside the kettles.'

'But why would do they that, Stanley?' I say. 'You're pulling my leg.'

'Cross my heart, I'm telling the truth, sweetheart,' says Stanley. 'It stops the kettles from furring up. My mother swears by it.'

'It's nice to see a man so fond of his mother,' I reply. I imagine her as someone like Madame Solange, very capable. Not like my mother, at all.

Now Stanley points to a jellyfish at the edge of the tide and starts to laugh. 'Look at that!' he says.

I peer forwards, and Stanley points again to the green design at the centre of the jellyfish. 'Just like a four-leaf clover,' he says. 'A good luck emblem.' He draws his sleeve up, past a faded tattoo of a blue rose that now resembles a bruise. Then he slides a woman's bracelet off his wrist and shows it to me.

There it is, in the palm of Stanley's hand, with its interlocking square brackets of gold, and its dainty safety chain. But since Papa died and Maman re-married, I never set much store by wedding rings. In fact, these days, all jewellery makes me feel suspicious. So now, as I peer at the bracelet with its interlocking square brackets of gold, its dainty safety chain, its scintillating diamonds and rubies, like tiny stars, I'm not sure what to say.

'My mother's,' says Stanley. 'I've worn it all through the war, and now the war's over, I'd like you to have it.'

My fingertips trace the metal, smooth and jagged at the same time. 'Is it costume jewellery?'

'Oh no,' says Stanley. 'It's a good one. Eighteen carat gold.'

Yes. I can tell by the weight of the bracelet in my palm, the way the links tumble over each other, like a metal waterfall. A heavy, hesitant jangle.

'Oh Stanley, it's beautiful,' I say. 'But I'm not sure I can accept it. Madame Solange said, 'never accept anything from a gentleman you can't eat or put in water.'

Stanley pauses for a moment, but then says, all in a rush, 'Could you accept it if I asked you to marry me?'

I pick up the bracelet from the palm of his hand, touch it gently. 'I need time to think about it,' I say. 'May I tell you this evening?'

Stanley squeezes my hand, still holding the bracelet. The heat of his hand is reassuring, but the bracelet feels like my tongue against my teeth, smooth and jagged at the same time. I'm still tongue-tied.

'Ah say yes, little wren,' he says, borrowing my mother's nickname for me, 'and we'll have oysters for supper.

THE WHITE GLOVES

That evening, Stanley and I sit opposite each other at the dining-table in my mother's cottage. There are candles on the table and an empty plate of oysters in front of us. I am wearing the diamond and ruby bracelet, and Stanley has adjusted the clasp so that it fits my wrist. I'm working on a tapestry, but sometimes my fingers stray from my needle to the links in the chain.

Meanwhile, Stanley's fingertips are inky with perplexity, and every so often he lets out a sigh or a groan over a letter he's trying to write.

Finally, I'm compelled to say, 'Who are you writing to, *chéri*? Your mother?'

'Ah, no,' says Stanley. 'She's next on the list. No, I'm writing to a girl back home.'

'Oh?' I say, quickly.

'Yes,' says Stanley. 'I'm telling her she shouldn't wait for me any longer.'

'But Stanley,' I say, putting the tapestry canvas down, biting my lip, 'I don't want to be the cause of anyone else's suffering.'

Now Stanley puts his pen down and looks straight across at me. '*Chérie*, you have a good heart,' he says slowly. 'But it really isn't anything like that. What I feel for her is more of a brotherly feeling. She was good to my mother when my father died. But what I feel for you is... what a man should feel for his wife.'

What I might say next, I don't know, because suddenly there's a loud knock at the front door. Stanley jumps up to answer it. Michel Delmare, a volunteer gendarme, enters the dining room, tugging at the fingers of his white kid gloves.

'Stanley,' he says, nodding at him.

'Michel?' says Stanley.

'I'm sorry to disturb you both this evening,' says Michel, a shade defensively, 'but I need to interview the young lady.'

'About what?' asks Stanley.

'A private matter,' says Michel, after a moment or two.

Stanley gives me a questioning look, but he is too polite to pursue it further.

'It's all right, Stanley,' I say, 'I'll talk to him. I've done nothing wrong.'

'If that's what you want,' says Stanley, and he walks towards the parlour, then pauses at the door. 'But I'm just going to be on the other side of this door. Call me if you need me.' He passes through, into the other room.

Michel Delmare sits down opposite me, in the chair that Stanley has vacated. He leans forward. The skin of his white kid gloves stretches taut as he splays his hands across the dining table.

He should have been a soldier, like his brother Frank, but he suffers from colitis. So instead, he's a volunteer *gendarme*.

And his gloves are immaculate.

I remember that time, many years ago, when I lent Maman my gloves for church. They came back grimy from the hymnbooks, and the dust-filled stoup. Only a pair of gloves, and yet I was so sad about it.

But after I went to live at *Les Hirondelles,* Madame Solange showed me what to do. First I should put them on, lightly rub them with soap, and sponge them with milk.

'Don't forget to change the milk when it looks dirty, Odette.' Then put them to dry away from direct heat and sun - although, before they are bone dry, gently stretch the fingers in all directions.

I tell you, after all that, I'd never lend them to Maman again. Besides, I didn't trust her with them anymore.

'Now, Mademoiselle Rivière,' says the *gendarme*. 'Let's go through this together, shall we? You know (*tu sais!*) that there have been stories circulating in the village about you (*toi!*) and a possible relationship with Lieutenant Franz Liebhart. It's my job to discover the truth.'

'I don't see why,' I say. 'Loving someone isn't a crime.'

'No, Mademoiselle, but collaboration with the enemy is.'

'I'm not a collaborator,' I say. 'But when you fall in love, you don't think about the nationality. You just love the person.'

'So, Mademoiselle, you (*tu*) admit to a relationship with the German officer?'

'Not a German officer,' roars Stanley, erupting back into the dining room, his face like thunder. 'A British one. I'm the young lady's *fiancé*.'

'Oh,' says the *gendarme*, unlocking his gloved fingers. 'That makes a difference. If Mademoiselle Rivière would sign a statement to that effect, we'll pursue the matter no further.'

'"*We*?' says Stanley. 'Who's your superior?'

'Henri Rolland,' says the *gendarme*, lacing his hands.

'Ah yes. The pharmacist. Perhaps you can tell Monsieur Rolland, from me, that he should keep a better eye on his own daughter, rather than trouble the virtuous ladies of the village.'

'Certainly not,' says the *gendarme*, the tips of his ears turning crimson.

Stanley reaches for his wallet, draws out the papers which give him police status in Ver, and offers them to the other man.

'I say you will,' he says quietly.

Michel Delmare snatches them, examines them, hands them back. He stands up, bows stiffly, and departs.

'Why were you being so evasive, Odette?' asks Stanley, not bothering to conceal the fact that he was listening at the door. He folds up the papers and returns them to his wallet.

'*Bah*, I don't know,' I reply. Then, sensing something more is required, 'I didn't like the way he spoke to me. He was calling me *tu*.'

'Jumped-up little jobsworth,' says Stanley, with another flash of anger. Then he smiles at me. 'But now that we're getting married,' he teases, 'Can I call you *tu*?'

Just for a moment, there's something in his voice that reminds me of Jacques. You can call me whatever you want, I think, only don't make my heart ache like that.

THE KIT BAG

Another evening and Stanley is out on curfew patrol. I am sitting at the dining-room table, idle for once, letting the links of the gold bracelet turn over and spill into my hands.

158

Suddenly, there's another loud knock at the door, and a deep voice calls out, 'Please let me in. I don't have my keys.'

I recognise the voice straight away. My stepbrother, Paul. Home from Stalag VIII C, the prison camp in Germany. Has he marched all the way across Europe? Because he looks dreadful. Standing there in the doorway, he's skeletal, wearing a dark prison uniform many sizes too big and dragging a beaten-up kit bag behind him. His skin is grey, his eyes are hollow, and his head's been shaved. Blond-white stubble peppers his scalp.

He steps into the parlour. I want to throw my arms round him, but his cool, appraising look won't let me. He's silent for a moment, then bursts out:

'Is Augustine safe? And the children? It's terrible to see *Les Hirondelles* like that.'

'They're safe, they've been allocated a cottage just down the road. But your mother-in-law…' I hesitate. 'What about you, though? And, please, what happened to Jacques? We had the telegram, but it didn't tell us anything.'

Paul glances at me again with that same faint distaste. 'Jacques killed himself,' he says finally.

Mon Dieu. OhGodOhGodohGod. I want to be sick. I gulp, then stare at Paul.

'What happened?'

His eyes mist over, and then he says, 'It was after Guy Rolland got that letter from his wife, hidden away in a frame behind a photograph. He said something about it to Jacques that night, before lights-out, and then, well, I thought Jacques didn't look right. He was trembling. So I motioned to him to come out of the dormitory, and he did, meekly, you know, like he could be, but not really himself either. And then when I said to him, 'What's up?' he started crying.'

'What did you do?'

'I put my arm round him. I asked him again what was wrong, but he wouldn't tell me. He was stiff under my arm. He wasn't right. So I thought I'd go and have a word with the prison doctor the next day. But then, in the morning, he seemed fine. He was shaving and laughing at something

Sabatine said. 'Everything all right now?' I called out and he nodded. And I thought, well, a man feels things at night he doesn't want remembered in daylight. Still, I wish I had said something to the doctor now. Because that evening, out in the exercise yard, Jacques wasn't with us. And then the next thing we heard was old Schlutt, shouting from the dormitory.'

'Shouting?'

'Well, of course he'd seen dead men before. But he didn't expect to find one in the dormitory. Then it was put of bounds to all of us, except for Sabatine, who got told to take away the body and clean the place.'

'Did you speak to him?' I say. 'Did you find out what happened?'

'I did,' Paul replies. 'I had to know. Jacques cut his throat with a razorblade, Sabatine said. Suicide. A mortal sin.'

Mon Dieu. But surely it isn't true. It can't be true. I shake my head from side to side, then raise my hands, bash them against my temples.

'Oh God. I wish you hadn't told me. I'll never be able to stop thinking about it now. Never.'

Paul seizes my hands and holds them down. He's stronger than me.

I collapse against him and burrow my head in his chest. After a moment, he puts his arms round me, but they're stiff, unyielding.

So I step back from him and try to think. 'What was in Guy Rolland's letter? Did you ask him?' But even as I say it, I already know the answer.

'*Bien sûr* I did,' says Paul. 'His wife was repeating village gossip. First she wrote that his sister Louise was getting a bad reputation. Then she added that Madame Solange threw you out because of your affair with the German.' He stares at me and now there's no compassion in his eyes. 'Jacques couldn't bear it, you know. If he couldn't believe you were waiting for him, he had nothing to keep him going.'

'But it isn't true, what she said,' I protest through my tears. 'It's just vicious gossip. My God. Jacques should have written to me for the truth, anything, rather than do that.' And then I realise what his letters never said, how depressed, how desperate he must have felt, even before he heard the rumours.

'What do you mean?' asks Paul. 'What is the truth?'

I shake my head and try to swallow the lump in my throat, but I can't. It rises up, and then my mouth starts trembling.

'Ask Augustine,' I say, before I can stop myself. 'She'll tell you.'

'What will she tell me?' says Paul, very slowly. He stands absolutely still, as if he's waiting for the words that will destroy his homecoming, the illusions he cherishes about his marriage. His brown eyes meet my gaze.

Something, almost a look of complicity passes between us. He knows, I think, *he knows*. That's why he came here first, to speak to me, rather than search out Augustine. And then I realise I can't say anything. Not so much for Augustine's sake, which surprises me, but for his. He's suffered so much, already.

So instead I take a deep breath, and say, 'You don't know what it's been like here. The other women, they spy on you, slander you, for any little reason, if you have a new dress, or a hat, or even if you just talk to a German. And Franz was living with us, was kind to all of us,' I add. 'He saved me from a work camp. That alone was enough to stir up gossip. Ask Augustine about that.'

'Oh, I intend to,' Paul replies. Then he hesitates. 'You don't know what it was like for us, either. All of us with pictures of our wives, children, *fiancées*, pinned to the wall beside our bunks. But we have to wait three months for your replies to our letters, just to find out that you're safe and well. And then when there's gossip, we're so far away from you all, how do we know who to trust, who to believe?'

Suddenly his eyelids flicker and he looks very old and very tired. He leans forward and gives me an awkward pat. 'Odette, if you're telling the truth, then I'm truly sorry for your loss.'

THE WEDDING DRESS

Louise Rolland attends to my wedding dress and even offers to teach me dressmaking. She's grateful for any work, any company, she can get these days. Her brothers and the other freed prisoners came home and punished her in whatever ways they could devise. Even her father's intervention couldn't save her.

That's another strange thing. All through the war, Monsieur Rolland pretended to be a staunch Vichy supporter, and then, actually, he turned out to be a member of the Resistance. Admiral Ramsay, who organised the Neptune Operation and commanded the landings, made his headquarters at the Rolland pharmacy.

They say that because of his war efforts, Monsieur Rolland might be made Mayor one day. Though his daughter...

The returning men smash her shop windows and daub *swastikas* on the walls.

'So much prejudice. Anyone would think I was a Jew,' she mutters to me, dipping her brush into a bowl of soapy water. It takes her half an hour just to scrub away the 'F' of '*Femme tondue.*'

Later she unwinds her headscarf and shows me her scalp. Her brothers shaved it, and now it's pitiful to see, a white egg, dusted with gold. Then she wraps her fledgling hair up again and finds her tape-measure.

My dress isn't the ivory silk from my father's shop. That's consecrated to the memory of Jacques. Once I'd wrapped it in tissue paper and stowed it away at the bottom of the *armoire*, I couldn't bear to take it out again.

No, I wear Augustine's wedding dress, altered to fit my size. It still carries her scent. Very faint at first, then stronger. Sweet almond oil and pear tree blossom. The scent of the sun and the rain.

This is what it feels like to be Augustine, I think, as I glide past the church pews on my wedding day. To be inside her. Wearing her long white robe, soft as swan's down, as cool to the touch as a glass of water.

At the altar, votive candles, splattered with ghostly wax, stand next to a Madonna and child worked into black marble relief on the pale walls. There are no stained glass windows, though, to shed their colours across the white dress. The pieces are stacked away inside packing cases marked '*Vitraux: Fragile.*' They'll only resume their place as soon as the stonework is repaired. Then the windows will dance light across Augustine's face and eyelids, turn her unshaven head the colour of autumn leaves.

'Do you take this woman?'

Except, of course, that Augustine isn't at my wedding. Paul still had his doubts about me and wouldn't let her come. He made her choose him, or me.

Though of course, I know that today, of all days, my head shouldn't be filled with thoughts of her. On our wedding day, it's Stanley who's the important one.

Maman couldn't come to the wedding either. She was ill - another migraine or *la grippe,* she said. But at least things are better for them now that Bertrand has his insurance job. He's able to take good care of her. And that's what marriage is all about, after all, isn't it?

So, a quiet wedding, all-in-all. Only Stanley and I appear in most of the photographs. Him, standing beside me, resting his hand on my shoulder. Me, sitting beside him, the beautiful folds of the wedding dress draped round me.

'Are you all right, Odette?' asks Stanley, just before the photographer's bulb flashes in our faces.

'I'm fine. Why do you ask?'

'You look a bit paler than usual, that's all.'

'It's this dress,' I say.

And in the end, I'm glad to go back to our commandeered room and change out of it, into my little black suit. Then we enjoy our first walk along the beach as a married couple. Stanley takes my arm even as I clutch at my pillbox hat, with its rosette fluttering against the breeze.

'Always wear a hat,' Madame Solange used to say. 'It makes you look like someone.'

'Who?'

'Like someone who always wears a hat.'

Now I peer through the black scrap of veil at the desecrated beach. Behind the veil, everything blurs, even the rusted hull of a landing craft moored in the sand.

Stanley climbs inside it, then gives me his hand and pulls me up. It smells…well, rotten, metallic and decayed.

'I don't like it,' I say. 'I want to get down.'

'Wait a minute,' says Stanley. He pulls me close to him.

I squint against the bright white sun, and then, dazzled and dazed, the sand becomes the sea. The liner begins to bob up and down. Lulled by its imaginary motion, we're happy enough together, sailing away to England.

A different place. A new start. England. Coloured rose-pink on the map at school. London, of course. Then Liverpool. Manchester. Chester. The Yorkshire and Lincolnshire Wolds. Wolds? Does that mean hills? How high? But Stanley says Fitz is so small it isn't even on the map. A dot of ink, or a speck of dust, that's all.

'It'll be a new start for us, though,' he says. 'In a tiny village where they keep oysters in kettles.'

But I've already decided, I'll be a different person when I live in England. Someone taller, grander, wiser and more beautiful. I'll meet important people, because Stanley is so important himself. There'll be feasting and dancing and chandeliers. Satins and silks for summer. Velvet and furs in winter. And snow.

A veil of falling snow.

THE BASIN

Our room in my mother's cottage has a big brass bedstead and plain oak furniture. On the dresser at the end of the bed is a silver-backed brush and comb and a large pewter jug. It's a nice room, nice of my mother to let us have it, but night after night, my heart keeps me awake by beating too fast. Then, each morning, my head feels like its under water, and shoals of bright colours dart in front of my eyes.

'You look quite green,' says Stanley, as he pushes the hair back from my face, holds the basin out in front of me. 'Are you sure you're going to be well enough to travel?'

'It's nothing,' I say. 'Maybe I caught a touch of Maman's *grippe*.'

'I hope not,' says Stanley, a little frown appearing between his guileless blue eyes. 'Because, sweetheart, I'm sorry to tell you this, but I'm not going to be able to travel with you to England.'

I look up hurriedly from the basin.

'What do you mean *chéri*? We paid for two tickets.'

'I know. And my superiors will refund the cost of mine. Because they want me to stay in Ver until a replacement can be found.'

'But won't they refund my ticket too? After all, a husband and wife shouldn't be parted so soon after their marriage.'

'I did ask them, but they said no.'

'Well, but, I want to stay with you, *chéri*.'

'But Odette. We can't afford to lose the money on your ticket. You know that,' he says.

Well no, I didn't know. Of course, Stanley's only on Army pay. His pockets aren't lined with gold. But still… Then he gives my hand a gentle squeeze, and I realise, it isn't about the money.

'What will I do without you?' I say.

'Sweetheart, you came through a whole war without me. And I'll write to my mother in Shrewsbury. She'll look after you, I promise, and then I'll join you as soon as ever I can. It won't be more than a couple of months.'

'A couple of months?' I repeat, in a small voice, then make another sudden grab for the basin.

THE CAMEO

Its haymaking season, but as we begin our journey, there's the scent of rain in the air. In the small car borrowed from the Lelédiers, we drive along the rutted road towards the port at

Dieppe. We pass the white stone pillars still standing at the entrance to the farm - stalwart guards of a vanished place.

The sacred spring still froths at the edge of the fields.

Then, fields give way to Ver's scattered houses and shops. We pass the dressmaker's, the tavern with the old men sitting outside playing chess, the baker's, shut as usual on a Wednesday afternoon. Red and green bottles gleam in the pharmacist's window, beside a white pestle and mortar. Then we round the corner, past the cemetery, the graves with their bunches of primroses, or tangles of weeds.

Across the village square, the church waits for its stained glass to be restored.

'I won't ever see it again, will I?' I say to Stanley as the rain starts to fall.

'Course you will,' he replies, as we circle past some railings, where just beyond, the reconstructed *château* rises from its bed of gravel. 'I promise.'

Just for a moment, I long to lay my head against his jacket sleeve.

We approach the bridge that leads out of Ver. We're just about to drive across it, when a woman emerges from its shadowed arch. One hand clasps a striped umbrella, the other is waving at us.

I slip out of my seat and run towards her, hoping that she's really there, that she isn't just a mirage of mist, and rain, and the rising haze from the fast-flowing stream.

But what she crushes into my hand is real enough.

'Ouch,' I say, as it pricks my palm. The pin of her mother's cameo brooch.

'I can't take this,' I say. 'She wouldn't have wanted me to have it.'

'Yes, she would have, in time,' says Augustine. 'She thought the world of you, you know. Even after everything that happened, she used to say that she missed you, that you'd been like a second daughter to her.'

'I didn't know that,' I say, 'I thought she hated me…'

'Don't think about that now,' says Augustine, her sea-green eyes filling with tears. 'Just remember how we all once were at *Les Hirondelles*, Maman, Jacques, you and me.'

But after all, there's only just time to kiss her goodbye before Stanley calls me back to him. 'Odette! Sweetheart! Come on! You'll miss the boat!'

'I have to go now,' I say, and then I walk over and climb back inside the car. 'I'll write,' I shout, as Augustine grows smaller and smaller beneath the dot of her umbrella. She shouts something back, but now we're too far away. The sound of her voice is lost as road and stream wind away from Ver.

THE SILVER CROSS

A gull darts out into the sky, whilst its reflection dives beneath the waves. I lean out further over the ship's railings, crushing my chest. But I can't see Stanley anymore. I may as well go below deck. Because it's *still* raining. And as the boat tips and heaves, my stomach gives a sudden lurch. Seasickness or…?

But who is that down there?

Not Stanley. Not Augustine. But a woman on the quayside, wrapped in a dark coat, her hair white against the overcast sky. Black-and-white, like a nun, or the photograph of one. Maybe she's wearing a silver cross. Maybe she's Maman's old friend Thérèse, sent by her to say goodbye.

I shut my eyes. Outlined against my eyelids, I can still see the holy lady.

For a moment, the words of my mother's lullaby mingle with the insistent patter of falling rain… '*Ne pleure pas petite chose…*' Then the clouds disperse, and the rain gives way to hazy sunshine. So I stay on deck for a long time, watching the ship force a white path through the green sea.

Part IV
Shrewsbury and Normandy, 1945-1956

THE RED VALISE

Is this it? Is this all there is?

Because just like that, everything's different. - like I'd just turned round from playing Grandmother's Footsteps.

My mother's lullaby dissolves, into wind, waves and salt spray.

Now all I can hear are the loud voices, the easy laughter of the soldiers who've stepped out on deck. One of the soldiers keeps playing around with a lighted match, trying to set fire to the other one's hair. But I can hardly understand a word they're saying. I seem to have forgotten most of the English I knew when I was a girl, chatting to the American pilots.

We're all called below deck. Through the porthole, I glimpse rows and rows of half houses, like rotten teeth, with gaping holes from fallen bombs. The few remaining chimneys give out smoke the same colour as the sky. And suddenly I know my baby will be a girl. I know she'll be a girl, because I want a boy, blue-eyed, dark-haired, like his father. But things aren't always how I hoped they'd be.

Several hours later, the train pulls into the station. My heartbeat speeds up. My palms begin to sweat so that I can barely grasp my needle. What if I'm in the wrong place? What if they've painted out all the signs, like they did in Ver? But no. Here we are.

Shrewsbury.

I take a deep breath and tug the needle through the canvas. One last cross-stitch in a bunch of embroidered forget-me-knots - a gift for my mother-in-law, Mrs Morgan.

That's my name now, too.

But on the platform, no matter how often I peer at the creased, grey photo of the elegant lady, Stanley's mother, it doesn't help. She isn't here. So I take another deep breath, count to ten, then drag the cases, the red valise, to the taxi rank at the front of the station. There are no cars yet, just a man in uniform, smoking a cigarette.

'Fitz,' I shrill. 'Fitz.'

He looks at me, a little startled, puffs out his cheeks, then stares at my valise.

'Fitz, love?' Then he says a whole sentence I don't understand. I shake my head.

'Stay here, love,' he says. He mimes someone driving. 'Taxi. Taxi in a minute.'

Soon I'm sliding into the back seat while the driver puts my cases into the boot. Then he pokes his head through the door.

'Where do you want to go?'

Home.

I show him the address Stanley scribbled down for me on the back of the ship's pass. He nods and we set off.

'That's the River Severn,' he says, pointing to a stretch of water far wider than our stream in Ver. 'Fitz lies between that and the River Perry.'

We drive past the tavern that juts out from the hill that overlooks the river. At the foot of the hill, after the bridge, begins a road newly planted with sycamore trees. They're thick with leaves, ruddy, golden or greenish yellow as army uniforms. The road leads directly to some redbrick houses. From the car window, I glimpse the yards grow smaller, the houses closer together, the hedges disappear. Then we sweep past a square, dominated by a red sandstone building,

'The old schoolhouse,' the driver says.

On the other side of the square, there's a vicarage, also built of redbrick. And behind that... From his rear-view mirror, the driver catches me staring at the redbrick church.

'Saint Peter's and Saint Paul's,' he says.

Peter and Paul. Oh.

I'm just starting to think there's altogether too much redbrick round here, when we circle past the railings behind the church. A black, wrought-iron gate opens out onto a wide avenue, struck by sunlight, and lined with cedar trees. A few leaves tinged with russet again herald the approach of autumn.

Then, through the leaves and sunlight, I glimpse the mottled frame of a manor house, half-timber, half white daub.

'Oh,' I say, sinking back into my seat. *'Si belle.'*

But instead we judder along a long road full of potholes which runs the length of some fields, towards a few grey houses huddled together. Then the driver stops and switches off the engine.

'This is where you want to be,' he says.

'Vraiment?' I say, as I climb out.

THE APOSTLE SPOON

Now the taxi and its driver disappears back down the long road. I drag my suitcases and my valise towards the peeling blue gate of the garden in front of the house, where an old lady is standing.

'Bonjour Madame. Je suis Odette,' I say.

'Odette?' she says, in a quavering voice. She peers at me. 'Are you Welsh?'

I try again. *'Où est Madame Alice Morgan? Je suis Odette, sa belle-fille.'*

'I'm Alice,' says the old lady, screwing up her eyes against the sunlight.

Mais non. Impossible. Ma belle-mère is an accomplished lady in a smart costume, standing beneath the cedar trees outside the manor house. Whereas this woman, well, her shawl's crooked and her hair's tumbling from its tortoiseshell comb.

I reach for the photograph in my handbag.

'Madame Alice Morgan?' I repeat, pointing.

'Yes, that's me,' says the old lady. 'A long time ago. Stanley took it.' Then she catches sight of the gold band on my ring finger. How bright and new it looks. Moments pass whilst she ponders, whilst I gaze at the wisteria clouding the inevitable redbrick façade.

Her faded blue eyes widen. 'You're Stanley's wife,' she says. She peers into my face. 'You're not Welsh, are you?'

I smile at the old lady and shake my head. Then she says a whole sentence I don't understand. So she removes some of the words and tries again.

'Apostle spoon,' she says, and mimes someone stirring.

I presume she's offering me a drink, and I nod. Then she confuses me by adding, 'Stanley knows how important it is.' I feel I ought to understand what she means. Because, of course, the words, *Stanley* and *importante* are the same in French.

Her eyes narrow and she glances past me, towards the road and fields.

'But where is Stanley?'

Finally, a question I do understand.

'France,' I say.

'No dear, this is Shropshire,' she replies.

THE WAX APPLES

I follow her up the path towards the house. The garden is a blur of green, except for a whitewashed building I later learn used to be a pigsty, and a few dark red roses peeping over the neighbour's fence.

'Welcome to Park Cottage,' says Alice Morgan, pushing open the front door. The brick doorway leads into a narrow passage with a coatless coatrack. Here, the floor is covered in peeling lino, exposing the grey cement beneath. Further down the passage is the kitchen with its ancient cooker, and then a parlour with a frosted glass door, a few pallid-looking plants, and no gramophone, only a wireless.

Climbing the stairs with the valise is almost too much for me. I pause half-way up to catch my breath and notice a print of a woman draping her long, dark hair over a glazed earthenware jar. When I reach the top, there's another narrow corridor lit by a single lightbulb, plugged into a socket, and left bare.

But to my surprise, Stanley's room - our room - isn't bad. Instead of blackout cloth, there are real curtains, striped, burgundy, with garlands of flowers blooming on a cream background. And when I draw them back, there's the neighbour's roses and chestnut tree, the glimmer of the river.

Only I don't want to spend the rest of my life, looking out of the window, into the neighbour's garden.

I cross over to the bed, peel back the candlewick bedspread, test the feather mattress. Then glance up over the brass bedstead to the bookshelf. A few Boys' Own Adventure Annuals with bright, colourful spines. A faded French Grammar, a copy of *Coral Island* and a cloth-bound prize book for Latin composition. And over on the mantelpiece, set out as if to fight, are some badly painted lead soldiers, and a shallow glass dish, full of red wax apples.

I lie down on the bed and shut my eyes for half an hour. I don't feel well.

When I wake up, Mrs Morgan is standing over me with a wineglass of yellow liquid. I take a sniff. I have to be cautious. On board the boat they said they'd run out of Ovaltine, whatever that is, and offered me something called 'toast water.'

But this smells like ginger. I gulp down a mouthful, then hold the glass up towards the light, to catch the fitful rays of the setting sun.

'Thank you,' I say, trying out one of my few English phrases. And I really mean it.

THE TIN OF SPAM

That evening, Mrs Morgan reaches for a tin of spam. Her fingers twist the key over and over. But the exposed line of meat makes me feel sick. It's like a thin, pink wound.

'Oh dear,' says Mrs Morgan, catching sight of my face. She brings me some more of the same golden drink. 'Ginger ale,' she calls it.

After supper, she gestures for me to lie down on the narrow *chaise-longue*, the 'sofa.' At first, I think I won't stay there long. But as I shift and turn, struggle to catch my breath, a sharp pain shoots down my side. I have to stay lying still just to get rid of it - half-dozing, half-listening to the clatter of crockery and knives from the kitchen.

I so wanted to please her. But all I can do is sleep. And dream that *ma belle-mère* is standing at the sink with her sleeves rolled up, muttering, 'That lazy girl. That lazy, good-for-nothing girl that Stanley married.'

'*Je ne suis pas une bouche inutile,*' I shout as Franz fastens the gate to the work-camp. 'I'm not,' I shout again, and the sound of my own voice wakes me up.

To find Mrs Morgan, standing over me, miming opening and closing a book.

'Stanley's grammar books?' she says, then something else I don't understand. 'I'll look for you,' she adds, then disappears. But she re-appears a little while later, shaking her head. She hands me a copy of *Jane Eyre*.

I thank her, pause to admire the red-tooled leather cover with its gilt lettering. The flyleaf pages are also pale gold, with a pasted-in plate with a school-motto, and some handwritten words: '*Awarded to Alice Dutton, for good conduct.*' But the title page is creamy vellum, with the publication date, *1847*, in fine, black print. Oh. It was published nearly a hundred years ago.

But for now, the plate and the date are about the only things I can understand - at least until the little French girl, Adèle, arrives at Thornfield. *Merci Adèle, pour parler ma langue,* and for making Jane and Mr Rochester speak it, too. Though certain other words still don't make sense. They swarm in front of my tired eyes, elusive as spectres: *Red-room, Temple, Burns...*

I wake suddenly, hours later. The fire's dying down in the grate, and I'm alone.

Except that through the thin walls, I can hear the neighbour's child, crying in the dark. A weak and fretful wailing. Then louder, more definite, and more anguished. Pierre used to cry like that sometimes, such a *boucan*. I could never get used to it, never, that note of forsaken despair.

Suddenly I sit bolt upright on the sofa, absolutely furious. Why doesn't the mother rock its cradle, rub ointment into its sore gums, walk up and down with her crying child?

'Crying child?' Mrs Morgan repeats, the following morning. Then she shakes her head. 'No dear,' she says, sadly. She taps the copy of *Jane Eyre*, then taps the side of her head. 'Too much Brontë if that's possible,' she adds, with a sudden, mischievous grin.

THE CHANDELIER

Red. Room, Apples, Roses, Blood. Unfurling its sticky petals across the white cotton, more than I could have imagined.

'*Médecin,*' I beg Mrs Morgan. A doctor, please.

'Medicine?' she says. 'Ginger ale? Or some stout? It's important to build up your blood.'

'Yes. Blood,' I say, clutching her hand. But she doesn't understand.

So I stumble down the path, then out onto the long, rutted road to try and find help, a doctor. I'm not sure how, but I manage to force one foot in front of the other, till I reach a sharp corner. Then, there it is: the manor house. Turrets, gables and balconies all mixed up together. Cedar branches and green shutters banging in the breeze. A granite gentleman with a cocked hat bows low to a lady with a broken arm, covered in lichen.

And there, on the dark, smooth lawn, is a rocking-horse, painted white, with red spots.

If I can reach that horse, touch its mane, I'll be well again. It's the simplest things that make you well, *I know*.

Only the horse won't let me. It rears and starts, then charges towards me. Red spots dance in front of my eyes, until they're all I can see. Or are they the crimson carpets, no, the crimson curtains of the manor house, swaying in the breeze? Then the statue leans over me, says something, rests my head in her ample lap.

When I open my eyes again, I'm lying on a sofa beneath a white and gold ceiling. Above me are great plaster roses, and a chandelier, shimmering with glass drops, beautifully flawed.

'The blood,' I sob. Tears pour down my cheeks, tears tip and sway above me.

'That's all stopped now,' says the pale lady in French, 'and your baby is safe.' I'm so surprised to hear someone speaking *ma langue*, I don't think to ask how her she knows. Then she continues, 'You're very weak and you need to rest. The doctor said to ask you, have you been short of breath lately?'

I nod and stare at the lady. She looks to be in her late thirties, a few years older than me, no more. She has brown eyes and dark lashes that relieve the pallor of her complexion. Light brown curls cluster round her white forehead, tangle with the long strings of amber beads that contrast with the severe cut and colour of her black tunic.

She smiles at me and continues, 'The doctor thought so, thought you were very anaemic, even before he realised you were losing blood.'

'Augustine was anaemic when she was pregnant,' I say. 'They told her to eat liver and *rosbif* for the iron.'

'You've come to the wrong country for that,' says the lady. 'Not that it matters much to me. I was vegetarian, even before the war, and now I grow my own.' She gestures towards the garden on the other side of the bay windows that fill the room with light.

'Hmmm… stout, or no, nettle tea, that should help,' she says. She smiles, then continues. 'Augustine. That's a pretty name. Your sister? But what's your name, *chérie?*'

'Odette,' I say. 'Odette Morgan.'

'Pleased to meet you, Odette. I'm Sophy Arbuthnot. Sophy with a 'y."

'Y?' I say, being more used to the French spelling.

'Why not?' says Sophy in English, and then I realise, I've tumbled into an old joke.

'My father's mistake,' she adds. 'And now that we're friends,' she says, 'Let me tell you, you haven't been taking care of yourself.' She smooths her tunic over her turquoise trousers, then continues, with gentle condescension, 'In fact, I rather think you've let yourself go.'

Her smile takes some of the sting from her words. Then she pats my arm with her pretty, ringless hand, and says she'll go and boil some nettles for me.

THE HEAD OF RED CLAY

Later, when she hands me my cup, I notice sky-blue paint wedged beneath her fingernails.

'Are you an artist, then?' I ask. Like Jacques.

Sophy nods. 'When I found you, I was painting a portrait of my rocking-horse, out on the lawn.' She smiles. 'When I found you. Odette, you're *un objet trouvé*, like Duchamp's urinal. Like the chandelier.'

'The chandelier?' I say.

'Yes,' she says, 'It came from a skip outside a pub. And the chairs were stored away in the attic. I brought them out, painted them, and covered the seats with fabric. And I re-gilded the mirror-frame with gold leaf. It took ages.'

'Make-do and Mend?' I say, repeating one of Mrs Morgan's phrases.

'More like, creating an illusion,' she replies.

'That's what my father and I tried to do, with the antiques,' I want to say. But suddenly, I'm too tired to speak. My eyelids start to close.

Sophy tiptoes away, leaves me undisturbed until the evening, when she brings in a head of red clay from the kiln.

'What do you think of it?' she asks.

'It's like the head in an Odilon Redon painting,' I say.

Sophy opens her eyes very wide at my cleverness. 'But don't you think she looks like me?' she says.

'Well, all art is a sort of self-portrait, isn't it?'

'That's what my husband always says.'

'Your husband?' I repeat. 'But you're not wearing a ring.'

From beneath her collar, Sophy pulls out a gold chain that loops through a diamond ring. 'I didn't want to get paint or clay on it,' she says. 'It was expensive enough. My husband's Sir Hugh Arbuthnot.' She says the name as if I ought to recognise it, but when I frown, she smiles. 'He's an MP. He works for the Treasury, so he's often away in London.'

'And you don't mind?' I ask, thinking of Stanley.

'Of course I mind,' says Sophy. 'But at least it gives me the time to pursue my art.' She nods at the clay head.

I twist round on the sofa to take a better look. 'There's something in her expression that makes me think she's suffering,' I say. Then, mindful of what she's just said about her husband, I quickly add, 'An old, old hurt, that's shaped her, marred her, made her what she is. It's that that's burnt her, not the oven.'

'An old, old hurt?' Sophy repeats, slowly. Then she tells me that when she was a little girl, she woke up one night and went looking for her drawing pencils in the parlour. But she was too small to reach the light-switch, and she walked into a knitting needle by mistake. It took out the retina of her eye. Then the doctors had to stitch it back together.

'Just imagine that,' says Sophy. 'A whole year with zigzag stitches. But it did the trick. It saved the eye.'

THE OPAL RING

As the weeks pass, I grow stronger. Sophy and I often sit out in the garden, beneath the flame-tinged cedar trees. Above us, swallows linger in the sky, confused by this luminous, golden autumn.

Then it's late October, and the season starts to turn. Leaves wither and shine, streaked with gold. The sun moves in and out of the hazy clouds, casting long shadows across the lawn. Sophy tips her head back to look at the sky, dislodging her hair, twisted round combs and pinned to the top of her head.

'Not quite so warm today,' she says.

'No, not quite,' I say.

'I suppose we'll all be complaining soon about the cold.'

'I hope not,' I say, thinking of the swallows, returning to their winter homes. And thinking of Stanley, who even as we speak is entering the long dark tunnel on the railway line to Shrewsbury. I shiver and rub my arms.

'There's a shawl over there, if you want it,' says Sophy, returning her attention to her jewellery box. I shake my head and bend over my cross-stitch.

'You know,' says Sophy, after a moment or two. 'Your embroidery is exquisite. And your sewing. Maybe you should try and do something with it.'

'I will be,' I say, 'I'll be making clothes for the baby.'

'Yes, but something else, too. Oh, there isn't much call for the decorative arts round here,' she says, 'but there might be for dressmaking…'

'We'll see,' I say, as I push the last bright coloured thread through the canvas. 'There, finished. For you.' An avenue lined with trees leads up to the words *Ma Maison,* stitched in purple letters.

'Oh,' says Sophy, 'Lovely. Thank you.' Then, 'Here you are,' she says, tipping two rings into my palm. 'I was trying to choose a going-away present for you, but I couldn't decide which one. So you can have both.'

'Oh,' I say, 'that's too much.'

'No,' says Sophy. 'It's just about enough.'

I clutch at them, greedy, despite my dislike for jewellery. One ring is gold, with a green stone at its centre, and the other is silver, with a pale milky stone - an opal perhaps? I slide the silver ring onto my finger.

Then Sophy says, 'Here, let me have that one back for a minute and I'll tell you if you're going to have a boy or a girl.'

'What do you mean?'

'Losing my eye, and then regaining my sight, did something to me. Sometimes I can tell what's going to happen before it does.'

'How?'

'Well, if I concentrate on something, a piece of jewellery or an object that's absorbed a person's energy, my mind sometimes lets me colour in their future.'

Madame Rolland used to dabble with tarot cards, but I've never heard of anything like this before. Psychometry, Sophy calls it. Somehow, I don't quite like it. But I hand her the opal ring. As she concentrates, she twists it this way and that. Now the stone is mild as moonlight. Now it flashes, red as fire.

Then Sophy gasps and drops the ring. 'It burns,' she says.

She bends to retrieve it from the grass, then stares at me with her good eye, the other, almost as good, but slightly unnerved, blinking.

'That never happened before,' she says.

THE JUG

Finally, Stanley returns from France and together we wonder if Park Cottage might ever feel like our home.

Park Cottage, where the lower half of the kitchen wall is painted dark blue, whilst the upper half is a pale sky-blue. Wedged up against it in the corner is a large, off-white larder. There's a white sink with silver taps, and above it, drawn across the window, a white curtain with a pattern of plums and bees. Beside the sink is a white stove with a copper kettle and a silver saucepan, with charred string wrapped around the handle.

Next to the sink is a green, mottled marble-effect dresser with two pull-out drawers and an assortment of pots and pans arranged untidily on its surface. Above the dresser is a framed photograph of the young Princess Elizabeth; beneath it are bright brick-coloured floor tiles. At the heart of the kitchen is the table, spread with a red-and-white vinyl cloth.

Alice Morgan, Stanley and I are sitting at this table together. She's frowning and rubbing her eyes as if she's very tired, so I say to her, not to worry, I'll take care of his supper.

'What about these?' she says, gesturing at a carton of new-laid eggs. A gift from a local farmer to welcome home the hero.

'They're very precious,' says Stanley. 'We have to be careful with them.' I nod to show I've understood, so that he doesn't have to say it over again in French. But his mother's reply confuses me, and he translates it.

'The goose that laid the golden egg,' says Alice, pleased with herself, thinking, perhaps, of yellow, runny, yolk. I smile at her. Just for a moment, I wonder what it would be like if she got better, if she became like everybody else.

But in the middle of the night, all she remembers is that her boy has come home, and she must feed him. So she gets up to boil him an egg. She sets a saucepan of water on the stove and lights the gas. There's a hiss as the blue flame spurts up. She feels the haze of heat against her face.

It troubles her. She wanders off to the bathroom to find a cooling flannel. But the flannel wipes away all her thoughts of cooking. She returns to bed.

I wake just as the clock in the hallway is striking two.

The reassuring bulk of Stanley's body sleeps beside me. I give him a quick shake.

'Whatsamatter?' he mumbles and rolls over.

'I can smell something,' I say.

There's a sudden click and then Stanley's staring at me, the pupils of his eyes reduced to pinpricks in the dazzle of the bedside lamp.

Cautiously, we push open the bedroom door. Out in the corridor, the smell of burning, of singed rubber, metal and gas is much stronger. Stanley takes my hand and leads me, barefoot, down the stairs. Then, wreaths of blue smoke push past us from beneath the kitchen door, wrap themselves round the banisters, the lightbulbs, the picture-frames.

Stanley shoves the door open. A wall of smoke hits his face. Straight away, he starts coughing.

I rush to the sink and fill a jug with water. I hurl it over the flaming saucepan.

'Your mother,' I say to Stanley when the fire is finally out, and he nods.

The next day, when we're standing on stools, scrubbing smoke stains from the ceiling, I suddenly remember that old game of Augustine's. What if I were to scream 'Egg' at Alice, louder and louder? Would it work? Would her faded blue eyes fly open? Would she finally wake up?

THE PINK TEACUP

Later that day, Stanley gazes at the hairline crack beneath the glaze of the pink teacup. Then, 'She can't help it,' he says softly, so that she won't hear him from the parlour.

He lifts his *lunettes*, rubs the bridge of his nose. A nervous, fidgety gesture I hadn't ever noticed in Ver.

'Her husband and daughter are dead. I'm her only son,' he continues. 'All the time I was away, she kept hearing about how other people's sons had been killed or had disappeared. When she couldn't get in touch with me, it sent her a bit funny.'

He pushes the teacup towards me for some more powdered milk.

'But didn't you know?'

'How could I?' he replies. 'I was working for Intelligence. No-one could get in touch with me, and even if they could've, what would they have said?' He takes back his cup, spoons in his own powdered milk, and adds, 'Do you seriously think I would have sent you to live here by yourself if I'd known?'

I shrug. 'It's just, none of this is what I thought it would be. And I still miss Ver.'

'Yes, I know you do,' says Stanley. 'I see the clocks you keep on French time. But we'll save some money and…'

'For the baby?' I say.

'No, so that you can go and see them again, in Ver.'

I'm quiet for a moment. When he says *Ver*, it's as if he's picking at a scab and that makes me sound harsher than I intend. 'Well, we can't stay here now,' I snap. 'It's not safe. Not with the baby coming. What if she did it again?'

Stanley blinks, as if he's startled by the sudden change in subject. Then he says, 'But you'll see. Now that I'm back, Mammy's mind will settle. She'll get better.'

'No,' I say firmly, one of my few English words. Then, in French, I add, 'I don't want my baby brought up here. You must get someone to look after your mother, pay them.'

'Who?' says Stanley.

'I don't know, a neighbour, a friend. And when you've done that, you must find us a place of our own.' With crimson curtains and golden mirrors, a rocking-horse and a chandelier…

Stanley mutters something in English about money. In French, *monnaie* means coins, so I understand what he means.

But, 'What's that?' I say, my voice rising an octave. Because really, after everything Maman went through with Bertrand,

I've always thought a married man should be able to provide for his wife. Really, he should.

'Nothing,' Stanley says, and sighs.

I peer into the dregs of my teacup and try to make out our uncertain future.

THE GLASS OF MILK

'She's calmer today,' Stanley says, a week or so later, placing her empty glass of milk on the bedside cabinet. He draws back the curtains, then leans across the bed to give me a good morning kiss.

His mouth is still wet from baking soda.

'Ugh,' I say, and turn my face away.

'Suit yourself,' he replies, picking his way through our packed boxes and cases. Then he reaches into the wardrobe and pulls out the only shirt left hanging there.

After he's left for the insurance office, I flick through yesterday's copy of the *Daily Mail*. It's easier to understand than literature, especially with the illustrations. There's an article entitled 'What every newly wed should know' with a 'Day-to-Day Plan' for new brides. Apparently, yesterday, I should have done some light personal laundry, followed by the ironing. And I'm just reading that today is for polishing the silver when there's a knock on the bedroom door.

'Come in,' I say.

Alice steps into the room. Her wispy hair is still in flypapers. The buttons of her bedjacket are all in the wrong holes.

'Oh Mammy,' I say. 'What do you want?'

She twists her hands in the thick brush-cotton. 'I wanted to say...' she says. Then, all in a rush, 'I'm so sorry. I know it hasn't been ideal for you.'

I know enough English by now to recognise an apology. And the word 'ideal' is almost the same in French. But somehow, I can't forgive her.

'No,' I say, bitterly, 'It hasn't.'

Alice gives me a quick, startled look. Then her pale blue eyes fill with tears, the easy tears I can't bear. But she manages to hold them back.

There. I always knew she could, if she wanted.

'Please, don't be like that,' she implores.

I sigh and sit up in bed. The bump of my two months' belly makes the sheets stick out. I stroke it through the linen. 'It's just,' I say, at last, in English, 'you're so like my own mother.' At her most irritating. Before she sorted herself out.

Alice, of course, understands the words, but not their import. The anxious look fades from her eyes. Two redcurrant dimples appear.

'Thank you,' she says, popping a button back into a buttonhole. Then she mimes pulling open a door and reaching inside. I stare at her for a moment, and then I realise. She wants to give me something from her stock-cupboard.

'*Bah*,' I say later, running my fingers along the dust-covered shelves. '*Rien ici*.' Because if my morning sickness is better, the food hasn't improved. There are as many farms in Shrewsbury, as fine, or finer than *Les Hirondelles*. But the farmers here aren't allowed to sell us anything, only the food suppliers.

Alice frowns and forces some hard-won tins of fruit and a bottle of orange juice extract into my hand.

I sigh. The red wax apples in the dish upstairs look more appetising. But I suppose she thinks they're a luxury... What with meat rationed, eggs rationed, butter rationed, lard rationed, margarine rationed, tea rationed, cheese rationed, sugar rationed, jam rationed, even toothpaste, all rationed...

Dear Lord, please let me not think of early mornings crunching russet apples in the orchard. Of the bowls of ripe plums and pears that Madame Solange kept on the kitchen dresser. Of the explosion of juice against our tongues from the greengages that never lasted till Sunday and Sunday lunch.

The memory makes me smile. Without understanding why, Alice smiles back.

Well, she means well, I suppose. It's not her fault that this is Austerity Britain. As Stanley keeps trying to tell me, not everything is his mother's fault.

THE PINK TEASET

In our new lodgings, we take our first meal properly alone together, *tête-à-tête*.

Stanley leans forward, with an expectant look, heavy silver-plated spoon clasped in his hand.

'No soup today, I'm afraid,' I say. I didn't want to be in the kitchen with all the other tenants speaking English at me. 'Since we've such a good fire in here, I boiled some water over it.'

'So we're having?'

'The last of the eggs your mother gave us.'

'I don't dislike a boiled egg,' says Stanley, as egg-white slithers down his throat. He glances at the wind-once-a-week clock on the mantelpiece as it starts to chime. *Din dan don. Din dan don.* Seven. A singing chime we hear every quarter of an hour, even with our heads buried in the pillows - but we like it. Next to the clock is one of our wedding pictures, tucked into a framed photograph of the landlord's mother and sister.

'I know what,' says Stanley, suddenly, jumping up. He crosses over to a suitcase and starts to unwrap the pink tea set from its newspaper nest. His mother's wedding gift to us. He wipes two cups carefully with his handkerchief, then finds some tea leaves in a tin. He takes the kettle off the flame and pours a stream of boiling water into the porcelain teapot.

Wisps of steam settle in his sparse hair as he brings the tray over to the table. But when he tries to drink, his fingers are too large for the cup's handle. He puts it down and stares at it for a moment. It's made of porcelain, coloured halfway between blush and apricot, gold-rimmed, and delicate as eggshells.

'Poor Mammy,' Stanley says, and sighs.

Later that evening, I read over my own letters from Maman. She wants me to have a little girl, she says. They all do. '*And then*, she writes, *when I meet her, perhaps it will be like meeting you, all over again, Odette. You grew up, grew away from me so fast, I never had the chance to enjoy you properly.'*

That night I dream of Maman. She's lying on her bed, staring at the blue-gold light at the heart of a candle-flame. But the face she wants to see there is still unformed. She tries to pray, because the flame reminds her of clasped hands. Her mouth moves, wanting to shape the words. But instead, she screams and then her baby slides into the world, wailing at all it has lost, its protest at being born.

Now Maman can see my face in the candle-flame. And when they place me beside her, her lips move against the curve of my cheek. She says my name.

THE HANDKERCHIEFS

Monday is washday. Each week, I rinse out a pair of pyjamas, a vest or a shirt, collars, socks and handkerchiefs for Stanley. I scrub his long johns on the draining board. I rinse cardigans for both of us in the sink, and boil skirts and blouses in a tub for me. And stockings. And underwear. Lift them, flatten them down again, force the water through the cloth, over and over, to rinse the dirt away. Then squeeze them through a mangle and hang them out to dry.

Perhaps all this washing is what's making my skin itch. Though when I scratch, there are little raised pink lumps, like fleabites. I'm not sure why. And walnut patches have been appearing on my face ever since I became pregnant. These days, I'm almost as plain as Yvette. Really, quite foreign.

Sophy's right, I have let myself go. Papa used to say that the antique mirror was a reminder that what you collect is always yourself. But it used to be that the stains were only ever on the surface of the glass. Now they're on me.

THE PETROL LAMP

'But we're comfortable enough here, aren't we Odette?' Stanley says one evening, frowning, creases appearing between his brows.

I nod and his eyes return to the columns of figures ruled off in his ledger. Insurance gives him a great deal to do. He has to find customers to increase the budget. Even on a Sunday

Then he looks up again, fixes me with the intensity of his blue-eyed gaze.

'We'll have to try and save some money.'

I nod again. I've heard all this before.

'No, I mean, so that we can go and see your Maman after the baby's born,' he says.

'And Augustine,' I add.

These days, they're often on my mind. When I'm lighting the petrol-lamp at seven o' clock in Fitz, Augustine is lighting her lamp at eight o' clock in Ver. And perhaps Maman is pulling herself close to the red and gold shade, to make something for the baby. She frets over her failing eyesight, but she likes the polished ivory feel of the crotchet hooks.

If I keep the clocks on French time, then I'll always know what they're doing.

Though I haven't heard from Augustine since I came to England. It's my fault. I said I'd write first, and I haven't. But I can't find the words. I don't know what to say. Even after our farewell, I haven't quite forgiven her.

She wasn't at my wedding.

I understand her reasons, about Paul, and everything... but still.

I can't write that, though, can I?

'What's wrong now?' asks Stanley, glancing up, taking off his *lunettes*, rubbing the bridge of his nose. Now there's a phantom pair, marked out in red creases on his brow.

But before I can answer, the petrol lamp starts to smoke, casts flickering shadows across the ceiling. While Stanley sorts it out, I try to explain, about Augustine. But of course, he's a man. He doesn't really understand.

THE SHEET

In my dream, Augustine steps towards me and drops a sudden curtsey, as if it's a country-dance. Then she bobs upright, and hands me the runched-up corners of the bed sheet. But a breeze pulls it out of our hands, starts to tug it open. So we step apart and lay the four corners out on the courtyard's cobblestones.

At the centre of the sheet is my baby, pink and smiling.

I wake up suddenly, stretch in the armchair, rub the small of my back. I wonder, if I have a girl, whether I should name her after Augustine, or Maman. Of course, Stanley wants to call her Alice, but I don't think I'll let him. He's already got his own way about our moving back to Park Cottage.

'I can't afford to keep paying someone to look after Mammy,' he says. 'Though she is much better,' he adds, hurriedly.

Besides, Stanley's ankles are covered in little pink lumps as well. There must be fleas here - little friends, we call them, though we don't really relish their company. Camphor and thyme might get rid of them. That's the kind of thing Madame Solange used to know.

'I'll tell you all the secrets,' she'd say to me. 'Because you're interested. Augustine doesn't care about things like that.'

Still, it doesn't really matter. We'll be gone ourselves, soon enough. I sigh, listen to the clock's *tictaquait*, loud in the quiet room. Then I get up and fetch the sheets in from the washing-line. As they billow round me, white sails of an invisible ship, I suddenly realise what I'm going to do when we leave. I'm going to take the clock.

THE LETTER

We return to Park Cottage and everything's fine until eight o' clock one Wednesday morning. Then the pains begin. Stanley drives me to Sheldon Hospital, Shrewsbury, in his friend Andrew's car, and I'm shown into the labour ward.

In the labour ward, there are seven white beds on seven black bedframes on either side of the rectangular room. Fourteen expectant mothers sit up propped against their pillows, their faces varying in expression from pain to hunger to anticipation to boredom. White-capped, white-aproned nurses hover by their patients' beds, whilst another nurse wheels a rickety tea-trolley down the ward's polished floor.

Throughout the day I lie there, tutting, in the furthest bed beside the door, staring at the last yellow lampshade in a row of yellow lampshades running the length of the ceiling. Four injections in ten hours. *Mon Dieu!*

An older nurse, Jenny, with a silver crucifix around her neck, must hear me, because on the evening round, she approaches my bed and says,. 'It's because your waters haven't broken yet. Baby can't be born until that happens.'

I sigh and turn my head away from her, in time to see Stanley, wearing a navy blue raincoat and a tartan bobble hat, and carrying a bunch of pink carnations, push through the ward-doors.

'Visiting time already?' says Jenny, glancing at the watch pinned to her dress. 'Here's your lovely husband.'

'How's my girl?' asks Stanley, beaming.

'Still waiting for the baby,' I reply. 'But carnations, Stanley, how nice!'

Jenny disappears in search of a vase. Stanley lays the flowers on the bed and leans across to give me a big kiss. No baking soda, this time.

'How are you all getting on without me?' I ask.

'We miss you,' says Stanley, 'but we're coping. Mammy seems much better. And I have some more good news for you, too.'

'Oh, what is it?'

'Only…,' says Stanley, grinning, 'a letter from Augustine.' He reaches into the pocket of his raincoat and pulls out an envelope. I reach for it and tear it open.

'Well?' says Stanley after I have been reading for a moment or two. So I read the letter out loud. Stanley's French is good enough not to need my halting translation.

Ma chère Odette, (she writes)
> *Thank you so much for the photograph of your wedding. You look so beautiful, and your Stanley is so smiling, that I have high hopes for your happiness.*
> *I'm very sad that I didn't come to the ceremony and kiss you both. I showed your picture to Paul, and he said to write and tell you that he's sorry, that he shouldn't have spoken to you like he did. And that you and Stanley must visit us as soon as ever you can. If you do, I may have a little surprise for you. In the meantime, ma chère Odette, I hope that a proper letter will soon follow your photograph.*
>
> *Je t'embrasse comme je t'aime.*
> *Augustine*

'I'm glad she's written,' I say to Stanley. 'But I don't understand what she means. I didn't send her a wedding picture.'

'No,' says Stanley, quietly, 'I did.'

THE MASK

Then, at midnight, it happens. My waters break. The baby's coming, but there aren't any doctors or nurses around. It hurts, *Mon Dieu,* it hurts. Madame Rolland, Augustine, Maman, why didn't you tell me?

After a very long time, the doctor arrives and says he'll help me.

He puts the mask over my face. Then the bed tips and heaves. I'm on a boat, sailing back to France, to Normandy, to Ver. To Maman. In her last letter, she said she'd be thinking of me, that she would know, in her heart, when it starts.

I open my eyes and say to you, 'Maman, the sister told me I was stupid to scream.' But you bend over me and kiss me.

Your mouth tastes of salt from swimming in the sea. Skeins of seaweed mingle with your long, red hair. Your limbs are silver-white as the foam they part, your eyes blue as the sea. *Ma mère est la mer...* And at the heart of the ocean lies the island I knew before I was born. A humming land of summer leaves

189

and ladybirds - the island's song, your song, lulling me, lulling me...

Two hours later, the sister wakes me up. It's just before 6am, judging by the open arms on her watch. She smiles and presents me with a baby.

'Mine?' I say.

'Yes,' she replies. 'A little girl.'

Just what you wanted Maman, and it ought to feel like a reunion. But it's all so much effort. I examine the baby, then turn my head away, exhausted, faint.

THE BOX OF BONBONS

Before I fall asleep again, I manage to write a few words to Maman. '*You are now the grandmother of a little girl of nearly 6lb. She has blue eyes that gleam black. She has a double chin, a dainty mouth, a chubby body and little hands and feet. Her fingers are like transparent film. Her hair is lighter than mine, but it may get darker as she gets older.*'

The next day, Stanley brings us another bunch of carnations, a box of *bonbons* with a *tricolore* ribbon round it, and the baby clothes I sewed - even though we're not allowed home for another week. He bends down and kisses my cheek. Then he bends lower and kisses the baby's forehead.

'What are those marks on her cheek?' he asks.

'From the forceps,' I say. 'They'll disappear. But don't you think she's pretty?'

'She looks like you, sweetheart,' Stanley replies.

'I think it's too early to say,' I reply. 'But she's certainly prettier than all the other babies on the ward.'

'That's what I meant,' says Stanley. 'Now what name are we going to tell the registrar when he comes round?'

'I should like - I should very much like to call her Monique,' I say.

'Oh,' says Stanley. 'Not Mary for your mother. Or - Alice for mine?'

'Oh, Stanley, you are clever, that's it. Monique Mary Alice Morgan it is.'

'A name like that deserves a christening,' he replies.

THE BLACK GLOVE

These days, I find English easy to understand, but hard to speak. But it's strange, not one single nurse or doctor is able to speak to me in French. Which is odd, really. Maman and Papa could both speak English quite well, and even Augustine and I could say a few words.

Of course, some English words are almost the same as the French. 'Stomach, stomach,' the nurses keep saying to me. I know that means *estomac*, but I don't understand why they're saying it. So to show me, one of them lies down on her front on an empty bed.

Of course. New mothers are supposed to sleep on their tummies, in order to flatten them.

So I lie face down, with my head squashed into the pillow. I've only just shut my eyes when someone whispers,

'Mrs Morgan? Mrs Morgan?'

'*Oui?*' I say.

I turn onto my right side to see who's talking to me.

A hand in a black glove.

I turn a bit more and find myself facing a nun.

'Thérèse?' I say to her.

Her look of astonishment finally wakes me up.

'Good morning,' I say in English.

'Good morning,' she replies. 'Are you Spanish or Italian?'

I suppose I really must look foreign.

'I'm from France,' I say in English. 'From where the Normandy Invasion took place. Do you understand me?'

'Yes,' she replies, but I know I speak very badly.

THE BOTTLE

My milk hasn't come yet, so I feed Monique with a bottle. I have to be careful not to give her any air bubbles.

She gulps down the milk, and then they take her away.

The nurses change the sheets. The doctor who delivered my baby takes me in his arms and places me in another bed while mine is being made.

When the sheets are clean, two priests come to visit me. The first one, a Catholic, is very old. He says he learnt French in Lille when he was young, and that he's forgotten a lot. The second one, a Protestant, was a prisoner-of-war in Germany for three years with some Frenchmen, which is how he can speak my language. I want to talk to him about Jacques, but I don't. Instead, when he's gone, I write my first letter to Augustine since the birth.

As I write, I can hear singing. The Protestant priest has taken some of the new mothers into the little chapel, two doors away. They sing hymns for a few minutes, and then they come back, purified. It's all so much quicker than a Catholic purification Mass. A good thing, really.

THE SPOON

Baby is doing very well. Her little nose, which was quite wide between her two eyes, is taking shape. Her cheeks, which were yellowish-white, are now pink. She's no longer blue round the mouth. Her hands and feet are not so thin, and they're whiter.

She turns her head. Her eyes, I think, are china blue. She smiles a little smile.

But when I give her the breast, even though she drags for ten minutes, her mouth won't latch onto the nipple. I can't feed her. The bluish milk runs down her chin.

I don't know what to do. Her head lolls away from me and she's screwing up her eyes, weeping with hunger, when Sophy arrives. Today isn't visiting day, but I suppose the lady of the manor has special privileges. She fetches a bottle and spoon and straight away, Monique drinks from it.

'Greedy little girl,' I mutter.

'No, she's adorable,' says Sophy. She hands me a bunch of eight red roses. 'You see, I remembered,' she says.

'What do you mean?'

'That you didn't want to be always staring at the neighbour's flowers. That you wanted some of your own.'

I remove Stanley's withered carnations from the vase and make myself a fresh bouquet. It's kind of her I suppose but I thought she knew I don't like roses.

Sophy promises to bring me some white wool, so I can knit a matinee jacket for the baby.

'Thank you,' I say, but then I yawn, right in her face.

'I'm so sorry,' I stammer, trying to keep my eyes open. But almost at once, they close again, as if the lids are weighted down. Really, I've nothing to say to Sophy today. She isn't Augustine and I just want to sleep.

THE SNAP-DRAGON

Back at Park Cottage a couple of weeks later, I'm sitting up in bed, rifling through the morning post. Something with a Royal Liver stamp for Mrs Morgan. A letter from the bank for Stanley. And yes - here at last, a reply from Augustine.

I lie back, ease my spine against the feather mattress. Then I open the envelope, take out the sheet of paper crisscrossed with Augustine's familiar handwriting. It's a nice letter. She doesn't have her brother's gift for writing, but she spices her words with herself.

She says that at first, she and Paul felt awkward with each other, modest even, after so long apart. But they soon got over it. And so now, she too has a new baby girl, *'Un enfant du retour.'*

I stretch out against the mattress, the sheets that bear the imprint of our bodies. Sometimes I think our souls imbibe a little of each lover's in the act of lovemaking. So, to my way of thinking, that makes the baby a little bit Paul's, a little bit Franz's, a little bit Augustine's.

Not that Augustine would be too happy to hear it. After all, she's named her new daughter Francine. A truly French child's name. And she's pressed a red and pink snapdragon to the corner of the page. As I turn it over, the flower falls, paper-thin, into the bedsheets.

Augustine writes that in France, there's a charity called *Gouttes de Lait* that provides germ-free milk for babies who can't breastfeed. She says I should try to find something similar in

England. And she asks me whether I'm going to have Monique christened in Ver.

Bien sûr, Augustine, I want to return to Ver for the christening. I've already talked about it with Stanley. After all, he's Catholic too. He converted to my faith even before he knew me. But he just says, 'We've already deprived my family of a wedding. Let them at least have a christening. The Church of Saint Peter and Saint Paul is Catholic, after all.'

I suppose he's trying to compromise. Because Mammy is Protestant and she wants a different celebration for Monique somewhere else, in an Anglican church.

I stretch out again. New mattress: old bedstead. Through the wrought-iron bars, I glimpse the curtains' garlands of flowers. Then I find the snapdragon among the sheets and return to Augustine's letter. She finishes by saying that in order to honour Admiral Byrd, the Americans have paid for new stained glass windows for the Church of Sainte-Marie.

THE KEY

The door to the church in Fitz is locked. No-one can find the key. Hugh and Sophy say we can use the manor house for the ceremony, but it's too far away. And Monique is starting to cry.

So the vicar rushes into his kitchen and fills a glass with water. Then he fetches some cooking-oil from his cupboard. He returns to the churchyard and anoints the baby. He christens her right there among the waving flax, and the bluebells peeping out among the graves.

Bluebells.

'No,' I shout, then open my eyes.

There, on the bedside cabinet, is Maman's latest letter, saying that until we have the baby christened, she doesn't have a place in Heaven.

So I pick up my pen to reply. I tell her we're doing our best to return to Ver, that our passport goes from London to Liverpool, then from Liverpool back to London, accompanied by a letter from the French Consulate. And that we're going to try to be the first in line at the custom's office, for Monique's sake.

Monique is lying beside me in her cradle. Her chubby limbs are still, but her eyes are wide open. I put down the pen and start to sing my mother's lullaby, *'Monique a perdu son grand pierrot, toujours en satin blanc...'* I break off when she smiles. Perhaps it's just the sound of my voice, or perhaps she knows, she's going to be christened in Ver-Sur-Mer.

THE CHRISTENING SHAWL
Ver-Sur-Mer, September 1946

I drape it over my arm. The lace-work shimmers in the lamplight. For a moment, it seems that the butterflies, hovering over the full-blown flowers, might flutter away.

'I didn't expect anything so exquisite,' I say, exhaling, a long-drawn out breath.

Maman flushes pink with pleasure.

'Well, you know,' she says, 'everyone helped.'

I imagine the women in her lace-making collective swapping bobbins and pins, extolling the virtues of various threads. Then I realise. 'They must all have forgiven me then,' I say, slowly. 'Or else they knew the rumours weren't true.'

'I think,' Maman replies, 'they realised you'd had a hard time. After all, everyone knows what Augustine can be like. Especially Yvette.'

'What do you mean?'

'She came to see me a few weeks ago, to try and tell me what she'd done. I said it was too late for all that. But she said she felt awful for having helped to drive you away, and could she please have your address in England.'

'I haven't received anything from her,' I say.

'And perhaps you never will,' says Maman. 'Perhaps she feels too guilty. We all make mistakes, after all, but we don't always find it easy to talk about them.'

I drape the christening shawl over the back of the *chaise-longue*, then glance at Maman. But despite her words, her blue eyes are guileless and round. I shrug, then smile.

Monique gurgles away in Paul's old crib by the hearth. Maman approaches her, trailing her scent of roses. She touches the baby's cheek with her fingertip.

'She looks so like you, Odette,' she says.

'No,' I say. 'I'm much darker.' My smile falters and I can't help rubbing the brown stains on my face.

'Not your complexion,' says Maman, hurriedly. 'But you both have a sort of faraway look.' She eyes me for a moment. 'Odette, if I were you, I'd try lemon juice mixed with rosewater on those patches. It's what I've been using on my freckles.'

My eyes fly to her face. It's true. She's no longer so speckled and witchy. But, 'Maman, how do you know that?' I say.

'Augustine gave me a book of her mother's remedies,' says Maman, approaching the sideboard. She rummages around in the drawer beneath the green glass vases. 'Here we are,' she says, taking out a slim book covered in brown paper.

'I didn't know you were interested in that sort of thing,' I say.

'Hélène Solange was my friend, too,' says Maman, softly.

I nod and take the book from her. Leafing through the pages, there's remedies for shining hair and flyaway hair, for impeccable hands and brighter eyes, for loosening a glass stopper, and keeping marble white.

'You can have it, if you want,' says Maman. 'I know most of them off by heart now anyway.'

'*Merci*, Maman.'

'Now if I could just find a remedy to remove my mole,' she adds.

'Don't be silly,' I say. 'People with freckles don't get moles.'

So Maman peels back her floral collar and shows me a little pink bobble just above her breastbone.

'Oh,' I say.

Later that evening, I start to read Madame Solange's remedy book more carefully. Next to '*Relieving aches and pains*,' '*Better digestion*,' and '*Balm for a sore throat*' are various comments, scribbled in the margins. '*Tried this. Didn't work.*' Or, '*Substitute radish juice if out-of-season.*'

But what really worries me is the handwriting. Too familiar. I don't think it belongs to Madame Solange. I think it belongs to Maman.

THE CANDLE

The villagers turn in their pews to watch the fourteen-year old godmother make her vows. Blurred rubies of candle-flame hover on either side of her as Juliette renounces the world, the flesh, and Satan and all his works.

But while she's renouncing, Monique wakes up and starts whimpering, a thin, mournful plaint, like a gull.

I take her from Juliette's arms and try to soothe her. As she struggles, Monsieur le Curé pours water over her head.

'I baptise you in the name of the Father, Son and Holy Ghost.' His deep, sonorous voice echoes through the church. Then he hands each of us a lighted candle.

'Jesus, the light of the world,' I mouth at Stanley, because after all, he hasn't been Catholic for very long.

'Shine as a light in the world to fight against sin,' intones Monsieur le Curé.

I glance at Maman in the front pew. She's smiling beneath a bonnet trimmed with lilacs, her hand resting on Bertrand's arm. But who's that in the opposite pew? The old lady, turning away from the altar, a black shawl pulled round her head? *Mon Dieu.* Surely not Malevola, the bad fairy?

But then she turns and faces me. Looks straight at me with her faded blue eyes. And all the little hairs stand up on my arms. *Que ce n'est pas possible.* If I didn't know better, didn't know she was safe at home in Fitz... Because the woman in black looks just like Mammy.

I shiver. And there must be a draught somewhere in the church, because my candle-flame flickers. I think it's going to go out. But I shield it with my hand, and it burns up bright again.

THE MILK BOTTLES,
Fitz, September 1946

Back on Park Cottage's doorstep, there are three full milk-bottles. Frothy yellow scum floats towards the top of the first one. It's three days old and starting to curdle.

The unusual number makes our milkman bang on the door. But Stanley and I don't answer. We can't, we're not there. We only hear about it afterwards. At the moment, we're in the Church of Sainte-Marie in Ver. So the milkman tries to force the lock. When that doesn't work, he breaks down the door.

And there's Alice Morgan, lying face down at the foot of the stairs. The slipper that tripped over the curling drugget lies beside her.

'Ah, the poor girl. The poor, poor old girl,' the milkman says. He turns Alice over. Her eyes are closed but she is still breathing. He reaches for her pulse, which trembles, weak and frantic, beneath his grasp.. 'Alice? Can you hear me, love? I'm going to go next door to get help. Nod if you can hear me. For a moment, Alice seems to smile. But he waits in vain for a nod that never comes. So he runs next door to use their telephone and calls for an ambulance. He gets her into hospital and then manages to contact us by telegram.

Mammy dies a few days after our return.

'At least she got to see her granddaughter again,' says Stanley.

But I've never seen a man cry like that before. I don't know what to say.

At the funeral service, the choir sings, 'Abide With Me.' Stanley joins in, his whole heart in his voice, lending it a Welsh lilt.

'Come not in terrors, as the King of Kings
But kind and good, with healing in Thy wings...'

As I listen, I'm suddenly glad that we moved back to her house. That we were able to spend those final few months with Alice. Because, after all, she meant well. I remember, when we first returned to Park Cottage, she saw me poring over Augustine's letter. So she fetched her hat and scarf and went straight to the Post Office. She queued up for ages for some Christmas cards and then again for the right stamps.

'Here you are, dear,' she said, on her return. 'You'll be able to send them to your mother and all your friends now.'

'Oh,' I said, 'Thank you so much.'

Her redcurrant dimples appeared. But when I showed the envelopes to Stanley, he frowned.

'I'm sure I paid more than that when I posted that photo to Ver.' He took off his glasses and rubbed his eyes. 'I know what she's done,' he said as he replaced them. 'She still thinks you come from Wales.'

Now I smile at the memory. My fingers slip into Stanley's hand and matching my voice to his, I join in the hymn's final words:

'*Heaven's morning breaks, and earth's vain shadows flee.
In death, in life, O Lord, Abide with me.*'

We bury Mammy in the Protestant churchyard, beside her husband and daughter. On the Mothering Sunday before her last, fatal bout of scarlet fever, her little girl gave Alice the silver Apostle spoon she was looking for the day I first arrived in Fitz. Saint Peter perches on top, holding open Heaven's Gate.

THE SEWING-MACHINE

I open the kitchen cupboard and start to write an inventory for the back of my recipe folder. A list of jam-jar lids, tins of corned beef and spam, a netful of corks, an envelope filled with string. The war, and rationing, has turned us all into hoarders.

Though really, there's less need for that now, at least for Stanley and me. The Royal Liver paid out a high dividend on Mammy's life insurance policy. So these days, we're a bit better-off. We're able to pay the mortgage on Park Cottage and invest in a Singer sewing-machine for me - black and gold, with a fine, severe pedal.

I turn over the list. There, on the back, are bits of a condolence letter from Augustine. It's less irreverent, more spiritual than usual, full of words like *motherhood, sacrifice, children* and *soul*. These days, family relationships really seem to preoccupy Augustine.

But me? Do I have a soul? Or did Augustine suck it from me when we played at vampires as children?

Because really, I can't seem to feel anything the way I should. I fold my grief away, like anonymous letters, hidden in cupboards and drawers. I hoard my secret sorrows, like Papa and his antiques, or Madame Solange and her ornaments.

Now I lean over and shut the cupboard door. Then I find a cloth and start to polish it. The highlights that play on the surface of the wood ease my troubled heart.

My little kingdom, firmly under my control.

THE THIMBLE

Sophy is standing on a kitchen-chair while she and I debate the proper length for her blue skirt. On the floor beside us, Monique plays with the bobbins and cotton-reels.

'*MamMamMamMam,*' she sometimes babbles in time to the rattle of the sewing machine. Not sure if I'm Mum or Maman, she picks her own way through her mother-tongue and her mother's language. Monique, *ma chérie*, like nobody at all, except perhaps yourself.

'*Dehors,*' I say to Stanley now, peering in at the door. 'This is women's business.'

My business, in fact.

But Stanley doesn't want to go outside. It's late summer but it keeps raining, a steady, persistent drizzle. So he stands and watches whilst I tack Sophy's skirt. I like the way the pins make such precise, silver stitches.

But, "*Needles and pins, Needle and pins, when a man marries, his trouble…*" mutters Stanley.

Sophy frowns at him, then smiles down at me. Gracious as the statue of the Madonna in the Church of Sainte-Marie.

'My little French dressmaker,' she says.

I smile back up at Sophy.

She sneezes. Hay fever. Or else she's suffering from the warm steaminess she's brought into the kitchen. And her stockings are damp, and stained brown, from the insides of her scuffed leather lace-ups. Because not even the lady of the manor's clothing coupons stretch to a new pair of shoes.

Still, my mind skips forward, to a time when Sophy and some of her friends, maybe Miss Jones and Miss Shapcott, will ask me for the New Look - the petal-shaped skirts that Christian Dior's introducing in Paris. The Labour MPs may complain that the New Look wastes material and manpower, but it's a vast improvement on the stiff taffeta gowns that ladies wear round here.

Despite my dreams, winter comes, and everything changes. My business starts to fail with the falling snow. No-one wants to come for a fitting - it's just too cold. And at Park Cottage, the gas is on at such low pressure, it's reduced to a blue ghost.

Oh, I keep trying to work, with a balaclava and a scarf over my head, mittens on my hands, and a rug round my legs. But the mittens make my fingers clumsy. Then I get chilblains. Then it's even harder to clasp the needle, push it through the fabric.

To keep myself going, I switch on the wireless.

'There was no possibility of taking a walk that day,' it grumbles. *Jane Eyre*, for the book's centenary. But then they ration the electricity, so I have to limit my listening. And the light. So If I'm dealing with black or dark blue cloth, it's like working in the dark.

Though sometimes I step outside with Monique for some fresh air, both of us wearing snow boots and bundled up in an old fur-lined coat. Then the glitter of white light is dazzling. The world has disappeared beneath the snow. Just the tops of hedges show white, the tips of reeds, silver.

In the evenings, Stanley and I take Monique into bed with us, to keep her warm. All three of us huddle together under sheets, blankets and homemade eiderdowns. And winter coats, carried up from the wardrobe at the bottom of the stairs. All three of us still wearing the socks that protect us from the frozen floorboards.

The thaw doesn't come until March, round about when Jane leaves St. John Rivers and searches out Mr Rochester. As I listen, I sort out my needles and pins, my thimbles and thread. Ready to start my business, all over again.

THE LETTER

'Qu'est-ce que tu as là?' asks Stanley, glancing up from the sports pages.

'Another letter from Augustine,' I say. 'But Stanley, you and Monique promised me you'd only speak to me in English. Otherwise I'll never improve.'

I read English books, English magazines, listen to the wireless. I've become a magpie with words, stealing precious gems from others' sentences. I understand far more than I can say. But when I try to speak, I jumble all my meanings. I make flaws from others' *bons mots,* striving and failing to find my own gleaming language.

'Sorry,' says Stanley. 'You're right. It's just quicker to speak to you in French, that's all.' He lowers the newspaper, gives me his full, contrite attention. 'What does Augustine have to say for herself?'

'I'll translate,' I say. 'It'll be good practice.'

Stanley rests his head against the cloth I've placed over the armchair, to protect it. He puts his pipe down and half-shuts his eyes.

'Come on then,' he says. 'Hurry up.'

'Wait a minute, where's the start, yes, here we are.'

"*Petite Monique has just turned four, hasn't she?*' I read. '*Happy Birthday Monique! Too young to start school though and give you some peace. Unless you have des écoles maternelles in England, too?*"

'...*des écoles maternelles?*' What's that in English, Stanley?'

'Nursery schools, I suppose. But carry on, you're doing well.'

'All right. Well, then she says, '*We may have the vote now, but a mother's life doesn't change much.*' Then she describes, um, a red,

202

sleeveless top I think, and a swirly black skirt with those little, what are they called, spots?'

'Polka dots?'

'Polka dots? Like the dance? Well maybe. Because then she talks about a ball at the Auberge d'Or, *'in honour of the new school and new square, just opened in Ver. Paul took us to see the ceremony the following afternoon. There were balloons, flags, and a speech from the Mayor. The new Mayor, that is, Monsieur Rolland.'*

'That arrogant little pharmacist?' says Stanley.

'He's the great man of our village, these days. And listen to this, *'Ver itself has been awarded the Croix de Guerre.'* And Admiral Byrd was there. He made a speech, because they named the school and the square after him.'

'He's more my idea of a great man,' says Stanley. 'I'd like to have met him. Who else was there?'

'It's a small village, Stanley. Not that many famous people. But, oh, the next bit's easy. Augustine says, *'the children sang the 'Marseillaise.' Then the Mayor cut the ribbon, and we all trooped round the new classrooms to take a look. I tell you what, wouldn't it be lovely if Monique and Francine could go to school together in Ver, like we used to do…'*"

'Same old Augustine,' says Stanley, trying to smile. 'She hasn't changed.'

'What do you mean?'

'Only that she's as thoughtless as ever.'

'I don't understand.'

Stanley stares at me. 'Her letter,' he says. 'Making you want things you can't have.' From behind his glasses, his blue eyes are guileless and round. 'D'you think I don't know, Odette,' he continues, 'how you long to be back in France? Back in Ver-Sur-Mer, with the two little girls going to school together, like she says?'

I drop my eyes. I don't know whether to feel ashamed, or not.

Stanley leans forward, places his fingertips against my cheek. So cold. Stanley Winterhands, I call him.

203

'It's all right,' he says, softly. 'I'm not blaming you. It's only natural really, that you should feel like that. Only...' He pauses, and I look up. 'Your home is in England now, Odette,' he continues, very gently. 'Don't you think you should be making the best of your life here?'

I bite my lip. *'J'essaie,'* I reply. Then, *'C'est difficile.'* And then I realise. I'm still speaking in French. And in fact, in all the years I live in England, I never lose my French accent. And that night, and every other night, for all the rest of my life, I dream in French.

THE BASKET

On my birthday, there's a letter from Maman. Crisp blue envelope covered in thin strokes of ink. Send it back. I don't want to read it. I don't want to read the word we can't ever bring ourselves to say. *Cancer.* The same in both languages.

I prop the envelope against the teapot, away from Monique's birthday drawing, Stanley's bunch of daisies, the loaf of bread. Then I glare at my reflection in the concave mirror of a breakfast spoon. Forty-one. How did that happen? My skin's still smooth, but there's a fine fretwork of lines round my eyes. And those eyes, still two hazelnuts, like Jacques used to say, but no longer so certain, so bright.

Yesterday's loaf. 'None of that,' calls Sophy through the kitchen window. 'Look what I've brought you.' She holds up a basket full of strawberries. And a book with the words *French Country Cooking* emblazoned across the cover, beneath a pen-and-ink illustration of a bulb of garlic.

'Bon anniversaire,' says Sophy a few minutes later, kissing me on both cheeks.

'Elizabeth David?' I say, peering at the book. 'Her name isn't French.' I start to flick through the coarse-grained pages. 'And she sounds more like a schoolteacher than a cook.'

'Odette, sometimes there's no pleasing you,' Sophy says, taking the book from me. 'I was going to make us some strawberry compote,' she continues, finding the right page, marking it with Maman's letter. 'Only,' she glances at me, 'you'd do it so much better.'

'All right,' I say, looking at the recipe. '*Bah* - she hasn't got it right. I think I'll make my own version.' So I add the strawberries to a saucepan, twist of sugar, sprinkle of vinegar. Then I place some eggs, cream, sugar and vanilla pods into a large bowl and whisk it. I take what's left of yesterday's loaf and cut it into four thick slices. Then I heat a frying-pan over the blue flame of a low heat and throw in a glug of oil. I dip a slice of bread into the egg mixture to coat it evenly.

I wonder if it's true, that when we cook, we re-make our mothers. 'The artist at work,' mutters Sophy and then I realise. I'm not Maman. I'm Madame Solange.

I drain off the excess egg, can't help licking my fingers, but wash them quickly under the tap. Then I tip a couple of slices of bread into the pan and fry them for a few minutes. I transfer the slices into a baking tray and place them inside the oven, to keep them warm. Finally, I fry the remaining slices of bread.

'De-lic-ious,' Sophy sighs, as we eat them, laden with spoonfuls of strawberry compote.

'You know, Odette,' she continues, 'You should really think about growing your own fruit. You have the space, and it would be better than all that Bird's Eye quick-frozen stuff.'

'Stanley says the seeds get under the plate of his teeth.'

'Men,' says Sophy. 'Do you know, Hugh doesn't like fruit cake? Don't you think that's odd? But anyway, it doesn't have to be strawberries. Oh, sorry,' she adds, and dabs at the glob of compote that's fallen on Maman's envelope. 'But you haven't opened it,' she says.

'I don't want to.'

Sophy stares at me. 'There's nothing bad in it,' she says. 'I'm certain. Would you like me to read it for you?'

I nod.

Sophy licks the crumbs from her fingers, then tears the envelope open. A handmade card, white, with a pale yellow tissue-paper flower. A scrap of lace for its leaf. A bit silly. Like something Monique would make, really.

'*Birthday greetings to ma chère petite Odette,*' Sophy reads. '*Love to Stanley and Monique.... Bertrand says he's never seen a cabbage that size before...Augustine hasn't been round much lately. I could have done with her support when I went to see the doctor.*' Ah, here we are. '*He said...*' She pauses for a moment, then looks up. 'Odette, this round of blood tests were fine. She doesn't have cancer. Just there's a few more tests to come, she says for anaemia and white blood cell count.'

I let go of my breath, wait for my mouth to stop trembling, wait until I can speak. 'What shall I grow in my garden?' I say, at last.

THE PLANT-HOLDER

There's a plant-holder in my garden, shaped like a swan. Wild strawberries, redcurrants and raspberries climb the fence. On the sapling Stanley planted for me, apples show their rosy bloom.

The fruit goes into tarts and pancakes, soufflés and mousses, even pies. I make compotes of apples and pears. I bottle cherries, greengages and plums. I make feasts for Monique and Stanley and urge them to eat. Soon my daughter grows plump as a child in a fairy-tale, as Mademoiselle Madeleine. And Stanley...he likes my home-grown fruit and veg. They appeal to his Austerity mentality. But to my surprise, for himself, he prefers flowers.

'They're truly a sign that the war's over,' he says. 'No more Digging for Victory on the Home Front. And when we've been married for ten years,' he adds, 'I'll plant anniversary rose-bushes, with red and white flowers. Only it'll be Fitz and Ver, instead of York and Lancaster.'

I haven't got the heart to tell him, I don't like roses. Anyway, perhaps it's Monique who's the flower. Our funny hybrid rose. English in England, but French in France. A proper little *jeune fille,* just like I used to be. She sips her National Health Ribena and pretends it's Holy Communion wine.

Myself, I prefer a cool glass of water, a cup of camomile tea, or a sip of coffee, sugarless and black. Black as a moonless lake, where my white swan glides.

THE TEA-SET

Every evening after school, Monique takes her books and toys down from the shelf. Then she pauses and contemplates the empty space. It contains her silence. She can sit and look at it, take her time, decide what to put back, what to throw away.

Just like Papa and I used to do in the antiques shop.

But it's in the window of a toyshop in Shrewsbury that I spot a doll's pink tea-set, the perfect miniature of Mammy's. A complete assortment of rose-coloured cups and saucers, and teapot and jug and sugar basin, laid out among the sailing ships and spinning tops.

On her birthday, Monique removes the wrapping paper very carefully, liking its sheen and the shiny rosette. Then she lets her hand linger over the teapot's gleaming lid, its porcelain smoothness, its blush-pink tint. The cups don't hold more than a thumbful of liquid. The handles are too small even for her fingers.

'Thank you, Mummy,' she says, then starts to arrange the tea-set on top of her bookcase, just so.

'Aren't you going to play with it?' I say.

But Monique shakes her head, adjusts her hair-ribbon, then reaches for her duster.

THE PIGEON-HOLES

If Monique favours the bookcase, the bureau is sacred to Stanley. Its rows of pigeon-holes contain cheque books, old diaries, address-books and receipts. Here too is the mottled leather blotter embossed with gold. And rows of ink-bottles glow like ancient potions of red, black, purple and blue in the pharmacist's window.

The lid opens out to make a writing shelf. Here stands the stapler, the hole-puncher, the penholder. The airmail envelopes contain foreign thoughts on feather-thin paper. Though *our* envelopes never lose their stamps, Admiral Byrd.

Monique knows where the key is kept. Not in the outside lock, but beneath the base of a standard lamp. She unlocks the bureau and reveals the sacred treasures of its inner drawer. Stumps of scarlet sealing-wax and a gold seal ring, paperclips and drawing-pins, a box of pen nibs, and buttons cut from her grandfather's army uniform.

When Stanley catches Monique murmuring over the contents of the drawer, as compelling to her as rosary beads to me, he isn't angry. He smiles. He shuts the bureau lid and pulls out the top drawer beneath. He rummages through a stack of files marked *Mortgage, Insurance, Bills*. The bottom file is called *Me*.

'Here,' he says to her. 'You can look at this if you like.'

Monique flicks through it.

'Real stories?' she says. She pulls out a page, reads slowly, *"Watch yourself, soldier. That's a mine." He knew what a mine could do. He'd stepped on one a couple of hours earlier."*

'Did you write that?' she asks.

'Nobody would publish it though,' he replies. 'I sent my stories to all the magazines after the war, and no-one was interested.'

He leans forwards, ruffles her hair. It's a mass of dark curls, not thick and straight, like mine.

'When I was your age, I was determined I was going to be a writer,' he says. 'I was convinced I was going to make it. Then the war came, and then, after that, I wanted to be a policeman. But now I sell insurance. And so what do you think the moral of the story is?'

Monique shakes her head, wide-eyed, clinging to the folder.

'The moral of the story is, never let anyone stop you from doing what you want to do. Never give up.' Stanley tries to smile again, but this time, his mouth doesn't quite manage it.

At least I don't think so, as I peer at them through the frosted glass of the parlour door. It's hard to tell without my *lunettes*. I left them on top of the bureau. I was reading that folder of stories he's showing to Monique. That he's never showed to me.

THE STRING BAG

I put the invitation on top of the bureau, ready for Stanley to see. Then I turn and face Monique.

'Shopping,' I say, 'is as much a daughter's duty as it is a wife's.' So as well as my leather handbag, we search out a string bag for her.

'What's wrong now?' I say, as her blue eyes cloud over.

'The holes are too big,' she says. 'All the shopping will fall out.'

So we put newspaper in the bottom, and then the stolen clock chimes the hour, and we have to run for the bus.

'Keep close to me,' I say, when we finally reach our stop outside the Town Hall. Impressive enough, I suppose, with its tiers of white columns, its statue of the Mayor, its inevitable redbrick facade. The marble man gazes out across the town, as if his sightless eyes can contemplate the twists and turns of the fast-flowing River Severn.

'Don't smile at strangers,' I say to Monique.

'I was smiling at the statue,' she says, reaching for my hand. 'He looks lonely.'

Then she pulls me along, to the Square, with its covered market. First stop: Mrs Jenkins. She sits behind a trestle table, with her butter and cheeses arranged in front of her, a dragon-queen guarding her ingots.

'Are you still coming to me for a fitting next Wednesday?' I say.

'Oh yes,' she replies, 'I'm looking forward to it.' So I buy half a pound of her butter, pale gold and gleaming, with its own individual crest shaped like a crown on top.

Next stop: the butcher's stall, for Cumberland sausages, potted meat, and black pudding. Then we buy all the vegetables

I don't grow in my garden, cabbages, cauliflowers, leeks and onions. Finally, we cross the cobbles of Grope Lane, and pop into Lipton's for tea and sliced ham. Two different counters, so two different queues. Monique likes to put the money into the cans that whiz overhead, to the central cash desk. Then they come back with change, wrapped in the receipt.

But what Monique hates, really hates, stamping her black buckle shoes in protest, is the trip to the Co-op for knickers, socks - and a liberty bodice.

'You'll need it for when you start St Anne's in September,' I say. But as a reward for enduring the Co-op, we stop at the baker's for a fruit scone. I break it in half, and we share it between us. It falls apart in our hands, and again on our tongues, sweet crumbs and raisins sticking to the roofs of our mouths. Then we make our way up Pride Hill and into Bullogh's.

The department store, with its fine lights and corridors of carpets. Our feet sink into thick, dense pile, soundless and welcoming. - more crimson, and less threadbare, than those at the manor house. Normally, we just buy what we can afford: reels of cotton, press-studs, lavender-scented notelets to send to Augustine. But today is different. Today, I ask the girl behind the counter to pull out a bolt of pale pink silk. Blush-pink, I want to say. Like the pink tips of daisies.

'Is that enough, Madam?' she says, holding up her tape measure.

I nod my head at the crisp snip of the pinking shears. I imagine the flutter and shimmer of sequins beneath high windows.

The stained glass windows of the Church of Sainte-Marie.

'What do you think?' I say to Monique, as imaginary colours hover across her cheekbones, thread glowing jewels through her blue-black hair.

'Oh Mother,' she breathes. 'It's beautiful. Are you going to wear it to Ascot?'

'Ascot? Really, Monique, I don't know what gets into you, sometimes. The material's for you, not me. Or rather, for you and Francine. You're going to be bridesmaids at Alain and Juliette's wedding.'

THE TABLE-CLOTH
Ver-Sur-Mer, Normandy, 1956

When they re-built *Les Hirondelles*, they tried to follow the old architectural plan. So it doesn't feel all that different when Maman and I stand by the parlour's new French doors. We watch two farmhands carry something from the barn. We can't quite tell what it is from this angle.

Then the farmhands walk towards the fields, to put the tents up for the wedding.

At sixty-six, Maman's still spry, still silly, her flaming mass of hair now wisps of flyaway curls. *Petite Maman.* The doll I used to want to keep inside my pocket. A widow-doll, dressed in black, who says she's getting old. She won't marry again, now.

'The bamboo's from Africa. The silk's from India,' she whispers. 'There's going to be stalls with fish, meat and *canapés*, and then a great central tent for the sit-down meal.' A feast, in fact, for one hundred and seventy people. They'll eat for four or five hours, and then again the following day, and again the day after.

'That's right,' says Paul, joining us, making us jump with his booming voice. 'We're going to show the village how a proper wedding should be done.' He offers Maman his arm into dinner, bending solicitously over her tiny frame. But he still casts longing glances back at Augustine.

At dinner, he raises his glass in fond, foolish, middle-aged salute to his wife. Then uses the tablecloth to dab his broad, too red lips. I don't know why, but whatever that man does still annoys me.

The quiche's soft cheese falls apart against the roof of his mouth. He savours the gnarled, grilled aubergine.

'Remember all that fuss over our wedding?' he mumbles with his mouth full. 'I swear, if it had gone on much longer, I'd have abducted you.'

He laughs, and after a moment, so does Augustine. But her fingers pluck at the tablecloth that Maman made them all those years ago.

Then Paul uses the tongs to dip a sugar lump in his glass of wine. He sucks on it, an old trick to renew the appetite - and loosen the tongue. He turns towards Juliette's fiancé, Alain.

'That's what I'd advise you to do with my daughter,' he says, 'Abduct her.'

Alain tries to smile. He's thirty-five to Juliette's twenty-four, but he's young beneath his prospective father-in-law's gaze. His Adam's apple bobs painfully above his highly starched collar.

'Paul,' says Augustine. *'Les enfants.'* She nods towards Monique and Francine.

'Please, what's 'abducted,'?' says Francine, though from the glint of her eyes, I'm sure she already knows.

'There, now look what you've started,' Augustine mutters.

The tips of Paul's ears turn beetroot. But he shrugs and helps himself to some more green beans.

'Don't you know?' says Monique in her eager French. 'It's when a gentleman in a carriage carries away a lady so that she'll marry him.'

Augustine and I exchange glances, grateful for this interpretation.

'When *I* get married,' says Francine, *'I'*ll wear a red dress. But I won't wear a veil.'

'Why not?' I ask.

'Because,' says Francine, 'my husband will want to see my beautiful face.'

'Where do they get all this from?' asks Paul, shaking his head.

Before bedtime, Francine drags Monique for a walk round the kitchen garden. The scent of crushed sorrel, sage, and green leeks wafts through the open window. I watch as Francine taps a dry poppyhead into Monique's open palm. Monique smiles at the black pepper of seeds.

But later that evening, I find her half-asleep, her head resting against the curlicues of the banister at the bottom of the stairs.

I wake her, as gently as I can.

Her eyes dart across the black-and-white tiles. 'Francine wanted to play abductions with me,' she says. 'I was nearly asleep when she pounced. So I escaped and came down here.'

Poor little soul. I carry her back up to bed, settle her down, then glare at Francine, pretending to be asleep. Pretending to be a good little girl.

An hour or two later, Monique glides past my open bedroom door. Dazed and dreaming, she climbs the stairs to the attic room - the one that, in the old house, used to belong to Franz. Suddenly I wonder if, on nights when the moon is full, the old house hangs like gauze around the rafters of the new. Mysterious corridors of silver and glass might appear, facets of a prism refracting unearthly light. And what if Franz still lives there? What if he never went away? The ghost inside my looking glass. The *revenant*, who always returns - but never does.

Now I follow Monique up the stairs. Inside the attic-room, apples are laid out in rows on sagging benches. Through the skylight in the roof, moonlight washes over them. Monique, still asleep, kneels down, rests her cheek against the seat of a wicker chair filled with moon-dappled apples. The white light softens her face, blends the shadows of her curved cheeks, dark lips, staring eyes.

She's a pale, gleaming bird in a nest filled with round, green eggs.

I pick her up. But this time, I'm careful not to wake her. My arms are gentle. I protect her dangling feet from every sharp doorway, every abrupt stair. I cradle her, little, sleeping girl, in tender arms, against my cardigan of fox-coloured, home knitted wool.

Down the stairs we go, then along the black-and-white corridor. I like the *click tap* of my shoes measuring out its long silence. My door opens again, pushed by a breeze from the window, from the orchard, whitening beneath the moon. The sudden gust of air is cool against my cheek.

Monique sighs, stirs in her sleep. I take her into my own bed and hold her close. She's so warm and she smells faintly of apples and cinnamon. I start to drift...

Suddenly, sweating and panicked, Monique twists round in the bed and kicks me. Her eyelids fly open, and she stares at the strange blankets, the unfamiliar walls, the lantern hanging from the curtain-rod.

'Abducted,' she whimpers.

'Ssssh, *chérie*,' I say, as bodies stir above us. 'I'm here. I'll keep you safe.' But Monique moans and shivers, refuses to be comforted. So I take one last breath of the salt-laden air, then pull down the window sash.

Now the lantern splits the window's rectangle of moonlight into four squares, superimposing bars, the outline of a crucifix, across our bed. In the pane's glass, the reflection of my face is white and pinched from lack of sleep.

Today's their wedding day. Summer is nearly over.

Part V
Shrewsbury, Normandy and Surrey, 1959-2003

THE TELEPHONE

On the night of Alain and Juliette's third wedding anniversary, I hope to dream of *Les Hirondelles*. But I don't. Instead, the long-ago curving moon house appears, bobbing gently on the sea. I wave and a light in the parlour window flickers. A child perhaps, signalling messages with her candle. Then a voice calls her away. The flame is extinguished.

So I follow a path of moonlight down to the water's edge. Then, suddenly, rearing up in front of me, much larger than I remember it, is Barthonien - that I used to call the Egg-Rocks. I rub my hands all over its chalk-buds. I rest my head against them, and then I notice what I've never seen before.

A cave, hollowed out from the heart of the rock. It smells of damp sand and clotted blood.

Its walls are jutting slate, ridged and shiny. From somewhere inside, I can hear the steady drip, drip of salt water.

There's a little girl inside the cave. She moves forwards from the shadows but stops short of the nervy moonlight.

'How did you get here?' I say. 'I thought you were at home, fast asleep.' Then I see her face. My mother.

'This is where I live now,' Maman says, with a wave of her hand. 'I'm always happy here.'

Her face is smooth and round. No frowns etched into it.

'You're so little,' I blurt, and I reach forwards to touch her. She backs away from me and I look at my hands. My nails are dirty, wedged with sand.

'It's time for you to go,' she says.

She stands at the mouth of the rock and waves me off. A fairy-doll with a porcelain face, smooth as eggshell.

'Goodbye Marie-France,' I call, because I know I'll never see her so dainty, so child-like again. I'm straining for my last glimpse of her, when somehow I lose my balance, slip and fall into the sea. But it feels like the opposite of drowning. It feels like I'm being pulled up through dank green water, to swim into bright white light, sharp as broken dreams...

Burr, burr. Burr, burr... I grope for the ringing telephone's receiver, then hear Augustine's voice, crackling from a long way away.

'I'm so sorry to tell you this, *ma pauvre*. We just lost your mother.'

I cradle the receiver against my cheek, listening to the hiss and crackle die away, like the sound of the sea.

'Odette, Odette, are you there?' calls Augustine.

THE HEADSCARF

It's Maman's funeral on Wednesday.

I suppose, sooner or later, she knew she would return to the sea. She couldn't survive on land. She wanted to, but she failed. So now she takes Pierre's hand.

'It's just a game,' she whispers, so he won't be frightened. She knows he doesn't like the sea. Not even paddling in the ripples at the water's edge.

But when he's calmer, they wade in further together, taking it very gently - allowing him time to get used to the deep, dark water, the crashing waves. They start to laugh as their clothes billow out around them.

Then Pierre is very tired. He wants to sleep. Then the sea holds them both in its arms, rocks them like a cradle. They lie down together at the bottom of the ocean, where nothing more can ever harm them.

They'll be safe forever.

Except, of course, Maman didn't drown. She was ill for ages, with the breast cancer their tests didn't find, and by the time they did, it was too advanced. She saw a specialist or two, but by there was nothing they could do. Their chemotherapy and radiotherapy didn't help. It shrivelled her up into a little old woman, melted her, like a child's doll thrown onto the fire.

All burnt up, her hair fell out, another *femme tondue*.

When I was a child, I said I wanted you to burn. But I didn't mean it, Maman, honestly, I didn't. I sent you headscarves and kisses in the post, so you'd know I was thinking of you. But before I could save up the money to come and visit you, you died.

And now, when I say I'm sorry, you can't hear me.

THE ROSARY
Ver-Sur-Mer, Normandy, July 1959

I don't know what I'd do without her. Augustine lends me some money, enough for the fare to France, and says she'll look after Monique while I visit the presbytery.

So I pick my way between the cemetery and the church, along a path leading down a narrow garden, enclosed by shrubs and iron railings.

A very secluded life for one they say is young and kind. Though perhaps he's too young to know about death. Not that I really understand it myself. And it's been so many years since I was last here, for my confirmation classes with his predecessor.

But as I step into the hallway, I realise it still smells the same: dust and dregs of communion wine. And inside the parlour, the same curtains of closely woven cotton, still stretch across the window-frame. The same ceramic screen by the grate still shields an unlit fire.

There's even the same crucifix above the fireplace, with a rosary coiled round it, little carved wooden beads, like juniper berries.

Different picture of a different Pope, though. And the goldfish, flicking back and forth in its aquarium, that's new. And the shallow-topped stove, with orange peel curling over it. I shut my eyes and, ignoring the dust, inhale the mingled scent of citrus and communion wine. It comforts me.

Hem-hem.

I open my eyes to find Monsieur le Curé, regarding me with a concerned expression. He must think I'm praying. Or mad. But then, it's a long time since a priest thought I was holy. He invites me to sit down. He clasps his hands in the lap of his black *soutane*. Long tapering fingers he has, like those on a tombstone figure. He clears his throat and begins.

'You know,' he says, 'I performed the Last Rites for your mother. I also heard her last confession.'

I start to say something, but he stops me with a look.

'Your mother made it clear that I should share what she said with you, if she died before she could speak to you herself.'

'Is that permitted?'

'I mustn't reveal her confession. But her conversation, which was substantially the same, that's allowed.' He clears his throat again. 'You know, of course, that there was a time when your mother was very unhappy.

I nod.

'That level of despair, it's almost a state of mortal sin. Such a shame she never sought counsel from my predecessor. But I understand that after your father's death, she felt alienated from the Church.'

'And from all of us,' I add. Even me.

'Well, it was a very strange time in our history, Madame. People were trying to wean women from the Church, to promote their own suffrage and Republican causes. And I believe that your mother was heavily influenced by one such person – a Mademoiselle…'

'Madeleine,' I say, and compress my lips.

'Yes, but even this friendship brought her no real solace. She said that one day she walked down to the sea with your little brother… And she felt a strong, terrible urge, a compulsion she called it, to throw herself into the water. So she told - Pierre, was it?'

I nod.

'She told Pierre to go back home and wait for you. He was nearly at the door when she plunged into the water. But your little brother, he ran back to her, screaming for her. So she started to swim back to the shore.'

My mouth is suddenly dry. I run my tongue over my lips, to moisten them. How much of this is true?

Monsieur le Curé continues, 'Your little brother, Pierre, leaned over the side of the promenade. But he leaned over too far, and the promenade was slippery. He lost his balance and fell into the water.'

He pauses, as if he can't find the words. He laces, then unlaces his long fingers. The signet ring on the littlest one gleams red.

Then, 'His death was an accident. That's what your mother wanted you to know. It was a terrible accident.'

'Bb-b-ut,' I stammer, wiping tears from my eyes, 'it's what I always feared. My mother tried to commit suicide. She doesn't deserve to be buried on holy ground.'

'Madame Morgan, you're obviously very upset, and no wonder. But thoughts are not sins, and besides, your mother did repent of her despair. She was coming back to Pierre, came back, to you. And one day, you will see her again, in Heaven.'

Like it says on the inscription I'd planned for her black marble headstone:

*'I will go and see her one day,
I will go, far from the earth,
On the heart of my mother,
Resting without returning.'*

'No,' I say. 'No headstone.'

Monsieur le Curé looks at me. His eyes are blue as the sea, but there's a fleck of brown in one iris.

'But what will people say?' he asks.

I shut my eyes again, but now all I can smell is vervain tea and the faint aroma of roses. 'No more than what they've said already.' Two tears slip out from beneath my eyelids. I wipe them away. Two tears. That's enough. More than she deserves.

THE TALL CANDLES

The church bells toll loudly, a long, slow thunder of iron upon iron. Rolling through the village, and into the surrounding fields.

Paul, Jojo, Alain and another man from the farm carry the coffin out of her cottage. They load it onto a cart draped in black crepe. The cart lurches over the ruts in the road; the coffin slides backwards and forwards. When they reach the Church of Sainte-Marie, the four men heave it out of the cart, carry it up the aisle and deposit it on the waiting bier.

Monsieur le Curé lights the tall candles flanking the coffin on each side. The flames flicker, cast shadows across the wall, then one of them goes out. He reads aloud from the Bible,

'In my Father's house are many mansions: if it were not so, I would have told you. I go to prepare a place for you.'

But what of my mother's final resting place, its compact, solid walls?

After the Mass, we leave the church and walk towards the cemetery, where I've chosen a quiet corner for her. Beside a hawthorn seeded in wild grass, next to a blackened brick wall. Close enough to the church to be included in the company of the righteous. At sufficient distance not to cause offence.

Clouds cover the sky, leaving no trace of blue. The men lower my mother's coffin into the ground, and heap soil over it. Earth to earth. Ashes to ashes. Dust to dust.

It's always men who take charge of the coffin, never women.

Though Stanley was right. I shouldn't have dressed Monique in black. She looks like a young crow, laying a bouquet of purple daisies beside her grandmother's grave.

No headstone.

A poor funeral, I'm sure everyone's thinking, like a pauper's.

Light rain brushes against my face, a vaporous veil of mourning. Then raindrops fall onto the flowers' petals, making up for all my unshed tears.

THE RED VALISE

T-t-t-t! Look what Monique's done now! Propped the red leather valise up against the wall. I remove it, but no, it's too late. An oblong of grime disfigures the whitewash. I hope it'll scrub off.

And those green leaves on the wallpaper. So faded. Or else my vision's distorted. But Paul, my stepbrother, set such store by them. His own mother picked out the pattern and then, after she died, he felt as if he was in charge – the keeper of the house.

So Maman never really had a chance to make anything of the place. Not until Paul moved up to the farm to marry Augustine. To go and pester *her* when *she* was trying to dust.

At least Stanley isn't like that. Sits in his armchair, newspaper on his lap, dreamy, faraway look in his eyes.

'Put some elbow grease into it, girl,' he teases, but he lets me get on with it. One good thing about marrying him, I suppose.

Plenty of polishing to do here, as well. Dust animals run along the skirting board, mingle with skeins of my mother's long, red hair. She must've carried on dying it even after it was falling out. Because *les vieilles filles* don't have red hair. Even if my own chignon is still fairly dark at forty-nine.

I give it a complacent little pat.

Hair balls, cobwebs, dust puffs. And a damp, malign odour. Probably a dead mouse somewhere. Or else my senses are heightened with the beginning of a migraine. But I'll call Monique in, and she can help me get the place clean. Then we can sleep here tonight and tomorrow I'll talk to Paul about renting it out to holidaymakers. Because, under the terms and conditions of my mother's will, Paul and I have jointly inherited the cottage. I swear she did it deliberately. She knew we don't get on.

Her little moment of power from beyond the grave.

No wonder the wallpaper's faded. Just look at that sunlight ricocheting off the walls. With Paul up at the farm, and Bertrand dead, there was no-one to tell Maman to keep the shutters drawn. Her last years spent in a blazing hive of sunbeams. Her hair (dyed) a halo of red and gold.

Perhaps I won't talk to Paul about renting out the cottage. Perhaps Monique and I will stay here for a bit, have ourselves a little holiday. I can show her the old family albums, sort out the jewellery that was left to her.

Maman's First Communion bracelet, the gilt crucifix she wore round her neck on Sundays, the topaz brooch, the pearl choker from her wedding-day. And two wedding rings, one silver, one gold. Though really, for the life she led, two husbands, one rich, one poor, it's not much of a hoard.

Though there's always my father's antiques. I ought to start compiling an inventory of the household contents, like the lawyer suggested. It's just, my mind's been in too much turmoil. Every time I try to write, it comes out the wrong way, back-to-front, upside-down. Like Monique and her mirror-writing. And I'm not sure what to do with all these things I've inherited. They won't look right back in our new bungalow in Shrewsbury.

As I said to Stanley when we bought it, the advantage of a bungalow is that you don't have to worry about falling on the stairs. Now if Monique and I lived here for good, I'd have to get some banisters put in. The steps are very steep, and even though she's nearly thirteen, *Mon Dieu,* she's clumsy.

Still, nearly made it up the stairs. There should be some dusters in that cupboard on the landing. Right by the window.

My eyes water with the sudden light. Sunbursts coax the primroses out. And patches of blue sky show through the clouds. Suddenly, I remember when I was a little girl, looking up from the watercolour pictures in my illustrated bible.

'Are your eyes sky blue or sea blue, Maman?'

'China-blue, *chérie,*' she said, and gave me a kiss on the lips. Monique has those same eyes. And Stanley, blue eyes as well, that take their colour from the weather. I hope the frost doesn't get to them. The flowers, that is. Because it's too cold for summer. More like an awkward spring, an Easter egg, not sure whether to hatch just yet.

There's Monique, legs dangling, brown and scratched, from the upside-down bowl of the chestnut tree. T-t-t-t! I tap on the glass and waggle my finger at her. She stares back at me, then draws her legs in and crouches on the branch - poised, wary.

Thirteen. *L'âge ingrat*, Maman used to say. The tender age. Or else, the graceless, ungrateful age when your little girl is growing up and doesn't love you anymore.

Still, Monique always was Daddy's girl. When we first arrived, she insisted we telephone him from the farm, to let him know we were safe. Then she picked out a picture postcard for him, swans on a lake, if you please. Followed by a long letter with rows and rows of kisses. And each morning, she lifts her head with the shuffle of the letter flap, then runs to the letters tumbling onto the mat, then droops and sighs because there's no reply.

No reply. How could there be, to the words that were said before we left?

'I don't think it's a good idea for you to take Monique to the funeral,' he'd said. 'It's morbid, a child that age dressed all in black. She already has nightmares. And she hardly knew her grandmother, anyway.'

'And whose fault is that?' I'd snapped back. 'If you earned more money, we could have had regular holidays in France. I wouldn't have become so cut off from my family.'

'You and your old gramophone-groove,' he replied. 'That trouble with your mother began years before I met you. Don't start blaming me just because you feel guilty.'

'Guilty? You're the one who should feel guilty. All this scratching around, make-do-and-mend. Not even the money to send Monique to private school.'

'We're already paying for her uniform, gym clothes, hockey stick and tennis racquet. We can't afford school fees on top of all that. And she'll do just as well at the grammar school. It's not as if she's poor little Sadie Thomas, shunted off to secondary modern.'

'But I wanted Monique to have the best possible start in life,' I say. 'I had to leave school when I was thirteen, remember.' No prize books for Latin composition for me, Stanley.

He didn't say anything after that. Just pressed the tobacco into the bowl of his pipe and puffed away. Lost himself in wreaths of smoke.

England, with its skies the colour of smoke, the land of reticence, of no reply.

At least Maman's husband let her have her own way. Well, he let her re-decorate upstairs, anyway, though they couldn't afford it. The parlour may conform to Paul's mother's austere taste, but upstairs, the bedroom is entirely Maman's. Pink wallpaper roses twine round the mirror, bloom round the window-frame. Bottles of scent, a cedarwood box, a silver-backed brush and comb on the dressing-table. And a picture of the Madonna over the bed, looking a bit like Mademoiselle Madeleine, with her dark, soulful eyes.

With a bright halo round it. No, that's just my migraine. The flickering aura of lights that herald the attack.

Piles of her pillows are plumped up in the centre of the mattress. Maman again, trying to pretend it was a big, single bed. Trying to pretend she didn't hate sleeping alone. Though if she'd liked her own company better, she'd never have married Bertrand Carpentier so soon after Papa died.

There it is, their wedding-day, captured in a framed photograph on the bedside cabinet. Black-and-white, but I remember them in full colour. Bertrand, in his stiff, freshly starched suit, which he hadn't worn since his previous wedding. Maman, still so young, with her wide eyes, and wildflowers in her short *garçonne's* hair, flicked back in auburn waves.

She made her choice.

But the photograph's full of bubbles. I'll just prise open the frame and smooth them out.

Oh. There's another photograph behind it. She's even younger in this one, sitting down, with a baby, me, on her lap. Both of us shelter beneath the sleeves of Papa's dark serge suit. That's how she was. That's how we all once were, together.

I swap the two pictures over. I arrange the frame just-so on the bedside cabinet. I'm trying to put everything back together again, how it used to be.

'Monique, Monique,' I call out the window. I want her to come and look at her French family. I'm not sure yet when we'll be returning to her English one. Maybe Stanley can join us out here. Or not. Just as he likes. If he can find the money, and the time. He hasn't been back to Ver since Monique's christening.

Phul-phul- phu…Birdsong? No, Monique whistling. I can hear her, but I can't see her. Though she's making far too much noise. A crowing cock and a whistling hen are an insult, both to God and men…

I reach over to tap on the windowpane, to make her stop. But my sleeve catches against the photograph frame. It judders and falls forward.

I pick it up. Now there's a crack running down the sheet of glass. My parents are separated. I'm split in two. Half Papa's *fille*. Half belonging to my mother.

I glare at her. What was it she'd said, all those years ago, when I told her I wanted to live with Augustine on the farm? 'No, you can't just go where you please. I absolutely forbid it. A child should not be separated from her family. Are you listening to me, Odette? *La famille, c'est la chose la plus importante.*' Message understood, Maman. But Mon Dieu - even now she's dead, she's still telling me what to do.

Death. This is the bed where she died. This is where they laid her out, dressed in her best clothes, hands crossed on her breast. Paul kept vigil over the corpse. Round here, you have to sit with the dead for three days, and three nights. That's the custom. And of course, people trooped in and out to pay their last respects. Augustine, Juliette, Alain, Jojo. The women from the church.

Three days and three nights on that bed.

Maybe I should try and stop thinking about it. It isn't doing me any good. And I feel so strange. Although perhaps that's just the migraine coming out. Such a peculiar, one-sided headache. I never had them before this last trip to Ver.

Maman's legacy, perhaps.

I turn away from the window, walk towards the dressing-table. Nothing to fear. But nausea jabs at my insides; shadows lurch; objects loom. Like this silver-backed hairbrush, with her hairs trapped in it.

The house is full of my mother's red, red, red.

I hold one up, then let it go. It drifts into the hearth and disappears into the blackness of the chimney.

Then there's footsteps on the stairs. The floorboards along the corridor emit their oaken reproach. *You weren't here, You weren't here, You weren't here.* Each creak is louder than the last.

Now the dressing-table mirror flickers a warning. Huge, scared eyes, white, pinched face. There once was a girl who thought she saw her mother's face in a magic mirror. Then she grew up, and realised it was her own. The End.

The bedroom door swings open. I want to be sick. I'm numb all down one side.

But really, there's nothing to fear. It's only Monique, running into the room. She stops short in front of me, but I throw my arms round her. She wriggles, then acquiesces, her bones digging into me through my cardigan.

'Mot-herrrrr,' Monique sighs, staring up at me. My head hurts so much now. But if her eyes were a different colour, I could bear it better.

THE LADYBIRD BROOCH

In an alcove in my mother's cottage, there's a little bottle of holy water. A white bottle from the Lourdes spring, shaped like Madame la Sainte Vierge. Her clasped hands are a white flame of prayer. Her blood is water and flows purely in her veins. She wears a blue screw-top for a crown. It always looks too heavy for her head. Holy Mary, Blessed Virgin, always has a headache.

After our disastrous morning in my mother's cottage, Monique and I go and stay at the farm. 'I need you like I need a hole in the head,' I snap at her, when she comes into my bedroom early one morning, before I'm even dressed. *Mon Dieu.* I can't help it; she's getting on my nerves.

'Wear the fox-coloured cardigan,' she pleads, as if I have nothing better to do than gratify her whims. And when I say no, she begins her litany of complaints.

'I don't like Francine. I don't want to share a room with her. She snores. Why can't I sleep with you?'

'You're too big. I don't want to wake up in the night squashed right to the other side of the bed.' Besides, the desperate embrace of Monique's nightmares is not an experience I care to repeat. I need my sleep.

Because I'm not sleeping very well at the moment. I can feel the shadows burning beneath my eyes. Augustine gives me curious glances and makes me cups of camomile tea. There's something she wants to say, I know. But not yet.

And these migraines... *Mon Dieu.* I never knew what Maman suffered with them, till now. Night after night after night, that same relentless headache, boring into my skull.

'Offer them up to the Virgin,' Paul mutters at breakfast, through a mouthful of crumbs. I glare at him, then at Augustine. She has no right to tell him my private matters. After all, I myself keep many things secret from my husband.

But perhaps Paul is annoyed with us being here? It has been nearly three months. And he and I never rubbed along together particularly well. I give him my sweetest smile. A smile I learned from Augustine, when she wants her own way.

'That's a very good idea, Paul. Suppose you drive us all to Mont-Saint-Michel? It would be good for Monique to see the chapel before we leave.' There, a sudden spoonful of sugar, thrown in at the end of the sentence. Paul raises his head quickly from his *croque-monsieur* and stares at me.

'You're leaving?' says Paul. 'So soon? Surely not!'

Really, I have no intention of leaving. My mother's cottage may not have suited me, but *Les Hirondelles* has always been my true home.

Augustine is rapt, pink-faced, with the prospect of a day out. She places her hand on Paul's arm. 'Please, pretty please, *chérie.*'

Paul grumbles, 'The one who drives is always the the chauffeur.' All the same, he will do what she wants. He no longer has the upper hand in their relationship. Over the years, there's been a shift. While he was away, a prisoner-of-war, *Augustine* was in charge, making decisions about housing and the family. She had to raise Juliette and Jojo alone, impose discipline, oversee their education. And Paul? Well, these days he's like almond paste in her hands.

We load up the voiture - a Citroen 2CV, Paul tells us. He bought it second-hand, but it was more expensive than a new one, because that meant he didn't have to wait for it. He's so proud of it, but the car is so little, like an umbrella on wheels. Still, it manages to hold all of us and our picnic basket.

Monique takes a cautious sniff at the interior. I hope she's not going to be car-sick when we travel. But no. She beams, says she likes its smell: leather, cigars and petrol. And as the Citroen speeds along, Francine starts to sing. We all join in. Even Monique. Even me, with my headache.

'Un p'tit village, un vieux clocher
Un paysage si bien cache
Et dans le nuage le cher visage
De mon passé...'

'*A small village, an old church tower*
A hidden landscape
And in the clouds, the dear face
Of my past.'

We stop the car beside a stream, where fallen poplar leaves rush past in patches of copper. Augustine hands me a bottle of red wine, unlabelled, and a small glass, wrapped carefully in a napkin. Then, for dessert, we swallow whole loaves of newly baked bread, inserting squares of dark chocolate into them.

Monique grins at us, chocolate oozing through the gaps in her teeth. She pats her stomach, says it aches with pleasure.

But after lunch, everywhere we go, there's dust, rubble, chaos and confusion. Repairs are under way - although some cathedrals and churches still stand. That's down to robust construction, and the fact that, even in the midst of the bombing, efforts were made to spare them.

When we arrive, Paul helps me out of the Citroen. Well, he could always play the perfect gentleman, when he wanted to. But then he smiles at me, and the tide of wariness between us two old adversaries subsides.

I smile back, and just for a moment, I wonder if Paul will sit up late one evening, and tell me stories about him and Jacques, working together on the farm. Because I know I'd like to hear them. To build, after all these years, a causeway, where friendly feeling might pass. Like Mont St. Michel, which sometimes, after all, decides to be part of the mainland, its marsh and mud.

And suddenly, as we step onto the causeway, there it is. Its stout walls and towers, capped by grey roofs, rise up from the absolute flatness of the surrounding wastes. High-buttressed walls, supported by a great platform on which the abbey buildings stand. Pierre's longed-for model fort, grown to giant's size.

We pass through the entrance gate onto the narrow street, where little houses and shops cling, limpet-like, to its steep slope.

'Biscuits de beurre, biscuits de beurre, broches et porte-clés,' call the tradeswomen. Francine stops at one of the shops and buys herself a ladybird brooch, with three black spots.

'Ladybird, ladybird, Fly away home. Your house is on fire, Your children are flown,' mutters Monique in English. Then, to me, still in English, 'Daddy taught me that.'

'What's that?' says Francine.

'Nothing,' says Monique. 'Here, let me see,' she adds, reaching for the brooch.

'Mais non, Bibendum,' teases Francine, holding it behind her back.

'What did you call me?'

'Bibendum. You know, the Michelin man,' she says, nodding at Monique's thighs, bunching out from beneath her shorts. Or rather, Jojo's shorts, belted round her waist. Because nothing we brought with us fits her at the moment. Too many slices of bread with gruyere cheese.

I frown at Francine, but she just laughs, and throws her arm round Monique. Her movement pulls taut the cotton of her sleeve, accentuates the graceful curve of her shoulder.

Monique holds up her hand against the bright sunlight. It shadows her eyes, which sometimes seem too large, can be disconcerting. But even when she was a baby, her eyes were blue, beneath fluttering, transparent lids, like iris petals.

'All babies have blue eyes,' said Stanley, but all the same, I could tell he was pleased. He thought it meant Monique looked like him, like his mother. I didn't remind him, my mother had blue eyes as well.

Monique's eyes turned a sort of slate grey-blue as she grew older, with a hazel fleck in them that reminded me of a boat, drifting on the sea. Drifting... drifting... when I asked her about her homework. But alight with blue fire when Stanley talked to her about racehorses or told her one of his war stories.

'I don't believe she understands half of what you tell her,' I said to Stanley. 'She's not even six.'

'Yes, she does,' he replied. 'It's all in her eyes.'

The others want to take the guided tour, to wander through vaulted halls and stumble up-and-down stone stairs. So I leave them to it. I cross the cloisters and then slip into the side-chapel, where I kneel down, and confront the statue of Mary.

Madame la Sainte Vierge. Quite different to her incarnation in the Church of Sainte-Marie. The sign says that she's modelled on one found at La Délivrande, where she was buried to save her from the ravages of the Vikings. Here, she's cast in bronze, and is shown praying for the sinners. Her feet are placed on a writhing serpent, which she crushes. But I think that the reddish tinge of her dark gold skin, and the almond shape of her blue eyes give her a look of... well, Maman...

So I offer up a prayer. *'Je vous salue, Marie, pleine de grace...'*

Nothing. Not the wink or the flicker of a painted eye. So I try again.

'Forgive me, Maman,' I say. *'Petite Maman, pardonnez-moi.'* When I was thirteen, I broke her with my anger. But seeing her broken saddened me. I had to learn to love her again.

From somewhere over the haze of lighted candles comes a faint sound, like a sigh. Then there's an explosion of flashing lights. Another migraine aura. And another long-ago Madonna, painted seaweed-green, swims into my mind. Only now she isn't broken. Now she holds out her arms to me and - she's smiling. Smiling through tears, falling down the curved lines of her face. But a statue can't cry. Though my mother often did. She didn't want me to see it, but sometimes she couldn't help it. But her lullaby echoes through clouds of incense. *'Ne pleure pas, petite chose...'* Our reunion. Our mending of what once was damaged. Because sometimes, even when it's broken, it can still be fixed.

But the voice of the history guide cuts into her song:

'St Aubert was bishop of Avranches in the eighth century. He is credited with founding Mont Saint Michel. According to legend, he had a vision in which the Archangel instructed him to build an Oratory on this rocky island at the mouth of the river.' The guide steps forwards. The insistent thump thump of the tourists' feet follows him across the cloisters' stone floor.

My poor head.

'Aubert did not pay attention to this vision at first, until, in exasperation, Michael appeared to him again, this time driving his finger into his skull and ordering him to complete the task.' But no, they're not coming in here. The guide continues: 'The relic of Aubert's skull, complete with the hole where the archangel's finger pierced it, can still be seen in the church of St. Gervais in Avranche. It is generally believed nowadays that the skull is in fact a prehistoric relic, showing evidence of trepanation.'

His voice dies away. I think they're heading towards the oratory, where Aubert is reputedly buried. I wonder if trepanning would help me? Because now my head feels too heavy for my neck. My eyes peer out from behind a wall of pain. But maybe Augustine has a cachet for me in her handbag. So I clatter across cobbles, leave the dungeon darkness of a winding passageway, step out into brilliant sunshine.

After all, it's not too hard to guess where the others are. In a little first-floor restaurant, enjoying a coffee and one of Madame Poulard's famous omelettes. 'You should have one too, Mum,' says Monique. So La Mère Poulard fetches another egg from a black wire basket, cracks it on the edge of a cup, lets it slide down. She whisks it, then dangles it into a pan slick with melted butter. A sudden hiss, then a swirl of yellow. She shakes her omelette over the fire, adds a few herbs, thyme, rosemary, and a little salt and black pepper. The secret, on display for all of us to see, but none of us will ever make omelettes like Madame Poulard.

Delicious, but I can't each much. Instead I gulp down an aspirin with a mouthful of black coffee and then we trudge back down the hill towards the Citroen. Monique links arms with Francine.

'I thought you didn't like her,' I hiss in English.

'I do now,' says Monique simply. 'I prayed to Saint Aubert and now we're friends.'

But later that evening, when it's time for them to go to bed, she stares up at me with imploring blue-grey eyes.

'I want to sit up with you. I want to drink liqueurs with you and *Tante* Augustine,' she says. 'I'm not at all tired.'

How does she know about the liqueurs? Unless it's the scent on my breath when I slip into their room to kiss her good night. Because Augustine always puts a nip of something good into my camomile tea.

'That should make you sleep,' she says, but it never does.

Augustine nods in agreement as I say to Monique,

'Children of your age are never tired.' Then, 'You can't sit up with us,' I add. *Tu n'as pas bonne mine. Tu devras dormir.'* I peer inside her eyelids, check the whites of her eyes. Thankfully, no anaemia. But like me, she has dark circles. Poor little soul, with all those nightmares, she isn't sleeping well either. Not because she doesn't like Francine. But because…because…

'Yes, I miss…'

'Off to bed, *chérie.*'

After the girls have gone to bed, Augustine makes me a nightcap. Stirs a tot of rum into my tea. The vapours of steam waft round her, like incense on an altar. 'Don't you think,' she says, her voice very soft, her eyes very wide, 'that it's time you went back home, to England? Monique needs her father. It's her insecurity about him that's making her cling to you.'

I glare at her. This is our true home, here, *Les Hirondelles.*

'Don't leave it too long,' she continues. 'When Paul came home, after the war, his children hardly knew him. You don't want that for Monique.'

As if Augustine can tell me what to do. She's hardly a paragon of fidelity, the patron saint of wife and motherhood. Though I know how she justifies her relationship with Franz. Paul was gone for five long years. Their best years, their beautiful years. Their young years, when they needed each other most.

Oh Augustine, compassionate, fallen saint, pray for me.

Because, of course, she's right. I should go home. To Stanley.

And as I acknowledge the truth of her words, my excruciating perpetual headache begins to lift. A miracle.

THE MEDALLION

Alain and Juliette turn up at the farm to say goodbye. Whilst Alain stammers out his farewells, I gaze at Juliette. Such strange brown marks across her eyelids. The shape and colour of the wooden spoons I gave her, for her wedding anniversary. I thought the third year was wood, but I made a mistake. It's only leather.

Augustine takes one look at her eldest daughter and drags her into the kitchen. A hurried conference, then Juliette emerges, head bowed, but with a little smile playing at the corners of her mouth.

'I'm pregnant,' she announces.

Francine throws her arms round her sister.

'I'll be an Auntie,' she says. '*Tante* Francine.'

'Will I?' asks Monique.

'No,' says Francine, looking up from Juliette's embrace with glittering eyes. 'You won't.'

Juliette detaches herself from Francine and reaches for Monique.

'Of course you will,' she says, 'Of course my goddaughter can be an auntie.'

'But she isn't related to us,' says Francine, with fine disdain. 'She lives in *Ennnnge-land.*'

'*Ennnnnge-land?*' echoes Monique.

And even though Juliette glares at Francine and protests, 'She's family,' I realise it's definitely time to take my daughter home.

A few days later, we tread down from the ferry's gang plank onto Victoria Pier – and there is Stanley, sauntering towards us with cod-and-chips wrapped up in a newspaper in one hand and a little tin of barley sugar in the other. The sky is blue above him; the sea is blue beside him; the gulls circle overhead. He appears blithe, unconcerned. However, these days he is a little pale and thinner, so that his linen suit hangs off him. On his head, he sports a tartan hat with a bobble.

I'm carrying the suitcase; Monique, the red valise. Then Monique catches sight of her father and runs towards him, shrieking, 'Daddy!'

Stanley catches hold of her and hugs her so hard, he squeezes the breath from her. Then he lets her go.

I approach him more slowly. 'Stanley.'

'Welcome home, sweetheart,' he says. 'I bought you some cod-and-chips. I remembered not to put vinegar on them, like you like.'

'Oh, Stanley, how nice,' I say. 'And you're wearing the hat I bought you in Edinburgh too.' I take the cod-and-chips from Stanley, and he takes the suitcase from me. The barley sugar is for Monique, so she won't be carsick, although actually, she was fine in Paul's Citroën. Together we trudge towards our Mini in the carpark, Monique running ahead of us. Stanley opens the car door. The Saint Christopher medallion glued to the dashboard for safe travel flashes and gleams silver and emerald. Stanley's face flashes and gleams with smile

THE PAPERBACK

'Who are you meeting?' I say.

Mon Dieu, that hairdo! The beehive, she calls it. More like a bird's nest, sprayed with lacquer. My hand slides to my own chignon, neat and wispy.

'Oh, you know, just Sadie and...'

'Her brother, and probably some other boys too,' I say, accidentally stabbing myself with the sewing needle. I feel the blood tingle at my fingertip. 'Tell the truth, Monique. You're not all dressed-up *comme une putain* for Sadie's sake.'

Monique stands still, watching me, while my words prickle in the air between us. The moment lengthens, then she tugs the safety chain loose. She pulls open the front door and goes out, slamming it hard. The glass shudders in its frame.

Mon Dieu. I can't believe I just said that. It doesn't sound like me at all. I shake my head to try and dislodge the memory of Madame Solange, red-eyed, wild-haired, shaking her fist, mouthing obscenities at me in a part-furnished parlour with flickering lamps.

I take a deep breath and switch on the wireless. On Radio 4, a man called Barker is reading aloud from a book about peregrines. '*The peregrines are dying,*' he begins, in his mellifluous baritone. I bite off another length of thread, but now my hands are shaking so much, I can hardly steer it towards the needle's eye. '*Pesticides build up in their tissues, so there's less calcium in their eggshells, which makes them flimsier, more fragile, liable to break.*'

Stanley buys me Mr Barker's book a few days later, for my birthday. I peel off the wrapping paper, admire the neat beige cover with its pen-and-ink and wash illustration. Inside, peregrines blaze across a landscape of close-set print, leaving a trail of redshanks and lapwings, commas and apostrophes, in their wake.

When I've finished reading it, I force the paperback between Monique's *What Katy Did* and the old, illustrated Bible on the shelf in the parlour. Then I make myself a cup of black coffee, trying to ignore the sudden thought that some peregrines squash their eggs in the nest rather than hatch them.

THE BOUQUET

The first time that Monique's boyfriend Simon visits us, I show him all the old pictures of Monique, even her christening and First Communion photographs. Then I pull out another manila folder from the bureau marked *School Reports*.

'Monique tells me you studied languages, like her,' I say as he glances down at the scrawls of *Making Progress* and *Must Try Harder*. 'French and Italian?' Because Simon reminds me of Louis Jourdain with his dark, smooth features, dark floppy hair, and broad, generous mouth. Less suave perhaps, a little more *gauche*, but then he's only young. They both are.

'Spanish and Portuguese,' he replies.

'Well, that's very impressive,' I say. 'I expect you did very well, graduated with Honours, like we want Monique to.'

'I got a Third,' he says, biting a bit of dry skin from the corner of his mouth.

'I expect your parents were very proud, all the same. And your father, he works for...?'

'He's a gardener,' says Simon.

'Oh well,' I say, 'So pleasant to be among the flowers. You must say thank you to him for this beautiful bouquet.' Red and white roses that exude a heady scent, their velvet petals dishevelled by the rain.

Only, if Simon knew me better, knew *my* language of flowers, he'd know I don't care for roses.

236

'I bought those,' he says now.

'You should save your money for Monique,' I say. 'Courting's an expensive business.'

'Well, Monique's worth it,' says Simon, trying to smile. He turns over another page in the family album and lifts the covering sheet. Freed from her tissue-paper prison, my daughter smiles and smiles, her arms clasped round the neck of Augustine's old bobble-furred poodle.

'Yes,' I say. 'And I suppose the Crown Agents pays you well?'

'Not at the moment,' says Simon, with a short laugh. The tips of his ears turn crimson, and for a moment, he becomes very engrossed in the photograph of Monique's patent leather shoes. They're so glossy, they reflect the lawn where she sits, a grey blur, with white daisies.

Just then, Monique returns to the parlour with her grandmother's pink tea-set. With a glance at me, she tells Simon how she always loved it, ever since she was a child.

'That's why Mum bought me a doll's tea-set that looked just like it. Though it was so precious, I never dared to play with it.'

'It's funny how attached people can become to objects,' he replies. He starts to tell a story about his time in Spain, how, though he had no money, he bought himself two carved wooden figures of Don Quixote and Sancho Panza and kept them on his windowsill. They were his friends, companions for him in a strange land while he struggled to learn its language.

But when he arrived back home in England, his mum confiscated the wooden figures.

'Because I hadn't bought her a present. I was too broke,' he said.

'I can't believe she did that,' gasps Monique, with another glance at me.

'I think it's all right,' I say.

'It's fine,' says Simon, with a proper smile now, one that reaches his eyes. 'I don't mind. Besides, one day, when she's not looking, I'll take them back.'

237

THE POSTCARD

Sudden clatter of Monique's sandals on the stairs.

I look up from the gingham skirt I'm trying to mend - my last chance before she goes back to university. Out of the corner of my eye, I glimpse an old postcard tucked into a silver frame. *La Joconde,* sent from Paris, where Alain and Juliette went for their honeymoon.

Monique pokes her head round the door. She has something important to tell me, she says. About her and Simon.

Does she want to tell me that he's leaving England? But I know that already. Last time he visited, I asked him to dig over a corner of my back garden, to make it ready for the rockery. As the bright edge of the spade bit into the soil, he muttered something about how he'd be on double pay when they send him out to Kenya.

'Kenya? So you'll be leaving us?' I said, trying to keep the note of relief out of my voice.

Simon didn't answer for a moment. Then,

'I think I'll stop now, for a beer,' he said.

'See if you can keep going until supper,' I said. 'You know what they used to say during the war, "Dig for Victory."'

'Patience isn't my virtue,' he replied.

I remember this conversation now, as Monique stands in front of me, smiling and waiting, looking just like the Lady in the Louvre. Hopeful and fearful and craving – what? Three russet apples in a morning?

Mon Dieu. She isn't, is she? *Enceinte?*

'Are you preg…..?'

Monique interrupts. 'As soon as I've finished my degree, I'm going to join Simon in Africa. And,' she adds, 'that means we'll have to bring the wedding forward.'

Africa. I release my clenched fingers, stare at the indentations of nails across my palm. That's not what Katy did next. The storybook heroine went to Europe. It revealed itself to her like a set of picture postcards or the stereoscope's

238

double-imaged cards. The Tower of London. Click. The Louvre. Click. The Sistine Chapel. Click.

'I thought you wanted a long engagement,' I say now. 'You're not even twenty-one yet.'

Two young girls peep out from behind a heavy brocade curtain, their whole lives ahead of them. Click.

Monique throws her arms round me. Her chin is pointed, digs into my shoulder. Her crinkly plait is very black, as though it's been dripped from a bottle of ink. It crackles, heavy with static, against the new wool of my cardigan.

'You and Dad will be all right without me, won't you?'

Kenya. Click. The stereoscope's light goes out, and I'm in the dark again. I glance down at my lap, at the blue-and-white checked squares of her skirt.

'Maybe I can make your wedding-dress,' I say, at last.

Monique lifts her head from my shoulder, her cheeks burning red, her eyes gleaming black.

'Oh Mum, would you?'

Later, I watch her walk to the car's open door. Her shoulders are slumped from the weight of her case. She's wearing a thin white blouse, with flounces at the cuffs and collars, and a long, flowing crepe skirt, embroidered with flowers.

Pain is a red rose, the flame-tips of a chrysanthemum, the sharp points of petals and thorns. *She loves me. She loves me not.*

Stanley hoists the red valise onto the roof rack, then eases himself into the Mini, ready to drive her to the station. He crouches over the wheel while Monique presses her face to a window full of pale sunlight and the quick moving shadows of trees. Then I screw my eyes up against the sun's white dazzle. I can't see her anymore, but I keep waving.

THE PAPER SLEEVE

I make my way back along the path that shimmers like a spilled bolt of silk. And as I pull the cardboard box out from the bottom of the wardrobe, I imagine the play of light against the cloth. I take it out, shake free its folds, and for one brief moment, there it is, a white rush of wonder.

Then I lay it out on the carpet, and my heart sinks. Augustine's wedding dress carried the scent of summer, of sun and rain. Her clothes chest in Ver was sweet-smelling cedarwood. But this length of silk is musty, redolent of mothballs and mahogany. I hold it up, begin to twist it, this way and that.

Perhaps if I unpick what's left of the hem, there'll be enough material for a bodice or a sleeve. So I start to pull out the stitches. They leave little holes, like clawed fox tracks in the snow. Then I pin a paper sleeve to the hem, a thin, white shadow, smooth to the touch. I trace its outline with tailor's chalk, even go so far as to reach for the pinking shears.

Then I pause, push my *lunettes* into my chignon, rub my eyes. What's it all for? A faded dream of cloth. A ghost in the grey daylight.

Once, when I was a child, ten or eleven perhaps, and alone in the antiques shop, I wrapped this piece of silk round my body, over and over again. Then I tried to catch a glimpse of myself in the froth-framed mirror, beneath its patches of rust. The shop door was open to the sunlight, Papa was whistling in the street, his cane tapping over the cobbles, but suddenly I was afraid.

I was certain that hidden beneath the folds of the silk were the bones of Marlene's little brother from *The Juniper Tree.*.

Then Papa returned to the shop, with a parcel of books under his arm, smiling and pleased to see me. Nothing bad had happened, and I forgot, or told myself I had forgotten.

Now I unpin the paper, stretch the cloth out flat. After all, it's thick with dust, yellowing with neglect. I said I'd do it, but… there are some promises I can't keep.

I rub my cheek. I can still feel the imprint of Monique's kisses. *She loves me.*

THE ENGAGEMENT RING

At the manor house, Sophy takes Monique's engagement ring in her hands. Then she closes her eyes.

'I see a green forest, and dark men with gleaming teeth,' she whispers, 'and a house set far back among palm trees.'

Simon grins and takes a sip of brandy from a glass resting in front of him on a tarnished silver tray. But Monique frowns. She knows her Aunty Sophy already knows she's going to Africa.

'What else?' she says.

Sophy opens her brown eyes very wide. Then, 'Young man,' she says, turning to Simon, 'None of this holds any interest for you.' Simon puts down his glass, starts to protest, but Sophy turns to Monique and says, 'He knows something that you haven't realised yet.'

'What's that?'

'That we carry within us all the wonders that we seek outside.'

Simon nods. Sophy locks eyes with him. 'So I'm sure,' she says, reaching over, patting his arm with her slender, ringless fingers, 'you'd much rather have a look round the house than listen to us. There are some masks and ebony elephants along the corridor in the East Wing.'

Simon kisses Monique's cheek, then gets up and leaves the room. But he's scarcely pulled the door shut when Sophy hisses, 'He's not the right one.'

'What do you mean?' asks Monique.

'If you marry him,' says Sophy, fingering the diamond solitaire, 'You'll never meet your true soulmate.'

'B-b-but I love him,' Monique protests, looking first at Sophy, then at me.

'Sophy,' I interrupt, 'Don't tell her things like that. She doesn't need to hear them.'

'How can you say that, Odette?' asks Sophy, 'After what happened to Jacques?'

Now it's my turn to stare at her. Of course, over the years I've told her many things about my previous life in Ver. I think

I even said, 'There's always one you can't have.' But I'm sure I never mentioned Jacques by name.

'Who's Jacques?' asks Monique.

'Augustine's brother,' I say, remembering our kiss in the shadow of the hayloft, the day he went away. 'A boy you never knew.'

'A boy I never knew?' Monique repeats. Then she looks at Sophy. 'If I do marry Simon,' she says, 'No, *when* I marry Simon, what happens then?'

'You never meet your true love,' Sophy says, sliding the ring onto the tip of her finger, letting the diamond make rainbows of the chandelier's fractured light. Then she yawns. 'If you do marry Simon,' she says, 'I see another house, near a park with a stream. And babies, one and two, pink and blue.'

She pauses. For dramatic effect? Or is there something else? Something she doesn't want to say? Because her brown eyes darken, become blacker than I've ever seen them, so black it's impossible to distinguish the pupil from the iris.

But, after all, I don't think I want to know. So I glance away from her, at the white porcelain ornaments on the mantelpiece, at the white lace of crocheted cloth, folded along the back of the *chaise-longue*.

Sophy yawns again, right in our faces. 'I'm so sorry,' she says. 'I stayed up all night working on a commission. A painting of Olivia's cat. And now...' Her head nods and dips. 'Let me just shut my eyes for a moment,' she mumbles.

Her chin sinks into the folds of her black tunic, until it's resting on the chain where she keeps her own wedding-ring. Suddenly she's asleep.

The droop of her head, the sag of her shoulders, makes her look old. There are silver threads running through the abundant brown curls.

Oh Sophy, don't grow old. You're my dearest friend in England. Don't go away from me into being old.

Monique nudges me.

'Come and help me find Simon,' she says. 'You know the house better than I do.'

We take the third turning down a long, silent corridor. There are doors at both ends. We push open the one half-concealed by a tapestry of a forest where fruit and blossom grow on the same bough.

The door opens onto an oval staircase. Our feet clop on the marble, then clatter across the scarred tiles of the great hall. Then out into another corridor, where, through archways and open doorways, I glimpse suites of chambers unfolding, one out of another, like a series of Chinese boxes.

Finally we reach the East Wing. The heads of stags hunted and captured in the Vienna Woods vie for space on painted white panels, their antlers interlocking. But they soon give way to masks with strange, elongated features, and elephants carved from ivory and jade.

Simon smiles when he sees us and puts his arm round Monique's shoulder. Through the open doorway of a guestroom, he points out the canopy of a four-poster bed, hung with peacock feathers. Then we twist and turn on a staircase so white, it dazzles. For a moment, it's as if we're walking among the facets of a cut diamond.

Then we're lost.

'Typical,' says Simon. He tugs open a high, lattice window and looks out. 'I can't see the garden,' he says. 'Just a little, shut-off courtyard.'

'Let me see,' I say. But, after all, I'm not tall enough to look out of the window. So I set off in search of something to stand on.

Inside an old oak chest with brass feet like lion's claws, I discover a *pri-dieu* embroidered with a faded *fleur de lys*. I thump it, and clouds of dust rise up. Then I carry it back to the window, only to find that Monique and Simon have disappeared.

But music, delicate, silvery tones, reverberates from the end of another corridor. A long-ago waltz, sweet and sad. It leads me on, to the anteroom where Sophy keeps her collection of jewellery boxes. On the window-ledge, there's a white sandalwood box, with an open lid. A minute lord and lady pirouette in time to the tune, beat out by tiny tongues of raised steel.

Hem-Hem. As I clear my throat, Simon and Monique draw apart, her face hidden by the dark curtain of her hair. Then, as the music fades, we hear Sophy calling, 'Odette, Monique, where are you?'

THE PEARL CHOKER

Monique peers into the mirror of my dressing-table. Her face is flushed beneath her wedding-veil. Her black curls fall in thick clusters all round her shoulders. She's so lovely, and she doesn't even know it. But when I open my mouth to tell her, 'You're wearing the wrong necklace,' tumbles out.

Monique raises her eyes to heaven.

That's not what I meant to say. Though you are wearing the wrong necklace. A gift from Simon's mother, all hearts and flowers and stars on a silver chain. More like a charm bracelet. And I don't want you to wear silver on your wedding-day. If you do, people will think we can't afford gold. That's not what I want for you, at all.'

'What do you suggest?' Monique drawls.

'There's a necklace here that used to belong to my mother,' I say. I reach inside the top drawer of the dressing-table, pull out a long green box. I flip back the lid, let my fingertips revel in the crushed velvet interior, the tiny teardrop beads that make up a rope of pearls.

'A choker?' says Monique. 'It looks so heavy. The other one's more delicate.'

'But this will go better with the pearl beading on your dress,' I say.

'Oh,' says Monique, 'That thing.' I bite my lip. She still minds, then, about my broken promise. But I think I'll give them her grandmother's tea-set as a wedding gift. Then she'll be happy.

'Trust me,' I say. 'I've got a good eye for detail.'

So Monique loops back her hair and veil and unhooks the clasp on the silver chain. She reaches for the pearl choker. I help her fasten it, and together we stand, mother and daughter, in front of the mirror. Then she leans forwards, traces the outline of the choker with her fingertips. The glass spills her beauty back into her face.

'You're right, Mum,' she whispers.

I smile at her in the mirror. She's going to have a beautiful wedding-day.

But years later, when she's ill and I'm looking after her children, I find her diary. It tells a different story.

THE PIPE

I take down Mademoiselle Madeleine's copy of the Brothers Grimm from the shelf in the parlour. After all these years, it's still as black, red and white as if it was new, still those same *swastika* colours. I start to read it over again, from the beginning, the first story, the story of stories, *The Juniper Bird*.

Over in his armchair beside the hearth, Stanley reaches for his pipe. But one look from me stays his hand. I know he wants to pack it with tobacco, press it down into the bowl, light it, draw on it, discolour the wallpaper with his smoke. That man. These days, it's as if everything he thinks has to be sucked in through his pipe.

I wonder what happened to the real Stanley, my Stanley... When we were first married, he used to drop light kisses in the hollow of my throat. One time, he said he could smell nettles through my pores, a clean, green scent, because of all the tea. And then, when my belly grew round, he rested his face against it - as if my warmth and smell was his home.

Ver was always my home. My seaside village with its deep, rutted roads, a path across the cliffs, then a sudden drop down onto the shingle and sand. Like a birth. The cry of the gulls. The sun on my face. The taste of salt on my mouth.

Your mouth. Your lips speaking against my belly. You said it reminded you of an apple, its roundness, its milk-white flesh, its faint pinkness.

'Can you hear the baby?' I said.

'Maybe,' you said. 'Or maybe it's just your heart.'

I started to say something. *Love Love Love* was what I started to say.

But now... now I ignore you, keep turning over the gold-edged pages, trying to find the part where sister and brother are reunited, where they return to their home, rejoicing. Only, somehow, I go past the place, reach the end of the story, without finding it.

The reunion hasn't happened. So I put the book down on the shelf and watch as Stanley takes out a silver spike-tipped instrument, then something else that resembles a spoon. He starts to clean his pipe. But as the spiky thing glints in the light, I suddenly realise something. The problem with Sophy's gift of prophecy is that my real life never glittered like the one that she predicted. Just a few lit-up moments, that's all I ever had - like the images inside the stereoscope.

The rest is darkness.

THE TELEPHONE

'*Aidez-moi*,' I say, a few days later, cradling the receiver against my chin. My lungs have stopped breathing. My heart's stopped beating. But I swallow hard, manage to force down some air.

'I'm sorry, you'll have to repeat that,' says the voice on the other end of the line. '*Aidez-moi*,' I say, and then I remember. This is England.

'Help me, please. My husband needs an ambulance.' As soon as I've said the words, my heart starts up again. I feel it beating, all through me. Because I know my husband is dead.

He woke up just now and was sick down the side of the bed. When I came back with a sponge and some towels, he was gone. Just like that.

I didn't know what to do. I dialled Monique's number first, then put the phone down. Wrong number. I'd forgotten the dialling code. So I tried again, stammered out what had happened. And Monique became my mother, insisting, very firmly, that I ring for an ambulance.

Now I rest my cheek against Stanley's hands. They're so cold, but then he often had cold hands. Stanley Winterhands,

246

I used to call him. When they warmed up, you knew it was spring. I press my lips against the veins on his cold hands, try to ignore the faded tattoo on his wrist. The blue rose that looks more like a bruise. Tears leak out of my eyes, soak into his skin. I shut his eyes. Now I hear in song the answer to the long-ago riddle: '*A rock needs no rain, and yet it can grow. / True love can blossom, bloom through the years/ And a heart can yearn, cry without tears.*'

But he isn't Stanley anymore. Instead, I glimpse the death mask of the unknown soldier that arrived in Papa's shop all those years ago. And then, for one awful moment, Papa's face, colourless and creased, against starched hospital sheets.

There's nothing to do now except wait for them all to arrive.

THE UNDERCLOTH

It doesn't take long for the ambulance men to pronounce Stanley dead. Simon helps the undertaker to carry him down the stairs. Just as well I had that new banister rail put in. Something for them to grab hold of, if they start to fall.

I sit at the dining room table, head in hands, staring at the pattern of flowers on the cloth. The plastic undercloth I've only ever found in Normandy. But I can't make out the shapes anymore - just patterns of red and green. As they blur, I rub my temple. If I can stroke away the headache, perhaps the rest of me will stop hurting.

Monique clatters into the room. I don't look up, but she pulls my hands away from my face.

'Why did you wait so long to call the ambulance?' she says.
'What?'
'Why did you wait so long? If you'd called them earlier, they might have been able to help.'

I'm not sure if she's right, or not. Though it did take me a while to fetch the towels. I thought I heard a bird, scratching across the roof-tiles. Then I was frightened. I stood still for a moment and listened. I needed to know. I needed to know if it sang the Juniper bird's song.

But I can't say that now. Instead I mumble, 'I didn't think it was anything serious. He saw the GP up at the surgery today. They said it was acid indigestion.'

She isn't listening, anyway. All the bones in her face are rigid and her deep-set blue eyes are unrecognisable - nothing at all of her father or my mother staring out of them. So I reach over and touch her shoulder. She shakes my hand off and glares at me. Then the anger falls out of her eyes. Her face creases up. Her lower lips trembles.

The front door slams and Simon steps into the room.

'Stop that,' he snaps at Monique but at least he hides her in his arms, tries to make her pain go away. But I see it travel all through her, to the very ends of her long dark curls. And I hear it. A whimpering sound like a baby or a bird, a thin cry, like a gull.

I glance down, start to twist the buttons of my black cardigan. I'm a widow now. Who'll comfort me?

THE FOX-COLOURED CARDIGAN

I'm wearing the fox-coloured cardigan that Monique used to like, when she was a little girl. The wool is soothing against my skin, jagged and smooth, as I pace the length of the hospital corridor. When I reach the end, a solid-looking man in blue overalls nods at me.

'All right, love?' he says, then grinds his mop against the side of the bucket.

But these aren't tears, I want to say to him. It's just the scent of disinfectant, making my eyes water. Though I wouldn't have thought they'd need to worry about germs, here.

Monique turns away from me when I approach the bed. And - oh - her long dark curls have gone. She asked the hospital hairdressers to cut them all off. And they did. The doctor says it's good for her to have her own way at the moment.

She wipes away the kiss I give her with the back of her hand. She refuses to meet my gaze. But I try not to let it hurt me. Because I know she isn't my Monique at the moment. My Monique's a proud young woman in a black gown and mortarboard. A graduate. A French teacher. A beautiful bride wearing her grandmother's pearl choker. Not this little boy impostor, wide-eyed and terrified.

I reach for her hands again, try to warm them. Because now she looks just like Pierre...

And Simon... He used to be so good-looking, like a film-star, like Louis Jourdain, but these days...

When I get back from the hospital, he wants to make sausages and mash for dinner.

'Let me do it,' I say. 'The children don't like lumpy mash potato.'

I approach the potato rack. But the *pommes de terre* have green eyes, and long, snake-like roots dangle between the mesh of red plastic.

'We can't eat these,' I say. 'When they're green, they're poisonous.'

Simon turns abruptly red. 'It's you who's poisonous,' he says as the veins bulge in his temples. 'It's all your fault that Monique's... Monique's...' He gives a great, shuddering sigh.

I want to say – I know what I want to say, '*Mon pauvre, je suis désolée...*' But the anger in his eyes is so intense, my own anger springs to meet it. I scream something at him in French.

I don't remember what. I never remember when I've said something bad.

Simon stares at me for a moment, as if he can't quite believe what I've just said. Then he draws his sleeve across his face, and mutters something which sounds like, 'Old witch.' Which is worse, really, than when my grandson called me 'Frogface,' though that made me cry for ages.

Well, like I should have told the man in overalls, I'm not crying now.

Though when I'm back in my own home, I peep into the dressing-table mirror. Not that there's any reassurance in my reflection. Searching for the face I've always known, I don't find it. I'm just not lovely anymore. Sparse grey hair sprouts from a little, wizened face. And my skin is creased and lined, like a withered russet apple.

Apple of the earth. The old crone's poisonous apple.

THE CARD

I remember my blue-eyed girl running home from school, drawstring PE bag in one hand, a card she'd made for Mothering Sunday in the other.

'Mummy, Daddy, Me,' she gabbled as she showed it to me. I'm four foot nine in high heels, but she'd drawn me taller than Stanley.

'It's wonderful,' I should have said. 'How clever you are.'

'*Pas mal*,' is what I actually said. Not bad. And then all the hope-light faded from her eyes. I put the card in a kitchen drawer, and forgot about it, for years and years and years.

Until now, when she's in hospital, and then I try, *Mon Dieu* how I try, to find it.

I even pray to Saint Anthony of Padua. Not that he takes any notice. Because we're not in Park Cottage anymore. Not even in the shiny Shrewsbury bungalow, all mod-cons. So, even though I tip drawers inside out, turn the whole kitchen upside-down, Monique's card is gone. Gone for good. Lost now, and too late to do anything about it.

To control my nerves, I start to wander in imagination through this new house, that we bought to be nearer the grandchildren. And Monique, of course. One by one, I list all the possessions I've accumulated over the years: my larder, china cabinets, cupboards. My inherited antiques. My well-tended furniture. But it doesn't work. That forgotten drawer. That sealed-off space inside my heart. There are gaps in my life that can never be filled.

THE RING-BINDER

A few days later, still looking for that card, this time at Monique's house, what do I find? Her old diary.

Tucked away inside a recipe ring-binder, with all the plastic peeling at the edges. Of course I read it. I know I shouldn't. I know. But - well - I wipe the diary free of crumbs and break the padlock on the front. Wrinkle my nose at the cheap scent from the pink pages - and…take a look.

'Granny, Granny, it's time for *tartines*,' James shouts, running into the kitchen.

'In a minute,' I say, managing to decipher one of Monique's few legible sentences. *'Crying for something you can't have.'* How on earth did she pass her exams, with handwriting like that? And mostly, it's peculiar stuff. A muddle of scribbles and doodles and fragments of phrases. *'A wedding-dress, with leg-of-mutton sleeves.'* And scraps of stories. Bits of dreams. Poetry, I suppose, but no rhyme or reason, hard to make sense of it, really.

'Mummy always lets us have something to eat at four o' clock,' chimes in Rachel.

'Well, your mother isn't here,' I snap. Then I quickly look up from the diary, 'I'm so sorry, *chérie*. I didn't mean that.'

Rachel tries to smile, but the startled look remains in her tear-bright eyes.

'Mother in tears at the wedding. Dad said, 'He who pays the piper…'

Did Stanley really say that? It doesn't sound like him. It makes me think of the Pied Piper. That I read to Jojo and Juliette. I put the diary down next to the cutting board and hold my hands out to my grandchildren. James, a miniature version of Stanley. And Rachel, like no-one else at all in the world, except, perhaps, me.

They pull me towards the fridge. We take the bread out of the bag and put it in the toaster. When it pops up, James tests the knife against his thumb. Rachel digs another knife into a pot of blackberry jam. She licks the jam from the blade.

'Careful,' I say. 'Don't cut your tongue.' While they're crunching toast, I turn back to the diary, flick through the pages. The early part's more of a sketchbook, really. Drawings of women with long, flowing hair, stars, moons, pastry-cutter people and teapots. Children's drawings I glance up again.

James is swirling his crust round the edge of the plate, to mop up the remnants of butter. Then back to the diary. Towards the end, there are certain phrases copied from biology textbooks, just showing off, I suppose. Then, on a clean page, a whole paragraph, dated some twenty-five years ago:

'A memory? (Monique writes) *A real memory or was it a dream? Anyway, I want something - I don't remember what. A rabbit, maybe? And I'm crying, crying, can't stop crying (spoilt little girl!) because Mother won't let me have one. And yes, I suppose I am making a terrible racket. So Mother grabs a paperknife. And holds out her arm. And says, 'Is this what you want, that I should cut off my arm? Because Mon Dieu, I don't know how else to make you keep quiet.' And it all seems so real, so vivid. And I can't remember if it's a dream, or not.'*

I snap shut Monique's diary.

'What's wrong, Granny?' asks Rachel. 'Your face is funny. Do you feel sick?'

I nod. 'I'll have some dry toast,' I say. 'That'll help.'

But my hands are shaking so much, I can't make the handle on the toaster go down. Rachel has to do it for me.

Oh Monique. Of course it was a dream, *mon enfant*. When I was a child, I used to escape from life, the realities of life, by reading fairy tales. As long as I believed they contained all the answers to my every need, I felt safe. For a time, they completely altered the tenor of my mind, rendering it as shifting, various and multi-coloured as the plumage of an exotic bird, or the tilt of a kaleidoscope. It became almost impossible for me to view the world in a simple, realistic way.

Then I grew up. I learned that dreams, no matter how vivid, are just dreams. But how to tell you that, Monique, now you're in hospital? How to tell you that what you keep telling the doctors isn't true?

Because they'll keep you on medication, won't let you go home until you stop saying it, stop believing it,

'My mother, she killed me.'

THE BLUE-BACKED NOTEBOOK

All the girls at Rachel's convent school are doing French Exchanges. Francine's daughter Justine, she's eleven now, the same age as Rachel, came over to England for a visit earlier this year. We took her to see the Tudor ovens at Hampton Court. And now Rachel and I are going to Ver-Sur-Mer.

I peer over the railings, at the back and forth swish of the blue-grey sea. When we reach the mid-point of *La Manche* we'll exchange our English for our French selves.

Rachel's long brown hair dips into the pages of her notebook. She glances up. Her mother's eyes, that same blue that takes its colour from the sea. But it's so easy with this one. Why couldn't it have been like that with Monique?

Perhaps that's what grandchildren are. Our second chances for the mistakes we make with our own children.

'Are your practising your French?' I ask Rachel, smiling at the memory of her *San fairy ann*, her *bon jure*, and *silver plate*. Her *mercy*.

Rachel shakes her head.

'It was supposed to be a diary of the trip,' she says, 'but we haven't gone very far yet. So I'm writing a story about the ghost at school.'

'The ghost?'

'Yes. They say she was a nun who fell in love with a man and got pushed off the belltower by another nun. The Grey Lady, they call her.'

I smile. So she's going to be a writer, is she? A better one than Stanley, I hope. But the name The Grey Lady, pulls me up short. That's me. I remember now, when Monique had been back home from hospital for a few months, I passed James and his school-friend on the stairs.

'Eugh – what's that?' said the school-friend.

'That's my grandmother,' said James.

'Your Ghost Granny,' said the school-friend.

Yes. A Grey Lady, returning to her former haunts. Because I'm seventy-seven years old and I know that this is the last crossing I'll ever make to Normandy. And perhaps the last time

I'll ever hear Augustine's voice, singing along to her ancient wind-up gramophone.

> *'When Nature has turned green again.*
> *When swallows homeward wing their way,*
> *I love to see my Normandy,*
> *The country where I saw the light of day.'*

But for now, the sea seems the right place for us ghosts and hybrids, floating somewhere between England and France.

THE TAP

After all, it isn't Francine who comes to meet us at Le Havre, but Juliette. She kisses us solemnly on both cheeks.

So does her daughter, Marguerite. At twenty-six, she's no taller than my granddaughter at eleven.

Of course, Juliette herself is a tiny woman.

But Marguerite…sparse hair, dry skin, flat features. Down's syndrome, they call it nowadays. Mongolism, they used to call it, back when I was young. She rubs her cracked lips against our cheeks and smiles.

'*Bonjour,*' she says, and then gabbles a mangled salad of French and nonsense words, her own slang.

Her father Alain died a few weeks before she was born. And since his heart-attack, Paul can't do much manual labour anymore. So these days, it's Juliette who runs the farm for her mother. Fragile, tiny, indomitable: I never met anyone with so much courage as Juliette.

We clamber into the van. My granddaughter takes a wary seat in the back, next to Marguerite. Perhaps she remembers the girl roaring at them through the banisters, she and her brother screaming happily, 'Marguerite's a monster.'

We had to explain to them why they shouldn't call her that.

Many years ago, before Rachel was born, Stanley and I brought Marguerite a huge doll in a golden dress. Straight away, she snatched it from us and undressed it. Since she's like Jojo, a perpetual child, an egg that never hatches, I sometimes think we might just as well bring her the same doll, over and over, every time we visit.

But no. This year, my granddaughter's brought Marguerite a jewellery box.

'*Si belle,*' I said, 'But why give her that?'

Rachel looked at me 'I want Marguerite to have something that makes her feel pretty,' she replied. 'Something that any girl would have.'

Any girl. But Marguerite 's not that, is she? Still, if she never changes, some things do.

At the foot of the hill, after the bridge, begins a road newly planted with beech trees, which leads directly to some recently built houses. Then we circle round some railings, where the *château* nestles against a gravel path. A statue of Diana, the huntress, stares at us through the railings, with her finger to her lips. And the brass plate gleams on the gatepost. The owners' names are different now, but the *château* is still the finest house in the district.

On the other side of the square are posters with Gothic lettering, advertising ancient inns, traditional cider and Calvados. *La Mere*'s this and that, everything from new-laid eggs to strawberry jam. Then the van tilts round another sharp corner and we sweep into Ver-Sur-Mer's Place d'Or. Past the village church, with its wooden roof beginning to rot at the top, its paintwork, pitted with black. Past the cemetery, with the family graves. More gravel here too, covering over the grass.

I wish they hadn't done that.

There's a pavement now, streetlamps and bus-stops. Road signs, cafés, and a social club.

Across the road are the pharmacy and the baker's. Oh. The baker's gone. And Monsieur Rolland's pharmacist window, which used to be full of ancient glass jars, red and green, now sports a tub of whistle-pops and a plastic leg wearing a sheer-weave nylon stocking.

I remember mine and Augustine's gravy stockings, and I start to smile.

Half a kilometre later, there's the sudden scent of grass, wet earth and manure. Now tall poplars and chestnut trees flick like feathers as the wind stirs them. Then we proceed slowly down a long rutted road, past the sacred spring.

The white stone pillars welcome us back to the farm. The van slides past the henhouse, the hayloft. The farmhouse floats on its green lawn, its beds of purple daisies and pink snapdragons.

I look towards the wasteland for the white blossoming tree, where Augustine and I played at First Communions and weddings. Where Augustine kissed a German soldier and Yvette threw up in the nettles.

But something acid and bitter jabs at my insides. The wasteland's gone. Flattened, levelled out. Even my tree's been chopped down. Because they're building a guesthouse. The farm hasn't been doing so well lately, and they need to make some money.

But me - I need a space for my green, alluring memories, my broken dreams.

Due to the building work, Augustine and Juliette have decided that we won't be staying here, after all. So after we've said our *bonjours* and *au revoirs,* handed over our *cadeaux,* we're traipse along the road to Francine's house.

Past my mother's old cottage. Its windowpanes are dust-smeared and cracked. Obviously, the holiday company Paul and I sold it to aren't doing so well these days either. They don't bother to keep it in a good repair, and so it stays empty. But I pause for a moment and turn on the outside tap. Though now there's no cool, baptismal promise of water. The pipes creak and then rusty liquid dribbles out through my fingers, sluggish and brown.

THE JEWELLERY-BOX

A porcelain cat in a black velvet pouch for Augustine. My granddaughter chose it herself, bought it with her own pocket-money. Cufflinks for Paul, the perfect gift for a retired gentleman farmer.

Scottish shortbread for Francine, because she always gives us Normandy biscuits thick with butter, yet never eats any herself.

A silver brooch for Juliette, shaped like a pen's squiggle. She turns it over, lets it sparkle in the light. 'It's very nice,' she says, at last. She glances at her work-worn hands. 'I don't get many opportunities to wear jewellery, but still…'

For Justine, a heart-shaped garnet on a burgundy ribbon. *'J'aime bien ton petit coeur,'* she says to Rachel. 'I like your little heart.'

And then, finally, Marguerite removes the padded jewellery-box from its cellophane. She disregards the pearl beads, the pale blue satin, in her effort to open the lid.

My granddaughter watches her, biting her lip.

Marguerite pulls back the lid and stares inside the empty box. She tugs at the runched-up satin interior.

'It's to put things inside,' my granddaughter says, in a rush. 'Whatever you like. Even this, if you want.' She gestures at the porcelain cat. Then a silver glint gives her pause. There's a mirror inside the lid of the box.

'Oh, I didn't know that was there,' I say. 'She'll break it. She'll hurt herself.'

'*Bah.* You worry too much,' says Juliette.

Marguerite peers at her reflection. No rapture, no disgust, just curiosity. She touches the silver glass, then rubs the smooth satin against her cheek. She starts to grin. '*C'est beau,*' she says at last. '*Tu es très gentille.*'

Rachel gives her a tremulous smile.

THE CHANTICLER MOSAIC

Justine and Rachel share a room at the top of Francine's house. A wicker chair that they particularly love hangs from the ceiling. And a special fan-shape of blue glass is fixed above their door. Along the corridor, there's a beautiful black-and-white mosaic with an embossed golden Chanticler.

I tap across him in the middle of the night. There's a terrible pressure on my bladder and I need the *cabinet*. Though to get there, I have to pass through the room where Francine and her husband Vincenzo sleep. While I'm there, I accidentally tread on a loose floorboard. Francine sits up suddenly. Her pale face gleams with alarm.

'*Je vais faire pipi*,' I whisper. Francine nods, sighs and settles back into sleep.

I reach the staircase, grope for the banister, make my way down. The third stair creaks too. If I open the back door, will I find myself a girl again, with Minouche, chained up and howling in the yard? But of course, there's no dog outside, nothing but the moon, hiding, nun-like, behind a veil of cloud.

Whatever happened to Maman's old friend Thérèse? Did Maman ever hear from her again? And then there's Yvette… is she standing outside in the moonlight, clutching the torn-up pieces of her anonymous letter, saying,

'I'm so sorry *ma pauvre*. Really, I didn't mean it…'

THE PORCELAIN FLOWERS

I know I won't ever see Yvette again. The next day, Francine tells me she had a stroke six months ago, and now she's in a nursing home in Bayeux. Oh, I suppose she's being cared for, well enough, but she might not recognise me - even if I were brave enough to go and see her.

Too many questions, and Francine doesn't know all the answers. But in the afternoon, she offers to take us all to the re-built *château*. So we drive up to the tall, white wrought iron gates. We peer through them at the pink manor house with its ninety-nine windows. But the gates stay shut.

Bah. Francine should have checked the opening times.

Instead, she drops Justine and Rachel in town and drives me back to the church. I walk beneath its shadowed porch. Those two marble plaques outside the door, they're new. One is in memory of the English soldiers who shed their blood on our sands. The other commemorates the French soldiers killed in the last war.

Oh. Jacques's name is on it.

I make the sign of the cross, say a few words of prayer, then walk away from the church, towards the cemetery. I search out Maman's grave, over in the corner, beneath the hawthorn tree.

When Stanley came to Ver for Francine's wedding, he was appalled by my mother's neglected grave. He used to take flowers every week to the family plot in the Protestant churchyard. He trimmed the patch of turf round the grey stone, kept it neat. But all Maman had was one dry flower hanging down from a metallic hoop cross.

'Not even a headstone,' he said, with a questioning look. 'You must buy some porcelain flowers, some pink and red roses, perhaps some daisies,' he added.

'I don't like them much,' I replied.

'But it's a way of showing respect,' he said. 'I know you're not here to look after it, but at least the porcelain flowers will honour her memory, will live on even when we're gone.' I remembered that's how I felt about my father's antiques, after he died. So I did what Stanley suggested, bought some porcelain flowers, arranged them over her grave - and my heart was lighter for it.

Now I shake the soil and dust from their sharp, frilled edges and listen to the breeze, trying to catch the sound of my mother's lullaby.

THE WATCH

Later, I walk back to the farm, and spend the evening with Augustine. *Bavarder et tricoter.* Chatting and knitting. Watching the embers fade in the hearth.

Though the kitchen's been rebuilt, it doesn't look that different to me. Just a new cooker squeezed in next to the range. And a new fridge, bright white that juts out behind the back door. But then, not everything was destroyed in the war. Same wooden table, same carved dresser stacked with plates and bowls. Even the same marble shelf, where the eggs are still kept.

Bah. Too much attachment to objects, I scold myself. They're not really a substitute for people. Papa found that out when he opened his antiques shop, after his first wife died. And nothing here consoles me for the loss of Madame Solange. Nor the porcelain flowers for Maman.

But then, objects survive - not people.

As the afternoon becomes evening, Jojo enters the kitchen through the side door, followed by his basset hound. Augustine gets up and props a chair against the kitchen door, to keep the dog inside.

'I don't want him shedding hairs all over the furniture,' she says.

Vain attempt. There are many doors to this house, and none of them stay shut.

'Mmm-aman, Mm-aman, Ma-mman,' Jojo stammers as Augustine pours him a glass of cider. Her hand trembles. I offer to do it for her, but she shakes her head, and grips her arm steady with her other hand.

'*Voila*,' she says, pushing the glass towards him.

He drains it in one gulp. His eyes water in his sun-tanned face. Then he grabs at the basket of greengages, and one-by-one, pops them into his mouth. The juice spurts all down his chin. He smacks his lips.

'*Si bon*,' he says and spits the oval stones into his palm. Then he wipes his hands on a napkin Augustine embroidered for him - a crooked cross-stitch rabbit wearing a lorgnette.

Jojo glances at his watch. The watchstrap suddenly irritates him. He starts to undo it, tries to loosen it, then do it up again. But it's too fiddly for him. His fingers start to tremble. He must do this and this and this, and his watch might fall off if the strap's too loose, and then how will he know the time?

He holds out his wrist to Augustine.

'Mm-maaman, Mm-maaman.'

'I can't,' she snaps. 'You know that.' She turns to me. 'The tremors,' she explains. She gets up, crosses over to the sink, and splashes cold water on her shaking hands.

I take hold of Jojo's thin forearm and help him with his watch. His wrist is passive, inert, but his eyes are hopeful. Stanley was so patient with him, that time he came over for

Francine's wedding. Dabbing a crumb from Jojo's face, helping him fasten his watch, his belt. Jojo never stammered when he talked to Stanley.

Whilst I'm fastening the watchstrap, Victor the hound seizes his opportunity. He thrusts his long nose at the chair, pushes it away from the door. Scrape. Crunch. Crash. His stumpy tail wags as he breaks free from the kitchen.

Jojo smiles.

THE BLACKBOARD

Loud barks from the hall. Victor dashes back into the kitchen, followed by the two girls. Rachel hangs back in the doorway, but Justine steps forward and drops a kiss on her grandmother's white head, and another one on my cheek.

'*Bon soir,* Mam'Odette,' she says. She pushes past my oak-backed chair and reaches for two white bowls from the dresser.

After she's filled them with hot chocolate, Justine approaches a blackboard in the corner of the kitchen. It's been there for decades, to teach children their letters. She tries to get Rachel to write a sentence, in French, about their afternoon's outing: *'J'aime faire les courses.'*

But my granddaughter can understand French better than she can write it. On the blackboard, she forms her letters carefully, but she gets the meaning wrong.

'Je t'aime,' she writes. Oh. That was the first sentence Monique ever wrote in French. I placed my hand over hers as she grasped the pencil, intending to guide her over the page. But she shook herself free. She said she could do it, all by herself.

I shrugged. 'You'll only make a mess of it if I don't help you,' I said. But what she wrote was, what she wrote was…

'I love you,' Justine drawls, a French girl pretending to be American, then she shrieks with laughter.

Next Rachel draws a picture of a dog, and confuses everyone by pointing to it, and saying, in English, 'Tail.'

Marguerite enters the red kitchen. When she realises the girls have been window-shopping without her, her mouth turns down. '*Et moi?*' she says to each of us sitting round the kitchen table. '*Et moi?*'

Rachel, quiet already because of her bad French, grows quieter. She knows what it's like to feel left out. From Justine's chat, we learn that they bumped into a schoolfriend of hers. Sandrine Delmare. They spent the afternoon with her. But Rachel couldn't really keep up with their conversation.

Ma pauvre. I remember what it was like when I first came to England, and no-one to talk to except Sophy and Stanley.

But Justine's all chat chat chat, her brown eyes sparkling. 'Sandrine said we could spend the afternoon with her again tomorrow,' she says. Then she stops and looks at Rachel. 'But perhaps you'd prefer it just to be the two of us.'

Rachel doesn't say anything for a moment. Then, 'Yes,' she says finally, 'Just us. - *les deux ensemble.*'

'*Les trois,*' mutters Marguerite, and Justine puts her arm round her cousin's shoulder.

'*Bien sûr, les trois,*' she agrees.

But Sandrine Delmare?

'Is she a relation of Yvette's?' I say.

Augustine shrugs.

'Yvette's granddaughter,' she replies, looking at Justine, then at Marguerite. 'These days, the old animosities don't seem so important. All the children play together now.' She smiles, her eyes green and gentle as dock-leaves for nettle-stings.

THE CAMERA

The next day, Augustine shows me their new bedroom on the ground floor. That huge double bed, how did they ever manage to get it down the stairs? But it was necessary. Her legs are often so bad. Parkinson's disease has got her now, as it will have me, in time.

Augustine points to the new wallpaper. Big pink and red flowers in a geometric design.

'I see my friend in it,' I say, and she smiles, then opens the window. Now the orchard is painted on the glass. And white towels on the washing-line lift against the breeze, strain against the blue and white pegs. Further away, in the fields, are the sheep they keep not to breed, but to kill and eat.

Vincenzio walks past the window and nods at us.

We smile at him, then I cross to the opposite window. From here, I can see the gap beneath the house, where they keep the firewood. Threading through it are weeds, and late summer leaves. And there's half a plastic bottle - and a bird's mauled wing. Beyond that is the house's shawl of green and crimson ivy, its open double doors. And the cobbled courtyard, from where Rachel's voice rings out, sudden and panicked.

'Where are you Granny? I can't make my camera work.'

THE PHOTOGRAPHS

My eyesight's not good enough to help her. I can see to read, but not for fiddly things like this. When we get back to England, I might go to the opticians, get some new lenses fitted. But that's no help to Rachel now. She wants to take photographs at the war museum in the village - though I'm not sure she's allowed. Besides, I've told her, there's nothing much there.

Still, we find Vincenzio, overseeing the building work. He helps her load a new reel of film into her camera. Then, in the afternoon, I take her to Musée América at 2, Place Amiral Byrd.

The sign outside confuses her.

'I thought the museum was about the D-Day landings, when you met Granddad. So why's it called America?'

'Part of the museum is about the D-Day landings on Gold Beach,' I say. 'But the America was the name of an aeroplane, with American pilots, that landed here before the war. Back in 1927.'

Her brow stays creased. Her lower lip protrudes.

'Don't you remember, how I told you about the American pilots who were supposed to take the airmail to Paris, but landed in Ver-Sur-Mer instead?'

'Oh, but I thought that was just a story,' she replies. 'I didn't think it actually happened.'

Nor does she seem impressed with the dioramas charting the various flight paths. She shrugs when I point out the twinkling lights that commemorate the America's forty-two hour flight. And not even the *papier mâché* models of Byrd, Acosta, Balchen and Noville hold her attention. I suppose the Science Museum, and Madame Tussaud's in London, have spoilt her for anything else. Still, I can't blame her really. None of the models look anything like the men I remember.

We reach the part of the museum devoted to the D-Day landings. From one of the posters, I read out to her: 'The events in Ver-Sur-Mer, lasting only one and a half hours on the morning of 6th June 1944, were a vital part of the successful invasion in Normandy, the liberation of France in 1944 and Victory in Europe in 1945.'

One and a half hours. Is that all? And yet the consequences last a lifetime. Monique, Rachel and James, they're all a part of *Jour-J*'s aftermath.

Rachel glances at a steel helmet, dredged from the sea. It's covered in lichen and barnacles.

'Why's that here?' she asks.

And then I try to tell her that history also resides in the minutiae of our lives. In ordinary, everyday objects. But she's not listening. Instead she copies her name down in Morse code, then peers at every faded photograph.

'Be careful, *tu vas abimer tes yeux*,' I say.

'You'll hurt your eyes,' I repeat as she leans into the glass covering yet another black-and-white image. 'Are you trying to see whether the soldiers polished their boots?'

She darts me a reproachful look. 'I'm trying to find a picture of Granddad,' she says.

I don't have the heart to tell her that he wasn't actually part of the D-Day landings. Especially when, in her best-schoolgirl French, Rachel scribbles a sentence in the visitor's book about her grandfather, the war hero. And then, in English, chats to the museum attendant behind the desk about all of Stanley's imagined adventures.

Just a *papier-mâché* hero, I want to say, but I don't.

264

A large, red-faced man suddenly bursts through the doors of the museum and lurches towards the desk. Drunk, at two o' clock in the afternoon. Disgraceful.

'*Mon père était là,*' he says, gesturing towards the photographs of Gold Beach. The attendant nods and glances down at her neat striped blouse. The man stumbles past us. Without paying the entrance fee.

'*Il faut payer,*' the attendant says, raising her voice after him. But he throws up his hands.

'*Mon père, tué,*' he says, and strides forwards.

The attendant calls out, 'This little girl's grandfather was also here during the war, but they still paid to see the museum.'

The man waves his hands at us and enters the darkened room, only lit up by the aeroplanes' flight paths. So I unhook the clasp on my black leather purse and reach inside for a five franc note. I pay the drunk man's entrance fee. It hurts me to do it. After all, I'm a widow now. I don't have Stanley's pension to rely on. But there are some things in life that hurt more.

Mon père, tué.

My father, killed.

THE PAPER BAG

On the last day of our visit, Francine drives us back to Le Havre. She hasn't had time to make us a packed lunch, but she throws a brown paper bag onto the back seat. It's full of sweets shaped like cola bottles and flying saucers. And sticks of spearmint gum. And cheese crackers in a cardboard tube, with their own chocolate dip in a plastic holder at the side

I shake my head in polite distaste, but after a moment's hesitation, Rachel reaches for a blackberry chew.

Justine works her jaw on some gum. Then the van starts to leak petrol. The mingled smell of ethanol and spearmint is horrendous. Rachel turns pale.

'Granny,' she whispers. Then again, more urgently, 'Granny.' She leans out of the window and vomits down the side of the van.

I commend her presence of mind.

Francine parks the van. She finds a tissue in the glove compartment, turns round and wipes my granddaughter's mouth. But later, when we reach the port, Francine just shakes her hand. She doesn't want to kiss Rachel goodbye.

Justine glares at her mother, then throws her arms round Rachel and smacks kisses on both her cheeks. She kisses me goodbye too, then reaches for the chocolate dip. With a sidelong glance at her mother, she smears chocolate all over her own mouth and fingers. Then she approaches her mother, as if to kiss her as well. Francine escapes, climbs back inside the van.

Justine throws back her head and laughs, a merry peal, an echo of Augustine. Then she too gets back inside the van. The last thing we see is her waving goodbye to us, with her chocolate-covered fingers.

The next day, back in Sutton, Rachel and I arrange for an appointment for me at Boots' opticians. While we're there, we drop off her camera film to be developed. When we pick up the photographs, there's Augustine and me, smiling, screwing up our eyes against the sunlight. Our heads just touch: mine, shot through with silver, hers, white as a little bird's feathers.

Angel feathers, we used to call them when we were young, twirling them round and round, seeing who's could twirl longest, then watching them fall, like apple blossom. Like sudden snowflakes, beneath a glass dome.

THE SAFETY PIN

I'm lying on the sofa of my house in Sutton, beneath a crocheted patchwork quilt, staring at the clock on the mantelpiece, that I stole from our lodgings all those years ago. It's still on French time.

In Ver, during the war, the town hall clock may have run on German time, but in our homes, we kept French hours. So now, when I say ten o'clock or half past two, I don't mean the shrunken time of towns, but something wilder, more intangible, a stray beam of light across the kitchen table, a sparrow hopping beside my window.

Behind me is the staircase which leads up to three rooms, two of decent size, one only big enough for a single bed, a dresser and a built-in wardrobe.

The living room, where I am now, leads into the dining area, with a rectangular table covered in a vinyl cloth patterned with birds, green leaves and red flowers. The dining area leads to a sky-blue-tiled kitchen.

Now there's a sudden loud rap at the front door and I hear Rachel shouting from outside: 'Granny! Let me in!'

So I wrap the crocheted blanket around myself, slide my feet off the sofa and into my slippers, then head to the front door, take the safety chain off, unbolt it, twist the key, heave it open.

There's Rachel, twenty-one now, in a denim jacket and black skirt, wide-eyed and hopeful.

'Have you quarrelled with your mother again?' I sigh.

'No Granny, I want to tape your memories of France for a college project.'

'You'll have to be quick about it,' I say. 'I'm eighty-seven. I might not be here much longer.' After all, I'm an old lady now, living on borrowed time, but it's mine, all mine. My posthumous existence. Rachel enters the house and sits down on one of the forest-tapestry chairs, then rummages through piles of newspapers and magazines.

Now I make us cups of camomile tea.

'*Camomile, pour les vieilles filles,*' I mutter as I spoon the herbs into the pot.

Then, 'Come and fetch your cup,' I call. But Rachel's looking for the magazine she left here last time. *Marie-Claire.* She wants to show me a picture of a dress held together with safety pins. *Le pauvre modèle.* No-one to stitch it up for her, like I used to do for Augustine.

We sip our tea. Then, 'Puss, puss,' I call into the shadows. I want to make sure he's safe inside before I shut the house up for the night.

Augustine gives me a perplexed look.

'You don't have a cat,' she says.

It isn't Augustine.

It's Rachel, my granddaughter.

Now we sit side-by-side on the sofa and sip out tea. Rachel switches on the tape-recorder, keeps an eye on the whirring spools, as I begins to reminisce.

'Often, I think about the strange process of mental association, in which everything is linked to everything else. Returning, obsessing, resurrecting, coming back. Rather like birds. A trajectory of flight which becomes a complete circle, which is my life, and my name.

O for Odette. The shape of the Easter eggs I used to paint. The sand eggs I hid in the shadow of Bathonien, that day with Pierre. Or wandering along by the sea, worrying that the Egg-Rocks might get worn away. Then Papa told me that the waves must be charged with grit and stone before that could happen.

And how could I forget the character of Odette in *Swann's Way*? The great love of his life. I wonder if I was named after her. I know Jacques used to think so. Because of all those yellowing novels my mother used to read. Books stuffed among the cushions, wedged into the needlework-basket, or languishing in the orchard, drenched by the rain.'

THE ENVELOPE

The following morning, I shuffle round the living room in my navy-blue dressing-gown and slippers, trying to locate my *lunettes*. There they are, on the mantelpiece next to the clock. Now I have them, I balance them on my nose.

Suddenly, the letter-flap edges forwards on its metal hinges, then snaps shut. An envelope flutters to the doormat. I don't want it. Send it back. I don't want to deal with it, neat white rectangle, French postage stamp, French handwriting, all loops and bars across the sevens. And a black border round the edges.

I haven't seen a black border for years. Not since Maman died and we sent out her photograph, edged in black. I didn't know they still made envelopes like this. *Faire-parts,* they're called.

But this one feels light, too light for something which carries so much meaning. My sweaty fingers smudge Paul's neat black handwriting.

He could have phoned. How hard would it have been just to pick up the phone and tell me - tell me she's...

No, for us to have a polite conversation, about *this*, would be impossible.

Now I take the envelope over to the table where Rachel is sitting, eating a piece of toast with apricot jam. I prop it up against the teapot, stare at it.

But Rachel is staring down at the *Daily Mail*. The headline reads, 'PRINCESS DIANA DEAD. Any other morning and I'd have read the paper from cover-to-cover. But the black-bordered envelope is the only thing that exists for me now. Unnerving, implacable, against the porcelain.

'Augustine's dead,' I say at last..

'Eh? What do you mean?' asks Rachel.

I point to the envelope. 'The black border. Paul's handwriting.'

Rachel picks up the envelope and opens it. Then she closes her eyes for a moment. When she opens them again, she stands up and hugs me very hard. My head barely touches her shoulders.

'I'll stay with you for a few days, until you feel a bit better,' she says.

Later that day, I read the newspaper. Princess Diana is dead, killed in a car crash in a tunnel just outside Paris. The mourners leave masses of flowers for her outside Westminster Abbey.

Augustine died alone in a hospice, in the middle of the night. I press a snapdragon for her between the pages of my old, illustrated Bible.

THE BLACK-AND-WHITE TELEVISION

'Mexican fajitas,' says Rachel another time. She's cooked me my dinner.

'Hope they're not too spicy.'

'No, you'll like them,' she promises. And I do.

We eat with plates balanced on our laps, in front of the black-and-white television. Black-and-white because the license is cheaper. And more restful on the eyes, I always say. Rachel wants to watch the last match of the World Cup. France is playing at the new *Stade de France* in Paris.

And France is winning. Three-nil against Brazil.

Then, at the end of the match,

'We won, Granny,' Rachel shrieks. 'We won.' She jumps up from her armchair, pulls me to my feet, dances me round the living room. She kisses me over and over again.

And she's not the only one celebrating. Paul, these days my most faithful correspondent, writes that there are street parties and festivities all across France. He tells me that on the day of the match *Le Monde* discussed the racial mix of the players under the headline, 'Playing together.'

That'll show Le Pen. Except, of course, with all the World Cup publicity, he has to pretend he isn't racist. He proclaims, very publicly, that anyone can become a French citizen providing they love France and share its interests. *Bah. Hypocrite.* Though on my fuzzy nine-inch television screen, it's hard to tell who's black and who's white anyway.

THE GLASS JARS

When I die, I'm going to split this house in three, leave it to the three of them. My grandson, my granddaughter, and - Monique. I'd better see a solicitor, draw up an inventory of household contents...

Though some of the things I love most, I can't leave in a will. Stanley's flowers, my fruit. And the spices, nestling in their glass jars in the cavernous regions of the cupboard. Cardamon, cinnamon and black pepper. The purple veined bulbs of garlic. Oriental twists of ginger. As many herbs as can be picked in flower, then slowly dried. A little wild oregano. Marjoram. A few juniper berries. Some thyme, but never enough.

'I'll tell you what I want, what I really really want...' scream the Spice Girls on the radio. Baby Sporty Scary Posh Ginger in her Union Jack dress.

What I want. What I really really want. Is to know that it hasn't all been in vain. That I haven't made a mess of it. Even though the recipe of my life didn't...quite turn out how I expected.

THE SHAWL

I wake in the near dark. The stars still shine and there's a pale strip of light in the lower sky. I strain to hear the crowing cockerel, the pigs pushing through mud to find their food, the cows in a distant pasture. And beyond that, the plash of morning waves.

The snow rattles against the windowpane, trying to get in. Or is it the bird that chitters against the glass? There's a patch of red upon its breast, and its tail feathers are green.

If that bird were caught, it would probably die.

No. Perhaps not. You can't always die when you want to.

It's a dark, cluttered, narrow room, with mirrors gleaming from corners, a shawl slung over a chair, a cat sleeping in its wicker seat.

No. No cat. And then I realise, I'm not on the farm anymore - though I know, too well, the shape of every shadow, every cobweb.

'Claire, Claire,' I call. But it's too early for her to have started her shift yet. There's only that woman on the front desk who pokes her head round the door every half hour. So I turn over in my bed, shut my eyes, and try to go back to sleep.

THE PATCHWORK QUILT

The patchwork quilt slips from my shoulders. I'm too old and stiff in my bones to pull it back. But I'm supposed to keep myself well wrapped up. The damp is killing me. I am, these days, a *frileuse,* a shiverer, suffering inordinately from the cold. I never used to be like this. My blood must have got thinner.

The clammy aroma of boiled cabbage mingles with the tang of stale urine and disinfectant. If I can ignore the smell, the voice proves more insistent. A thin, high voice calling, 'Biddy, Biddy, Biddy,' over and over again. Her sister's name.

One of the nursing assistants tells her that Biddy lives a long way away in Ireland and won't be coming to visit today. Another tells her, brusquely, that Biddy died a long time ago, and to stop all that racket. To no avail.

'Oh Biddy, Biddy, Biddy. Oh, Biddy, Biddy, Biddy.' The same high-pitched, monotonous wail, all morning, all afternoon, and late into the night. As if she's chanting a spell to bring her sister back. Finally another assistant tells her to shut her eyes, and try to sleep, and she might see Biddy when she wakes up.

Or in her dreams, perhaps.

But I, I dream of Augustine. Not ravaged by Parkinson's disease like the last time I saw her in Ver, but restored to health, youth and gaiety. Dancing round the parlour in her summer-dress.

The snapdragon, blooming red and pink, open-mouthed.

I lean towards Augustine as she moistens her lips and begins to speak.

'Do you dare?' she says.

'No,' I reply, shrinking away from her. 'I don't.'

'I don't want anyone except you,' I say, later that day. Thin, high-pitched, querulous voice. Much whinier than I'd intended.

Claire, the nice nursing assistant, hazel eyes and freckles, pats my shoulder. 'Unfortunately, Odette, we don't always get what we want,' she says. 'Irene is perfectly lovely, perfectly capable. You'll be in good hands. And I told you I was cutting down my shifts here so I could go back to college.'

'I hope you fail all your exams,' I say. It sounds spiteful. I didn't mean it like that. I meant I hope she'd fail so she wouldn't leave the nursing home and I wouldn't be deprived of her company.

'Oh Odette,' says Claire, sighing. 'You're just having one of your crotchety days.'

Crotchety days. That's what she calls it. She doesn't know I overheard her talking to Monique just outside my door.

'You must understand,' she said. 'Parkinson's is a neurological disorder. It's affecting the way her mind works. Sometimes she can't help what she says.'

'But sometimes she can,' said Monique. 'Sometimes it's just Mother being Mother.'

I think I prefer Claire's version. Now she smiles at me, and I love her. *Petite Claire de la lune.* Let your perpetual light shine upon me.

That's the prayer for the Holy Souls in Purgatory. *Le Purgatoire,* I call this place. But if you make the pilgrimage to the Chapel of Saint Gerbold on the first feast day after Easter, you're granted a hundred days less in Purgatory. Jacques told me that. Though, after all, we never did find the lost chapel. Only the Lélediers think they did, with their stories of desiccated bones.

'What's that Odette?' says Claire. 'Are you praying? You don't want to see a priest, do you?'

'I do not,' I say, 'I've had enough of them to last me a lifetime.'

Let me rest in peace.

THE BIRTHDAY CARD

A woman who isn't Claire thrusts a white oblong beneath my nose.

'What's that?' I say, groping for my *lunettes.*

'Oh Mum,' sighs the woman. 'You asked me to get a birthday card for that nursing assistant you're so fond of.'

A voice is calling me from a long way away. I listen hard. The sound gets closer and closer, the tones more confiding.

'Oh Mum,' says the voice. It's my little girl. My Monique. My face wants to break into a smile. Love is like a waterfall, a radiant rush of wonder. Let it wear away the stone. Let it seep through the cracks, then surge across my heart.

'Where's Claire?' I ask, glancing all around the room. Past the ornaments and the pictures, and the patchwork counterpane slung over the low-backed chair. Where have you hidden her? *Ma Claire de la lune.*

'Now Mum, you know it's one of her college days. But you'll see her tomorrow and you can give her this then.' She takes the card out of the envelope and shows me the picture. A kitten asleep in a bed of pink roses.

There's a hopeful, expectant look in Monique's blue-grey eyes. Eyes like the sea when the storms have fled, but lifting at the corners when she smiles. She gets them from Stanley. Those blue-eyed foreigners. I can't bear it. Stop looking at me like that, Monique. Stop it.

'*Pas mal,*' is what I find myself repeating now, the words rising unbidden to my lips, the easiest, and most hurtful phrase. 'You don't get everything wrong, after all.'

The roses have thorns, the kitten, claws.

Monique arches her eyebrows, makes a *mou* of disdain. On a younger, slenderer woman, such a gesture would be impressive. She opens the card.

I reach for my fountain pen. I try to sign my name, but the tremors take over. My hand starts to dance. Very gently, Monique guides it across the page. '*With fondest love, Odette Angèle Elise Morgan.*'

THE SUGARED ALMONDS

I dance when I want to walk. I walk when I want to stand still. I reach for the bag of sugared almonds that Monique brought me. I manage to grip hold of the bag. Then the cellophane starts to tremble in time with my tremors. I force the bag still and bite a hole in it with my teeth. B-b-b-bang.

One of the nursing assistants sticks her head round the door.
'Everything okay, Odette?'
Mrs Morgan, I think, you should call me Mrs Morgan.

Then she sees the sugared almonds scattered across the floor. Pink, mauve, white. Some of them intact. Some of them crushed. Like eggshells.

'Oh dear,' she says. And then I think, Claire, none of this would have happened, if you hadn't gone.

THE LOOKING GLASS

Ah, but she's come back…she's reading to me. On and on and on. Can't really understand what the story's meant to be. And my back hurts. I told them this chair was no good. They might as well just prop me up in bed and leave me to…

My stomach's rumbling. There's a sour, metallic taste in my mouth.

'When are you going to feed me?' Claire hasn't heard me. Louder. 'When are you going to feed me?' Oh. I've already eaten? Well, but… and the light's making my eyes sore. Switch it off and…that's better. Now there's just the little lamp by the bedside, so that Claire can carry on reading. But the story still doesn't make any sense. May as well just stare at the ceiling. T-ttt-ttt-t-t. The nurses should have long-handled brooms to get the cobwebs down. It's something that needs to be done every week. Spiders always re-build their homes, impatient to eat the flies.

Home? Where's that? Perhaps it's inside Claire's voice, with its gentle lilt, so like Augustine's. Soothing as the crunch of gravel outside the kitchen door, or the sight of a distant horse, ploughing the fields.

And Jacques will steady the horse, guide the plough.

No. Of course he can't, he died a long time ago, in Stalag IV. A very long way from home.

I glance round at my high, narrow room. Most of the antiques have been sold, to pay the nursing fees. But one or two things, I managed to keep. The bronze statue of Pan, the looking glass with its stains the colour of tea.

'Who did this to me?' I mouth at the speckled old lady who lives there. But she shakes her head slowly, from side-to-side. She doesn't know.

The girl who used to live there, she'd know. Was it Claire? Did she step out from behind the mirror to keep me company here? In this city where it's always winter. Where only frost flowers bloom against the windowpanes. Where grass doesn't grow, and birds don't sing.

No. Sometimes they sing, but I don't like to hear them. *Ky-witt, Ky-witt, what a beautiful bird am I.*

There it is again, that sound of scratching, scuttling among the roof-eaves. A trapped pigeon perhaps? But Claire says that all old houses have strange noises. She turns back towards the page.

I wonder when I became so old that all she can do is read me children's books. Still, she means well. It's a book about a swallow called Odette. *Une hirondelle*, who dies, heartbroken, one very cold winter.

I shut my eyes, and just for a moment, I'm a child again, back in my bedroom at the top of the curving house by the sea. It's raining outside, a steady, persistent patter, but beams from the lighthouse sweep across the ceiling and cover us in light. I whisper to you that every light is a story. The rays across the ceiling are stories going out across the waves. One of them is yours and one of them is mine.

THE CLOSED BOOK

Claire helps me into bed. She covers my sheets with a blanket, smiling to herself as it catches in her auburn hair.

'Not still cold, are you?' she says.

I shake my head. Suddenly I know that outside my window, the snow is starting to melt. Ditches become puddles, puddles, streams, that join the River Wandle winding round the town. But what if the process were reversed? Water slipping backwards through my open fingers, starting to solidify, becoming ice?

Now the stream beside the sacred spring is frozen over, white as the moon. The village children skate upon it. White lines sketch in the fences and gates as snow falls in gentle folds on the farms and fields of Ver.

Snowflakes like white feathers, shaken from a pillow. Snowflakes, like forgetting, but like remembering, too. The drift of white muslin on my First Communion Day, the pale transparency of Augustine's wedding veil. And the snowstorm

I broke those many years ago is mended now, mended so that I can hardly see the cracks.

Oh. A packed wad of snow catches me squarely on the jaw. And there's Yvette, grinning beneath her uneven fringe, her eyes glinting with mirth and mischief. I rub my stung cheek and stare at her. And suddenly Yvette's frizzy hair falls into dark curls, her pock-marked complexion turns smooth as porcelain. It's not Yvette, after all. It's my Monique. She drops her handful of snow and waves at me, the tips of her fingers pink and chilled at the end of her fingerless gloves.

It's strange, I'm not cold at all. The snow is as gentle as a feather eiderdown, as comforting as freshly laundered blankets and sheets, as Maman tucking me up in bed.

'Sleep well, *chérie,*' she says, closing the book, bending over me, her good night kiss scented, as ever, with vervain tea and attar of roses. 'I'll keep the night-light burning for you.' Because she knows that in the dark ship of the night, what saves you is a single light.

'Thank you,' I say to Maman, my eyes round to take in the snowstorm om the bedside cabinet. Inside it, the snow settles on Ver's moonlit streets and houses.

'Good night,' I say to you, as my head slides to the centre of the pillow, collides with your dark, dreaming head.

'Night, Odette,' my little brother mumbles, then turns away. And so, we sleep, we dream.

By the same Author:

In Valerian - Part I of the Valerian Trilogy
The Dragons of Blue Lias – Part II of the Valerian Trilogy

Coming soon:

Collodian Star - Part III of the Valerian Trilogy

Printed and bound by CPI Group (UK) Ltd, Croydon, CR0 4YY
06/04/2024
03765029-0001